IRON
BUTTERFLY

ROBERT BRACE

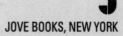

JOVE BOOKS, NEW YORK

THE BERKLEY PUBLISHING GROUP
Published by the Penguin Group
Penguin Group (USA) Inc.
375 Hudson Street, New York, New York 10014, USA
Penguin Group (Canada), 90 Eglinton Avenue East, Suite 700, Toronto, Ontario M4P 2Y3, Canada
(a division of Pearson Penguin Canada Inc.)
Penguin Books Ltd., 80 Strand, London WC2R 0RL, England
Penguin Group Ireland, 25 St. Stephen's Green, Dublin 2, Ireland (a division of Penguin Books Ltd.)
Penguin Group (Australia), 250 Camberwell Road, Camberwell, Victoria 3124, Australia
(a division of Pearson Australia Group Pty. Ltd.)
Penguin Books India Pvt. Ltd., 11 Community Centre, Panchsheel Park, New Delhi—110 017, India
Penguin Group (NZ), Cnr. Airborne and Rosedale Roads, Albany, Auckland 1310, New Zealand
(a division of Pearson New Zealand Ltd.)
Penguin Books (South Africa) (Pty.) Ltd., 24 Sturdee Avenue, Rosebank, Johannesburg 2196, South
Africa

Penguin Books Ltd., Registered Offices: 80 Strand, London WC2R 0RL, England

IRON BUTTERFLY

A Jove Book / published by arrangement with the author.

PRINTING HISTORY
Jove mass market edition / April 2006

ISBN: 0-515-14118-6

JOVE®
Jove Books are published by The Berkley Publishing Group,
a division of Penguin Group (USA) Inc.,
375 Hudson Street, New York, New York 10014.
JOVE is a registered trademark of Penguin Group (USA) Inc.
The "J" design is a trademark belonging to Penguin Group (USA) Inc.

PRINTED IN THE UNITED STATES OF AMERICA

10 9 8 7 6 5 4 3 2 1

Among the trucks parked out front there was a perfect primrose-colored E-type Jaguar. It was a convertible. The top was down. I went over to admire it.

The wheels had chromed wire hubs. The long hood was lined with ventilation slots that the engine would appreciate on a desert run like this. California plates. The car was probably forty years old, but it was in pristine condition—whoever owned it was obviously fastidious. I looked at the odometer to see what sort of mileage it had. As I leaned inside I saw a silk scarf on the driver's seat. I could faintly smell it, too, something I couldn't quite identify. I picked up the scarf, brought it close to my face, and inhaled deeply. Roses, overlaid with something harder and spicier, cedar wood perhaps, giving the scent a balanced but remote, ethereal quality, like a perfect dream that drifts just out of conscious reach. Whoever owned this car smelled pretty good.

"Forget your handkerchief?"

I stood and turned.

She was five six, give or take. Big mass of wavy dark hair, cut a little shorter than shoulder length. Long, slender limbs. Smooth, brown skin. Tight jeans hugging narrow hips. Boots. Tank top that didn't reach her belly button. I was pretty sure that belly button would be cute, too, but it was obscured right now by the butt of an automatic pistol jammed into the waistline of her jeans . . .

To Joan Brace

ACKNOWLEDGMENTS

The author wishes to acknowledge with gratitude the generous and professional help of his agent, Caitlin Blasdell, and also Liza Dawson, of Liza Dawson Associates, and his editor, Leona Nevler, and also Tova Sacks, of Penguin Group (USA). He also wishes to especially thank Erika Wessel.

ONE

IT took me awhile after waking up to realize that I was tied to a chair. My head was pounding, and I was too groggy to have yet opened my eyes, but I could feel the bindings tight across my chest. The chair was stiff-backed and hard, a kitchen chair maybe. I tried to think how I might have become tied to a kitchen chair, but I had a hangover the size of a mountain, and it hurt too much to think.

One at a time, I gently tried my arms and legs. All four were secured, arms behind, legs to the front legs of the chair.

The binding was rope. Secure, but not professional. A professional would have used handcuffs or duct tape; rope loosens. My shoulders ached—nothing compared to the blacksmith's shop inside my head, but enough to tell me that I'd been tied to this chair for a long time.

I tried thinking again. It took awhile, sorting through the hazy fragments of broken memory, getting events into the right order, but eventually I had a more or less coherent recollection of what had happened. It wasn't pretty: my very last memory was of being shot to death.

If I was dead, then it occurred to me that I had an urgent need to establish just exactly where I was. I forced my eyes to open.

In front of me was a face, an ugly one, not six inches away, bloodshot eyes staring right into mine.

"Hello, asshole," it said.

A bad sign—I was pretty sure that this would not be a common form of address in any desirable postmortem sphere. The creature before me continued to stare, grinning inanely, apparently pleased with his own wit. He had that inbred, malnourished countenance of a hillbilly: sunken cheeks, wild eyes, unshaven beard too wispy to cover the acne scars.

I tried asking where I was, but my throat was as dry as the Kalahari, and nothing came out.

"Cat got your tongue?" he said mockingly. He poked out his own tongue in emphasis. It looked like mine felt, coated in something unpleasant and furry. His halitosis wasn't doing my stomach any good, either.

"Breath mint," I managed to croak.

"What?"

"You need a breath mint."

He jerked back and stood up straight, unamused. His upper lip curled, baring what remained of his teeth: moss-covered little stumps occasionally separated by the gaps of fallen comrades. This wasn't the man who shot me. The man who shot me had good teeth. I could remember him smiling as he pulled the trigger.

"So you're a funny boy, huh?" Billy-Jo-Bob hacked a bit, then spat on the floor at my feet. Or perhaps onto my feet—he didn't strike me as being overly concerned with accuracy. "See how funny you think this is."

He reached under his loose shirttails and pulled out a large handgun from the waist of his jeans. I recognized it as a Colt Anaconda, one of those massive .44 Magnum revolvers suitable for stopping cars or elephants or narrow-gauge locomotives. This one had the extended eight-inch barrel. I focused for a moment on the chambers—all four that were visible were loaded with hollow nose rounds that would make a mess of anything they hit. He tried pointing the thing at me, but Billy-Jo-Bob was a little excited, and the muzzle was waving around all over the place. Although it was technically point-blank range, I figured that if he pulled the trigger now there was only a fifty-fifty chance of him actually hitting me.

Not that it mattered much. How many times can you get shot to death?

The gun that had shot me was big, too. I'd been cornered in some dark and anonymous alley, the usual narrow, trash-strewn thoroughfare common to most American cities. I'd been backed up between the wall and a Dumpster, looking for a sign of hesitation or distraction, hoping for an opportunity to make a last desperate move. But my killer had been calm and professional: eyes fixed on the target, gun raised in a steady two-handed grip as he closed range, then assuming the firing stance at twenty feet—too far to get rushed, too close to miss.

I would have done it the same way myself. In fact, I had done it the same way myself.

"You had a loaded weapon with the safety off stuffed into your pants," I said to my companion. "Are you contemplating a career as a contralto?"

Billy-Jo-Bob pointed the Anaconda at my head.

"How'd you like a career as the Headless Horseman, asshole?" There was no doubt that Billy-Jo-Bob was a master of repartee, but the eight-inch barrel sagged. A fully loaded Colt Anaconda would weigh in at something like four pounds, heavy for a handgun, and obviously more than his thin wrist could support for an extended period. If he pulled the trigger now, I'd be the

Chestless Horseman. I would have given him some brief instruction on the correct handling of small arms, but he didn't seem amenable to free advice.

"Where am I?" I asked.

"Where am I?" he mocked, his voice pitched high. He wasn't that far from a contralto already. "Don't you worry 'bout where you are, asshole. Only thing you got to worry about now is *me*." To emphasize this last point he tapped himself on the chest with the muzzle of the Anaconda. Billy-Jo-Bob was in desperate need of a firearms safety course. I tried again.

"Why don't you just tell me what's going on?"

His mouth smiled, revealing the erosion within. Billy-Jo-Bob was in desperate need of a firearms safety course and a dentist. He leaned down close again.

"So you want to know what's going on?" His breath would have dropped a camel. I looked more closely at his eyes and realized why that weapon was waving around so much: his pupils were the size of dimes, so dilated that there was no iris visible. Billy-Jo-Bob was high.

He raised the Anaconda and managed to hold it steady enough to jam the business end of the barrel squarely between my eyes. He pulled the hammer to the rear. "I'll tell you what's going on, asshole. I'm going to ventilate your friggin' head."

For the second time in twenty-four hours, I was in the ridiculous position of being about to be shot to death by a man I'd never met, and for reasons that I'd never know.

BACK when I commanded a Force Reconnaissance unit, the lieutenant colonel who ran our group was a man called O'Hara. His first name was John, but out of his hearing he was inevitably referred to by officers and troops alike as Scarlett. Scarlett O'Hara and I used to sit on the selection boards to review candidates from regular marine units who had applied for special operations training. He was a good commander, a gritty old guy who'd come up through the ranks—hard as nails but with a quick wit and ready intelligence. We got along fine and usually had little difficulty in agreeing on whom from the many applicants we'd select for those few much-coveted Force Recon slots.

But there was one candidate we couldn't agree on. I liked the guy—his fitness reports were excellent, his academics were near the top, and he was in good physical condition.

But old Scarlett just shook his head. "No trigger," he said. "Kid's got no trigger."

"Begging the colonel's pardon," I said, "but what the hell are you talking about, sir?" That's the way we talk in the marines—weird, but you get used to it.

Scarlett claimed that some men have an internal trigger, and that it was the first thing he looked for in a special forces recruit. He said he didn't know how, but that he could always tell who's got one and who hasn't. If it's there then it's always there, he said, potent and ready, like a Rottweiler on a leash.

In time I came to agree with him. No doubt the "trigger" is just biochemical—somewhere some gland releases an enzyme, which in turn generates a massive flood of adrenaline if and when the occasion arises—but it makes the difference between those who succumb and those who go down fighting. The strange thing—something Scarlett never mentioned—is the mental change that it induces. When the trigger is pulled, your mind enters a state of almost supernatural clarity. Suddenly all distractions have disappeared. Nothing is vague anymore; there is no uncertainty. You see only the relevant, stark and clear, and no longer just in the appearance but in the essence, too. It's as if you've been given the power to know the very nature of things.

When Billy-Jo-Bob pulled back the hammer of that gun, the pounding in my head was suddenly gone. I no longer felt any ache in my shoulders. My mind was as clear as a cloudless midwinter's day. I understood with complete lucidity that I was about to have my head blown apart, and that the one possibility of avoiding it—however slender the chance—was to use the only weapon available to me.

In an instant I had snapped forward and clamped my teeth into Billy-Jo-Bob's wrist, getting in touch with my own inner Rottweiler. Several things happened very fast. He instinctively jerked his arm away, but I had bitten down with all the force I could muster, and the only effect was to pull me toward him, which just gave me more purchase to really dig my teeth in. He screamed— thankfully whatever he was high on wasn't enough to dull the pain. He pulled away again—not just instinct now, but a deliberate and desperate attempt to get free. While doing so he twisted his hand below the wrist, the way you might when trying to get out of a genuine Rottweiler's jaws. The effect of this was to inadvertently point the barrel of the Anaconda back up and at him. He kept pulling, giving it everything he had, exerting so much effort that his fist closed in the attempt.

One of his fingers was still on the trigger. The gun fired.

I let go, nearly knocked unconscious from the shock and noise of the massive handgun discharging right in front of my face. The gun went flying, and Billy-Jo-Bob collapsed onto the floor.

I craned my neck forward to look down at him. Billy-Jo-Bob had managed to shoot himself in the face. He was still alive, squirming in a bloody mess on the floorboards, but at least he had resolved many of his previous dental issues. His good hand was on his face, his bad hand was flopping away at the side as if it had a mind of its own. Blood was pouring from where I'd chewed through an artery. He was making incoherent, guttural sounds that were ten percent cry, ten percent moan, and eighty percent gurgle.

"Well," I said out loud, "that pretty much puts an end to the operatic career."

But Billy-Jo-Bob wasn't done yet. His wild eyes went from the gun to me and back to the gun. Still prone on the floor, he began pumping his legs, trying to push himself toward it, but he'd lost a lot of motor control, and progress was slow. Without triage he was going to bleed to death soon—that much was clear—but the danger was that he would reach the Anaconda before doing so.

I was tied at the ankles, but my feet were on the floor. I pushed up on the toes, which lifted the front of the chair an inch or so off the floor. When I let go it fell back down and rocked forward slightly. If I got the timing right I was able to hop the chair along the floor.

We raced each other toward the gun. The word *race* here is a relative term—I was making about a mile a day, and he was alternating between the occasional flurry of legs propelling him a foot or so farther toward the gun, and those sudden aimless spasms into which the dying drift. He was quieter now, no longer making any sound beyond the wet, labored noise of getting air into lungs gradually filling with blood.

For a while I was beating him. If I got there first, then all I would need do was give the thing a flick with my foot, sending the Anaconda scooting along the floorboards and farther out of reach—he didn't have enough in him for a second attempt. But when I was nearly there, Billy-Jo-Bob must have gathered himself for one last big effort. Suddenly he was beside me on the floor. He was stretched out full length on his side, his head arched back looking at the Anaconda, and reaching out with his good hand just inches from the weapon.

I pushed back on my toes, then rocked forward with as much momentum as I could manage. My weight was momentarily forward, and the rear legs of the chair came off the floor. At the top of the motion I pushed off with my left foot, twisting the chair around so that hopefully the right rear leg was above Billy-Jo-Bob's head. As the chair came back down, I tried to put as much of my own weight into it as I could.

I felt a momentary resistance before whatever it was that the leg was over gave way. The chair came down with a hard, crunching squelch. I felt a moment or two of further struggle, then all was still. I could tell that he was dead because the wet breathing sounds had stopped. I didn't look down, my stomach wasn't up to inspecting the details of what had happened down there.

Instead I began working the ropes. I was tied at the wrists, but my hands were free. Hands are flexible things, the fingers amazingly nimble—it's what allowed man to rule the world. If horses had hands instead of hooves we'd all be neighing, as Swift would have wished. Nimble or not, it still took a long time—at least thirty minutes, perhaps an hour. By then my wrists had been worn raw by the movement, and the bugs that had gathered for the big Billy-Jo-Bob hoedown were beginning to take an interest in me. But at last I was free.

More than anything else, what I wanted to do now was floss.

I went in search of the bathroom. There was a small cabinet above the sink. It had a mirror, which was unfortunate: the face it reflected would have given Goya nightmares. I washed off the blood and cleaned my teeth, but it didn't improve matters much. My face had big, dark circles under bloodshot eyes, and was covered in a day's worth of beard.

So I'd been here overnight. Judging by the face in the mirror, whatever I'd been doing during that time, it wasn't sleeping.

When I came out of the bathroom it was time to get down to business. I picked up the Anaconda, carefully decocked it, and engaged the safety.

First task: scout and secure the area. I went outside. The building was a cabin rather than a house—not a permanent residence, and probably only inhabited during the hunting season. It was situated in a small clearing surrounded by forest. There was a rutted dirt track but no vehicles. Either someone was going to come back to pick him up, or Billy-Jo-Bob had intended to extract on foot.

Second task: locate an alternate extraction route. There was a trail in back of the cabin leading into the forest, a hunting trail most likely. I took it for about a hundred yards, enough to familiarize myself with it sufficiently to negotiate that far in the dark, then returned to the cabin.

Third task: environmentals. Judging by the fading light it was late afternoon. Overcast, and it felt like snow was coming—I needed to extract soon, before the snow started. It's easy to track people through snow.

Fourth task: check for intelligence. It's what I'd wanted to do all along: try to find out what all this was about. I went back inside the cabin and searched Billy-Jo-Bob's body. A few banknotes but no wallet and no ID. His watch had a date function, which confirmed what the beard on my face had already told me: that last memory I had was from the previous evening. There was a gap in my life, an eighteen-hour period with no memory from the moment I'd been shot last night until I'd woken up today, surprisingly alive, but tied to a kitchen chair.

My own watch was gone. Billy-Jo-Bob wouldn't be needing his anymore, so I kept it.

He had a duffel bag, and that proved more profitable. Sitting on top of a folded hunting jacket was a box of .44 Magnum rounds, 240-grain hollow points. I used one to fill the chamber vacated by Billy-Jo-Bob's inadvertent face-lift, and put the rest in my pocket.

Underneath the jacket I found the gun with which I had been shot yesterday, and now I understood why I was still alive. It was a dart gun, the sort of weapon used by researchers to drug wild animals so they can examine them in safety. I could still recollect that last sensation of the bullet pounding into my chest. I pulled up my shirt. Sure enough, there was a large bruise. But no bullet hole.

I examined the weapon more closely. Single-shot, bolt-loaded—a gun for someone very confident in their aim. The weapon had originally been a rifle, but the butt had been replaced with a pistol grip, and the barrel had been sawn off at the stock. The frame had been filed away where a serial number had once been stamped.

Someone had turned the rifle into an anonymous and concealable handgun—no wonder it had seemed big to me. But this weapon didn't belong to Billy-Jo-Bob. It belonged to a professional—a confident professional with good teeth. He would be coming back for his stuff.

I didn't want to waste any more time, but something else caught my eye. There was a hypodermic syringe, several as it turned out, lying loosely at the bottom of the bag. At first I assumed they were for the dart gun, but on closer inspection they were just ordinary plastic syringes, needles still attached but covered with plastic caps, not suitable for being shot out of a gun.

I rolled up my sleeves and checked my arms. On the left arm at the crook of the elbow I found the puncture marks. I counted the syringes: five. I counted the puncture marks: five. Each was surrounded by a bruise. The bruises were so big that they overlapped. Obviously whoever had done the injecting last night hadn't been a registered nurse.

So I'd been abducted and drugged. The absence of a gag was explained: presumably they'd interrogated me while I was under the influence of whatever had been in those syringes.

They would have been disappointed. Right now I knew nothing. These people were a day too early: I wasn't due to meet Dortmund until this evening.

If they'd gotten me after that, they would have hit the jackpot.

TWO

I ordered a dry martini, straight up with an olive. The steward nodded. He didn't ask the usual, "Vodka or gin?" which meant that at least they knew what went into a martini here. I took it as a hopeful sign that the drink would arrive well made. Dortmund ordered sherry. The steward retreated quietly, so as not to stir up the faint odor of corruption that hung like dust in the air.

Dortmund seemed disinclined to talk, so I looked around the place. From outside it hadn't seemed much: a pair of heavy wooden doors set deep into a stone-faced building in one of those quiet streets immediately west of the White House. No street number, but a discreet plaque reluctantly admitted that it was the Mayflower Club.

Inside and hidden from public view, there was no longer any need to be coy about the power and wealth concealed within: the interior was all marble and velvet and mahogany. A white-gloved butler had approached me, and from the look on his face he had instantly divined that I did not belong. He had been opening his arms to urge me back outside when I said the magic word: *Dortmund*. In the brief interval before his gesture melted into one of solicitous courtesy, I had noticed him nod to himself, as if to say that the ways of both God and Dortmund are mysterious, and thus it was sometimes necessary for them to invite the unlikely into their houses.

He had removed my coat. Perhaps he always wore gloves, or perhaps he had donned them especially for me. He managed to avoid an outright sneer at my ragged ex-navy pea jacket, but he handed it off to a porter quickly, obviously reluctant to remain holding anything but cashmere for the minimum time necessary. No tag. Here, they remembered your coat.

The butler had ushered me through a drawing room filled with old leather chairs with old leather men sitting in them. Some were alone, smoking or reading a newspaper. Others sat together, talking quietly, deciding the fates of others in the tone of those who have long ago taken for granted their right to do so.

All men. Perhaps women were barred, or perhaps the old men who clustered here had simply forgotten that they exist.

Dortmund was in the library. The room was otherwise unoccupied, which may have been a coincidence but probably wasn't. Bookcases lined one wall. The opposite was pierced by a fireplace, alight on a cold day like this, but insufficient to dispel the gloom of collusion that hung about the place. The carpet was old and Oriental, faded with the accumulated years of countless whispered conspiracies.

I looked at my companion and wondered how many of his victims had sat here like me. Dortmund was corpulent and severe, still with the Richelieu-like mustache and pointed goatee, presiding over his surroundings like a malignant Buddha. I had once inadvertently done this man a service, and the only other time I had met him had been at its conclusion. Normally a man is thankful for an unexpected favor, but to Dortmund it had just been an opportunity to see what more of me he could use. The powerful do not acquire their power through the unprofitable exercise of gratitude.

The steward returned. He served the martini, then placed Dortmund's glass on the table before filling it from a cut crystal decanter. It was a proper sherry glass: same size as a port glass but slightly narrower—what the Spanish call a *copita*. The amber fluid glistened in the firelight. Sherry is at home in surroundings like these, dark rooms in which plots that would not have survived the harsh light of public scrutiny were quietly murmured and agreed upon. When the glass was full the steward left the decanter on the table and retired—they knew Dortmund's drinking habits here.

Water beaded on the outside of my martini. We drank without ceremony, and I was grateful that at least Dortmund had felt no need to gild the occasion with the trappings of false bonhomie.

The astringent, ice-cold gin helped scour away the sour taste that I had acquired in this room. Dortmund savored the sherry a moment, then sat back and regarded me with cold appraisal.

"You are a soldier, Captain Dalton."

"Ex-soldier," I corrected.

"Yes, of course," Dortmund said. "I suppose that it really doesn't get more 'ex-' than a dishonorable discharge."

I didn't reply. It was not a subject open for discussion.

"So tell me," he continued, "what is it that wins a war?"

"Guns."

"Just guns?"

"And bullets," I added. "Last man standing wins."

Dortmund didn't look very impressed with this answer. "I have no doubt of your capabilities in the field,

Captain Dalton, but if you believe that, then you have a very naive view of the art of war."

I had a feeling that I was about to be enlightened. Dortmund took a large sip of sherry and rearranged his bulk as comfortably as could be managed before continuing. I wondered when he had last been able to see his toes while standing.

"In 46 B.C., following the defeat of Pompey, Julius Caesar returned to Rome, now in full possession of it. From that point on, the Roman republic existed in name only. Caesar was dictator, and his rule was supreme."

So I was going to get a history lesson. I would have preferred false bonhomie.

"But Africa was in revolt," Dortmund continued, "and in Carthage, Cato was raising an army. I speak of Cato the Younger, of course."

"Of course."

"When Caesar returned to Rome, he found the treasury empty. The depredations of half a century of social war had drained the state, and the provinces had been taxed into penury. How did Caesar respond?"

"Buy a condo in Naples and retire?"

"He raised funds," Dortmund answered, ignoring my reply. "He did so by confiscating the estates of those senators who had backed the conservatives, or those who he suspected of secretly sympathizing with them. Until then Caesar had always been generous in victory. He had restored to his defeated enemies their wealth and position and had asked nothing more than public obeisance. This policy had won him a hundred battles that arms alone could not have managed. But now he felt that he had no choice. He himself put it bluntly: 'Soldiers depend upon money, money upon power, and power upon soldiers.' "

I'm sure those newly homeless senators felt better when he'd explained it like that. Dortmund paused to sip the sherry before continuing.

"Of those three—soldiers, money, and power—the only one which can be obtained without the aid of the other two is money. And which is of course why Caesar began by seizing the estates—he had to get the money first, after which soldiers and power would naturally follow. And so it is today, as even the most casual perusal of a presidential campaign reveals: money comes first."

"Was Caesar abducted and interrogated?" I asked.

"What?"

"The deal's off, Mr. Dortmund. Your operation has been compromised."

"What are you talking about?"

I gave him a brief account of what happened. Brief and abridged: I did not trust Dortmund enough to admit killing a man to him, however much it may have been in self-defense, and so I left Billy-Jo-Bob out of the story altogether. And I changed the location, saying that I'd woken up alone in the wreck of an abandoned house in northwest D.C., where the shells of many once-fine homes stand gutted and empty, their only inhabitants cockroaches and crack addicts. If I was asked to locate it, I would claim to have been confused at the time, and be unable to do so—more believable than inability to locate a lonely hunting cabin in what had turned out to be rural Maryland.

Dortmund said nothing as I recounted this version of events. After I'd finished, he remained silent for several minutes, staring into the fire, his expression thoughtful but unalarmed.

While he contemplated, I drank. I downed the rest of the martini, then nodded to a passing steward for another. Getting the taste of Billy-Jo-Bob out of my mouth was going to be a multi-martini job.

Finally Dortmund roused himself. "Naturally this concerns me," he said at last. "But in the end it makes no difference. The basic reality is that there is nothing you could have told them."

"The basic reality is that they know I'm involved."

"Yes."

"Which means it's compromised."

"No," Dortmund corrected, "it means *you're* compromised. The operation itself remains quite secure."

"Which means I'm out."

"No, at most it means that you've lost the advantage of anonymity."

"You're not listening to me, Mr. Dortmund. I quit."

Dortmund shrugged. "As you wish," he said. He sipped his sherry before continuing. "What sort of flowers would you like for your funeral?"

"What?"

"You surely don't believe that these people are going to just leave you alone now, do you?" He smiled, the way an adult might at a child's admission of belief in the Easter Bunny. "My dear Captain Dalton, these people are *closers*. They complete what they begin."

I thought again of that man who had shot me, of the calm approach and steady aim. The smile as he shot me had not been malicious. My father had smiled the same way after completing a good piece of carpentry, running his hand along a length of timber planed so smoothly that he knew it was right even before checking with the straight edge. It was the satisfied but unself-conscious smile of a professional executing a task well.

Dortmund was right. These people would finish what they started.

"Last night, they presumably abducted you in order to interrogate you," he continued. "Today, they were saving you for further interrogation, but through some error they inadvertently left you alone at the precise moment you regained your wits. You escaped. Very good. But I think we can safely assume that during that time you at least told them all about yourself. In other words, they know your name, your address, your Social Security number, everything. There's probably someone at your vineyard right now, waiting for you to return so that they may close matters permanently."

My vineyard—the reason that I was here in the first place. Dortmund had some sort of operation going and needed an outsider. Me. In return for my services, he would relieve me of the vineyard's mortgage, and I would return to it free and clear. That was the deal.

It had seemed like a good deal at the time. It occurred to me that Faust had probably thought the same thing. The second martini arrived, and I was in sore need of it now. I took a big swallow, put down the glass, and faced Dortmund.

"So exactly what is it that you want me to do?"

His mouth didn't move, but he couldn't keep the smile from his eyes. Dortmund was a man who took immense pleasure in the successful manipulation of other people.

"I have found the location of Caesar's hoard," he announced. "I want you to use it to find my Caesar."

"Where is this hoard?"

"In the British Virgin Islands," he said. "Specifically, in an account held at the Trans Oriental & Occidental Bank. Despite the all-encompassing name, this bank has but one branch, which is located in the capital, Road Town, on the island of Tortola." It seemed that at last we were done with the historical allegories and getting down to facts. "The BVI are technically British, of course, but are largely self-governing and are not subject to British banking laws. There are really only two industries there: tourism and offshore banking. The latter is fueled by that one essential to offshore banking: legal nondisclosure guarantees. People use offshore banks for one reason only: to hide the loot. But you can't hide the loot in an account unless that account is anonymous."

"It's numbered?"

"No, accounts like this are named now, but the name

is meaningless. In these days of endless log-ins and PINs, no one can remember a number anymore. The name on this particular account is Iron Butterfly. You must find out who this Iron Butterfly is."

"I can tell you that right now: they were a rock band in the sixties. Had a big hit with a song called 'In-A-Gadda-Da-Vida,' I think."

He looked at me blankly. He had obviously never heard of the band, and I'm not sure what he thought I was saying when I'd told him the song title. "There has been no music written since Wagner died," he finally declared. For the first time in a long time, I felt an urge to smile. He picked up the sherry and sat back, apparently ending any further discussion on the subject.

"How much loot are we talking about here?" I asked.

"At the moment a million or two," he said dismissively. "Not real money."

"Dollars?"

"Yes, of course," he replied. To me a million dollars constituted real money. Actually, to me a single dollar constituted real money. "We expect the balance to increase," Dortmund continued, "and to increase considerably."

"Why?"

"Because it will fund the purchase of a particularly valuable commodity."

"What commodity?"

Dortmund didn't reply immediately. Instead, he shifted his great bulk forward and reached for the decanter. He had surprisingly small hands for such a large man. I couldn't help looking at my own in comparison, scarred and battered with wrists still raw from the rope, hands which knew the value of a dollar, and which would never see a million of them. Dortmund sipped with satisfaction from the refilled sherry glass before continuing.

"Are you familiar with the need-to-know principle?"

I nodded. It's a basic rule in the military: only those who need it are given classified access, and that access applies only to matters relevant to their particular work. It's meant to protect confidential information by not spreading it farther than is strictly necessary. I assumed that this principle applied even more in Dortmund's line of work, which is essentially the trade in secrets.

"Then you will understand why I would not normally answer your question," he continued. I understood: he wanted me to trace the money to its owner—there was no need for me to know what the money was for. "However, in this case I am going to make an exception," Dortmund said. "I am going to make an exception because I want you to fully appreciate how important it is that you not fail."

I shrugged my shoulders. If he wanted to tell me, that was fine; if not, that was fine, too. The gesture disappointed Dortmund—he could not understand anyone else not sharing his love of secrets. "The commodity I speak of, Captain Dalton, is plutonium. Black market plutonium, to be precise."

He let that sit there a little while, allowing me to absorb the implication for myself. The steward came, removed my empty glass, and replaced it with a third martini, unasked for this time. I must have looked like a man who needed a drink. I took an appreciative sip before continuing.

"Someone's making an A-bomb."

"They're trying to," Dortmund confirmed. "The NSA has made a series of intercepts over the last several months, indicating that a deal is being arranged. The suppliers appear to be Russian mafia, and the plutonium is likely to be Russian as well. It's the purchasers who concern us more. As yet we do not know their specific identity, but the general geographical location from which most of the intercepts have originated is that remote, mountainous border region between Afghanistan and Pakistan."

"Islamic fundamentalist terrorists."

"That's what we assume," Dortmund said. "Apparently negotiations are still proceeding. We understand that a small sample has already been transferred, probably just a fraction of a gram, but enough to enable the purchasers to be sure of the product. Should the deal go ahead, the parties have agreed that the vehicle for the transfer of funds will be this account at the Trans Oriental & Occidental Bank. We have of course mounted a major operation to identify and arrest the parties involved, and hopefully to intercept the plutonium itself. However, another way to put a stop to the deal would be to intercept the funding. No money, no deal."

"Any idea how much money we're talking about here?"

"Yes, we have a very good idea. The minimum amount of plutonium required to produce an explosive fission device is about eight kilograms, if your critical mass geometry is good enough. But Euclid and the Koran would make strange bedfellows, so let us call it ten. Whenever we hear of fissile material coming onto the black market—that is, plutonium or highly enriched uranium—we usually enlist a proxy or proxies in an attempt to purchase it for ourselves, which, apart from anything else, is the one certain way of keeping it out of the wrong hands. We therefore have a good feel for the market price. The going rate is around twenty-five million dollars per kilogram. Thus a quarter billion dollars should be sufficient to purchase the necessary ten kilograms, but let's call it two hundred million, in case they get a bulk-buyer's discount."

I guessed that even to Dortmund a quarter of a billion dollars was real money. We sat in silence for a while. I took a large mouthful of gin, sat back, and regarded my companion. I could not read him well, but well enough to know that there was more to this than he was telling me.

"I wasn't your first choice," I said.

"No," Dortmund admitted. "Nor my second. I regret that so far, the operation to locate the source of the money has met with failure."

"What sort of failure?"

"Persistent and terminal."

"Could you expand on that?"

"I'm afraid not, Captain Dalton. What's past is past, and we must look to the future now. I want you to find this Iron Butterfly. I want you to find him, and I want you to ensure that he will not be funding the purchase of plutonium through this or any other account in the future. Ever. Do I make myself clear?"

Very clear. Too clear.

"I'm not an assassin, Mr. Dortmund."

"I have access to your service records, Captain Dalton. All of them."

"I was in uniform then."

"And now you are out of uniform. A sartorial detail and entirely irrelevant. Only priests and fools mistake their garb for a binding moral imperative."

I let that go. I would make my own call on what to do, if and when the time came. The first thing was to find out who this Iron Butterfly was.

"Do you know anything more about the account?"

"No, but that is obviously the place to start. We have of course tried to penetrate the bank's network and access the account data, but this is not the routine matter that those occasional computer hackers one hears about would have us believe. Especially so in the case of an offshore bank, an institution whose business is the protection of identity, and who therefore takes pains to ensure that their firewall is secure. In short, we have been unable to access the network electronically. Therefore, you will need to access the network physically."

"Physically?"

He reached inside his jacket and pulled out an envelope, which he slid across the table. I picked it up and opened it. Inside was an airline ticket to the British Virgin Islands. The flight was scheduled for tomorrow morning.

Coach. Well, that's what happens to consultants.

"You must break into the bank, Captain Dalton." Now I knew at least one reason Dortmund was using me instead of his own people: if I was caught, they would simply disown me. There was nothing linking me to them. I would presumably spend the next five years or so doing time in some British prison, but for Dortmund that would be inconsequential. His only interest was in avoiding the embarrassment of having one of his own people caught spying on an ally's territory.

"And once I'm inside?"

"You need only find a data terminal and plug in," Dortmund said.

"Plug in what?"

"A laptop computer, which we will give you. If you connect it to a data port physically within the bank, it will do the rest."

"How does it work?"

"I have no idea, Captain Dalton—I am not a technical man. You will be given suitable instruction when picking the thing up. I had intended you to do this at Langley, but given the fact of your abduction, I think that is no longer wise."

He pulled out a notepad and wrote down an address, then tore off the sheet and passed it to me. The address was in Alexandria, Virginia—a Washington suburb.

"Ask for Harry," he said. "I will ensure that there is a Harry there tonight."

"A Harry?"

"I have more than one Harry, Captain Dalton. I have several Harrys, in fact."

"Several Harrys?"

"They are very useful to me."

Dortmund—a man with several useful Harrys.

He pulled out another item and passed it to me. It was a folder, an American Express folder. Inside were an itinerary, five thousand dollars in traveler's checks, and an American Express Platinum Card. The card was in my name.

"This will cover your expenses during the operation," Dortmund said. "Use the traveler's checks—the charge card is only for use in an emergency. You must keep the originals of all receipts, and we will of course require a strict accounting for all expenses incurred."

"Of course."

"Lastly, I have this for you." He pulled out a cell phone and passed it to me. "It is a normal cell phone, but the chip set has been augmented with one of our own. In all cases but one it will operate as would any other cell phone. However, there is one number which will cause it to encode the transmissions. These can only be decoded by another phone containing the same chip. When you dial this number it will briefly ring as usual, then when the other end answers, there will be a series of tones as the two phones synchronize. This will sound something like a fax line. When the tones cease, you have a secure connection. Even if the transmission is intercepted, it will be meaningless to a listener who himself does not have the decoding chip set." He gave me the number, which I spent a moment silently repeating until I had it memorized.

"Is it your number?"

"No, but it will be answered and can be securely transferred to me."

Dortmund finished his sherry, then placed the emptied glass on the table next to the emptied decanter. "Now, unless you have any further questions, I think that concludes our business. I will expect regular progress reports, and I will expect that you will have progress to report."

I took my time with my own drink, something which obviously annoyed my companion. One of the old leather men came tottering in, saw Dortmund enthroned by the fire conducting an audience like the Pope, then promptly turned around and shuffled back out. I finished the martini and stood to take my leave. Dortmund remained seated—getting up would be a major operation for him, an effort which would be wasted in showing courtesy to a hireling.

"Does the Mayflower Club have any female members?" I asked.

"Don't be ridiculous," he responded.

"It's the twenty-first century, Mr. Dortmund. You should let women join."

He looked at me with an expression somewhere between horror and revulsion. As long as he'd thought of me as an assassin he'd had no problem with my company, but now that I had suggested admitting women into his club, he clearly found my presence repugnant.

We parted with a nod. No handshake was offered to me from the man who had several useful Harrys.

THREE

SNOW was still falling outside the Mayflower Club, the same snow which had begun to fall this afternoon as I'd walked from the hunting cabin into the nearest town, eventually catching a bus back into D.C. But the snow there had been clean snow, country snow: big, dry flakes settling quietly on fields silent and fallow. I had enjoyed that walk, thinking of my home not so far away. I could imagine the vines as they would be then, standing lonely and serene in the leaden gray blue late winter light, austere dark skeletons against a fresh sea of white. I had longed to be back there.

Now I trudged through city slush, trudged through snow that was gray before it even hit the ground.

I realized that I was thinking of my home with Beth Houston still in it. During the fall we had drunk mulled wine in front of the fireplace, and I'd told her how lovely the vines looked in snow, but she never got to see it for herself. She was back in New York City now, an urban girl who'd been out of place on a remote vineyard in northern Virginia—something we'd both known all along. And in any case it must have been obvious to her from the beginning that I was manifestly unfit material for any lasting relationship.

I found myself at the end of the Mall, surprised at having come so far. I must have been thinking of Beth for half an hour, although it seemed like just a minute. I was annoyed to have found myself thinking of her again, when I'd thought I'd finally managed to force her out of my mind. I wondered what had prompted it.

I checked behind me, as I had done several times since leaving the Mayflower Club, watching for the friends and relatives of Billy-Jo-Bob. But the expanse was empty. The great institutions of the Smithsonian had closed long ago, the tourists were gone, and nobody else was stupid enough to be trudging late at night down the middle of the Mall during a snowstorm.

The Capitol building loomed ahead, immense and proud. I stood a moment to admire it. This is the building which best symbolizes Washington, not the White House. Every two-bit dictator has a palace, but elected legislatures are the preserve of democracies. I walked up past it and over to the city's eastern quadrants, where Washington shuns the tourist and embraces the outcast.

My hotel—Sal's—was small, dark, and catered to transients. I took the Anaconda in hand, covered it with the coat over my arm, and entered. Sal's Hotel was the sort of establishment where to pay by cash was the norm, and which was why I had chosen it. The floor of the small lobby was littered with cigarette butts. One of the fluorescent bulbs buzzed and flickered. A hand-lettered sign above what passed for a front desk announced, No Women after 10:00 P.M.

The manager was a greasy man dressed in an undershirt, with his feet up on the desk, smoking a cigarette and reading a newspaper. I asked him for the key, which he gave me wordlessly. I felt like asking if there were any messages, just to see if I could get a rise out of him, but he was immersed in the racing guide, so I left him alone to contemplate the horses. Perhaps it was Sal himself. I couldn't tell because he'd forgotten his courtesy name tag.

The rooms had no phones, but there was a pay phone attached to a wall in the lobby. The coin return had been used as an ashtray, but to my surprise the phone actually worked. I called the airline and upgraded to first class. Full fare. I charged it on the American Express card.

There was no elevator. I walked upstairs, going by the occasional furtive guest coming the other way, broken men who negotiated their passage past other human beings with heads lowered and eyes averted. I checked them out anyway, looking for footwear that was too expensive, or teeth too well cared for, or some other sign that they were not the genuine article. My finger was on the trigger of the Anaconda the whole time.

At the fourth floor I checked the door to my room. The little shred of tissue paper I'd jammed between it and the frame was still in place: no one had entered the room in my absence, or if so, they'd been clever enough to notice the signal and reset it on departure.

I opened the door. My room was clear. There was no need to check for anyone hiding; there was no place to hide. I gathered the drugstore shopping bag of items I'd purchased after checking in, went down to the bathroom at the end of the hallway, and spent the better part of the next hour there. With the two showers, three martinis, and multiple flossings since having left the hunting cabin, I was finally rid of the remnants of Billy-Jo-Bob.

LATE that evening I took a cab to the address in Alexandria. I had expected a dark, out-of-the-way office or perhaps a small electronics repair shop in which the proprietor—a wizened, chain-smoking old man named Harry—would occasionally perform customized work for Dortmund. But instead the place where the cab dropped me was the most brightly lit building on the block, with a huge marquee full of flashing lights, and large, backlit advertising signs at sidewalk level beckoning passersby.

The place was called Babycakes. It was a strip joint.

I approached the ticket booth where the cover charge was collected. There was an old man on the other side of the glass. He wasn't smoking, but he could pass for wizened.

"Are you Harry?" I asked.

"Nope," he said. "I'm George, if that's any help."

"Do you know if Harry's inside?"

"Can't say I know any Harrys off the top of my head, but you can ask the floor manager. His name is Joe, by the way."

I nodded and made for the door, but he stopped me by clearing his throat. "That'll be twenty dollars," he said, "which entitles you to admission and two free drinks." I paid the man and went inside.

The club was dark and smoky, and the music was loud. A steroidal mountain with arms and legs, presumably Joe the floor manager, conducted me to a table. Obviously the floor manager's real job was keeping the patrons in line. We passed tables occupied by men with women in various stages of undress draping themselves over them.

Joe led me to a table by a wall, where I sat on the bench seat facing out to the room. I tipped Joe and asked him if Harry was here.

"Not as far as I know," he said, "but then this isn't exactly the sort of establishment where we ask patrons for their names, if you know what I mean." I knew what he meant. After he left I sat back and wondered how I was going to identify my contact. Going from table to table and asking the staff to briefly disentangle themselves while I inquired into the patrons' identities wasn't a realistic option.

A woman came over to take my drink order. She was dressed in a filmy negligee and high-heeled stilettos. I asked her what she would recommend.

"The whiskey's drinkable," she admitted. "Everything else is rotgut."

I ordered whiskey. She left to get the drink, and with my eyes now adjusted to the low lighting, I was able to get a better look around. There was a stage in the middle of the room. Its base was rimmed with small lights. At the center was a fireman's pole, which ran up to the ceiling, and which was currently being used in a way that no fireman ever would.

Around the stage were individual seats occupied by a number of admiring patrons with dollar notes extended in eager anticipation. Beyond these were regular tables, some occupied singly, many with groups that occasionally included female patrons—wild office parties perhaps.

The woman returned with my drink. I tried again, "Do you know if Harry's here tonight?"

"Sure," she replied, "that's her onstage now."

We both looked at the stage. My contact—Harry—was currently hanging upside down on the pole, one leg twisted around it to support her weight, the other extended toward the audience in a pose that had garnered their complete and undivided attention.

"Harry's quite an athlete," I said.

"Yeah, she's good," my companion said in professional admiration. She looked back at me and lowered her voice. "Would you like me to ask her to come over after she's done?"

I said that I would, and gave her a tip. After she left I watched Harry go through the remainder of her routine. She was genuinely athletic, performing full splits while both upright and inverted, and able to stand one-legged against the pole with the other perfectly vertical. I could see a faint sheen of sweat glistening on her skin, which helped give definition to the well-toned musculature. She could probably do more one-armed pushups than me.

Finally she completed her act and went offstage to a chorus of appreciative hoots and hollers from the front row seats, who clearly thought they'd gotten their money's worth. Her place onstage was taken by the same woman who brought me the drink, and who turned out to be no slouch herself.

After a while another woman approached my table—I had thought to take the second drink order—but it turned out to be Harry herself. It was hard to recognize her with her clothes on. She was wearing a white blouse with a tie, a short tartan kilt, long white socks that came to just below her knees, and was carrying a satchel over her shoulder. To complete the schoolgirl transformation she had tied her hair into two ponytails that poked out cheekily from either side of her head. But no girl would have been allowed in school wearing the shoes: patent leather pumps with enormous platforms and nine-inch heels.

She stood before me, hand on hip, sucking a lollipop.

"Hi, mister," she said.

"Hello, Harry," I said. "You're impressive on the stage."

"I've been a bad girl," she admitted. "You may have to spank me."

"I'm not playing, Harry. Let's just get this done, okay?"

"No play, no present," she said.

I sighed in resignation. "Okay, so what is it we have to do here?"

"Well, now let's see." She gave her lollipop a thoughtful suck, as if giving the matter weighty consideration. "One laptop must be worth at least one lap dance," she concluded, holding out her hand. "Twenty dollars please, mister."

I gave her a hundred—it was Dortmund's money.

Harry thanked me politely and carefully tucked the bill into a shirt pocket. She put down her satchel, loosened her tie, and sat up on the bench astride me.

She removed the lollipop and said, "Keep your eyes on me while I say this." I kept my eyes on her. "The laptop's in the satchel I just placed on the floor. When you leave, just casually pick it up and take it with you." Before I could respond she licked me. Not just once but several times, all on the face.

"Thanks, Harry," I said when she'd finished. "Now I'm all sticky."

But she just smiled and pulled the tie over her head. "Unbutton me," she commanded.

I did my best. The buttons were small and tight. The shirt itself was tight—there was quite a bit inside that it was holding in check, and I soon realized that there was no undergarment performing support duty. When the blouse was unbuttoned, Harry leaned up and forward, her head above mine, her breasts in front of my face.

"There's a Category 5 network cable with standard RJ-45 modular plugs and boots inside the satchel," she whispered, rocking in time to the music. "When you access whatever network it is that you're accessing, make sure that you plug in the cable before powering up the laptop." Her hips were moving in time with the music, too. "The computer will automatically check for network connections on startup, and log itself on to the network as a system administrator."

"How will it know the password?" I asked her left nipple.

"Unless they use very sophisticated encryption, the machine will get it." She leaned back, removed the ponytail bands, and shook her hair free. When she came up and forward again, her long hair formed a private little cocoon around us. "Once it's on the network, the machine will look for database servers." A breast gently bumped me in the eye. "The weak link is the type of server. The software has to be either Microsoft or Oracle or Sybase. Those are the big three, so it's likely that your target will use one of them. But not necessarily. If it's some other server type—UNIX-based, for example—the system won't recognize it."

Harry flicked back her hair, sat down firmly in my lap, and removed the kilt. Again she had made do without the benefit of underwear. Apart from the shoes and socks, and a small piece of jewelry in her belly button, she was naked.

She began gyrating to the loud music, neck and head back, eyes closed.

"Once it finds the server, it will select from a library of drivers, make an ODBC connection, and commence a database dump onto the internal hard drive," she said, louder now and breathy. I was finding it a little difficult to breathe myself. "There's over five hundred gigs of memory, so there's unlikely to be any disc space issue. When the dump is finished, a window will appear saying, 'Job complete.' Nothing else, just that. When you see that, you're done."

She grabbed my shoulders and began grinding back and forth in my lap now, still with eyes closed and head thrown back. Suddenly she opened her eyes and looked at me.

"Can't you at least pretend that you're enjoying this?"

"I am enjoying this," I said. "Very much." Given what she'd been doing, I was unsure how she could have been unaware of that fact.

"Then act it," she commanded. "Touch me."

"Where?"

That stopped her. She sat forward, grabbed my head with her hands, and looked me in the eye. "Do you really need a road map?"

"Sorry," I said. "Please proceed."

I never did get that second drink.

FOUR

IT was 3:00 A.M. when I finally left Babycakes. I stepped outside. The snow had stopped falling, and the street was calm and quiet after the raucous activity inside the club. George was still in his booth, still wizened. There was a man in a dark suit talking to him. He turned to face me as I came out the door. He was smiling, and he had excellent teeth.

He recognized me at the same instant I recognized him. We both went for our hardware.

Neither of us were exactly Quick Draw McGraw that night. I had a good excuse: something as big as an Anaconda is difficult to handle smoothly at the best of times, and I had never really gotten it sitting right after having had my general comportment messed with by Harry. But Smiling Man had no such excuse: he'd simply been caught off guard. Perhaps he'd been watching the club and had become impatient waiting for me to come out, or maybe he'd just come over to ask George if there was a back door I could have exited by. Either way, he was as slow with his hardware as I was.

We ended up with our guns on each other.

"Don't do it, George," I said to the old man, without taking my eyes off Smiley. In my peripheral vision I'd noticed his hands slowly going under the counter, perhaps to an alarm, but since it was both hands more likely to a shotgun. George's hands came smartly back up on top of the counter.

"No, sir," he said.

Now it was time to do some rapid assessment. Smiling Man: alert, steady, eyes not leaving mine. Okay, nothing there. Weapon: Government 1911 model .45 automatic, the gun that under the military designation M1911A1 had been the standard-issue sidearm in the American armed forces for most of the twentieth century—in fact I had once worn one myself. Common model with a number of different manufacturers, but primarily Colt. Functions reliably. Leaves big holes.

Did he have any people backing him up? None that I could see, and if he did, they would have been in play by now. So it seemed that it was just going to be me and the toothpaste commercial.

Then I noticed something interesting about that Government 1911 that he was holding.

THERE are two things needed to make a bullet come out of a gun. Firstly, the gun needs to be cocked by setting the hammer to the rear. Secondly, the hammer must be tripped, causing the gun to discharge. In all handguns the trigger performs the second action, tripping the hammer. That's called a single-action trigger. But on many weapons the trigger can also perform the first action, too. That is, in one pull the trigger will first cock the weapon, then at the end of the pull it will trip the hammer. That's called a double-action trigger.

Automatics have less need for a double-action trigger, because the gun automatically recocks and reloads itself after each round. Except on the first round—that one you have to do yourself.

My weapon wasn't cocked, but it didn't need to be. Like many revolvers, Anacondas have double-action triggers. Not so Government 1911s. Government 1911 models only have single-action triggers. And with that warm inner glow that accompanies the sudden realization that things are going your way, I saw that Smiling Man's weapon wasn't cocked. The most harm he could do to me with that handgun right now was to throw it at me.

If he'd been faster getting his weapon out he'd have actioned it and had me cold. But he'd been too slow for that, and so he'd simply brought the gun onto me, uncocked and unusable, hoping that I wouldn't figure it out, and that he could therefore extract from the situation with an honorable draw.

"You lose," I said quietly.

He was silent for a moment, perhaps wondering whether or not to try bluffing, but in the end he acknowledged reality. He shrugged his shoulders in resignation.

"So what's next?" he asked.

"Seen your friend from the hunting cabin lately?"

He nodded. "We found him."

"You keep bad company."

"So Momma tells me."

"Who's we?"

"Save your breath and pull the trigger," he said. It seemed that Smiling Man wasn't feeling chatty tonight.

"Gun on the ground," I ordered. He bent at the knees and slowly placed the weapon on the sidewalk. Real slow; he was spending too long down there. "You surely can't be contemplating going for a backup," I said. He clicked his tongue in annoyance and stood up.

"Wall," I said. He walked over to the wall of the club and assumed the position without further instruction from me. Whoever he was, this wasn't the first time he'd submitted to a pat down. I jammed the Anaconda into the back of his head and went to work. The only things in his jacket pockets were two spare clips for the Government 1911, both full. He had cash in his trousers, plus keys to a vehicle, both of which I took. On his belt was a small leather pouch with a pair of handcuffs inside, which I also took. And on his right ankle I found what had been on his mind: a small Taurus .22 or .25 caliber automatic. Double-action with a chambered round. He probably wouldn't be using anything but double-action weapons from now on. I put that in my coat pocket along with the rest.

What I didn't find was a wallet, or a driver's license, or any other form of identification. He was a professional—right now an embarrassed professional—but still a professional: I wasn't going to get anything useful out of him, but I knew some people who would.

I backed off. "Sidewalk, facing the street," I said. He came away from the wall and went to the curb, where he faced out onto the quiet street.

I held out the car keys and said, "Which one?"

"Figure it out for yourself, asshole."

My, but they were an unfriendly bunch. I pushed the unlock button on the key fob. The quiet of the night was broken by a shrill double beep from a large SUV parked across the street. Its parking lights flashed on and off a few times.

"My guess is it's the big Chevy over there that's blinking like a Christmas tree," I said. "What do you think?"

He didn't reply. This just wasn't his night.

"George?" George had been watching the proceedings with keen interest. At his age, he probably found all this more entertaining than what went on inside the club.

"Yes, boss," George replied. So I was "boss" now— apparently I'd been promoted by the Anaconda.

"When I give the signal, call the cops."

"Okay," he said. "What's the signal?"

"You'll know it when you hear it." I backed around behind Smiling Man. "Vehicle," I said. "Nice and slow."

At 3:00 A.M. on a snowy night there was no traffic. Smiling Man stepped out onto the street and over to the Chevy. It was a big one, a Suburban, black, with the windows blacked out, too. I took a moment to memorize the license plates. They were probably stolen—perhaps the whole vehicle was—but Smiling Man had already made one mistake tonight, and so perhaps he'd made another.

I cuffed Smiling Man to a rear wheel, went over to a grating in the gutter, and dropped the keys to the handcuffs through it. Then I stood by the vehicle.

"Don't you know these big SUVs are bad for the environment?" I asked.

"Wouldn't have taken you for a tree hugger," he replied.

"I'm a farmer," I said. "I understand the importance of preserving what nature gives us." I raised the Anaconda and put a loose three-round grouping into the engine compartment. In the silence of the still evening the noise from the Anaconda was tremendous.

Smiling Man looked very angry—so the vehicle itself wasn't stolen. "Asshole," he said.

I was getting tired of being called that, so I turned and shot him before he knew what was happening.

After the gunshot echoed away there was a short interval of dead silence, followed by the sound of a tire deflating. Smiling Man wasn't smiling. His eyes were wide open, looking down at his shoulder where the bullet had passed through on the way to the tire that was behind it. It was actually the tire that I'd wanted to take out: those first three .44 Magnum rounds would probably have cracked the engine block, but taking out a tire ensured that—even if Smiling Man got free of the cuffs and there was a spare to the truck hidden somewhere—he still wouldn't be going anywhere very fast.

Generally, you should always shoot to kill. Shooting to wound can lead to socially awkward situations in the future. But since a nice fleshy part of Smiling Man had been convenient at the time, I had not been able to resist extracting a payback while taking out the tire.

His eyes were open very wide for three o'clock in the morning. The rear of the Suburban gradually sank as it came to rest on the rim.

"Profanity is the last resort of the ignorant," I said. "Didn't your mother ever teach you that?"

"You shot me," he said.

"Yes," I agreed, "a little."

I walked over and bent down for a closer look at the wound. It didn't seem to have hit bone, but blood was pouring out.

"Gee, that's got to hurt," I said.

"You bet it hurts, you—"

I interrupted him by jamming the barrel of the Anaconda into his open mouth.

"Don't be such a baby."

He made a wet choking sound, which may have been agreement to behave more stoically. I looked him in the eye and spoke quietly. "I'd call it about even right now," I said. "You shot me, so I shot you."

He made another wet choking sound and dribbled.

"Please don't slobber on my gun," I said. "The police will be here soon, and they're going to do something that I can't: they're going to find out just exactly who you are. It'll make the papers, and so then I'm going to know who you are, too. After that, I'm going to make it my business to know all about you. You understand?"

He nodded without dribbling this time.

"So we're square now. But if I ever see you again, even by accident, I'm not going to give you a chance to upset the balance."

Without waiting for an acknowledgment I stood and walked away, making it clear to Smiling Man that his agreement wasn't necessary. I was a hundred yards down the street when I heard a voice crying out behind me.

"Hey, boss."

I turned around. The old man was out of his booth, looking anxiously after me.

"Yeah?"

"Were those gunshots the signal?"

"Yes, George," I cried back. "They were the signal."

With George, as with so many people in life, you really had to spell things out.

FIVE

DORTMUND'S itinerary had me staying at a hotel in Road Town. Judging by the rates it couldn't have been much of a hotel. First thing in the morning I canceled it and booked into a luxury resort instead. It was high season, and the rooms were fully booked, but they had a suite available. The rates were steep, but not what you'd call real money. The credit card took care of it.

I bought a copy of the *Washington Post* to read with breakfast at a nearby diner but found nothing in the Metro section about the previous evening—either it had been too late to make the edition, or D.C.-area shootings which don't result in fatalities are deemed too insignificant to matter.

Before leaving for the airport I made a couple of stops, the first of which was a gym. It wasn't the sort of gym where girls in colorful leotards work out on weight machines without any actual weights on them. It was called Mick's Gym, and it catered to the nonleotard set.

I went to the front desk. The man behind it was bald-headed and pale-eyed; he could have been anywhere between forty and seventy years old. The ridge of his eyebrows stood out, bulging with the layers of scar tissue that boxers acquire from having old wounds continuously reopened and then rehealing. He was short but wide and without much fat on him—welterweight now, but probably fought as a lightweight. Judging by that brow line he must have come off second best in a lot of fights, but that never deters an Irishman.

Behind him the gym was dominated by a boxing ring, the canvas gray with dirt and age. On the perimeter there were some heavy bags and some speed bags, plus benches with brackets for free weights. There was a set of scales: proper scales with a long balance beam along which the weight slid. Boxers are weight conscious: a fraction of an ounce too much can send them out of their class.

No cardiovascular equipment. This wasn't the sort of gym where words like *cardiovascular* were part of the vocabulary.

The ring was empty, but one of the benches was occupied by a guy doing presses, with another guy behind him spotting. Both were black, both were heavily tattooed, and both ignored me. Presuming the big plates were forty-five pounds, and the bar itself about the same, then the guy was bench pressing well over three hundred. I couldn't bench press that to save my life. But then I have a gun, so I don't need to.

"Are you Mick?" I asked the little guy.

"Yeah," he said. "Who wants to know?"

"Lysander Dalton," I said. We didn't shake hands. Mick's Gym was the sort of place where you didn't wear leotards, and you didn't shake hands. "I'd like to become a member."

"That so?" Mick said. He eyed me for a moment in evaluative silence before continuing. "Let me see where I left those membership forms."

He opened the drawer of his desk. There were two

things inside, neither of which was a membership form. One was a snub-nosed revolver, a .38 maybe, and the other was a packet of cigarettes. He held the drawer open long enough to make sure that I'd seen the gun—his way of telling me what kind of joint this was before I made any hasty, long-term commitments—then his hand went to the cigarettes. He closed the drawer and took out a cigarette. It was unfiltered. He tapped it a few times on top of the desk before putting it in his mouth and lighting up. Mick's Gym was the sort of place where the staff smoke unfiltered Camels while on duty.

"You been here before?" he asked.

"No."

"Might not be your kind of place."

"You got lockers?"

"Yep."

"Then it's my kind of place," I said.

He nodded his head in understanding and looked around to make sure no one could overhear before continuing. "You been away?" he quietly asked.

"Not for a long time," I said.

"Where?"

"Leavenworth."

He put his feet up on the desk, took a long drag of the cigarette, then let the smoke out slowly, as if considering the merits of Leavenworth.

"Good prison," he said at last. "They got very good food there."

"And an excellent health plan."

Mick smiled. He had all his front teeth, which seemed unlikely in view of the brow situation. They were probably false.

"Well now, about fees. Let's see . . . Use of the health club—"

"The what?"

"Don't call it a gym no more," he said. "Call it a

health club now." He shrugged his shoulders. "Got to keep up with the times."

"Okay, so it's a health club," I said. *Healthy for bacteria, not doubt.*

He squared his shoulders. "So, as I was saying, use of the health club: that would be ten bucks a month."

"Very fair."

"And rental of a locker, that would be . . . forty a month."

"A little steep for just a locker."

"They are *very* secure lockers."

I handed over five hundred dollars. "That's for six months," I said. "The extra's to cover any unexpected expenses—like, say, postage."

"Postage?"

"In case I need something from my locker," I explained, "but am not in a position to pick it up personally."

He nodded his head in understanding. "And would you be needing that locker right now?" He eyed the *Washington Post* I was holding, in which the Anaconda was currently wrapped.

"Yes," I said. I held up the newspaper package. "For my gym shoes here."

He got up from behind the desk and led me to the bathroom, a squalid affair which even I, though having experienced many years of less than salubrious facilities in both the marines and Leavenworth, would be reluctant to put my bare feet upon.

"Come on, Mick. There is such a thing as disinfectant, you know."

"It's got character," he said. "That's what distinguishes my health club from those other joints."

He threw his cigarette butt at one of the lidless and cubicleless toilets. It missed and landed on the floor instead. Mick either didn't notice or didn't care. He went across to the lockers, a series of old battered metal boxes that were about as secure as the newspaper.

"You call these secure?"

"They got what you call perimeter security," he explained. "That means me."

I shrugged my shoulders. No reasonable thief would think a job in here worth the risk of contracting hepatitis B anyway. I selected a locker, put the newspaper-wrapped Anaconda inside, and closed it with the padlock I'd bought at a drugstore on the way.

I kept one key for myself and handed the other to Mick.

"Don't let anyone play with my gym shoes," I said. "They're loaded."

He nodded his head but said nothing further. We left the bathroom and went back to the front desk. The black guys were doing squats now, but they'd dropped down to middle-range plates and were squatting less than a hundred. Typical ex-cons, they were all upper body, with little leg strength, probably less endurance, and they wore sweats to cover their skinny legs. They wouldn't have made it through five minutes of the course at Camp Pendleton.

"Don't you think our prisons need to emphasize a healthier and more balanced workout regimen for their inmates?"

"Yeah, worries the hell out of me," Mick replied, lighting up a fresh cigarette. "I was thinking of writing my congressman about it, you know?" He handed me a business card, according to which I was indeed in Mick's Health Club. "You get a sudden need for them gym shoes, call me on that number."

"You'll hear from me," I said.

I left the gym and began heading across town to my next errand, resisting the urge to wipe my shoes on the grass until I was around the corner and out of sight.

* * *

THE next stop was an American Express office for more traveler's checks. I also made sure to find out exactly what was and was not allowable with the little piece of plastic that had been entrusted into my possession, for I had no intention of risking time in a British prison to achieve results that could equally well be achieved by the liberal application of Dortmund's money.

Later that morning I took the flight from Dulles to San Juan, then a puddle jumper over to Tortola, where a speedboat picked me up from the airport and took me straight to the private island on which the resort was located.

By the end of the day I was sitting on the terrace, drinking a daiquiri, watching the sun set over the Sir Francis Drake Channel, and thinking that maybe working for Dortmund wasn't so bad after all.

THE next morning I went down to the beach, and spent awhile reading before taking a walk along its length. Other guests were installed here and there, some families but mostly couples, sleek and moneyed.

There were two girls playing paddleball, lithe and tanned, wearing nothing but little bikini bottoms, hitting the ball back and forward while chatting to each other in French. The one facing me hit the ball too hard, over her companion's head. It came my way. I took a few quick steps, caught it on the fly, then walked over to return it to them.

"*Bonjour,*" I said. I handed the ball back to the one who'd hit it my way. "*Vous êtes trés forte, mademoiselle.*"

"*Oui,*" she giggled, agreeing that she was very strong. The other giggled, too. They were probably giggling at my accent.

I held out my hand. *"Je m'appelle Lysander Dalton,"* I said. *"Comment vous appellez vous?"*

The one who'd hit the ball shook my hand first. Her name was Mimi. The other was Fifi. They were perfect.

"Vous êtes en vacances?" I asked.

"Non," said Mimi, *"Nous sérons ici à faire un film."*

"Vous êtes des actrices?" Mimi and Fifi both nodded: they were actresses. I talked with them for a while. The name of the film they were in the Caribbean to make turned out to be *Les Nuits Chaudes dans les Antilles:* "Hot Nights in the Caribbean." It was not intended for theatrical release, instead destined to go straight to cable on whatever was the French equivalent of the Playboy channel.

"I have a proposition for you," I said. I said it in English. I don't know how to proposition a girl in French, a serious gap in my social skills. They giggled some more. When it came to being propositioned, it turned out that they were comfortably multilingual.

THE three of us returned to the hotel together. In the lobby we stopped by the concierge desk.

"Could you contact Bergdorf Goodman in New York for me?" I asked the concierge. "I'd like them to ship two outfits here overnight."

"Certainly," he said, as if this was the most reasonable of requests. He took a notepad and pen in hand. "What sort of outfits?"

"Fashionable resort daywear for these two," I said. "I'll leave it to the store to select something suitable."

"Certainly, sir. What sizes should I ask for?"

"Quelles sont vos pointures?" I asked the girls.

"Trente-quatre," said Mimi.

"Trente-quatre," said Fifi.

"Et souliers?"

"Trente-huit," said Mimi.

"Trente-huit," said Fifi.

"Do you wear each other's clothes?" I asked.

"We do all sorts of things together," Fifi replied, a remark which launched them into fresh spasms of giggling delight.

I turned back to the concierge, who watched this proceeding with admirable aplomb. "Both are dress size thirty-four, and shoe size thirty-eight. Those are European sizes, of course,"

"Of course," murmured the concierge. "And price range, sir?"

"Any price," I said. Then, to the girls, "Why don't you do some shopping while I attend to business?" They toddled off into the lobby store.

I gave the concierge the credit card details that he'd need when calling Bergdorf Goodman. Then I asked him to do one more thing for me.

"I'd also like to make an appointment at the Trans Oriental & Occidental Bank in Road Town. I need to speak to someone there about opening an account."

"Certainly, sir, I'll be happy to arrange it."

We settled on a time, and I tipped him generously before leaving. With any luck, when he called the bank to make the appointment, he would also pass on what I'd just made sure he knew: that I was a man who obviously had too much money.

THE resort's speedboat took us into Road Town. Bergdorf Goodman had gone for the Saint Tropez look: the sort of clothing that models who when in town hang out with rock stars might wear when on vacation, hanging out with rock stars who were also on vacation. Mimi wore a Cavalli outfit for which Roberto seemed to have forgotten the lining, and Fifi was in something by Versace that would have gotten her arrested in Salt Lake City.

We sped into the harbor past yachts and a cruise ship and the ferry from Saint Thomas. Activity on the dock stopped as we came alongside and disembarked. A car was waiting for us and took us through the town, past old colonial buildings with wide verandas, and into a small corporate park complex on the outskirts of Road Town. One of the offices was occupied by the headquarters and sole branch of the Trans Oriental & Occidental Bank.

We went inside. There was no counter with teller windows: this wasn't the sort of bank that did honest, straightforward banking business. Instead it was a regular open-plan office space. In front was a reception desk with a comfortable sitting area for visitors. Beyond that were low cubicle workstations with old-fashioned CRT monitors, and then at the rear were glass-walled offices. There were four people I could see: the receptionist, two clerks at the workstations, and a man dressed in a suit occupying the largest of the offices at the rear.

All four looked up as we entered. I was expected. Mimi and Fifi were not.

The two clerks frankly stopped work to stare. The receptionist took a moment to compose herself before rising from her chair.

"Mr. Dalton?" she inquired.

"Yes."

"I'm Hermione Watkins." We shook hands. Her name sounded more English than English names, although she was an islander. "I'll take you through to the manager, Mr. Smythson." Before moving she looked inquiringly at the girls, then back to me.

Mimi had found a fashion magazine among those scattered on the coffee table, and was flicking through it while chewing gum. She idly blew a bubble. That was a nice touch—Mimi was a real actress after all.

Fifi was trying out one of the armchairs. She was bouncing slightly, an activity which appeared sufficient to keep her fully occupied.

"Best to leave them here," I said. Hermione Watkins nodded—she obviously thought so, too. I followed her though to the office at the rear.

The occupant turned out to be the manager. He stood and pushed in front of Hermione to introduce himself as Henry Smythson. We shook hands, which was like shaking a dead fish. He was a pasty man, as pale as ice cream—genuinely English. It was not a suit he wore, but gray trousers and a blazer. The trousers needed pressing, and the blazer was flecked with dandruff. The tie was what the English call a regimental tie.

I once had to pay a visit to a man in Kuwait City. The city was occupied at the time by the Iraqi Army, and I was not a welcome guest. The man was a colonel whose name began with Abu and was unpronounceable thereafter—we called him Colonel Boo Boo. He was a protégé of the infamous "Chemical Ali," and ran a unit whose job it was to interrogate anyone Chemical Ali wanted interrogated, but in this case "interrogation" was just a pretty word for torture. We knew that they had set themselves up in the former Kuwaiti military headquarters and were enthusiastically practicing their craft on the locals. We knew the building, but we didn't know what the layout was inside.

The intelligence people found a British Army officer who had recently been on exchange with the Kuwaitis, and who knew the internal layout. They had him flown into the Saudi base we were operating from. Late one night I took him into Kuwait City with me and three of my people: Easy Black—my best sergeant who was also an excellent knife man, a radio operator, and a new kid in the unit who needed to get blooded—he was designated as the explosives guy.

Covert operations like these are usually complete successes or total failures. This one turned out to be a mixture of the two—we got Colonel Boo Boo and two of his associates, but the extraction was ugly: I lost the radio guy, and the Brit took a round. He was tough though, and we got him out. He spent a week recovering in the base hospital before they flew him back home. He turned out not to be English but a Scotsman, and a Scotsman who took the consumption of the national beverage as a solemn patriotic duty. When the nurses weren't paying too much attention I assisted his recovery by sharing a bottle of his favorite fluid. On our way to emptying it, he had told me about some of their strange customs in the British Army, including regimental ties, and had shown me his own: a blue and maroon striped tie with little shields on it that he referred to as "Orders of the Garter."

It was precisely the same pattern as the tie that Henry Smythson of the fishlike handshake was now wearing.

"Coldstream Guards," I said.

"I beg your pardon?"

"Coldstream Guards," I repeated. "You're wearing a regimental tie of the Coldstream Guards. Perhaps you know Jack Macgregor?—he served in the Coldstream Guards about the time of the first Iraqi War."

Hermione and I waited for an answer, but Henry Smythson was at a momentary loss for words. "No, I'm afraid that I don't know him," he eventually replied. Of course not: he'd never served in the Coldstream Guards, nor any other military, and had probably acquired the tie by mail order. "Thank you, Hermione," Smythson said testily. He would have preferred Hermione not to have witnessed this exchange.

Hermione looked at me and couldn't keep the smile from her face. "Nice to have met you, Mr. Dalton."

"And you, Ms. Watkins." She left the office with a jaunty stride.

Smythson invited me to take a seat, eager to change the subject.

"How might we be of service to you, Mr. Dalton?"

"I am interested in opening a bank account," I explained. "It would be important to me that the details of such an account be kept confidential."

"Yes, of course," Smythson replied. He smirked. I think the smirk was meant to convey that he was a man of the world, speaking to another man of the world with complete understanding, but all it conveyed to me was that his teeth were crooked. He went on to explain how the laws governing offshore banking in the British Virgin Islands guaranteed anonymity, and that given the importance of offshore banking to the islands' economy, these laws were unlikely to change. His eyes kept looking involuntarily over my shoulder as he spoke, glancing out beyond his glass-walled office to where Mimi and Fifi had draped themselves across the furniture. Can't say I blamed him.

Finally he asked the question that had been on his mind all along. "How much would you wish to deposit?"

"Eventually, who knows?" I said. "Right now, nothing."

Smythson cleared his throat. "Mr. Dalton, you must realize that in order for there to be an account there must of course be some money in it?"

I waved his objection away. "Yes, yes," I said. "When I say nothing, I mean nothing serious—not what you'd call real money. Of course you would need something to open the account. Shall we say, I don't know . . . fifty thousand?"

"Dollars?" he said. He wasn't a man of the world anymore.

"Yes."

"That will be most satisfactory, Mr. Dalton. How will you be making the initial deposit?"

"Wire transfer," I said. "If you give me an account number, I'll have my people do a wire transfer right now."

This was also most satisfactory. He opened the account from the computer terminal on his desk.

"We give our clients the opportunity to name their accounts," he said at one point. "That way it's unnecessary to remember a number. Is there a name you would like to give this account?"

I swiveled in the chair, as if trying to think one up. I looked out at Mimi and Fifi. Mimi was still reading magazines, lying back in an armchair with one leg over the armrest and her skirt hitched up. She was still blowing bubbles. Meanwhile Fifi had found the Xerox machine and appeared to be photocopying herself.

"Ménage," I said eventually, still looking out at the girls.

"Ménage?"

"Yes," I confirmed. "As in *à trois*."

Smythson swallowed. "Quite so," he croaked. He reverted to tapping at the keyboard, but more slowly now. I think he had difficulty getting the spelling right. Eventually the process was completed, and I had an new secret offshore account.

"Now," Smythson said, "the only remaining thing is to populate it, so to speak." He gently pushed the phone in my direction.

"Actually I'll use my laptop," I said, tapping the satchel beside the chair. "Could I borrow an office with a phone line connection?"

"Why yes, certainly," Smythson said, rising to his feet. He took me into the adjoining office, then returned to his own. The wall separating us was glass, and so he could see what I was doing, but he pretended to work at his computer while surreptitiously watching the girls and paid too little attention to me to notice that I had connected to a network port instead of a phone socket.

I turned on the machine. The display showed nothing out of the ordinary, but I could tell from the continuous low scratching coming from the hard disc that it was doing more than the usual booting up. What I hadn't counted on was it taking so long. After twenty minutes Henry Smythson had started to mix occasional glances in my direction with those at the girls. I took the cell phone in hand, turned my back to him, and put my feet up on the desk as if chatting with an old friend while waiting. Instead I called American Express and authorized them to make the $50,000 transfer that I had alerted them to before leaving Washington.

Eventually, nearly an hour after having first turned on the laptop, the little window saying *"Job complete"* came onto the screen. I shut down and disconnected the machine, then returned to Smythson's office.

"Sorry I took so long," I said. "You know how talkative those investment bankers can be."

"Yes, quite," he said, although he obviously didn't.

"Well, I think that concludes our business," I said. "You've been most helpful."

Smythson stood. "I do hope we've been of some service."

"Yes, certainly," I said. "I've gotten everything I came for."

SIX

DATA on a database is arranged in tables. The data in these tables can be accessed without the software by using generic server applications employing SQL—Structured Query Language. Notwithstanding the fact of named accounts, the unique identifier for each item on Trans Oriental & Occidental's database was still a number. The name and number were linked in a table called AccountNames. It took me most of the morning to discover all this, sitting by the resort's pool with the laptop on a table, frequently referring to the help menu, and using much trial and error to get the hang of SQL syntax. Eventually I put together the right command to return the Iron Butterfly's account number:

SELECT AccountNumber FROM dbo.Accounts. AccountNames WHERE AccountName = 'Iron Butterfly'

Once I had that number, it unlocked everything else on the database. I spent the afternoon systematically

going through each account table, running SELECT
statements with the account number as the condition,
returning anything connected with the Iron Butterfly account, and extracting the data to a text file. Soon I had a
complete history of the account's activity: the balances,
the cash flows, the orders. These last were orders for securities identified not by name, but by a nine-character
code, which, search as I did through the database,
I could find no description for. I made a note on the text
file to find out what they were.

Then at last, late in the afternoon, I finally discovered who the Iron Butterfly was.

Across the pool from me another person had also
been using a laptop all day. She wore dark sunglasses,
which must have made it difficult to use—in the glare
of daylight I found it hard enough to see the screen at
all. Black one-piece swimsuit. No tan, she hadn't been
in the islands long.

I shut down the machine and decided to swim laps. I
was surprised at having recognized the name of the Iron
Butterfly, and I needed to think. Swimming laps is a surprisingly peaceful environment in which to do this:
there are no distractions; it's just you and the water—all
you see is the bottom of the pool with the long black
stripe to follow, and which ends at precisely the right
place for a tumble turn and kickoff to go back down the
other end again. At every fourth stroke you turn your
head to take a breath, and for a brief interval you see
and hear the outside world again: a snatch of conversation, the clink of a glass being set down on a side table,
people coming and going—not enough to distract, just
sufficient to allow you to remain aware of what's happening beyond the water, and to quietly register any new
faces that show up.

The pool was quarter–Olympic size, meaning that
sixty-four laps was the half mile I had intended to swim.
The other people using the pool had politely kept out of

the lap lane, but at lap fifty-three when I was approaching the deep-end turn, I noticed that there was a leg dangling in the water, right where I would normally have
kicked off. It was a female leg, and it had no tan.

I stopped and grabbed the side of the pool. It took me
a moment to get the chlorinated water out of my eyes.
When I looked up, I saw the woman in the black swimsuit looking down at me, distractedly, as if she'd been
thinking of other things when I had shown up. I couldn't
see her eyes past those sunglasses, but she was smiling
faintly.

"Hi," I said.

"Hello," she replied.

She didn't seem inclined to say much else, so I introduced myself. "Lysander Dalton," I said.

We shook hands. She didn't offer a name in reply.
Instead she asked, "Where are your friends today?"

"My friends?"

"The French connection."

I realized who she must mean. *Les Nuits Chaudes
dans les Antilles* was being shot in a private villa over on
Virgin Gorda. Apparently Mimi and Fifi had been flown
to the BVI ahead of schedule to make sure that they were
appropriately tanned before it began. Now they were
filming on location.

"They left this morning."

"You're all alone."

"Yes," I agreed.

She seemed to have nothing more to say but was
content to just sit there with me in companionable silence. There is much to be said for companionable silence, but right now I was kind of busy—I needed to
talk to Dortmund. I wondered how to politely get rid
of her.

"Will you join me for cocktails this evening?" I
asked.

"Yes."

"Will you tell me your name?"

"No."

If she didn't want to tell me her name, that was fine by me. "Six o'clock, on the terrace?"

She nodded, a woman of few words. I gave her a little wave then kicked off to finish the remaining laps. By the time I returned to the deep end, she was gone.

THE little piece of tissue paper I'd left in the door to my room had fallen out, but all sorts of people come and go into guest rooms at a resort hotel: maids to clean it, supervisors to check on the maids, porters to restock the bar, and such like.

I inspected the markers that I'd left in the drawers: hairs off my own head carefully placed between items, but overhanging, so that even a gentle search would dislodge them. Both the hair in my shirt drawer and the hair in my underwear drawer had fallen out: my room had been searched.

Since I'd had both the phone and laptop with me by the pool, there was nothing for them to find, but the fact of the search bothered me. Perhaps they'd also bugged the room. I decided to make the phone call to Dortmund from somewhere outside instead.

I circled the grounds. The garden was luxuriant with palms and jasmine trees and big frangipani shrubs bursting with flowers—pleasant, but too dense to be sure someone hadn't come into hearing range. The beach was still occupied, but the dock was empty. I went down past the resort's speedboat, tied up alongside and gently bumping the fenders, and a flat-bottomed utility boat that was probably used for ferrying supplies. At the end of the dock I sat down with feet dangling over the water, checked that no one had followed, and dialed the number for Dortmund.

After the phone was picked up it went through half a

minute of mysterious noise-making as the decoders synched up. When finally a voice came on the line it was not human, but machine-generated, and sounded as if it was echoing down a very long pipeline.

"Hello?" it said.

"Dortmund," I replied. As at the Mayflower Club, it was the magic word, and a moment later the man himself came on the line, sounding only slightly less inhuman than the machine that had preceded him.

"Where have you been?" he said, dispensing with the usual polite preliminaries. "I have been calling you."

"I had the phone off," I explained.

"Off?"

"Off," I repeated.

I could hear a sigh being suppressed, or failing to be suppressed, on the other end of the line. "Mr. Dalton," he eventually said, "since you are on a mission to preserve us from nuclear calamity, perhaps you wouldn't mind leaving the phone *on*?"

"I know who the Iron Butterfly is," I said, a declaration which put an end to further complaints about the cell phone.

"Who?"

"There are three signatories on the account," I explained. "Each one has a name and an address. Two of the signatories are proxies for the third. Their addresses are both law firms, one in New York and the other here in Road Town. I presume that those two are lawyers, and are only there for technical reasons. It's the third person who is the designated principal."

"And the name?"

"Xerxes Antullis."

That shut him up for a while. I could hear him breathing heavily, echoing down the secure line, sounding like an asthmatic dragon at the end of a very long cave.

"Xerxes Antullis," he repeated at last. "You know the name of course?"

"Yes," I said. Not many people would not have known the name Xerxes Antullis, or the XA Corporation that he had founded.

"Assessment?"

"Well, I guess we know that he can afford the two hundred million," I offered. The software billionaire was so rich that he probably wouldn't notice two hundred million dollars missing in the first place.

"Yes," Dortmund agreed, "I think we can safely say that money is not an issue here. What about motivation?"

It was the question that had bothered me from the beginning. What would the founder of one of the world's biggest software companies want to do with a bunch of nuclear terrorists?

"I don't know," I admitted, "but I think he's got a reputation for being eccentric. Didn't he drop out of public life and go into seclusion a few years ago?"

"Yes, after he cashed out his interests in the XA Corporation," Dortmund affirmed. "Sold at the top of the market, if I remember correctly. Made a fortune and avoided the dot-com crash."

"So who knows the why? The fact is that it's his name on the Iron Butterfly account."

"Agreed," Dortmund said. "I will have to consider this further before we proceed."

Next I told him about my encounter after leaving Babycakes. I passed on the license plate I had memorized, along with my guess that the vehicle had not been stolen.

"How would you know?" Dortmund asked.

"He was really annoyed when I shot it," I explained.

"You shot his vehicle?"

"Yes."

"No wonder he was annoyed," Dortmund said disapprovingly. "Please do not go about shooting things in future."

Given his reaction, I decided against getting into the

detail about how I'd shot the vehicle's owner, too, and changed the subject instead. "I should get this database to you."

"Stay put for now until I consider the next move. Which reminds me—exactly where are you?"

"On a dock."

"That's not what I meant. Captain Dalton, I am informed that there have been some quite extraordinary charges rendered to your American Expr—"

"I'm losing you," I interrupted, and ended the call.

THE woman with no name and no tan was late. I sat at a table by the seaward edge of the terrace, looking out over the Sir Francis Drake Channel. She arrived all in black; perhaps it was the only color she wore. She said nothing as she sat, settling for a smile as greeting. She was still wearing dark glasses, which prevented me seeing her eyes. A waiter came over to take our order.

"Gibson," she said. "Two onions."

"Same for me," I said. The waiter left.

"You like Gibsons?" she asked.

"Only when I've run out of olives," I admitted. "Actually I would have preferred something brightly colored with a little umbrella, but I'd be embarrassed to ask for it now."

She laughed and then sat back, regarding me with the remains of her smile. She was still not talkative, and so I decided to match her.

"Aren't you going to ask me for my name again?" she said at last.

"No."

"Why not?"

"I assume you must have your reasons for not telling me."

"I do, but most men would nevertheless make an effort."

The drinks arrived, and we toasted each other. A Gibson is a martini garnished with a cocktail onion instead of an olive, which to me is a waste of a good martini, but the drink was pungent and ice-cold, a suitable drink for the tropics.

My cell phone rang. Then I realized that it could not be mine, since I'd left it off. She pulled out her own phone and hit a button which silenced it, but instead of listening to the handset she just read the screen—a text message, presumably.

It must have been a long text message, because it took awhile to read, and she had to scroll through it. Eventually she closed the phone and stood.

"Would you excuse me for a few minutes?"

"Of course." I stood as she left, then resumed my seat.

I wondered if she'd really had to respond to the message, or whether she'd just gone to search my room again, confident that with a fresh drink I could be relied upon not to return to it for a while.

If the latter, then she was doing a thorough search. After half an hour I'd finished the Gibson and was considering a second when the waiter came over with another drink, which he placed on the table.

"I didn't order that," I said.

"Compliments of the lady," he said.

"What lady?"

"The lady that was here before."

"Where is she?"

"She's gone," he said, with what I took to be a commiserating smile. "She checked out and left for the airport a few minutes ago." He lowered his voice. "She asked me to give you this."

He placed an envelope on the table, then quietly left.

The envelope was hotel stationery, and the note inside had been hastily written on matching notepaper. I could picture her scribbling it in her room, perhaps while waiting for the porter to arrive after having hurriedly packed. The first line was:

Now here's the drink you really wanted all along.

I couldn't help smiling. The drink was bright orange, served in an enormous parfait-shaped glass, and came with not one but two little umbrellas. I read the remainder of the note.

Since you apparently aren't picking up your calls, I have been asked to pass on the following instructions (He's livid, by the way, but because you obtained the database he'll probably refrain from having you terminated for now):

> *(a) Go to Los Angeles. Be in front of Grauman's Chinese Theatre at precisely 3:00 P.M. next Tuesday. Compare your handprint to Steve McQueen's. You will receive further instructions then.*
> *(b) Fly coach.*

By the way, my name is Harry.

P.S. It won't be necessary to deliver the database—I connected to your computer via a wireless link at the pool today, and downloaded everything. I will see that it gets to him safely.

P.P.S. Those 9-character security identifiers are called CUSIPs.

H.

Another Harry. I wondered how many useful Harrys Dortmund had.

I read through it a second time, committing the details to memory, then carefully folded the note and put it away. I finished the cocktail and returned to my room, where I tore up the letter and flushed the pieces down the toilet.

On the way back to the restaurant I stopped by the concierge desk and asked him to arrange a flight for me tomorrow to L.A.

"First class?" he asked.

"Yes," I confirmed.

My wealthy man's persona had served me well, and this was no time to break out of character.

SEVEN

THE air inside the terminal at LAX wasn't heated, it was air-conditioned. Winter it may have been, but Los Angeles is a city of eternal spring. I took a cab to the Mondrian, a fashionable hotel on Sunset Boulevard. The lobby was sleek and modern and laid-back in best Angeleno style, a marble expanse with long, wispy curtains wafting in the gentle evening breeze. The staff were deferential in a way that would last until they'd established that I was not a producer, or an agent, or a studio executive, which in Los Angeles means that you're nobody.

The front desk had mail for me, a small but heavy parcel, which I waited until I was installed in the room before opening. The Anaconda was inside. The weapon was still fully loaded—Mick of Mick's Gym had not paid attention to the United States Postal Service regulations regarding the safe transmission of firearms. I wedged a chair under the front door handle, put the weapon on the bedside table where I could get to it in a hurry, and slept the deep and peaceful sleep that only children and people with loaded firearms within easy reach enjoy.

* * *

I woke up early the next morning, still on Caribbean time, and had breakfast on the balcony looking out over the great basin of Los Angeles stretching down from the Hollywood Hills, past Century City, then out to Santa Monica and the Pacific beyond: a vast suburban sea washed with its diurnal vehicular tides—a place in which people live their lives by day in the dull vernacular, and at night dream celluloid dreams in heroic dactylic hexameters. Reality in L.A. is imagined reality, a movie set, a place where the idea of glamour is clung to like a saintly relic. Los Angeles is the most religious of American cities, for no matter what dreary ugliness the unforgiving Southern California sun reveals, here a persistent faith in an imagined glamour conquers all.

I went downstairs and approached the concierge desk.

"Where can I find a library?" I asked.

"A what?"

"A library," I repeated.

He looked at me as if I was from outer space—it was not a question he was often asked. In Los Angeles important people don't read books; they have books pitched to them. "What sort of library?" he asked.

"A public library. Preferably the main library."

He plunged into a directory, and soon his puzzled look turned to a smile. "Of course," he said, "Library Tower." He unfolded a map and pointed to the location. "Right here, downtown on Fifth Street," he said. "It's a big cylindrical building." He marked the spot with a pen. "You'll recognize it," he assured me. "It was the first thing that got zapped by the aliens in *Independence Day*."

It was a real building—it had been in a movie. I took the map and declined his offer of a cab.

"I'll walk," I said.

No one walks in Los Angeles, which meant that anyone who followed me would stand out, and was why I had declined the cab. But the idea that someone might walk was obviously as alien to the concierge as were books. He regarded me warily now, as if I might be about to do a little zapping myself.

THE main library was actually next door to the Library Tower, and from which the latter had taken its name. I went to the reference desk and told the librarian on duty there what I wanted. She suggested several resources, mainly newspaper and magazine archives. I went to work, and by lunchtime I had gotten what I'd come for: a basic background on the founder of the XA Corporation.

Xerxes Antullis was forty-six years old. Like the great corporation he had created, Antullis was known to friends and enemies alike as XA. He was generous, and he was ruthless. He was both a dreamer and an astute businessman. He was considered reckless but rarely made a move that wasn't carefully thought through in advance. He was charming and sophisticated but had not been seen in public for the last five years. In short, he was a mystery, different things to different people. A man of masks, difficult to grasp easily.

I decided to focus on the facts.

He was born in Pacifica, California, a comfortable middle-class community midway between San Francisco and the southern Bay area that was just then beginning to earn that sobriquet upon which Xerxes Antullis would rise to fame and fortune: Silicon Valley. He attended public schools, was a middling student, and thence UC Davis—an institution at the high end of the second tier. He didn't scorn education, but he didn't laud it either. One article quoted him as saying, *"Ten percent of my time in school was spent acquiring literacy, numeracy, and the ability to think logically, without which I would have been nothing. The other ninety percent was a waste of time, but it was worth it for that critical ten."*

At UC Davis he majored in computer science. He didn't do particularly well in the academic courses, but something in him clicked, and by his sophomore year he had started a business, headquartered in his parents' garage, and backed by a $500 loan from his mother. From the beginning he had called it the XA Corporation, as if certain from the start that it was destined to grow.

And grow it did. What began as odd-job programming tasks for local businesses soon expanded into serious contracts. His breakthrough had been a California government contract, entered into by a state bureaucracy that at the time was strapped for cash as a result of the tax revolt, and so willing to take a risk on a kid they would normally have avoided. The state needed an accounting system to quantify the market risk in their pension fund system. Xerxes Antullis built it for them. They were happy with the result, word got around, and the orders flooded in.

Without really knowing it, Xerxes Antullis had developed a new business model that was as yet untried in the emerging era of silicon. Unlike most software companies, he didn't build generic software and then sell it to whoever would buy. Instead, as he had done for the state of California, he continued to build software to do specific tasks for specific users. What he lost in economies of scale he made up for in hefty license and maintenance fees. Since his people built the software, it was only his people who could maintain it. He charged twenty percent of the license fee in annual maintenance, which meant that every five years he had effectively resold the same software.

Yet his customers were satisfied. His corporation was the subject of many lawsuits over the years—he was sued by other software companies for patent infringement, by governments for unfair business practices, once even by a mathematician for theft of intellectual property. But as I pored through the history of his company's legal disputes, looking for some clue as to what might have convinced him to bankroll terrorists, I could find no instance of him ever having been sued by a customer that wasn't either trivial or blatantly without merit.

Like Microsoft—the other great corporation taking off at the time—Antullis had recognized that software, not hardware, was the wave of the future. Years later, when *Forbes* magazine had XA on their cover, their interview quoted him as saying, *"In those days, the word* computer *was equated with IBM—people still thought of the industry in terms of beige boxes. But I knew that IBM would be just a tool for me, a producer of objects to be used as convenient, and disposed of when not, destined to be nothing more than railroad track to my software locomotive."*

The article was written in 1999 in honor of the first time the XA Corporation's market capitalization had exceeded that of IBM—the year before Antullis walked away from everything.

His personal life was as well-documented as his company's. If Bill Gates was the computer nerd's hero, then Xerxes Antullis was the antihero. He wore a suit and tie to work and was more comfortable in a dinner jacket than in jeans and sneakers. He had none of the fascination with code that characterizes the usual Silicon Valley crowd: *"Today's programmers are yesterday's coal miners,"* he proclaimed. *"Yes, they produce a needed commodity, but let's be honest: the work is deadly dull."* Whatever else one might say about him, Xerxes Antullis was certainly quoteworthy, and it was no surprise that there were so many articles about him: he was a great source of journalistic material. When asked which computer games he liked best, he professed to have never played one. *"Why would you waste time playing computer games in a world with women and martinis?"* he had responded.

Women. There had been a number of them. A weakness?

You would have expected modest beginnings—a neighbor he'd grown up with perhaps, or a high school sweetheart. But that wasn't XA's style—apparently the first woman who had played a major role in his life was the actress Sonya Peters, fifteen years his senior and fresh from a much-publicized divorce. It was to her that Antullis attributed having acquired a taste for martinis, among other things. *"She grew me up,"* he said.

There had been a succession of women ever since: a soap heiress, a singer, a porn star who ran for the state legislature, an East Coast writer and socialite, another actress (this time many years his junior), and at one time even a pretender to the Romanov throne.

His wealth and women had made him a paparazzi favorite. I found photographs of him at a Paris fashion show with the Romanov, going to the Metropolitan Opera with the socialite, at the Cannes Film Festival with actress number two (although the movie in which she starred, and which he had financed, was a flop). What was strange was that he didn't come across as a womanizer. Rather than treating the women as adornments to his own self, as is usual with the type, he seems to have genuinely liked them, and they to have genuinely liked him back. *"When he was with you the sun shone,"* the second actress was quoted as saying, *"and when he was gone, it was nuclear winter."*

There was a lack of scandal, too, that would unlikely have gone undocumented by the paparazzi had it existed. Each affair had apparently been allowed to run its course before another began.

Xerxes Antullis had never married and had no children.

Then at last, early in the year 2000, there had been the famous sellout. Without warning he had instructed his investment bankers to find a suitor. They had done so, and a month later Xerxes Antullis had suddenly divested himself of all interests in the company he founded. There had been no explanation, and the market had been wild with rumor. At the time the NASDAQ had been flirting with 5000. Six months later it was at 3000. And six months later still, it was at 1500—the great tech stock crash had wiped out three-quarters of the XA Corporation's market capitalization. The market commentators looked at Xerxes Antullis and said with a mixture of admiration and envy: *"He must have known. He must have seen it coming."*

But by that time Antullis was speaking to no one. He had dropped completely out of public life, and the paparazzi had to move on. Antullis bought a huge stretch of desert in Nevada, built himself a fortress of a home, and completely retreated from the world.

The man who had dated actresses and attended movie premiers and given interviews to magazines had suddenly become a recluse. What had made him do it? He wasn't saying, and there was nothing convincing or even suggestive among the speculation that I read through in the library. A soured business deal? He was out of business by then and had realized a fortune beyond imagination. A woman? The affair with the second actress was over, and she was the last of the line that had been publicly recorded. The breakup had been amicable, and they'd remained on friendly terms. Illness, perhaps? But there was no mention of ill health in anything that I read. On the contrary, he'd been a sportsman: a yachtsman and a racing car driver, among other things.

And so now what was Xerxes Antullis doing, apart from funding terrorists? There was no direct reporting anymore, but snippets here and there occasionally came to light. An article about last year's Pebble Beach

Concours d'Elegance mentioned that he was suspected of being the anonymous buyer of a number of the vehicles sold there that year—he was a well-known classic car collector, even before his withdrawal from the world. A court action involving the Sierra Club had revealed him as a major donor. An Italian trade journal identified construction of the Antullis estate as a significant source of the increase in the export of marble that year. And a *Sports Illustrated* swimsuit edition bio coyly reported that the model had recently spent, "some time at Xerxes Antullis's sprawling desert estate, but she's not talking either."

I returned the last of the back issues to the desk. It was time to make the three o'clock appointment.

IT took me a while to find Steve McQueen. The forecourt of Grauman's Chinese Theatre was teeming with tourists and hucksters. I bought a hot dog while searching. The actors in the prime spots were mainly pre–World War II, when the studios were still in Hollywood and the idea of capturing the ephemerality of the movies in the permanence of concrete had first occurred to the theater's proprietor. Steve McQueen was in back by Sophia Loren, not a bad place to be.

I checked my watch: 2:55. I would have liked to have the Anaconda out with the safety off right now, but the thing was too big to do so without being noticeable, and so I was forced to leave it tucked into the waistband in the small of my back, concealed by the jacket, and with the safety on.

I looked around while eating the hot dog. It was after three now. I expected to see a young woman approaching, one of Dortmund's Harrys, but the only person coming my way was someone in sandwich boards offering discount tours.

But people handing out fliers don't approach other people purposely, they just stand around catching passersby. And they don't come out of the way of the main foot traffic, over in back where I was. I dumped the remains of the hot dog and pulled out the Anaconda—noticeable or not, I'd been on the wrong end of a firearm too often lately.

That stopped him for a moment. I kept the gun by my side. Both his hands were visible, and the only things in them were fliers. When he saw that the gun wasn't raised, he nodded to himself, then continued approaching, more cautiously now. My eyes stayed on him. His eyes darted nervously between me and the weapon I was holding. He stopped ten feet away.

He was Hispanic, perhaps forty, short, balding. Very slowly, he held out a flier to me.

"See the homes of the stars," he said flatly.

"No thanks."

"You take this one," he said. "This one is for you."

"Who sent you?"

He shrugged his shoulders and said nothing, as if a baffling but unfathomable providence had caused him to come here today. He fluttered the leaflet slightly, urging me to take it.

"On the ground," I said.

He bent at the knees until the sandwich boards made contact with the concrete, then placed the leaflet on top of Carmen Miranda. He rose, backed off a few steps, then turned and plodded away with the dull resignation of someone too oppressed to question the mysteries of life.

I put away the Anaconda, stepped forward, and picked up the leaflet. The paper was stiffer and better quality than a flier. It turned out to be a brochure, not for tours of the stars' homes, but for the Getty Museum. It had a general description of the museum, directions, opening hours, a floor plan. One of the galleries in the floor plan had been circled in pen. Scrawled across the space was "Wednesday 11:00 A.M., Exhibit 47-06/T5."

It seemed that I would be making a visit to the Getty.

EIGHT

I stood on the terrace, looking out over the city. The Getty Museum sits perched in the Santa Monica Mountains, a vast cream-colored travertine complex from which you gaze out over the smog-enshrouded urban wasteland below, endless strip mall streets in endless suburban grids, a surreal dreamscape straddling a fault line. Why did they build a city here, a place without water on top of the cracking earth, choking on its own effluvium? For the movies, of course: the endless sunshine is good for shooting. Here at the Getty, with the afternoon heat rippling off the baked earth, you see Los Angles for what it is: a land waiting for something to happen—an earthquake, a call from an agent, anything. A baking city frozen with expectation.

I turned and went inside.

The gallery that had been circled in the brochure turned out to be space for temporary exhibitions rather than the permanent collection. The current show was titled *Art on Wheels: A Century of American Automobile Design*. There were original manufacturers' technical drawings, large black-and-white photographs of dream cars at the great Motoramas of the past, some clay mock-ups that the studios had put together in the process of arriving at a new design. But most of the exhibits were the cars themselves: an elegant Duesenberg, a massive black Packard fit for a gangster, a twenty-foot, three-ton Cadillac from the fifties, a revolutionary front-wheel-drive Cord that had been almost innovative enough to save the Auburn car company from the Great Depression, and a modernistic Studebaker Avanti which had similarly been unable to save that company thirty years later.

I went from one to the other, dutifully locating the plaque which identified the item and its provenance, and at the bottom of which was the museum's exhibit number. I finally found Exhibit 47-06/T5.

It was a Ford, but not like any Ford that I had ever seen. It was sleek and low, obviously a racing car, with a blue and orange paint scheme bearing the sponsor's name—Gulf Oil. The number six was painted on the doors and hood. It attracted quite an audience, at least twice as many as the other exhibits. I read the plaque.

Ford GT, retrospectively Ford GT Mark I,
then Ford GT40 Mark I.

Chassis number 1075. Original design 1964.

Winner of the Twenty-four Hours of Le Mans
in 1968 and 1969.

I looked again at the car. Rear-engined but with a huge, gaping grill up front, probably where the radiator was, as if it had needed to get every bit of air that it could to keep from overheating during those two long twenty-four-hour victories. The car was very low and had a steeply raked windshield. Big side scoops for the engine. Huge racing tires. Purposeful and taut.

The car belonged here; it was a piece of art. But apparently I was not the only one who thought so.

"Beautiful, isn't it?"

He was an old man, standing beside me. Someone who'd probably started off short and gotten shorter with age; he only came up to my shoulder. He was looking at the car.

"Very," I said.

He nodded his head. "The greatest American car ever built," he said. "Just look at it." I looked again. If he wanted it to be the greatest American car ever built, that was fine by me. Perhaps it reminded him of his youth. We stood together in silence for a few moments, admiring the automobile. "Do you think you can judge a man by the way he looks?" he suddenly asked.

"By looks?"

"I don't mean actual looks," he said. "I mean by the way he holds himself. By how he stands. By the way he looks you in the eye. By the way a smile comes too readily to his face, or never at all. By the way he looks like a fool or a liar."

"I guess," I said. I wasn't sure that I really believed it, but he obviously did, and I wasn't going to rile the old guy.

"Well, I think you can judge a car the same way," he announced. I hoped he wasn't going to tell me that the headlights were the windows to an automobile's soul. "When you look at this car, what do you see?"

I glanced at my watch. It was 10:45—I had a quarter hour to get rid of him and meet whomever I was here to meet. I thought it would be best just to go along with him.

"It's low and wide," I offered.

"No, no," he said. He waved a hand from side to side, impatient with answers that didn't please him. "What *qualities* do you see? You know, like the qualities you might see in a man."

It's just a car, I felt like saying, but that would only have invited argument. So instead I studied the vehicle and tried to come up with something that fit. No mom would ever transport the kids or pick up the groceries in one of these. It was built to win races—nothing else. "Single-minded," I said.

"Yes, yes, very good," the old man responded. "Definitely single-minded. Now, what else?"

The car had won Le Mans twice, a race that lasts twenty-four hours. And it had done so five years after being designed, an eternity in racing car time. "It has endurance," I said.

He cocked his head. "And what is it that makes men endure?"

I knew the answer to that question. After commanding a Force Recon unit, I knew the answer to that question without even thinking. "Will," I said.

He smiled at me, pleased with the answer. "Yes, exactly," he said. "More than anything else, this car embodies strength of will." I suspected that my little friend here was a disciple of Nietzsche. He turned back to the car. "Do you know the history of the GT40?"

"Only what I read on the plaque here."

"Bah, that's nothing." He waved dismissively at the plaque as he had my earlier answer. "The fools that wrote that don't understand." He was a man with little tolerance for things which didn't please him.

"What don't they understand?"

"Grit," he answered immediately. "That's what this car embodies above all: grit. Let me tell you the history of the Ford GT40. In the early sixties, Henry Deuce—that's Henry Ford II—was about to buy Ferrari. Suddenly Enzo backed out of the deal. No reason was given; apparently he just didn't want Americans owning his company. So what did old Henry do? What any man of grit would do: he said, 'Okay, then I'm going to build a better car than any Ferrari, and I'm going to beat you.' And he did just that. In 1966, just three years after beginning the program, Ford GT40 Mark IIs finished first, second and third at Le Mans, completely outclassing Ferrari. Then they won again in 1967, this time with the even faster Mark IVs. Not just Le Mans, either: the Fords won pretty much any race they entered. We beat the Europeans on their own soil, in their own races, under their own rules. So what did Enzo Ferrari do?"

"Build better race cars, too?"

"No, he had the rules changed. After 1967, they altered the regulations on engine sizes. This was supposedly done in the interests of safety, yet by strange coincidence the new rules just happened to *exclude* the Fords, but *include* the Ferraris."

He shook his head, as if Enzo Ferrari had personally affronted him.

"And that's where the story becomes truly great," he continued. "They couldn't win fair and square, so they changed the rules, and the Fords which had dominated the race were excluded. But what they forgot was that the original Ford GT40s, the old Mark Is, had smaller engines which *did* meet the new rules. So the Gulf Oil team resurrected these old warhorses, like chassis 1075 here, gave them a fresh lick of paint, and entered the race."

He pointed at the car. "She won. Then, to really rub it in, she won again next year. That's what I call grit." It was a good story, and he was silent for a while, allowing me to appreciate it. "What do you think of Chassis 1075 now?" he asked eventually.

"A great car."

"Good," he said, "it's yours."

"What?"

"It's yours," he repeated. "That is, it's mine right now, but I'm giving her to you." He turned and raised a hand. "Where's my assistant?"

"What are you talking about?"

He turned back to me. "It's perfectly simple," he explained. "I own this car. It is only here now because the museum asked to borrow it for this exhibition. I have owned this car for more than twenty years. I love her, but I am old. Soon the car must inevitably pass into the hands of someone else. Who shall that be? There's no shortage of potential buyers—I get unsolicited offers all the time. But would I really want my beloved Chassis 1075 to fall into the hands of someone who just wished to adorn themselves with her presence, to use her like a trophy wife—saying, 'Look at me, look at me, I'm a big shot because I own this car'?"

I shrugged my shoulders, not sure what to say.

"No, I will not allow that to happen," he said firmly. "You understand this car. You appreciate it. You will take care of it. I am therefore going to sign her over to you right here and now. We'll have the museum staff witness it, if my assistant ever shows up."

"I can't accept it," I said.

"Why not?"

"It's not right."

"Just exactly what *is* right? Would it be right for her to fall into the hands of some smarmy creature with more money than guts? The last nitwit who came trying to get his grubby hands on this car offered me fifteen million for it. You know who he was?"

"No," I said.

He lowered his voice, which up until now had been becoming increasingly loud. "Xerxes Antullis," he answered. "He's been trying to get me to sell him this car for years. My guess is that as soon as he hears that you've acquired it, he'll be giving you a call." Then he winked.

At that moment his assistant arrived, with museum officials in tow. The assistant was a tall, elegant woman, and very pale. It seemed that the California sunshine had not given Harry (number two) any more tan than she'd had in the Virgin Islands.

THE shrunken old man who owned the GT40 turned out to be Bernard "Binky" Benson, who'd made his fortune with a supermarket chain. The signing over of the car became a minor media event. Local news channel people arrived and began filming. Harry (number two) took charge and held an impromptu news conference with Binky and me standing smiling but mute in the background. During the question and answer period she let slip that I was currently staying at the Mondrian, and in response to the inevitable inquiry, "What does Mr. Dalton intend to do with the vehicle?" she said that I was going to drive it cross-country back to my vineyard in Virginia. The museum provided a private conference room for the actual signing of the papers. The officials stood back politely, allowing me to whisper a few quick questions to Binky.

"Is the car really yours?" I asked.

He nodded his head. "Still is, son, and don't you forget it." It had been a long time since anyone had called me *son*.

"How did Dortmund convince you to give it to me?"

"He's an old friend of mine," Binky said with a fond grin. "We were at Yale together when we were kids."

It was hard to think of Dortmund as having friends, or as ever having been a youth for that matter; easier to imagine him having been born Athena-like—fully dressed and already cynical—from the head of some malevolent but greatly relieved Zeus. Binky took a last, longing look at the car before leaving.

"Take care of it," he said.

"I will."

Binky looked me in the eye. "Well, that's good to hear, son, because if you so much as scratch this car, I'll have you emasculated."

I was first contacted two days later. I had just returned to the hotel room from a bookstore, where I had purchased a history of the GT40 in preparation for my role. The voice mail light on the telephone was blinking. The message was from a man who identified himself as Dennis Quire. "Q-U-I-R-E," he spelled out; perhaps he'd had a lifetime of people assuming it was written as it sounded: *choir*.

He said that he was Xerxes Antullis's executive administrator, and asked me to return his call at the first opportunity. The area code was 702, which I looked up: Clark County, Nevada. I didn't return the call until the following morning, not wanting to appear anxious. Dennis Quire was all business.

"I was calling on behalf of Mr. Xerxes Antullis," he said. "Mr. Antullis understands that you have acquired the Ford GT40 that had until recently belonged to Bernard Benson?" he said.

"Yes, Chassis 1075," I confirmed.

"Perhaps Mr. Benson acquainted you with the fact that Mr. Antullis has an interest in purchasing Chassis 1075."

"He may have mentioned it," I said. That silenced him for a moment. No doubt they had been planning to offer me much less than they'd offered Binky Benson, but now Dennis Quire wasn't sure. Eventually he continued.

"I will be perfectly frank with you, Mr. Dalton. Mr. Antullis offered Mr. Benson fifteen million dollars for Chassis 1075. He wishes to make the same offer to you."

"No, thanks," I said. "I'll keep the car."

Dennis Quire cleared his throat before continuing. "Although it is difficult to appraise the value of so rare an automobile, I can assure you that if you check the auction prices for other Ford GT40s, you will see at once that this is a most generous offer."

"I'm sure it is," I said, "but I'm not selling."

"Mr. Dalton," he said, sounding slightly exasperated, "far be it from me to impugn your motives, but for the record I must state that should you have expectations of Mr. Antullis increasing his offer, then those expectations are in vain. Mr. Antullis is, as I'm sure you know, a very rich man, and he is prepared to pay a premium over market price to acquire what he wants. What he is not prepared to do, Mr. Dalton, is to be played for a fool."

"You misunderstand me, Mr. Quire. The car is not for sale at any price. That's why Binky Benson gave it to me—because he knew that I wouldn't sell it."

"Very well then," he said, "and I am sure that your position is one which earns Mr. Antullis's respect. He only asks, should you reconsider, that you please contact him before selling the car."

"Of course," I said. "He would be the first person I'd call."

Dennis Quire sounded mollified by that. "Mr. Antullis has one other request, Mr. Dalton."

"Yes?" I tried to sound slightly irritated, as if I'd given him sufficient time, and had other things to do.

"Mr. Antullis understands that it is your intention to drive the car across the country to your home in Virginia."

"That's correct, yes."

"Since you will be passing by the Antullis estate, he would like to invite you to visit on your way through. In fact, he invites you to be his guest for several days. If you will not sell him Chassis 1075, he would consider it very kind if you were to at least give him the opportunity to admire it. And—with your permission, of course—to drive it."

"Where does he live?" I asked.

"Fifty miles north of Las Vegas," he answered. "The estate is called Quartz Peak, and I'm sure you would enjoy it."

"Fifty miles . . ." I said, as if that was a long way out of the way.

Dennis Quire lowered his voice. "I'm not sure how to put this delicately, Mr. Dalton, so I'll just say it. Mr. Antullis is more than just a rich man, he is also a great man. His society is sought by many but is granted to very few. Most people, even those who are themselves quite renowned, would jump at an opportunity to visit Xerxes Antullis. And the estate is surely one of the architectural wonders of the world, but seen by so very few. In short, I would urge you to accept Mr. Antullis's invitation—it will be an experience that you will savor for many years to come."

I said nothing for a moment, as if mulling it over.

"Okay," I said at last, "I accept with pleasure."

NINE

LEARNING to drive the GT40 was like learning to drive all over again. Perhaps fearing to do any damage, the Getty workers pushed rather than drove it out of the exhibition space and over to a service area closed to the public. There were no media this time, just riggers in work clothes and heavy boots—the men who do the manual work of packing and moving the exhibits—plus a lone museum official who had me sign a release before handing over the keys.

Getting into the car was not something achievable with grace. The roofline only came up to my belt buckle—the *40* in GT40 comes from the vehicle's height in inches, and had begun as an informal nickname emphasizing how extraordinarily low the vehicle was. The steering wheel was on the wrong side. The rocker panels were at least a foot wide, and to further complicate matters, the stick shift was located between the seat and the door instead of between the seats. The designers had tried to address these difficulties by having a portion of the roof attached to the door, so that it swung away to allow easier access.

I managed to get inside. The interior was all business—no carpet, no stereo, no air-conditioning, no anything that wasn't necessary for winning Le Mans. The seats were plain metal frames with canvas covers, perforated with grommets to allow air to circulate, and just enough bolstering to prevent the driver sliding around in hard turns. Strange to say, they were actually quite comfortable, although it was obviously weight-saving rather than driver comfort which had driven the design. The seat belts were four-point racing harnesses, one strap over each shoulder, one around each side of the waist. They all came together in a big round receiver at the stomach. If there'd been a fifth for straps between the legs it would have been the same as a parachute harness.

The metal dashboard was filled with analog dials and dominated by a big tachometer. The redline was a red zone: 6,500 through 7,000 rpm. There were many toggle switches, labeled with plain Dymo tape, including the special one for activating the brake lights without pressing the brake pedal, and which according to my book Jackie Ickx had used to fake out the Porsche 907 that had been hot on his tail at the end of the '69 Le Mans, causing the latter to brake just a touch too early at the end of Mulsanne Straight, and allowing the car in which I now sat to go on and win by the narrowest margin in the history of the race.

Most of the other dials were engine monitors: oil pressure, coolant temperature, and the like. The speedometer was the last in line, way over on the passenger side, canted toward the driver and obviously added as an afterthought—there are no speed limits at Le Mans.

On the far side was a fire extinguisher, the fact of which could either be reassuring or not, depending on your point of view.

I turned on the ignition. It cranked noisily a few times but didn't start. I pumped the gas pedal and tried again. Same result.

Some of the riggers were smirking, as if they could sense the beginnings of a good bar story. The official's face took on a look of contented *Schadenfreude*: he was a man who took pleasure in the misfortune of others. I felt sorry for the car. A back-to-back Le Mans winner reduced to smirks, like a once-great screen actress playing cameo roles as someone else's mother.

"Come on, sweetheart," I whispered. "Don't let them see you like this."

I put the gas pedal to the floor and tried again. This time the engine fired, and suddenly this inanimate collection of metal, rubber, and gasoline became a living thing—and a shrieking, furious, bone-shaking banshee of a living thing at that.

The noise was tremendous. I eased back on the gas pedal, and the car settled into a loud thudding that shook the bodywork, my spine, and the leaves off nearby trees. The engine was situated right behind my shoulder blades with only the thin firewall in between, so close that it felt as if mechanically connected to the driver.

Outside, the smirks were gone. The museum official had disappeared. In quake-conscious L.A., they don't like sudden, deep, loud rumblings.

The interior quickly filled with the smell of gasoline and burnt oil. Not only were the windows not electric, they didn't even wind down manually—the only air came from vents. Fifteen million doesn't buy much in the way of comfort. I wondered if I was going to die of carbon monoxide poisoning.

I put the thing in gear, upped the revs slightly, and very carefully released the clutch. The car shot forward—as I was to learn, it simply didn't go slowly. This made for an interesting drive back to the hotel through the stop-and-go traffic of the Hollywood Freeway: long intervals with the clutch depressed, allowing the cars ahead to get some distance, then briefly engaging gear followed almost instantly by the application of brakes to avoid rear-ending vehicles that had until a moment ago been well clear.

Lane changes were simply acts of faith: there were no exterior mirrors, and what little the interior mirror could capture beyond the massive mound of the engine compartment was made miragelike by the tremendous heat radiating from the motor.

On the way I stopped at a drugstore to purchase what I realized would be the two prerequisites for driving this car: earplugs and aspirin. Finally I made it back to the hotel, shaken and stirred.

In my room, I studied the road map. Originally I had planned to take I-15 straight through to Las Vegas, but twenty minutes of acquaintance with Chassis 1075 had convinced me of the need for open roads with no traffic instead. North of the interstate was an old highway that ran across the Mojave Desert and through Death Valley into Nevada—that sounded like the right route to take.

I called downstairs and asked them to prepare my bill. I also asked them to have a case of Evian put into the passenger seat. Between me and Chassis 1075, I was pretty sure that we would get through it by the time we'd crossed Death Valley.

UNTIL clearing Los Angeles, driving the car was more a strain than a pleasure. But beyond the San Bernardino Valley, where the desert begins, we left the freeway. At the bottom of the exit ramp I turned right at the stop sign onto the old highway. Suddenly in front of us stretched miles of two-lane blacktop disappearing into the horizon; and without another vehicle in sight. We were on a long straight. Empty.

I stopped and checked the gauges. The three essential fluids—oil pressure, coolant temperature, fuel level—were all good. The car felt poised and nervous, as if it, too, could sense the long stretch of clear blacktop that lay ahead. It was time to get to know Chassis 1075.

I revved up to 4,000 and dropped the clutch. There was a moment of rear-axle hop as the tires smoked on the pavement, but then they caught traction, and away we went. Suddenly the clutch, which had been heavy in traffic, was just comfortably firm now. The notchy gear shift was precise, and the suspension, which had seemed bone-jarring before, had become taut and businesslike. The car went singing up through the gears as sweetly as could be imagined, the tachometer needle steadily surging clockwise until each shift, then blipping back down and starting all over again. The GT40 was anchored to the roadway the whole time. I was careful to shift well before the redline, but the car felt as if it had no such thing, no limits at all, as if it could continue to simply go faster and faster all day, as long as it had the asphalt on which to do it.

The straight ended sooner than either Chassis 1075 or I wanted. I risked a quick glance across at the speedometer before coming off the throttle—130 mph, and I hadn't even gotten it out of fourth gear. If the car had been a horse, it had barely begun to canter.

I eased back and took it into the corner at three times the speed recommended on the yellow warning sign. The Ford rounded the curve as if it was riding on rails.

It was exhilarating, but the car wasn't really mine. I drove more slowly from then on—way above the legal limits, but well within the Ford's. I would approach the occasional car ahead and then flash by as if it was stationary. Towns were few, but when I slowed to 35 mph, it felt as if I could have gotten out and walked faster.

The car and I got empty about the same time. Ahead of us was a lonely roadside diner with gas pumps out front and a bar inside. I slowed and turned in.

Once a place like this would have thrived, but then when the interstates came, these old roadhouses lost their reason for being. This one looked as if it had been last painted during the Eisenhower administration, and if desert were jungle, nature would have reclaimed it by now.

I took the car in a big dusty loop in the parking lot, being sure to park it nose outward—like a horse, a GT40 is not good at going in reverse. I got out. The sun was high, baking an already overbaked landscape. There was nothing either way on the road for miles. A bunch of old rusting pickups were parked outside—locals, the only customers they would have left now. Inside I could hear a jukebox booming away with country and western music.

I parked to the side, figuring that with a few beers in them the local boys might not be all that careful when they got back into their pickups. But when I walked around in front I saw that not all the customers were cowboys. Among the trucks parked out front there was a perfect primrose-colored E-type Jaguar. It was a convertible. The top was down. I went over to admire it.

The wheels had chromed wire hubs. The long hood was lined with ventilation slots that the engine would appreciate on a desert run like this. California plates. The car was probably forty years old, but it was in pristine condition—whoever owned it was obviously fastidious. I looked at the odometer to see what sort of mileage it had. As I leaned inside I saw a silk scarf on the driver's seat. I could faintly smell it, too, something I couldn't quite identify. I picked up the scarf, brought it close to my face, and inhaled deeply. Roses, overlaid with something harder and spicier, cedar wood perhaps, giving the scent a balanced but remote, ethereal quality, like a perfect dream that drifts just out of conscious reach. Whoever owned this car smelled pretty good.

"Forget your handkerchief?"

I stood and turned.

She was five six, give or take. Big mass of wavy dark hair, cut a little shorter than shoulder length. Long, slender limbs. Smooth, brown skin. Tight jeans hugging narrow hips. Boots. Tank top that didn't reach her belly button. I was pretty sure that belly button would be cute, too, but it was obscured right now by the butt of an automatic pistol jammed into the waistline of her jeans.

"I was smelling it," I explained.

"Smelling it?"

"You have an unusual perfume."

"I don't wear perfume."

Slight accent, which I couldn't pick. Her mouth was wide and exaggerated in shape, peaked in the middle with two long, voluptuous curves either side—a mouth that could switch from pleasure to disdain in the blink of an eye. She didn't smile. With a mouth like that, she didn't need to. She walked up and held out her hand.

"If you're finished . . ."

I gave her back the scarf. What I wanted to do was nuzzle into her neck to see if she really smelled like that, but I resisted the urge and instead opened her door.

She got in and threw the scarf onto the passenger seat.

"I've always wanted to drive an E-type," I said. "Would you like to swap vehicles until the next gas stop?"

"Oh, sure," she said, starting the engine. "And what would I get—a Chevy pickup?"

"I'm a Ford man," I said, playing the part. "I'd rather push a Ford than drive a Chevy."

That got a laugh out of her. "Well, Ford Man," she said gently, "I'm afraid that you'll just have to admire my Jaguar's dust out of your Ford's windshield."

She reversed out. Before leaving she turned back, as if about to say something. But then she must have thought better of whatever it was, and instead just pressed the gas and hit the highway, leaving a wake of dust behind her.

I started counting to myself, "One-Mississippi, two-Mississippi . . ."

I decided against food. I went back around the side to the GT40, where it had been obscured from her view, fired it up, and brought it out to the pumps. The gas tank was in front and required not only the highest premium grade available but a can of additive as well: there was no such thing as unleaded gasoline back in this car's day. Eventually I had it filled. I got back in, restarted, and took a moment checking that all the gauges were in the black before leaving. By the time I hit the highway, I'd counted four hundred and ten Mississippis.

Call it seven minutes even. E-type Girl hadn't struck me as a docile driver. Say she averaged 80 mph, then she'd have about a nine-mile head start on me. I brought the GT40 up to a steady 120 mph. At that closing rate, I should catch up to her in about a quarter of an hour, thirty miles from here. I just hoped there were no state troopers along those thirty miles.

The road became flatter and the countryside more open—we were entering Death Valley. There had been only occasional vehicles before; now there were none. After ten minutes I could see nothing ahead, then twelve, then fourteen, but still nothing. After a quarter hour, during which the speedometer needle had crept even higher than 120 mph, I'd still seen nothing ahead. Eventually I gave up, thinking that she must have taken a turnoff, and was about to come off the gas when, rounding a bend, I caught sight of a car up in the distance.

Eventually I caught up to her and matched her speed. She was traveling at just under 100 mph. I closed the gap to a few car lengths. Her hair was being buffeted a little, but her posture was calm and relaxed, concentrating on driving and apparently unaware of the vehicle behind her. Cars traveling at 100 mph don't usually get caught up to, outside of a German autobahn.

I backed off a little and waited for a good time. Soon we rounded a gentle curve onto a very long straight. It was clear of traffic for as far as the eye could see. I hit the gas.

It must have been the suddenly deepening engine noise as I came onto the throttle that alerted her. I could see her stiffen as she realized there was a car behind her. I accelerated alongside, matched speeds for a moment, and gave her a little wave. She raised her chin and looked straight ahead, refusing to participate. I changed down and hit the gas.

There are not many cars in the world that can spin their wheels at 100 mph, but Chassis 1075 is an exception. The tires smoked for perhaps fifty yards before gaining full grip and thrusting the car forward like a bullet. There was no redline caution now—I took the thing to 6,500 in third (150 mph) and then again in fourth (180 mph). I finally came off the gas when the speedometer needle hit 200 mph, by which time the E-type was just a distant primrose dot in what I could make out through the rearview mirror.

I slowly eased back down to a little-old-ladyish 120. All the gauges were good: Chassis 1075 had endured twenty-four hours of Le Mans twice; 200 mph across Death Valley was just a Sunday stroll to her.

No wonder Xerxes Antullis had been willing to pay fifteen million dollars for this car. If you could spare the money, just to hear the whooping howl that at 200 mph had been coming from those header pipes behind me was worth fifteen million dollars all by itself. I sat back in the seat, feeling as good as I'd felt in a long time. I wondered how much of that was due to the car.

TEN

THE entrance to the Antullis estate looked more suitable for a military post than a rich man's residence: just two plain chain-link gates piercing plain chain-link fencing that stretched away for miles in either direction. Both gates and fence were at least twenty feet high, and topped by coils of razor wire. On the other side nothing but desert was visible. Security cameras sat atop each gate post. There was no indication of what the place was, just a lone tin sign on the left-hand gate declaring *Absolutely No Admittance without Prior Appointment. No Exceptions.*

This was not the sort of place where Avon would come calling.

There was an intercom on one of the gate posts. I was about to get out and give it a try when the sound of electric servo motors suddenly began. The steel bar that secured the gates pulled back, and the gates themselves slowly began to move. Whoever was at the other end of those security cameras had obviously identified the car. I pulled the GT40 forward and through.

Antullis maintained better roads than did either the state of California or the state of Nevada: the blacktop over which I now drove was perfectly smooth and free of potholes or repairs. For the first time since leaving Los Angeles the ride in the GT40 was not jarringly harsh. About a quarter of a mile down the road I came to a sign:

PROCEED TO GUARDHOUSE ONE MILE AHEAD
DO NOT STOP
DO NOT LEAVE ROAD
DO NOT LEAVE VEHICLE
LOW BEAM ONLY

Xerxes Antullis's version of the welcome mat.

Eventually I got to the guardhouse. It was a low concrete building that looked like a bunker. It was located by a ravine—probably a dry creek bed that only ran on those rare occasions when it rained. Now I understood why the guardhouse had been built here rather than at the entrance to the estate: the ravine formed a natural barrier cutting across the landscape. If it was big enough, a truck could simply ram through a chain-link fence, but no truck could cross that ravine, except via the bridge outside the guardhouse. And that bridge was protected by a double set of tire-shredding barriers: big, toothed, steel plates raised at an angle from the roadway. Nothing was going to get through here except with the owner's permission.

I came to a halt. I had expected some minimum-wage guy in a rent-a-cop uniform. Instead, there were two of them, and they were dressed in combat fatigues. Desert camouflage pattern, same as I'd once worn myself.

They split. One stayed by the guardhouse, his eyes never leaving the car. He carried a Tech-9 on a shoulder sling: not much penetration, but good for getting off a load of lead in a hurry. When the time came, he would be the one who approached me.

The other moved off about fifty yards to a position ahead and slightly to the right of the car, ensuring that the angular separation between him and his companion meant that they could not both be taken out by the same sweep, but not so much that he risked a friendly fire on his own guy. He carried an AR-15—a high-velocity 5.56mm weapon which would penetrate just about anything. In case of unexpected difficulties, it was also fitted with a below-barrel RPG attachment, illegal on anyone but a soldier. When he was in position, the first guy approached me.

This pair was alert and professional. These were not bored, minimum-wage rent-a-cops.

I showed both my hands then opened the door. The approaching guy stopped, and one hand went to the Tech-9.

"No windows," I quickly explained. "It's a racing car—they don't wind down."

The guy nodded in comprehension, then continued to approach. But his hand stayed on that Tech-9.

"Captain Dalton?" he asked.

Captain? I'd said nothing to Dennis Quire about having been in the marines, but obviously they'd already investigated me sufficiently to know what my rank had been. I wondered how much they knew about the circumstances of my discharge, or the court-martial which had preceded it.

"Just 'Mister' now," I replied.

"Photo ID?"

In other circumstances I would probably have refused—who gets invited to someone's house, then asked for photo ID? But I had a job to do, and that came first. I handed over my driver's license.

The guard checked the picture against my face before taking it with him back into the guardhouse. He disappeared from view, but I saw the light from a photocopier doing a scan. Then he came back out.

"Security always this tight?" I asked.

He nodded. "Tougher getting in here than getting into Camp Pendleton," he said.

"You're ex-marine?"

"Yes." For the first time his sneer was replaced by a smile—perhaps remembering better days—but his countenance quickly reverted to a sneer. "First Battalion, Fourth Marines," he said. "I was an E-7."

E-7: gunnery sergeant. By the time they make gunnery sergeant, most enlisted men don't like any officer below the rank of general.

"I worked with the Thirteenth MEU once," I said. Fourth Marines were part of the Thirteenth Marine Expeditionary Unit—MYOO, as we called them.

"What sort of work?"

"Force Recon."

Force Recon means special ops. The sneer was gone. He was silent for a while, as if debating whether or not to continue the conversation.

"Tried out for special ops once," he finally admitted. "Didn't work out."

"What happened?"

"Froze on the HALO."

High altitude, low open. Basically you jump out of an airplane at 15,000 feet over the Yuma Proving Ground and free fall for what seems a day before finally opening your parachute.

"Yeah, first time I nearly froze myself," I lied.

"Would have liked to stay for my twenty," he said, happier that we were both chickens, "but the pay for this gig was just too good."

I didn't stay for my twenty either. Even counting the prison time.

He handed back the license. "You're all clear, sir. I'll drop the barriers. Just follow this road straight to the house, about five miles."

"Five miles?"

He nodded. "Mr. Antullis likes his privacy. He puts a lot of land between himself and everyone else."

He turned and gave an all clear signal to the other guard, who shouldered the AR-15 and began trudging back. The first one returned to the guardhouse, and soon the steel barriers lowered to a position flush with the roadway. I pulled forward over them and across the bridge.

Soon I was past the ravine and the guardhouse was out of sight behind me. I was back in desert—Xerxes Antullis's desert. For a moment I thought about Dortmund—strange though the man might be, I had to admit that he had achieved the next-to-impossible: he had gotten me into the domain of the world's most famous recluse.

IT wasn't all desert. At one point I passed an airstrip, although *airstrip* is too minor a term for the huge expanse of concrete runway that stretched away farther than I could see, and which looked wide enough to accommodate a pair of 747s doing formation takeoffs and landings. In the distance I could see a control tower, hangars, and some aircraft parked on the apron. Not 747s, but a business jet and a helicopter, too.

Eventually the house came into view.

It was several hundred feet above the plain over which I had driven, built on a mesa that may have been the Quartz Peak after which it was named. The house was huge, constructed on many interconnecting levels which looked to follow the contours of the mesa, and faced in some sort of mottled reddish brown stone, as if the architect had wanted it to blend in with the desert landscape. But he'd had the ego of Xerxes Antullis to contend with and had obviously lost, for the sheer size of the place was so great that no amount of coloration or contour following could disguise the stark fact of its enormous presence: a gleaming and mysterious palace built high on a mesa in the middle of nowhere.

It's what the rich have been doing since the days of the pharaohs: building colossal monuments to themselves out in the desert.

The last mile or so of road was switchback climbing up to the house. I was used to the car now and so drove it fast, using singing downshifts for engine braking on entry, then exiting each turn at full throttle, seeing if I could squeeze out two upshifts before hitting the next corner and starting all over again. The GT40 took care of it like a mountain goat. If the guards hadn't already alerted them, then the noise of the engine would have given the estate's occupants plenty of warning that we were on the way.

I arrived at the house. The road widened and ended in a large forecourt covered in terra-cotta tiles. You could have parked a score of cars here, but the only other vehicle was a golf cart.

I shut down the engine and got out of the car. I had expected there to be at least someone from the staff to greet me, if not Xerxes Antullis himself, hurrying down the steps, eager to see the car he had craved for so long. But I was alone.

I stretched a bit and looked up at the house. It was built in a series of overlapping and interlocking terraces, the ones above providing shade for those beneath, and with few windows giving directly onto external walls—a sensible design for a house in a desert. The highest terrace was built into the mesa's tabletop peak. The lowest was about twenty feet above the forecourt. A wide set of steps led up to it. There was also an elevator here, seemingly built into the red rock of the mesa itself, and other doors in the base which presumably led to utility rooms.

The mottled brown stone I had seen from below turned out to be marble. No wonder the thing gleamed.

I heard an electronic beep, followed by the sound of an elevator car coming to a halt behind the twin steel doors. I was about to meet my first member of the Xerxes Antullis household.

ELEVEN

THE man who stepped from the elevator was not Xerxes Antullis. He was fortyish, balding, and wore a mustache. He walked quickly over.

"Mr. Dalton?"

I nodded.

"Dennis Quire," he said. "Welcome to Quartz Peak." He extended his arm and tried to smile. We shook hands.

"Lysander," I said. "Most people call me Lee." Actually, almost no one called me Lee anymore.

Quire's darting eyes went from me to the car. "So this is what all the fuss is about." He sniffed, apparently not thinking much of what he saw. It must have given him a lungful of the car's pungent burnt oil aroma. "My God," he coughed. "It stinks."

"It's a race car," I explained. "It's supposed to stink."

But he obviously wasn't reconciled to a fifteen million dollar car smelling like an incinerated gas station. He cautiously stepped closer and peered through the window. "And look at the interior," he exclaimed, "It's positively spartan."

"Yes," I agreed. "Race car."

Quire stood back with his hands on his hips, staring at the GT40, shaking his head in disapproval.

"He has strange interests sometimes," Quire said. There was no doubting who the "he" was. Like the spiritual presence of the supreme being to a medieval monk, I got the feeling that whether or not he was actually there in the flesh, Xerxes Antullis was the axis around which Dennis Quire's universe revolved. "Beats me why he wants it."

My father had been a taciturn man, not much for sharing his thoughts, but he had once unexpectedly given me some sound advice. *"Never trust a man who doesn't like machinery,"* he had told me, *"and never trust a man who doesn't drink."*

Quire again briefly turned his darting eyes to me. "Shall I give you the tour?" he asked.

"Sure," I replied, but he was already looking away. I wondered if it was just me, or whether he was this uncomfortable with people in general. He took quick, fussy little steps toward the golf cart, perhaps eager to get the tour over and done with. I followed, and we were soon on our way.

Quire stopped at the first of the hairpins leading down the mesa and swung the little cart around to face back up toward the house.

"This is the best place to look at it," he explained. "There's really no good place to see the house, which is by design. XA built it on top of a mountain so that he'd never have anyone looking over him. And on this particular mountain, even airplanes can't intrude on his privacy." He pointed to the west. "Nellis Air Force Base is over there, which is apparently where the government test their secret planes. This land used to be part of it. When they sold it off at the end of the Cold War, the

deal was that the airspace would remain restricted. No
transits, and our own aircraft must enter and exit on the
080 radial, directly away from the base."

We looked at the massive edifice shimmering in the
afternoon sun.

"Who was the architect?" I asked.

"There was a team of architects, but it was really XA
who designed it." Quire smiled. "If you knew XA, I
wouldn't have had to tell you that. There were engineering problems of course, trying to build something like
this on the side of a mesa. The house doesn't have a
foundation in the traditional sense: it's essentially a series of terraces projecting from near-vertical rock. The
architects wanted to use cantilevers to support the lowest terrace, with the others resting on it. But XA insisted
that there be no visible means of support—the terraces
had to appear to be floating. So in the end they had to
bring in massive rock drills of the type usually used in
mining, and bore horizontal shafts into the mesa, right
through the quartz after which it was named. They inserted rolled steel girders, pumped in concrete slurry to
fill the cavity, and then built the terraces upon the projecting ends of the girders. And he insisted there be a
separate set of bores for each level: all five terraces are
completely independent and self-supporting—truly
'floating.' "

It wasn't the Panama Canal, but as a piece of civil
engineering it was impressive.

"The real shock for the architects came with the
question of masonry. XA had made clear from the start
that he wanted marble. They had assumed that this
meant marble facing on a concrete foundation, which is
the usual practice. But no, XA abhors anything fake,
even if the fake can't be seen. It had to be one hundred
percent marble. This compounded the engineering issues: marble facing on concrete is much lighter than
sheer blocks of marble, and the big girders they'd just

finished inserting into the mountain had been selected with this assumption. They weren't sure they could safely support that weight of solid marble. Again XA solved the problem: he had them build a steel structure at each corner to support cross beams at the top of the walls, so that these cross beams would support the weight of the roof. The walls themselves would therefore not be load-bearing, and so could be made of much thinner slabs, and so having a much lower overall weight.

"Of course he'd thought all this through beforehand. He'd already decided to have a number of the external walls extremely thin, with the marble sliced so finely as to be translucent, in some cases almost transparent. This creates an interesting effect, which you'll see once you're in the house. During the day the walls themselves become sources of soft light, shimmering with it almost, and the effect changes throughout the day with the passage of the sun—quite amazing. The ancient Greeks apparently used to do the same thing with their temples."

Temples were the houses of the gods. Apparently Xerxes Antullis believed that his own home performed a similar function.

"There are more than a hundred different Italian marbles used in construction of the house," Quire continued. "Most are in the interior. The exterior is primarily composed of three marbles: Breccia Aurora, Rosso Magnaboschi, and Breccia Pernice." He pronounced all three with the easy confidence of an experienced tour guide. "XA selected them because in combination they match the changing colors of the desert. I'm told that building Quartz Peak used about two years' worth of the global supply."

So with the point made—that his boss built like an emperor—Dennis Quire turned the golf cart around and continued down the drive.

"Have you known him long?" I asked.

"Yes, I've been with him since almost the beginning," Quire said. "I started as a programmer. I like to say that I was the first head of development at the XA Corporation, which is technically true. Of course at that time there was only one developer: me. Until I arrived, XA had done all the programming himself, but by then he was too busy seeing projects through and no longer had the time. Later, as we began to build into a real corporation, XA needed an executive administrator. I moved from programming to that role, and have occupied it ever since." I wondered what an executive administrator was—it sounded like a secretary to me. "I was the only person he brought with him when he left the corporation," Quire added, speaking with the pride of an apostle.

We had reached the base of the mesa. Quire turned right, going west, beyond where I'd come on the way in. Quartz Peak was on our right now, looming above us, the great mass of the house perched high overhead. As we rounded the mesa the desert landscape ahead—red brown earth with occasional cactus and sagebrush—suddenly changed into verdant grass and trees. At first I assumed that it was a golf course, but by now I should have known better than to imagine something so prosaic from Xerxes Antullis.

"It's an oasis," Quire said, answering my unasked question. He took the golf cart up a path and through a long entrance lined with tall, slender palm trees into the oasis itself. It was essentially a mass of lush greenery, perhaps fifty acres, surrounding what was probably the ultimate expression of wealth in the middle of the desert: a lake. There were all sorts of tropical plants, among which I recognized sandalwood and jasmine trees and bright purple bougainvillea. A large square tent was set up near the water, the frame covered with translucent white linen drapery which gently undulated with the occasional breeze off the lake. The air was filled with the perfume of a thousand flowering shrubs and trees.

"Where does all the water come from?" I asked.

"Piped underground from Lake Mead," Quire replied. "Sixty miles away. Building that wasn't much cheaper than building the house itself."

He turned around and left the oasis. We continued our circumnavigation of Quartz Peak, and when we were halfway around we passed a turnoff leading down to an area surrounded by the same chain-link and razor wire as was the estate itself. We passed the turn without taking it. I asked Quire what was down there.

"Nothing," he said dismissively. "Used to be where the air force stored their explosives in the old days. There's just empty bunkers there now."

But I could see that the chain securing the gates was new. Why put new chain on something that's never used?

We eventually arrived at the airstrip I had passed on the way in. It was very long and wide. The concrete was shimmering with heat haze. The aircraft I'd seen earlier were still parked on the apron, despite the fact of two large hangars which could have accommodated dozens of them. When I mentioned this to Quire, he pointed at the nearest of the two hangars and explained that Antullis kept his automobile collection there.

"And the other one?" The other hangar was the larger of the two, and unlike its sibling was surrounded by chain-link fence and razor wire.

Quire didn't answer immediately. "I think the contractors keep their equipment in there," he said eventually. He hit the pedal and turned the golf cart around back toward Quartz Peak. We returned to the house in silence.

The ascent was slower then the descent, with the cart's electric motor straining up the hill. When at last we rounded the final hairpin and the forecourt came into view, I saw there was another vehicle parked behind the GT40. It was the primrose-colored E-type Jaguar.

Leaning on the hood, cowboy boots crossed at the ankle as if she'd been willing to wait for as long as it took, was the woman I'd passed earlier in the day. Apparently I was not Xerxes Antullis's only house guest.

Quire stopped short, startled by the new arrival. I got out without waiting for him, and walked over to the Jaguar.

She was still long and brown. Sunglasses covered her eyes, and she made no effort to remove them. The automatic pistol was gone—perhaps the pair at the guardhouse had confiscated it on her arrival.

I was right: her belly button was just as cute as could be.

"Ford Man," she said by way of greeting.

"Hello." I looked again at the Jaguar which she was currently adorning, long and subtly curved, just like her. "I still like your car," I said, "even though it's slow."

She briefly smiled an unwilling smile but soon had her mouth reset into a combination of mild disinterest for things in general, coupled with a more specific disregard for me in particular.

"It's not mine," she said. "It belongs to Mr. Antullis. I'm just delivering it."

"I hope you're not going."

"Are you inviting me to stay?"

"Yes."

"Even though it's not actually your house?"

"I'm sure Mr. Antullis wouldn't mind."

I heard fussy footsteps behind me. Quire had parked the golf cart and was now joining us.

"Ah, so I see you've met," he said.

"Not exactly," the woman replied.

"Then allow me to do the honors. Yamina, this is Lysander Dalton." He turned to me. "Mr. Dalton, this is Yamina Malik."

"You know each other?"

"Well, of course," Quire replied. "Yamina is the head of security here at Quartz Peak." Yamina Malik smiled and nodded her head. I tried not to look any stupider. "Now," Quire continued, "I'm going to fetch the staff."

He left us to go to an intercom by the base of the house. Yamina Malik leaned into her car, emerging with that scarf I'd smelled earlier. Her other hand held the automatic pistol. It was a Walther PPK, a German compact which fires 9mm *kurz,* a rimless shortened version of regular nine millimeter rounds, ammunition that in America we call .380 ACP.

"Mr. Antullis recently bought this car," she explained. "The man I'd assigned to pick it up called in sick, and I needed to be in L.A. anyway, so I decided to do it myself." She jammed the PPK into the waistband of her jeans, and looked at me directly. "Perhaps if you intend inviting anyone else to stay at Mr. Antullis's house while you're here, you might be good enough to check with me first."

She turned without waiting for a reply and walked away. It seemed that we had not gotten off on the right foot. I watched her passage across the forecourt and up the steps into the house. Wrong foot or not, that had to be the world's luckiest PPK.

TWELVE

THE inside of the elevator car leading into Quartz Peak was decorated with an impressive amalgam of wood and metal and sand-blasted glass that was part Art Deco, part Bauhaus, part Charles Rennie Mackintosh. The floor, a complex and highly polished rosette composed of inlaid woods, was an artwork in itself. The joins were precise and gapless—I knew from having as a child watched my father the level of carpentry needed to achieve such work. If the elevator was this sumptuous, it was hard to imagine what the rest of the house must be like.

Quire pressed a big chrome button for the second floor. Distant machinery gave off a deep hydraulic rumble, and we ascended. The buttons to the first and second floors were plain, but beside those for the third, fourth, and fifth levels were slots for security key cards. Apparently access to those floors, like access to the estate itself, was strictly controlled.

We were met at the second floor by another man, whom Quire introduced as Jeremy Caterno, the house manager. But for his bearing and dress I would have taken this to mean that he was the butler, but he was a young guy wearing a fashionably cut Italian suit that would have been at home on an up-and-coming advertising executive, and his manner lacked the usual deference. Perhaps Antullis had enough of that with his executive assistant.

Quire left us, and Caterno led me directly to my room. Actually it was a suite of rooms, luxuriously appointed, and bigger than most Manhattan apartments.

It turned out that guests like me, who had misplaced their own valet, were assigned one for the duration of their stay. Mine was introduced as Beckett. No first name, or perhaps it was no last name. In either case, Beckett was my idea of a valet. He was dressed in a black coat with tails, gray pinstriped trousers, and shoes which were either patent leather or had undergone hours of spit polishing. He bowed politely rather than shake hands on our introduction.

"Delighted to be of service," he said. He had an English accent, completing the picture. Caterno left, and Beckett the valet showed me around the suite. The sitting room occupied the northeast corner of the second terrace. The furnishings were fashionable and modern— the sort of stuff you'd find in the suite of a boutique Soho hotel. In the back corner was a bar, which I was pleased to see was well stocked. There was a kitchen, also well stocked. The bathroom was large, tiled in the same marble with which the house was built, and had a big tub. The bedroom had a walk-in closet, part of which I was surprised to find already occupied by my own meager possessions.

Beckett answered my inquiring look. "I took the liberty of unpacking sir's belongings while sir was touring the grounds with Mr. Quire," he explained. This mysterious third person he was referring to was apparently me.

I scanned the shelves. No sign of my gun.

"And what liberties did you take with the .44 Magnum?"

"Would that be the rather large firearm, sir?"

"That's the one."

He cleared his throat before continuing. "On sir's behalf I placed it in the custody of the security personnel," he replied sheepishly. "They asked me to assure sir that it would remain safe in an authorized firearm stowage for the duration of your stay. It will of course be returned on sir's departure, fully cleaned and correctly maintained."

So now I understood the circumstances of my arrival. Quire's tour, which had been long despite his obvious reluctance to conduct it, had been so that my gear could be thoroughly searched. When I returned, the whole thing was dressed up as the polite accommodation of a guest. It was a neat piece of theater. If I complained, they could always just say that the butler did it.

I considered pushing the issue but didn't. If the time came, I could do what needed to be done with or without a gun.

"What's this?" I asked, pointing to a dinner suit that was also hanging in the closet.

I could almost hear a sigh of relief as Beckett felt himself being let off the hook. "Mr. Antullis usually dresses for dinner," he explained. "I noticed that sir had obviously not been apprised of this, and so took the liberty of providing a dinner suit from the house wardrobe."

Antullis's house had its own wardrobe—now that's impressive. There was a dress shirt on the shelf above, and shoes underneath. They all looked more or less my size—that house wardrobe must have quite a collection.

"Am I supposed to wear this tonight?"

"I am informed that there will be no formal dinner this evening. Sir may therefore wish to dine in his suite.

I will of course serve. Would sir prefer flesh, fish, or fowl? I'm told that the chef has just received a shipment of excellent Scottish guinea hens."

"Sandwich and a beer," I said.

That took him aback. "That's all?"

"That's all. Any suggestions on the sandwich?"

He considered for a moment before replying. "Chef does make somewhat tasty sourdough rolls," he admitted, looking a little hungry himself. "I myself find that these go very nicely with a filling of fresh avocado, salsa, and crisp bacon."

"That sounds fine," I said. "You can bring it now, and that'll be all for today."

"Very good, sir." He bowed slightly and left.

NO one had offered me an elevator key for the floors above mine; apparently Xerxes Antullis did not give his guests the run of the house. In fact, he kept a very careful eye on them, and I was prepared to bet that Beckett had been assigned not for my convenience, but to keep tabs on me. I wondered to whom he actually reported: the head of household or the head of security.

I sat back in an armchair and considered my surroundings. The two exterior walls were, as Quire had told me, made of solid marble. Piercing each were floor-to-ceiling glass doors leading out onto two terraces—one a small, private balcony at the northeastern end of the building, the other a wide terrace facing the southeast and apparently shared with the remainder of this level of the house. The interior walls were wallpapered. The pattern was subtle, but it was enough—if there was a tiny microphone or lens embedded anywhere in that wall I could spend an hour searching and still not find it. Given the level of security I'd experienced so far, I had to assume that I was under surveillance in here.

I went out onto the private terrace, closing the door behind me. I looked around. Nothing but marble and fresh air here. If I needed to call Dortmund urgently, this was where I'd do it from.

I leaned on the rail and looked over the landscape. Since entering the estate this afternoon I'd looked at everything in recon mode: assessing, but not really appreciating. Now I took the time to appreciate. The lowering western sun had turned what was already ocher country into a deep burnt red. The desert air was fabulously clear, allowing an undistorted view to the horizon. The sky was still a luxuriant blue overhead, flowing through ever-darkening violet until at the eastern horizon it was already that deep indigo which is the last hint of color before nightfall. The long shadow of the mesa stretched out eastward, and in the distance I could see the ravine and the guardhouse, and then farther beyond that the line of razor wire and fence marking the boundary of the property, many miles away.

I could see why a man who had had enough of the world might choose to build a house out here. The desert was a sanctuary—a forbidding sanctuary, but a sanctuary nevertheless. But then I realized there had to be more to it than that.

Xerxes Antullis was a recluse—yes, obviously; the whole world knew that. But recluse implies retreat, and retreat implies defeat. Defeated men aren't builders, they are simply occupiers. If Antullis had been defeated, he would have retreated into a Beverly Hills mansion perhaps, or to some luxurious villa in the south of France. Men who have been defeated don't have the energy to build houses like this in the middle of the desert. And they don't build oases, either.

But if Xerxes Antullis had not left the world a defeated man, then why leave it at all? It occurred to me that perhaps he'd simply found the world inadequate to his needs and so had decided to build a better one here at Quartz Peak. That was fine, and the desire to be left alone explained the chain-link fence and razor wire around the estate. But what it didn't explain was the chain-link fence and razor wire around a supposedly abandoned ammunition bunker.

I went back inside then out to the main terrace shared with the rest of this level of the house. It was perhaps two hundred feet long and paved in terra-cotta rather than the ubiquitous marble—maybe even Xerxes Antullis realized that you could have too much of a good thing. I passed many doors and windows, vast areas of plate glass, but they were of bronze-mirrored glass, and all I saw in them was my own reflection. Maybe this was for privacy, or perhaps it was for protection against the morning sun. Halfway along was a set of stone stairs leading up to the third level. There was an iron grill gate at the bottom, locked shut. There was a slot for a key card, just like the elevator. There was no sign, but the fact of the gate confirmed what the elevator had already suggested: the floors above were out of bounds.

I could hear running water from above, which gave me an idea. I went to the side of the terrace, leaned out, and looked up.

Water erodes, and almost all buildings have to capture and direct rainwater to avoid that erosion occurring in the structure itself—from the simple guttering of a suburban house to the superb gargoyles of Notre Dame. The terraces of Quartz Peak would obviously need draining during the infrequent but often torrential desert downpour. I scanned along the base of the terrace above until I found what I had expected: a steel pipe projecting out a foot or more, designed to prevent the runoff from staining or eroding the levels below.

I went down to a point directly under it and stood up on top of the terrace wall. To the side there was now nothing but fifty feet or so of sheer vertical drop between me and the forecourt below. I looked up and reached out. I had intended to tap the pipe first, making sure that it was solid before entrusting my life to it, but Xerxes Antullis built everything on a grand scale, and the pipe was still a couple of feet out of my reach.

It seemed that I would just have to take a chance and jump. I jumped.

I caught the pipe one-handed and was left dangling in midair. The pipe held, no hint of bending, nor the crunching sound of masonry which would indicate that the sudden weight was yanking it free. I pulled up as if doing chin-and-dips. Getting the pipe to the level of my chin was the easy part. Now came the difficult bit. Using my free arm against the wall for some purchase, I had to do what was effectively a one-armed pushup: that is, pushing my body gradually upward to the point where my other hand could reach over the top of the wall.

In special ops school the master sergeants—triple-striped sadistic Torquemadas the lot of them—used to make us do a bunch of pushups, driving us to exhaustion. Then they'd make us do them all over again, but this time we had to clap our hands together and reset before coming back down. That was fun. Then they'd make us do them yet again, but this time using only one arm. I hated that last most of all, but now it paid off; I was able to get my other hand up and onto the top of the third terrace's wall before muscle failure set in, which would have left me in the awkward position of dangling hopeless from a drainpipe and calling for help.

It was easy from there: a knee onto the pipe, the other hand onto the wall, and then I was up and over. There was still some light, and so I stood awhile and looked around while catching my breath. I soon realized that I had entered another world.

Until now, what I'd seen of the interior of Quartz

Peak was luxurious enough, but nothing that couldn't be found in the better resorts of the world. That was no longer the case. The third level was much larger than the second—perhaps there had been a natural setback in the rock here that they'd used to advantage. The open terrace was vast, and there had been no retreat to terracotta: here, everything was marble. But the brown reds which I'd seen below were here used only for the exterior wall of the terrace. Beyond that, the dominant colors were blue and green and white: the colors of water.

And water was everywhere. There was a pool, perfectly rectangular and built in such a way as the water was precisely level with the terrace itself, so that it took a second look to realize that indeed there was a pool there. The pool and the inner walls were lined with mosaics: abstract arabesques executed in tiny, shimmering, glass tiles. There were many flowering plants and trees; some bushes were in huge pots, but the larger ones and the trees were growing in beds set directly into the terrace. There were two fountains at either end of the pool, and one of the mosaic walls had a waterfall.

This was not part of the modern world. This was the court at Constantinople, at the height of the Byzantine Empire.

But what took most of my attention was closer than any of these. Twenty feet away from where I stood was a white marble wall, alabaster perhaps, and so thinly cut that it was translucent. On the other side was the shadow of a naked female figure. She was washing her hair. The water I had heard from below was not the fountains or waterfall but the shower on the other side of that wall.

She was tall, full-breasted, and she was enjoying that shower. So far the only woman I'd met on the estate had been Yamina Malik, the head of security. Yamina was tall, but not that tall. Her hair wasn't as long as the hair hanging down as this woman threw her head back. And Yamina was slender and svelte, too much so to match the curved shadows on the other side of that alabaster wall.

Whoever she was, she'd been worth the climb. I went and found the elevator, grateful that the button for my own floor required no access key.

THIRTEEN

WHEN Beckett came with the sandwich and beer—plus, of all things, a plate of cookies and a glass of milk—I asked him where the staff lived.

"On the first level, sir."

"All of them?"

"Yes, all staff who reside on the estate are quartered on the first level."

"Who lives on the third?"

He didn't immediately answer. After a while he must have given up trying to invent something, and replied with his head hanging a little. "I really don't know, sir," he said to the carpet, obviously a lie.

"You don't know, Beckett?"

"My duties usually don't take me to the third floor, sir." He managed to look me in the eye this time—that at least was true.

"Why is there a key card system?"

"It's part of the security arrangements at Quartz Peak, sir. All staff who work on the estate are assigned a clearance which limits their access. The lowest is no access at all: that is, permitted only onto the estate's grounds, not into the actual house—this is for the gardeners and contractors and so on. Next are those only permitted to the first and second floors—typically this is for kitchen and maintenance staff. Then general house staff, such as myself, have access to all floors but the fifth. Very few are allowed to the fifth level, and even then only during specified times."

"What's there?"

"That's where Mr. Antullis lives, sir."

"Alone?"

"Yes. His quarters occupy the entire fifth level. And the entire top of the mesa, too—or so I am informed."

I thanked him and let him go for the rest of the night.

Beckett had made a good recommendation: the sourdough was still warm from the oven, and the sandwich was excellent. I quickly finished it, then sat back with the beer to consider what I'd seen on the third level.

Whoever the woman was, she lived like a princess: luxuriously, but in isolation. Perhaps she was well-known, someone whose face would have been instantly recognizable, which would have explained the need to keep inquisitive guests separated by gates and security keys. Or perhaps, like the man whose mistress she presumably was, she simply liked her privacy. I finished the beer, wondering if I was ever going to get to meet the woman who had been on the other side of that thin alabaster wall.

DESERTS get surprisingly cold at night, a fact I'd come to know well during my marine days in the Middle East. I pulled on a black turtleneck sweater. My trousers were dark, and my shoes were black. I would have liked to put on some face black, but that would have been impossible to explain. I took the packet of cigarettes and matches I'd bought as a prop, then went outside and down the stairs.

The Ford was still parked in the forecourt, but the Jaguar was gone—presumably it had joined the rest of Antullis's collection in the hangar. I looked over the car, playing the anxious owner for anyone who might be watching. The interior was still warm from the heat of the day. I opened the hood, which is actually the trunk in a GT40. There was a flashlight stowed in the corner, which I took and stuffed narrow end first into a trouser pocket. The house lights provided illumination here, but beyond the forecourt the desert was just a mass of black, and I might need that flashlight later.

I checked the time and looked up. The stars were visible, brilliant points of light out here in the unpolluted desert sky. Visible stars meant that no cloud cover had come in, something which I was counting on. I couldn't risk using the flashlight close to the house. Moonrise was in a few minutes, and I would be relying on it to get to where I needed to go.

I smoked a cigarette while waiting, trying not to cough. It wasn't much of a prop—if I'd wanted to smoke outside, I need only have gone to the terrace—but it would have to do. On schedule the moon rose, yellow at first but soon turning a soft white and bathing the desert in pale silver light—not much illumination, but enough to navigate by. I struck off along the road leading down the mesa.

It took three-quarters of an hour to reach the ammunition bunker. I was hoping that by some extraordinary oversight the gates might have been left unlocked, but people who rely on hope are bound to be disappointed, and I was that night: the gates were firmly secured.

I pulled the top of the turtleneck over my head, brought my arms inside, and wrapped the bottom around the lock before turning on the flashlight. It wasn't perfect, but encased by the turtleneck the flashlight would not be easily visible from far away. I studied the lock. The chain was made of thick links and constructed of

galvanized high-tensile steel: unless hydraulically powered, even a bolt cutter would have been unable to cut
through it. The surface of the metal was unweathered,
meaning that the chain had not been here long. The lock
itself was a big, solid padlock, and it, too, looked new.
Recent scoring around the keyhole confirmed what I'd
already suspected: Quire had lied—the bunkers were not
abandoned after all. The only question was what they
were being used for.

I turned off the flashlight and squared away the
turtleneck. This was really all I'd come for: confirmation that there was activity here. I decided to do a loop
of the fence before returning to the house, in case there
was an obvious vulnerability, like a gap in the razor
wire allowing me to climb over the top.

Three-quarters of the way around, in a corner, I
found something. I heard it at first: a gentle sucking
sound, very quiet, something that you would miss altogether among normal ambient noise, but which was just
detectable in the vast silence of the desert night.

It was coming from the other side of the fence. I
looked closer. About ten feet away were a set of metal
boxes, four in total, mounted on posts so that they were
standing at about chest level. I could make out dials and
switches. A small green indicator light was blinking in
one of them. It was some sort of control station I
guessed, but controlling what?

If I turned on the flashlight to find out, there would
be no disguising it under a sweater here: anyone who
happened to be looking in this direction would be able
to see it for miles. But the ammunition bunker was on
the western side of the mesa, out of view of the house,
except perhaps its uppermost level.

It was worth the risk. I switched on the flashlight.

I was immediately disappointed: it was just a meteor-
ological station. The box closest to me contained the
standard instruments for recording the weather: wet and

dry bulb thermometers, anemometer, barometer, a graduated glass cylinder for measuring precipitation. The next one had a single instrument, just a rectangular box with some control switches, but there was a metal label pop-riveted to the face which gave the name of the manufacturer and the instrument type: it was a microbarograph.

Usually barometric pressure is simply read at each observation—hourly at a real weather station, probably just daily here. There was already a barometer for doing that. But for some reason they'd also felt the need to continuously measure and record barometric pressure, the task of a microbarograph. I wondered why they would take such an interest in air pressure.

The next box contained another instrument, the one with the blinking light. This, too, had a label, but with just three letters: *TLD*. It meant nothing to me. The fourth and last box contained more instruments, too far away for me to make out any details, but I had a sense that the faint sucking sound was coming from there—perhaps they had an air sampler checking pollution levels, which could never have been high way out here.

I turned off the flashlight, disappointed. All I had discovered was that Xerxes Antullis recorded climate data. Perhaps he was a compulsive recorder, like those people who commit to diaries the quotidian minutiae of their lives for the doubtful illumination of posterity. Or maybe he was just a compulsive collector: he collected automobiles and weather observations.

Every man needs a hobby. I began the long trek back to the house.

ABOUT an hour later I returned to the forecourt. It was early morning now, 1:00 A.M. I quietly opened the hood of the GT40 and was leaning inside to replace the flashlight when the muzzle of a gun was jammed into the back of my head. I heard the hammer being pulled to the rear.

"Don't move," I heard Yamina Malik say.

"I won't if you won't," I said. I felt the pressure of the barrel ease.

"Mr. Dalton?"

"That's me."

"Sorry about that." The gun pulled away. "I didn't realize it was you."

"Can I turn around now?"

"Yes, of course."

I turned around. Yamina Malik was wearing a thin little T-shirt and a pair of white underpants. Nothing else. Her long legs looked good in moonlight. She had big feet. There was a spare magazine tucked into the elastic of her underpants. She was squinting down at the weapon, concentrating as she eased the action forward. When the gun was safe again, she looked up at me.

"I didn't have time to find my glasses," she said apologetically.

"Is that meant to be an explanation?" Best defense is offense, as they say.

"I heard someone at the car," she said. "My room's just up there." She nodded to the set of first-level windows above the stairs leading into the house. Like a good field commander, she'd made sure that her own quarters were by the access point, where she could see for herself that the perimeter security was holding up. Unlike a good field commander, she didn't sleep in uniform.

"I wear contacts by day," she explained. "Not at night, and I wasn't going to waste time finding my glasses if someone was messing with a fifteen million dollar car on Mr. Antullis's property."

The cold of the desert evening had gotten to her, something that the T-shirt was too thin to disguise. She must have suddenly realized how little she was wearing—she took a step backward and crossed her arms, still with gun in hand. Her look slowly turned to suspicion as she came to the realization that it was not strange that she was out here at 1:00 A.M., it was strange that I was. "What are you doing out here anyway?"

"I came outside for a cigarette."

"For which you needed a flashlight?"

"I went for a walk."

"Where?"

"Around."

She wasn't happy with that answer, but I wasn't giving her any more. We were silent for a little while—she looking at me with undisguised distrust, and me looking back at her with as neutral an expression as I could manage. I wondered if she realized how very attractive she was, annoyed and near naked in moonlight.

I could see that she didn't know how far to push for a better explanation. Perhaps cold or fatigue got the better of her—eventually she just shrugged her shoulders and unloaded the weapon.

"Best not to walk around the desert at night," she said at last. The magazine slid into her hand. "If the cougars don't get you, then the scorpions will."

For the second time that day, she turned her back on me and walked into the house without waiting for a reply.

FOURTEEN

BECKETT brought breakfast to my suite the next morning. It came rolling in on a tray covered with a white linen tablecloth, and the dishes were topped with polished silver domes. He served it on the private terrace. The GT40 was still parked in the forecourt—I wondered when Antullis was going to ask me to show him the thing that he'd invited me here to see. I asked Beckett what was on the program today.

"I understand that Mr. Antullis will be occupied today, sir," he replied. "I can bring you anything you may need." Translation: please confine yourself to the suite. I tried to think of something that he couldn't bring me, something that I would have to go and get myself.

"Is there a library?" I asked.

"Yes, sir," he replied. His face dropped as he realized that selecting a book was something that a guest would have to do for himself.

"Where is it?"

"On the fourth level."

"I'll need your key card then."

"I can show you the way if you like, sir."

"I'll find it myself—fourth level, right?"

"Yes, sir." I could see he wasn't pleased with the idea of me wandering around the house unsupervised. "If you turn left after exiting the elevator, the library is at the end of the hall."

"I'll probably just take the stairs," I said.

His face dropped further. Taking the stairs meant going via the third floor. I was pretty sure they would prefer me not to go to that third floor, but it would be awkward to stop me now. There was nothing more for Beckett to say. He reluctantly placed the key card on the table and left.

TWENTY minutes later I was finishing breakfast when the telephone rang. It was Dennis Quire.

"Good morning, Mr. Dalton. Did you sleep well?"

"Just fine."

"I'm sorry that Mr. Antullis is busy today. I wonder if this morning I might occupy some of your time instead?"

"How?"

"I'd like to introduce you to Mr. Antullis's other house guests."

So they had decided to precipitate events. It seemed that I was going to meet whoever was on that third floor after all.

QUIRE came to my suite half an hour later. He led me along the terrace and up the stairs to the third level, and past that same alabaster wall through which I had seen the shadow of the woman the previous evening. We went up some more steps onto a raised level, fifteen or so feet wide, which ran the remaining length of the terrace, perhaps a hundred feet in total.

Now that the alabaster wall no longer obscured any of the view, I could see in its entirety the area that I had merely glimpsed the night before. At that time it had been obscured in evening shadow, but now the golden and sapphire mosaic tiles were glistening iridescent in the morning sun, and the water flowing everywhere sparkled with light. The raised platform gave the impression that we were looking over a sunken garden, a grotto perhaps, although that term connotes too dark a picture to accurately describe it. It was a pleasure garden hidden from the world, a light-filled private domain perched high in the sky.

The pool was perfectly flat, reflecting a perfect blue sky. Up here on the raised area I was able to see that the blue and green marble terracing had been inlaid with complex geometric roundels, perhaps six feet each in diameter, made of subtly different colored marbles: it was a floor of stylized stone flowers. Fountains and flowing water and flowering plants were everywhere. There was a rose garden, the most formal part of the entire domain, and I could recognize Larkspur, a luxuriant cream-colored flower, and Lancastrian, with petals the color and texture of red velvet. There was a large trellis for climbing varieties. Other flowers and shrubs dotted the domain, including the palm trees I had noticed yesterday, and great sprays of purple bougainvillea came down the walls here and there. Almond trees, hibiscus, oleander, silver and green buttonwood, jasmine, bird-of-paradise. The interior three walls were flanked by a peristyle—a columned and arched walkway—from which carved wooden doors led to the interior rooms. Long white curtains of translucent material hung down where these had been left open. A grand piano, painted white, sat out on the walkway under the shade.

But what dominated the scene was none of these. What dominated the scene were women. Beautiful women, several of them, lounging or sitting by the pool or bathing in a fountain, wearing bathing suits or white robes of translucent material not unlike the curtains.

Now I understood what this place was. The woman whose shadow I had seen the previous evening was not a mistress, she was a concubine. I had entered a harem.

Quire opened the palm of a hand, gesturing to the scene before us. "Mr. Antullis's other guests," he explained. "Allow me to introduce them to you."

We went down the steps into the pleasure garden. Quire led me toward a woman lying on a chaise, stomach down, resting her chin on crossed hands. I couldn't see her eyes through the dark sunglasses, but I could tell that she was watching us. She had shoulder-length dark hair, was deeply tanned, and was wearing only bikini bottoms. I could tell from the swell of flesh as she lay upon her chest that she was full-breasted, but her hair wasn't long enough to have been the woman I had glimpsed through the alabaster last night. She came up onto her elbows and smiled as we approached.

"Julia, this is Mr. Dalton," Quire said to her. "Mr. Dalton, Julia Carpentaria."

Julia Carpentaria extended her right hand and held her left across her chest in a token gesture of modesty, but it would have taken a dozen hands to have covered those breasts.

"Lysander Dalton," I said. We shook hands.

"Hello, Lysander Dalton," she replied. "Welcome to Xanadu."

"Xanadu?"

"That's what I call it. Fits, don't you think?"

"No dome," I replied.

"I don't think Coleridge was being literal."

"And I haven't actually met the Kublai Khan yet."

"Then you have a treat ahead of you."

I looked around at the scene before us, then back at her. "Impossible to beat this," I said.

But she shook her head, as if we were discussing a

serious point. "No, we're all just satellites in his orbit."
She looked around. "Pretty satellites perhaps, but satellites just the same. You'll see."

"Intelligent satellites, too."

Julia shrugged her shoulders, as if the compliment
was trivial. "He despises stupidity, that's all," she said.
"I hope you're smart," she added with a grin.

"Me, too."

She rested her chin back down on her crossed palms,
a gesture which I took as a polite dismissal.

Quire continued to introduce me around. There was a
girl studying sheet music at a table. Her name was
Bettina Wittig, and she was the only girl dressed in
anything substantial: white cotton pants, black T-shirt,
black espadrilles. She told me that she was from
Braunschweig—Brunswick in English—a small univer-
sity town in central Germany that had once been the seat
of the royal family that now ruled the British throne.
There were two girls sitting by a fountain playing
backgammon, their feet in the water, the board between
them. The one in the bikini, Carla Fuentes, was an Argentine, and the other, wearing a one-piece, was Jodie-
Ann Palmer from Houston, Texas. Jodie told me that
she'd completed her postgraduate degree in astrophysics
at Rice, and was giving herself a sabbatical before returning to the inevitable fate of space engineers—a government job at NASA—until she'd gained enough
experience to land a position with real pay at Lockheed
or Boeing or the like.

She was a rocket scientist—it seemed that Xerxes
Antullis did indeed like his concubines smart.

Next to last was an Eastern European woman—
Katerina Lazarovic. She was strikingly beautiful and
very tall. She wore a loosely tied white robe revealing
an elegant, spare, narrow-hipped, flat-chested body. She
was sitting at a table, writing in a notebook, Cyrillic
script flowing across the pages. Katerina spoke little

English, but enough to reveal that she was a model by profession.

The last woman was apart from the others, tucked into a little private alcove away from the pool and separated from the rest of the area by a series of fountains worked into a chest-high grill of intricate mosaics. She was supine on a chaise, wearing only sunglasses and suntan oil, but unlike Julia she made no effort to cover up on our approach. Instead she just put aside the magazine she had been reading and smiled slightly.

I knew at once that this was the woman I'd seen in the shower last night.

Quire politely looked away, declining to stare. Me, I just returned the woman's smile. She took off her sunglasses, her smile widening as she registered what must have been the look of surprise on my face.

Quire performed hurried introductions. "Lysander Dalton, this is Sorrel Tyne," he said.

I already knew that.

"Ms. Tyne is a dancer," he added.

I already knew that, too.

He exited the alcove and backed around somewhere out of sight on the other side of the grill. I think he expected me to follow. I stayed where I was and looked at the woman I had last seen ten years ago.

"Hello, Sorrel."

"Hello, Lee," she said. "Imagine meeting you here. Are the marines invading?"

"The marines and I parted company some time ago, Sorrel."

"Yes, of course," she said. "And no doubt you are here because you're now working for Mr. Antullis." Her smile broadened. "He does seem to have a penchant for hiring thugs."

"Is that so?"

"Oh, yes," she said, still smiling. "You should see

some of the violent psychopaths he employs—I'm sure you'll feel right at home."

"What does he employ them for?"

"Didn't he tell you that when he hired you?"

"Actually I'm here as a guest of Mr. Antullis," I explained. "We haven't discussed the hired help, Sorrel. Thug or otherwise."

The smile became a little less certain. She ran a hand through the long, chestnut hair for which her parents had named her, and sucked on the end of her sunglasses as she looked at me afresh. I could guess what she was thinking: Xerxes Antullis does not invite ordinary people to his house, which meant that in the last ten years I must have become somebody. Perhaps she was debating whether to ask why I would get an invitation from the world's most famous recluse, or maybe she was merely doing the mental calculus, trying to figure out if walking away ten years ago had been a missed opportunity.

I looked her over. She seemed more or less unchanged. Same tilt of the head that cautioned men not to take her for granted. Full breasts, which would have pleased many women but not Sorrel: most ballerinas had small breasts, and her own were in her view a liability. She had been so flexible that she had been able to stand on one leg and rest her head on the sole of her other foot bent back behind her. Her calves were shapely and slender—too slender, Sorrel used to complain: she lacked the lower leg strength to dance for extended periods *à pointe,* one of the marks of a ballerina destined for the big time.

Quire reappeared. "Mr. Dalton, if you're ready?"

It seemed that the tour of the harem was over; Sorrel Tyne was the last. Six women. Perhaps, like God, Xerxes Antullis rested on a Sunday.

FIFTEEN

THE library at Quartz Peak was a large gallery split into two levels by the addition of a mezzanine. The lower level had a series of alcoves with bookcases. The upper level was reached by a little wood-and-iron spiral staircase in one corner, and the mezzanine ran around all four walls, with bookshelves built directly into them. High overhead, the ceiling had a skylight of milky glass which lit the room so well that no artificial light was required, despite the fact that there were no other windows.

I looked around. There were paintings hung on the wide expanses of blank wall separating the alcoves on the lower level. When conducting me to the library Quire had explained that the room also served as a picture gallery.

"Mr. Antullis collects American art from the century 1870 to 1970," he told me. "Roughly from the Impressionists through to the Pop Art movement."

After he left me alone I went to the books. They seemed to be arranged in no standard cataloging system, just lumped together generally like with like. As well as books there were magazines and pamphlets, and one bookcase was brimming with the annual reports and 10K SEC filings of publicly traded companies. I got the impression that this was not just a rich man's showcase but a real working library, a place where Xerxes Antullis spent a lot of time.

I found the reference area: rows of encyclopedias, a series of dictionaries including a full *OED,* atlases and a map drawer, plus many other specialist reference works—everything from philately catalogs to the standard pharmacopeia.

I took out a book of abbreviations and looked up TLD. It wasn't there. I tried the *Britannica* next, same result. Then I located a scientific dictionary. There was no entry for TLD. I looked up microbarograph instead:

> **Microbarograph** Measures and records barometric pressure. Used chiefly in meteorology and in the interpretation of radiation exposure data (as changes in atmospheric pressure affect the escape of naturally occurring radioactive gases, like radon and thoron, from the earth).

The instrument that had made the sucking sound remained a mystery, but remembering that I had assumed it was some sort of pollution measuring device I was able to track down a likely candidate:

> **Particulate Sampler** Collects airborne particulate matter by pulling air through a filter. Used for assessing airborne pollution, pollen and spore levels, and the presence of radioactive particles.

Two references to radioactivity. I decided to go through all the *T*s, trying to locate TLD in its long form. Eventually I found it:

ThermoLuminescent Dosimeter (TLD) Determines ambient natural background levels of radioactivity. Used in setting a baseline for the measurement of radiation from other, nonnatural, sources.

It wasn't hard to guess what the "nonnatural" source would be; plutonium doesn't exist in nature, it is entirely the product of man.

So Xerxes Antullis had set up a radiation monitoring station on his property. And not just anywhere on his property but at an ammunition bunker, which was supposedly abandoned and yet was surrounded by chain-link fence and razor wire and secured with a relatively new lock and chain. I sat back and considered what I'd learned. There seemed no way to interpret this other than the obvious one: Xerxes Antullis was not only funding the purchase of nuclear material, he apparently intended to keep the stuff here at Quartz Peak.

Why? Temporary storage maybe, a place to hide it until the terrorists were ready to take delivery? Or perhaps the terrorists were simply a front, and he actually intended to keep the plutonium and make an A-bomb for himself—the ultimate gun nut, one of those people who believed the Second Amendment's right to bear arms extended to any weapon imaginable, but in this case a gun nut with a checkbook big enough to make the unthinkable happen.

Either way, it didn't matter. The evidence wasn't conclusive, but it was close. I had yet to meet Xerxes Antullis, but I knew now that I was probably going to do what Dortmund had wanted me to do all along.

Suddenly there was a voice above and behind me.

"It's a Whistler."

I turned and looked up. The man I had just been contemplating assassinating was standing on the mezzanine, hands on the railing, looking down at me, and wearing the smile of a showman who knows that he's just made a good entrance.

"Untitled," he added, briefly glancing up. I followed his look to a painting on the wall in front of me. Apparently he had assumed that I'd been sitting here admiring it, when in fact I'd just been staring blankly ahead while wondering whether or not to kill its owner. "His most famous work is of course known to the world as *Whistler's Mother.* But he himself never called it that. Do you know what title he gave to that painting of his dear old ma?"

"No."

"Arrangement in Grey and Black Number One." His smile broadened to a grin. "Whistler was not a sentimental man, I think."

Antullis walked along the mezzanine to the stairs, although *walk* is too general a term to convey the quick, confident energy of his movements. He really *bounded* along the mezzanine to the staircase.

"How did you get up there?" I asked.

"Secret passage," he answered as he clattered down the stairs. "This place is full of them. Back when the air force owned this land they used the mesa as a lookout post, a natural thing to do since it's the high ground. They built a number of observation bunkers and had a network of tunnels connecting them with a central control station dug deep into the rock. I incorporated them into the design when I built Quartz Peak—the control station is now my wine cellar. I'll show you later."

I closed the scientific dictionary as he came across the library. I tried to do it subtly, so as not to draw Antullis's attention to the fact that I'd been using it to look something up, but I'm not good at doing things subtly, and I could tell that he'd noticed. Xerxes Antullis was not a man who missed much.

He came and stood in front of the Whistler. He was

of middle height, with a boyish, rounded face, alert eyes, and what seemed to be the permanent half smile of a man who enjoyed life. He wore working clothes: khakis and a white cotton shirt rolled at the sleeves with button-down flaps over the pockets. His whole de-meanor radiated energy: the young Howard Hughes per-haps, or better still the young Orson Welles playing the young Howard Hughes. No introduction, no handshake, no formal greeting—maybe in his long seclusion he'd forgotten the standard social courtesies, or perhaps he'd simply never had the patience for them in the first place.

Antullis turned to the painting, a brooding, enigmatic interior. "He did it in 1878. At the time Whistler was en-gaged in a long legal battle with Ruskin, which is per-haps why he never got around to giving it a title. He sued Ruskin for slandering his work, and the whole af-fair became a *cause célèbre*. Whistler eventually won but was awarded precisely one farthing in damages. A bad idea really: if I'd sued everyone who'd slandered me I'd never have had any time to do real work."

Or perhaps he had come up with another plan for dealing with his critics.

I looked again at the painting. "James Whistler sounds like he was an unhappy man."

Antullis looked at it, too. "Happiness is overrated," he said after a while. "A man who is not in conflict is not alive."

"A strange sentiment for someone who sold every-thing and became a recluse."

"At the top of the market, too," he replied with a sly grin. "Shall I tell you the truth, Mr. Dalton? It was dumb luck. One day, just for a laugh, I decided to calculate how much I was worth. I was at my desk. I put aside my work, put up my feet, and figured it out on the back of an envelope. It came out to $8.6 billion, give or take a hundred million. I wasn't yet forty. Then I imagined what I would have done back when I was a struggling computer science student if I had suddenly acquired that kind of money. Of course I would have quit school and had fun for the rest of my life. At that point I realized just how stupid it is to keep working to make money when one has already made more than one could ever need." His eyes were penetratingly on mine, as if inviting me to challenge the proposition. I remained silent. Eventually he laughed. "Come, let me show you the rest of the collection."

As Quire had already told me, all the paintings were by American artists, and all falling in the period between the ends of the Civil and Vietnam Wars. Besides the Whistler there were several nineteenth-century oils, occasional landscapes and seascapes, but more often portraits depicting the comfortable bourgeois of the Gilded Age. The twentieth-century paintings were better: an Ashcan School industrial scene, a number of midcentury abstracts, and one Hopper—a winsome nude looking out a New York brownstone window—that must have been worth a fortune. There was a Warhol print, a self portrait endlessly repeated, and a Jackson Pollock that looked like the result of a child having been left unattended with the paints.

It wasn't a huge collection, perhaps two dozen in all, but by and large they were genuinely engaging. I had the impression that Antullis was that rarest of art collectors: someone who purchased paintings for what they were rather than for who had painted them.

"Is the collection ever shown together?" I asked.

"It's never shown at all," he answered. Apparently his reclusiveness extended to his artworks.

"Then I'm a fortunate man," I said. "I've seen many beautiful things of yours today."

Antullis looked at me quizzically a moment, then grinned. "Ah, yes—the girls," he said. "They're adorable, but I don't think that you've yet met my favorite." He walked over to a telephone on a writing table, picked up the handset, and pressed a button. "Would you ask Maria to come up to the library, please? I would like her to meet Mr. Dalton."

Maria arrived a few minutes later. She was perhaps five feet tall and must have weighed 250 pounds. She had gray hair pulled tightly back into a bun, wore flip-flops and a big apron, and was drying her pudgy chapped hands on a dish towel as she entered the room.

Antullis stood and bowed slightly, apparently not having lost the social graces after all. *"Buena sera, signora."*

Maria gave a little tilt of her chin, a queen reluctantly acknowledging a not-too-favored courtier, but was otherwise silent and continued to dry her hands while examining me with mild curiosity.

"Mr. Dalton, Signora Maria Traversi."

"Pleased to meet you," I said.

She nodded at me and smiled briefly before looking back at Antullis and resuming her mild scowl of disapproval at having been interrupted. She was aptly named: cross indeed.

"Signora Traversi is my cook," Antullis explained to me. "Her English is limited, and my Italian is nonexistent, which allows us to get on very well together. She is the one person working on this estate without whom I would be lost. Are you hungry?"

"Sure." One thing you learn in the marines is to never say no to food.

Antullis turned to the old woman. *"Maria, pasta rustica por due?"*

She considered the request a moment, then nodded. She would agree to make us pasta. She turned to leave the room.

"E vino?" Antullis added.

Maria gave him a dismissive wave, as if the additional request to bring wine was too obvious to be worth even a nod, and closed the door behind her.

"If only competence and silence coexisted more frequently," Antullis said when she'd left. "In fact, I'd just settle for the competence."

"Has she been with you long?"

"Yes, many years," Antullis replied. He walked over to a cabinet by the wall and opened it with a flourish. No books, just booze. He began mixing drinks. "I value competence and am in the fortunate position of being able to afford to keep it when I find it. There is not a high turnover of staff at Quartz Peak. Dennis Quire's been with me for twenty years."

"What about Yamina Malik?"

"She's new. I had to fire her predecessor awhile ago."

"Not competent?"

"Very competent. Came highly recommended from the agency we use to hire such people: well-trained and very experienced in security matters. But the one thing he apparently couldn't secure against was himself: it turned out that he was a thief."

"What did he steal?"

"Coins. I have a collection of ancient coins, many of them very valuable. He helped himself to some, apparently in the belief that were I to notice, the person I would naturally ask to investigate would be him."

"What happened?"

"I did the investigating myself: I hid a small motion-activated video camera by the cabinet and caught him red-handed."

He brought over the camparis and soda. We sat and talked, or rather he talked and I listened. He related the story of the house's construction, much of which I had heard yesterday, but Antullis recounted it with an enthusiasm Quire lacked, and which turned the story into an adventure. The door opened, and Maria came in with a tray table. There were two big bowls full of some long, flat pasta—fettuccine perhaps—in a sauce of mushrooms and Italian sausage and whole garlic cloves that had been sautéed in oil. The bread was a round peasant loaf from which we both tore chunks, and there was a bowl of olive oil for dipping. It was a simple peasant meal—rustic, as Antullis had called it—not the sort of thing you imagine billionaires eating, but it was hard to think of how it could have been better. Conversation was more or less deferred while we ate.

The one thing that was not rustic was the wine: it was Lafite, and tasted too good to be true. It wasn't until Antullis was opening the second bottle that I saw the year.

"Do you realize what vintage this is?" I asked.

Antullis looked at the label. "Nineteen sixty-one," he read out loud. He burst into laughter. "My God, no wonder it's so good."

The year 1961 is a legendary vintage, one of the greatest ever for the first-growth Paulliacs like Lafite Rothschild. I wondered if Maria knew what it was she'd chosen. Most likely not—she'd probably just gone down to the cellar and picked something red to go with the pasta. Or maybe she'd noticed the year and decided that it was old and needed to be gotten rid of.

Antullis stood, smiling as always, and glass in hand. "Mr. Dalton, I think we should take it as a sign. Here's to things done well."

I stood and joined the toast. "To things done well."

We both drained our glasses. Antullis threw his empty glass into the fireplace. I followed suit.

Antullis put his hands on his hips. "And speaking of things done well, Mr. Dalton, will you show me that GT40 of yours now?"

"Mr. Antullis, it would be my pleasure."

He reached for the phone, grinning like a child on Christmas Eve. "Please have all the airfield floodlights turned on. Why? Because Mr. Dalton and I are going for a drive, that's why."

* * *

THE light had gradually faded while we had been dining in the library, and by the time we got outside it was nearly dark. Downstairs we were met by Dennis Quire, who looked displeased at being disturbed by this sudden whim, and Yamina Malik, who showed no emotion whatsoever. The forecourt lights were on, and Antullis approached Chassis 1075 like a pilgrim approaching a religious shrine.

"She's magnificent," he said.

He took a swig from the bottle and passed it to me. I drank the same way. I was pretty sure that we were the only people likely to have ever chugged '61 Lafite straight from the bottle. Quire looked appalled, whether at the general fact of drinking that way, or the specific detail of what it was we were drinking, I couldn't tell.

"I can't wait to hear it," Antullis said.

I got in and fired it up. The car started right away, as if it had been waiting to put on a show. All the gauges registered correctly. I got back out.

Antullis was standing with his eyes closed, listening to the booming exhaust note resonating in the still night air. Two of the girls I'd met earlier in the day—Carla Fuentes and Jodie-Ann Palmer—had come down and were admiring the car, too. Yamina Malik was speaking into a walkie-talkie, and a minute later a Humvee arrived, driven by one of her guards. It was a real Humvee, a military model rather than one of the domesticated versions sold to the general public, with heavy-duty off-road tires and a huge whip aerial tied down by the tip to the rear of the vehicle.

We set out in convoy for the airfield, Antullis and I in the GT40, Yamina in the Humvee with her guard, and Quire doing duty in the golf cart with the two girls.

The airfield was as bright as day, lit by huge banks of floodlights. The Humvee and golf cart stayed by the hangar area. Antullis and I drove to one end of the airfield. I pointed the car's nose down the strip.

"How long is the runway?" I asked.

"Twelve thousand feet," Antullis said. "They built it to accommodate fully laden B-52s."

More than two miles.

"If you're wondering how fast you can get it to go," Antullis added, "Mulsanne Straight at Le Mans is just a mile long. This car hit two hundred miles per hour on that straight every few minutes for twenty-four hours at a time. Twice. You should be able to hit that no problem."

But at the end of Mulsanne Straight the road didn't just end. At two hundred miles an hour I guessed the GT40 would probably need a thousand feet just to come to a stop. I put on the racing harness and made sure the individual straps were pulled down securely. Antullis did likewise.

When he was done, I revved the engine. "Ready?"

Antullis nodded. "Ready."

I released the clutch. There was a split second of nothing but tire squeal and smoke until the wheels gripped. The car yawed slightly as the tremendous power running into those rear wheels gained traction, then the GT40 took off like a rocket.

I took it to the redline through every gear. The engine spooled effortlessly, doing exactly what it was designed to do, moving from the low churning growl at idle to an ever higher-pitched scream as the car roared down the runway. We hit 100 mph in the blink of an eye, and 150 came up not long after. The last 50 was the longest, but there was still lots of runway left. I kept the pedal to the floor. At 210 mph, with the runway now rapidly disappearing and the front end beginning to display the unwanted aerodynamic lift that GT40s were known for, I came off the gas and applied the brakes. It took a long time to slow down, but gradually I sensed that there was more than enough room left, and eased up to prevent any fade or disc warping due to the excessive heat in slowing down a ton of metal moving at over 200 mph. We came to a halt with several hundred feet to spare.

Antullis didn't say anything. He didn't need to. I put the transmission into neutral and applied the hand brake.

"Your turn, I guess."

We got out and swapped seats.

So it went for several more runs, up and down the huge runway, pausing now and again to stop at the hangar for another pull from the Lafite. Antullis took Jodie-Ann as a passenger on one run, and I took Carla as a passenger on another. When we got back from that one I found that more '61 Lafite had arrived, along with a picnic, which was laid out on some grass by the side of the runway.

As the night wore on we graduated from speed runs to other games. Some cones were laid out, and Antullis and I competed to see who could make the fastest slalom run without knocking them over. The more we drank, the slower and less successful these became. Eventually we simply took turns making donuts, deliberately smoking the tires with the steering wheel on hard lock, leaving great circles of burned rubber over the concrete apron.

The last memory I have of that evening is of sitting on the airstrip with my back against the hangar, too drunk to drive anymore. Xerxes Antullis, also drunk, was hugging the GT40, his ear pressed against the engine cover. He was listening to the deep, low growl of the engine with the dreamy, faraway look of a philosopher who has discovered the music of the spheres.

SIXTEEN

I woke up early the next morning like I always do, hangover or no hangover. I've had better mornings, but I've had worse, too. At least this time I wasn't tied to a chair.

There was a note under my door, a single sheet of thick, high-grade paper in a matching envelope. Both envelope and paper were embossed with an interwoven X and A. The note was handwritten in an unusually elegant, flowing script, as if with a calligraphy pen.

Mr. Dalton,

I had immense pleasure in getting to know you and your car last night. I hope that you also enjoyed the evening, but that your head isn't paying the same penalty mine is this morning.

I regret that I will be occupied with business for the next day or so, but invite you to make yourself at home. My mechanic is on vacation, but the automobile collection is at your disposal—perhaps you might give some of them a run? And of course

Las Vegas is just an hour away, should you wish to try lady luck.

We have a little formal dinner every Saturday evening on the lawn at the oasis—I hope that you will join us. I also hope that you are in no rush to leave Quartz Peak—I am eager to find out if Chassis 1075 looks as good the morning after as she did the night before.

XA

So Xerxes Antullis was an early riser, too. I wondered what business it was that a man who has sold his business has that occupied so much of his time.

I took a carton of juice and a pair of binoculars out to the terrace and surveyed the damage while giving my stomach something nonalcoholic to settle down with. In the distance the runway lay stark white in the morning sunshine, except for the occasional patch of freshly laid black rubber. The GT40 sat by the hangar where I had last seen it in the embrace of Xerxes Antullis. The car itself looked fine, but I could see that at least one of those fat racing tires was flat. A flat tire was okay, but Binky would not be pleased if I'd bent a rim.

I continued to scan with the binoculars. The second hangar, the big one with the security fencing, had a door ajar. Not the main aircraft doors, just a regular people-sized door at the side. There was a black SUV outside, a big one like the truck to which I'd handcuffed Smiling Man. Presumably a contractor's vehicle, if Quire had been correct about the hangar being where the contractors stored their gear. Contractors usually have pickups, not SUVs, although there was a sign on the vehicle's door, the way contractors' vehicles do. I tried to make out the name, but it was too far away.

I surveyed the rest of the property over which I had a view—basically the eastern half of the Antullis estate.

There was the long road to the guardhouse that I had come in on, the sharp scar of the ravine which acted as a natural security barrier, and beyond that in the distance stood the chain-link fence and public highway. Nothing moved; everything was quiet in the still morning air. There was nothing of interest to the east. But of course I couldn't see anything to the west.

I ended the scan by looking directly down at the forecourt. I could see now that the occasional black tiles embedded into the terra-cotta there were not a random pattern. Seen from above, they formed a giant interlocking XA, big enough to have announced to overhead satellites to whom the property belonged.

I checked my watch. Too early to get a replacement tire, but early enough for the desert not to have yet gotten oppressively hot. The time had come for some reconnaissance over the western part of the estate.

WHEN I got to the base of the mesa I started by heading north across the desert, with the long runway about a mile over to my right. Basic military theory dictates conducting surveillance beyond your line of sight. With a unit on the move, you achieve this by sending out men ahead of the main body, a position called point. With a unit encamped, you conduct perimeter patrols, dawn and dusk at minimum. That's what I began now, a perimeter patrol in a wide semicircle covering the western half of the property. I started by taking six thousand strides due north—about three miles. Then I turned and took an angular measurement of the mesa with my arm extended and one eye closed. The mesa stood exactly one fist with outstretched thumb high. As long as I maintained that same angular measurement as I moved around the mesa, I would always be about three miles from it.

I began walking counterclockwise. The desert,

which had looked flat from the height of the mesa, was actually broken country when you got up close to it, full of small gullies and little rises. There was a surprising amount of plant life: cactus of course, but clusters of grass, too, and even the occasional stubbly shrub, sage--brush. There was also animal life, birds hopping about the grasses and lizards out sunning themselves on rocks. It wasn't until I came up over one of the rises that I found evidence of anything human. It was a bullet, and it went zinging past me.

I hit the ground. The first rule when the lead suddenly starts flying is to get as low as possible. I scrambled back down the little rise.

The shooter had missed me, and what I'd heard was a ricochet: the sharp crack as the bullet hit stone, immediately followed by that distinctive noise bullets make when—now subsonic and distended beyond the capacity for aerodynamic flight—they go whistling away. But I had no idea where the shot had come from.

I had to make a guess and act on it. He had to be ahead of me, not behind: if he'd been behind me, he would have gotten closer and wouldn't have missed. And he would likely have come from the house, which would place him slightly to the left. So I decided that he'd been on my ten o'clock.

He would expect me to retreat the way I'd come. I went to my right instead, keeping low along what contours there were, maintaining as much range as possible between me and the shooter while circling around in the opposite direction to the way he'd expect. Then I heard another ricochet, again bullet hitting stone, but much farther away now.

I decided to chance a look up. There was some good grass cover twenty yards away—I crawled up to it and looked cautiously through the thin, straight leaves.

The shooter was Yamina Malik. She was perhaps two hundred yards away, holding a long-barreled handgun in a two-handed grip. Whatever she was shooting at, it wasn't me. I saw her fire off a clip, do a quick magazine release and reload, then empty the fresh clip in a new direction. When she'd finished she checked her watch, then she put the gun down on a small table before walking out of my vision. I was pretty confident that I knew what she was doing, but it wasn't until she came back in view holding a pair of paper targets that I was sure. She was just practicing, apparently having picked this lonely piece of desert, miles from the house and roads, as an appropriate place to do it.

She had been doing a rapid-fire multitarget exercise: you set up two targets at varying ranges, take out the nearest with the first clip and then the other with the second. Score equals hits divided by time taken in seconds—a good, realistic exercise. In the marines we used to do them when out in the field and without proper combat range facilities available.

However, we wore more clothing. Yamina Malik had the camouflage pants and combat boots, just like we would have, but above that she was wearing nothing but sunglasses. It seemed that Yamina liked to work on her tan while keeping sharp on the firing range.

It was just as well I hadn't brought the binoculars, otherwise I would have been tempted to remain hidden a little longer than was strictly gentlemanly. Even without binoculars, what I could make out from this distance looked very good indeed: slender and smooth and even and very brown.

I backed down from the grassy area in which I was hidden, stood up, and then started whistling as I slowly walked back up the rise. I kept my eyes down: just a guy out for a stroll, watching where I was walking, whistling tunelessly and probably lost in thought.

"Hey."

I looked up and made myself search for a moment before locating the source of the cry. Yamina Malik had a tank top on now, but hadn't had time to tuck it in. I gave a little wave of acknowledgment and changed direction to head for her.

By the time I got down to her, the tank top was tucked in. It was plain khaki, tight, clinging to her narrow frame. Her arms were on her hips. She did not look thrilled to see me.

"You turn up at some inconvenient times in some unexpected places," she said.

"Morning walk," I said. "Good for the constitution."

"I shoot out here," she explained. "That could be bad for the constitution."

"Yes, well, now that I'm aware of that, I'll keep clear in future."

She looked at my attire. "And did you fall down while walking?"

I realized that I had failed to dust myself off after hitting the dirt. "No, I lay down," I said.

"Lay down?" Her voice was one of polite disbelief. "Fatigue, perhaps?"

"Checking tracks, actually. Those cougars you mentioned—I think I saw some cougar tracks."

"Really?"

"I tried to follow them, but it seems that I've lost the trail."

She looked at me without expression for a good thirty seconds before replying. It was hard to tell what she was thinking behind those sunglasses, but she obviously didn't believe my story. "Probably not a good idea to go chasing after cougars," she said at last. "Could end up in a case of the cat having killed the curiosity."

Besides the camouflage pants and combat boots she was wearing a regular holster, in which her own gun had been replaced, and a thigh holster, from which protruded the butt of Billy-Jo-Bob's Anaconda.

"Beckett told me that my gun was going to be safely locked up," I said.

"I thought I'd check it out."

"Check what out, exactly?"

She withdrew it from the holster and looked at it curiously. "I've never understood why some men are attracted to these hugely oversized handguns. Loud, cumbersome, more awkward than useful. I've always thought their ridiculous size must serve as some sort of psychological compensation for other, more personal shortcomings." She turned her gaze to me. "What do you think?"

"It's not mine; it's a friend's," I replied.

"And you're just keeping it safe for him?"

"Actually, he no longer has any need of it."

I walked over to the folding table on which the two paper targets were laid. They were standard NRA twenty-five-foot pistol targets, quite small, only six inches in diameter and with seven concentric rings scored from four in the outer ring to ten at the bull's-eye. At the range she had been firing most people would have been lucky to get any hits at all, even if it had been deliberate fire instead of rapid fire, but Yamina's targets were scattered with holes. She'd circled them with a pen as she'd counted them up. The first had two bull's-eyes with a scattering of hits in the other rings; the second—presumably the more distant—had no bull's-eyes, and the hits were clustered in the lower right quadrant.

"You're thumbing slightly."

"I know," she replied.

She'd completed the entire exercise in nine seconds—it was outstanding shooting.

"Since I'm here, perhaps we should have a little competition?"

She looked at me suspiciously. "What sort of competition?"

"Shooting. Rapid fire on two targets, once through for each weapon."

I could see that she didn't really want to do it, but she'd been challenged, and she wasn't the sort of woman who backed down from a challenge. She shrugged her shoulders and said, "Okay."

I picked up two targets and thumbtacks from the table, and headed out to the target posts. Yamina came with me.

"We should compete for something," I said while tacking the first of the targets. "Make it a real competition." I felt Yamina stiffen beside me.

"Like what?"

"I don't know. If you win, what would you like?"

"You to leave," she replied without hesitation.

I stopped mounting the target and looked at Yamina instead. She returned my gaze unflinchingly.

"Quartz Peak?"

"Quartz Peak," she confirmed.

Well, okay. It's always good for a man to know where he stands. I returned to mounting the target.

"And what if I win?" I asked.

"You tell me."

"If I win," I said, "then I get you."

She didn't reply immediately. I finished the first target and we walked in silence to the second post. Behind those sunglasses I couldn't tell where Yamina's eyes were looking, but her head was down slightly, and I got the sense that she was actually considering the terms, which I'd proposed only in order to ensure that her answer would be negative, allowing me to gracefully avoid the possibility of being required to quit the estate. I was frankly out of practice in shooting, which Yamina obviously was not, and I had no doubt that she would beat me.

It wasn't until we'd returned to the firing point that she spoke again.

"Double target rapid fire?" she confirmed. "Once through with each weapon?"

"Yes."

"One magazine each target?"

"Yes. Six rounds per magazine."

"What about the revolver?"

"No reload. Three rounds per target, but double score."

"And score is hit score divided by number of seconds?"

"Yep. We sum all three. Whoever has the highest total wins."

"And once through for each weapon, right?"

"Yes."

"I win, you're gone from here by nightfall?"

"Yes."

She bowed her head again, still thinking. I wondered what it was, that she wanted to get rid of me so badly. Then, without looking up, she quietly said, "Agreed."

I'd been going over the odds. She would obviously beat me with her own weapon: she'd just been practicing, and I had never fired it. But the Anaconda is a very heavy gun, and the trigger pull was stiff. And I'd recently had some real-world rapid-fire practice with it. I was just thinking that maybe I wasn't in such bad shape after all, when Yamina suddenly knelt and pulled up the leg of her camis, revealing an ankle holster.

She looked up at me. "We did say *each* weapon, right?" She pulled out a little snub-nosed automatic. "Para Ordnance P12," she explained. "Compact, but shoots .45. Why don't we start with this one?"

So it was going to be two weapons with which she was familiar, versus just one of mine. That's what she'd been thinking about: getting her questions worded just right to ensure that she would have the overwhelming advantage. I shrugged my shoulders in acceptance.

"Sure," I said. "After you."

She took a spare magazine and loaded six rounds of .45 into it—big rounds for a little gun. She placed the loaded magazine into an elasticized band on her webbing. They were designed to allow quick access to spare magazines—you just felt for it and pulled. Another advantage she would have over me—all I had were pockets.

There was a line in the dirt that Yamina had marked for the firing point. She toed it, and worked the slide on the Para twice, the second time ejecting the unfired seventh round and reloading with the first of the remaining six.

"Ready?"

I nodded. She held up her left wrist, pressed the button on her watch to start the timer, and a fraction of a second later was in a two-handed firing stance loosing off rounds in a rapid but controlled sequence into the near target. Small shards of wood went flying out from the backboard behind the target, and I could see the dark patches of torn paper. They were tightly clustered around the bull's-eye.

I looked back at Yamina, knees slightly bent, body tensed but not locked tight, eyes focused entirely on the view through the sights. She looked good when shooting. Not as good as when she'd been shooting topless, but still good.

When the action was locked to the rear, she seamlessly retrieved the second magazine with her left hand while hitting the weapon's magazine release with her right thumb, allowing the empty to fall to the ground. She slapped the fresh magazine home, actioned the slide, and began with the second target. All smooth, no rush, no fuss, just as clean as you could wish. When the action was again locked to the rear, indicating that the gun was once again empty, she reached up to her left wrist and hit the timer button as casually as if she'd had all day.

We retrieved the targets together. I could see as we approached the first that I was in trouble. The second was full of holes, too. We returned with them to the table.

Yamina laid the targets flat, and we leaned over to study them. We were close now, both looking down at those targets. Her arms were covered in a thin sheen of sweat. I could smell her, the same deep, good smell that I had first found in that head scarf, and her wild black hair brushed my face as she moved around, circling the hits in pen. I couldn't help wondering what it would be like if a miracle occurred, and I actually won this shoot-out.

Those fantasies disappeared as we counted the hits. Forty-nine on the first target, including three bull's-eyes, and thirty-two on the second. She showed me the timer on her wrist: 9.43 seconds. She rounded that down to 9, and did the division on a calculator, although I'd already done it in my head: $(49 + 32)/9 = 9$ exactly.

"Nice shooting," I said. Actually it was outstanding.

"Not bad," she admitted. "Now let's see what you can do." She handed me the watch and weapon.

I practiced with the watch first: it had a simple stopwatch function—you press the button once to start, again to stop, and the third time resets it to zero.

I practiced with the weapon next: easy magazine release, stiff action but smooth trigger pull. I loaded it with the same .45 JHPs—jacketed hollow points—that Yamina favored. Not suitable range ammunition—too expensive—but maybe Yamina wanted to practice with rounds that would give precisely the same kickback as when the time came to fire the gun in real life.

I picked up the second magazine from where it had fallen when Yamina had released it, dusted it off as best I could, and reloaded that, too. I toed the firing line, actioned the Para to load the first round, and quickly rehearsed in my head the sequence of movements I would make for the reload, the most critical part of the exercise. I took a deep breath, hit the timer button, and began firing into the first target.

When you fire a weapon, you know right away if you're doing well or not without having to actually check the target. As I fired off that first magazine I knew I was doing well: the foresight post was staying good and steady between the rear sights, and the trigger pulls were smooth and even. Soon the action was locked to the rear.

I released and reloaded, worked the slide, and took aim on the second target. Steady again, I pulled the trigger.

Nothing happened.

This is why multitarget rapid-fire exercises are good training: they drum into you what to do when something goes wrong. And the wrongest thing that can happen with a weapon is that you pull the trigger and it doesn't go bang.

Without thinking I came out of the firing stance, took my finger off the trigger, and pulled back hard on the slide, putting as much force as possible behind the action, giving it the best chance to clear the problem. The misfire ejected cleanly. I felt the action move forward smoothly, hopefully loading a new round with it. I went back into the firing stance and quickly put the remaining five rounds into the second target before hitting the stopwatch.

We went wordlessly to collect the targets and returned to the table. Again, Yamina circled the hits. In the first target there was only the one bull's-eye, but the grouping was tighter than Yamina's, so I got a 47, close to her 49. But the second target had only five hits to circle, and the score was just 24. The stopwatch showed 11.62, which Yamina kindly rounded up to 12. When she'd punched it all into the calculator, the score was a miserable 5.92.

"Too bad about the misfire," Yamina said.

I shrugged my shoulders and said, "It happens." In the special forces you learn not to complain.

Next was the Anaconda, and I offered to go first this time. I was accustomed to the weapon by now, and scored two bull's-eyes on the near target, plus another on the second. The time was just six seconds, much shorter because there was no reload, and the score was exactly 15. With the previous 5.92, that made 20.92.

Yamina was much worse with Billy-Jo-Bob's Anaconda than her own Para and ended up only hitting the second target twice. Still, she was fast and got enough to get an even 12, giving her 21 in total. Ahead of me, but closer than I'd expected. Closer than she'd expected, too: her mouth had tightened, and there was a thin line of sweat on the tank top between her breasts.

Yamina pulled out the third weapon, popped the magazine, and began unloading. There was a lot of unloading to do: the magazine held eighteen rounds, a huge number for a handgun. She looked up and met my inquiring glance.

"It's called a Gyurza," she said. "Nine mil."

Not exactly. Standard nine mil rounds, what they call 9mm Parabellum, are 19mm long. Gyurzas use a special extended 21mm round. Its purpose is to be armor-piercing, and the bullets are made with a steel rod embedded into the lead to help achieve that.

Gyurzas are quite rare, and I wondered how Yamina had acquired the weapon. I'd only ever seen a Gyurza once, at special ops school. They'd used one to demonstrate why we wear heavy flak jackets instead of the lighter and more convenient Kevlar, like the police use. In those Cold War days our focus had been on the Soviets, and our special ops counterparts in the Soviet military used Gyurzas. A bullet from a Gyurza can pierce twenty layers of Kevlar bulletproof vest, and that day the instructor had proven it to us.

Yamina fired first. If the previous problems with the Anaconda bothered her, they didn't show in her results:

she scored 91 in just 8 seconds, for a total of 11.375 and a grand total of 32.375.

I took my time getting to know the Gyurza. The hand-grip was unusually wide, built to accommodate those eighteen double-stacked rounds in the magazine. Most women wouldn't be comfortable with a grip that fat, but Yamina—like many tall, slender women—had big hands and long fingers. I pulled back the slide. The action was stiff and awkward. I would have liked to fire a few prac-tice rounds to get a feel for the kickback on those ex-tended nine mils, but wasn't about to ask. Instead, I assumed the position, and went to work.

When it was over, and we'd collected the targets, it was obvious that it was going to be close. I got two bull's-eyes and a total of 48 on the first target, and an-other bull's-eye on the second, but also a complete miss, and only 34. The stopwatch read 8:49, and so this time the rounding went my way: 8 seconds. But still the score was 10.25, not enough.

"Would you like me to radio ahead and have Beckett start packing?" Yamina asked.

"No," I replied, "but you might ask him to bring flowers and change the sheets."

"Huh?"

I held up the second target. "Maybe you should look again."

She took the target from me and spent a moment studying it. It took awhile, but eventually she found it: the hit in the bull's-eye had some tearing that distorted it, but there was something else, too. On the upper left there was a slight change in the curvature of the bullet hole, as if it was bulging out. There had been no miss after all. The missing round had in fact been a second bull's-eye, almost directly on top of the first.

While Yamina was studying it I worked the calcula-tor. My initial 82 with the Gyurza had in reality been 92, which made the third round score 11.5, and so the grand total 32.42, marginally ahead of Yamina's 32.375.

She put down the target. Her face, or what I could see of it behind those sunglasses, showed no emotion whatsoever.

"So you get to stay," she said.

"And something else, I think."

"Yes, of course," she replied matter-of-factly. "I hope you don't mind passion which is completely and obviously faked."

"Your virtue is safe, Ms. Malik. The truth is if you'd won, I wouldn't have left, so we're square."

Actually, I'd cheated. The Colt Anaconda has a windage adjustment on the back sight, a small screw on the right-hand side. After I'd fired, and while Yamina was retrieving the targets, I'd adjusted the back sight for maximum crosswind from the right, which of course makes the weapon fire to the right in compensation. But there was no wind to compensate for today. Yamina would have assumed that it was just her own problem of occasionally using too much thumb pressure, which also causes you to fire to the right. If it hadn't been for the cheat, I'm pretty sure I would have happily taken possession of the prize.

"You wouldn't have left if I'd won?"

"No," I confirmed.

"Maybe I would have insisted."

"Maybe you would have tried."

"Maybe I would have succeeded."

"Maybe."

She didn't reply.

I held out the Gyurza to her. The action was still locked to the rear, revealing threading on the end of the barrel. She took the weapon and immediately proved it, the way someone who's been well-trained does automatically whenever a weapon has been out of their possession, even if only for a moment. I wondered where she'd received that level of training.

Yamina wordlessly reloaded the weapon, thumbing the rounds hard into the magazine.

"Are you going to give me back the Anaconda now?" I asked.

"No," she replied without looking up. She slapped the magazine home, reholstered the Gyurza, and began reloading her backup.

"Why not?"

"I'm the head of security," she said. "It's my job to protect Mr. Antullis, not arm people who have access to him."

"If I had to kill Xerxes Antullis, a steak knife would do. Or any sharp object really—a pen, whatever. Of course a blunt object, too. Or nothing at all, if it came to that. Taking my gun from me does nothing to protect Xerxes Antullis. The only thing taking my gun from me does is prevent me defending myself against someone else who has one."

"Are you expecting to have to do so, Mr. Dalton?"

"You never know, Ms. Malik. There are some violent people out there."

She crouched and lifted up the leg of her camis as she replaced the reloaded P12. The slanting sunlight of early morning caught her at a good angle, the light and shadow highlighting the definition of her calf muscle and of the triceps and biceps of the long arm reaching down to the ankle holster. Yamina Malik was built as taut as a Thoroughbred.

She stood back up. "If you find any of these violent people," she said, "you let me know, and I'll have them taken care of for you."

Without waiting for a reply she turned and walked back to her Jeep. She fired it up with her right hand while talking on the radio mike in her left—checking in with her people, I guessed. A moment later she was gone in a cloud of brown red dust, the little open Jeep bouncing over the ruts on big off-road tires.

There had been no offer of a ride back for me. For the second time that morning, Yamina Malik had left me in no doubt as to my place in her world.

I shrugged my shoulders and resumed the perimeter patrol, but I was too lost in thought to look properly.

I had heard a ricochet—two ricochets—but in both cases there had been no sound of an accompanying gunshot. That means the gunshots had been muffled. There are many ways to muffle a gunshot—something as simple as shooting through a pillow will do it. But when I'd first seen Yamina, the handgun she had been holding had appeared long-barreled. Then later, the threading on the Gyurza's barrel had confirmed what I'd already suspected: she'd been using a silencer. Silencers are illegal in many states, which is probably the reason she had unscrewed and hidden it by the time I had made my way down to her.

But still the question remained: why would she have been practicing with it in the first place? Security people don't use silencers. Assassins use silencers.

SEVENTEEN

THE gymnasium at Quartz Peak was part Roman bath, part modern health club, part Gothic cathedral. There was a great basilica-style nave which must have been two hundred feet long, and much of which was occupied by a long lap pool tiled with natural gray green slate rather than the usual bright blue glazing. The exercise machines were in the aisles, hand-built precision pieces of equipment whose brilliant chrome contrasted against the dull stone; they were obviously well maintained. There was a transept, on one end of which was a Roman-style bath, plus a steam room and a sauna. The other side was given over to an open workout area, with an inlaid wood parquetry floor, floor-to-ceiling mirrors, dancer's rails. There were no windows, but the space where the transept crossed the nave was covered in a dome composed entirely of frosted glass tiles, and the gap between the aisles and the vaulting was pierced by a series of clerestory windows, so that by day the entire space was flooded with natural light.

I wondered what Mick of Mick's Gym would have thought of this place.

I was lying supine on a bench, struggling through a third set of bench presses on the Smith machine, when suddenly Sorrel Tyne's face appeared over mine.

"You used to do better than that," she said.

Actually I was lifting exactly the same weight as I used to lift in the marines. I engaged the stops and sat up.

Sorrel Tyne was dressed in a leotard and tights. Her hair was pulled back in a bun, the way ballerinas do to prevent it waving about. I saw the slippers in her hands.

"You still practice?" I asked.

"Yes."

"And perform?"

"No, no need to now." I understood: she was a kept woman—her days of struggle were behind her.

We looked at each other in silence for a moment. I found it hard to believe that I'd once contemplated marrying this woman. Perhaps she was thinking the same thing about me.

"What about you?" she asked. "What have you been doing since . . ." Her smile faded along with the sentence.

"Winemaking," I said. "I have a vineyard in Virginia."

"All red, I'll bet."

She remembered. I nodded. Her smile returned.

"Do you sell it?"

"To a distributor, yes."

"Do you make money?"

"A little," I said. It was a strange question. Money hadn't mattered to her much before, but it obviously did now. Or perhaps it had always been there, an avaricious seed lying like a cancer in her psyche, and which some time in the last ten years had suddenly metastasized. Maybe that was why she'd walked out the moment it had become clear I was going to do time in a military prison: ex-cons do not have good moneymaking prospects.

"When did you stop dancing?"

"A couple years ago. I was in the Los Angeles ballet."

So that's where she'd gone. I should have guessed—L.A. is the traditional destination of people who run away in America. Especially people who look like Sorrel; I was surprised she hadn't ended up in movies.

"Then?"

"Then, here." She looked down before continuing, quieter now. "When did you get out of prison?"

"I was only there for six months."

"Six months," she repeated. "That's not so long, I guess."

"Not so long," I agreed.

I could tell what she was really asking: *Why didn't you try to find me when you got out?* I didn't have an answer. I didn't know, myself. She left a pause for me to say more, but I remained silent.

"Well," she finally said, "I better go start my routine."

IN the afternoon I took a golf cart down to the airstrip. If Xerxes Antullis was going to store plutonium at Quartz Peak, something was going to have to bring it here. I wanted to inspect the aircraft.

The helicopter was still parked on the apron where I'd first seen it—a Sikorsky S-76, a civilian model that had no corresponding military version. It was painted black with a gold interlocking XA symbol on the fuselage, the same one as I had first seen on the letterhead this morning. I walked over for a closer look. The externals were routine: aerials for radio navigation aids and VHF communications, a pitot tube extending forward—used to measure airspeed—and a wire leading down to a terminal embedded into the concrete, grounding the helicopter. These were the things any aircraft would have. There was nothing suspicious, nothing like the equipment in choppers I was used to: no hard points for external loads, no weapons pods, no forward-looking IR for flying low at night, doing insertions under radar coverage.

I opened a door in the side of the fuselage and stepped up into the main cabin. The interior was fitted out with oversized seats upholstered in supple leather, well-spaced around a low table with indents for safely holding cocktails when airborne. There was a small bar and a head in the rear, and up forward an entertainment system featuring a wide plasma screen.

I'd flown in many helicopters, but the nearest thing I'd ever had to a seat was webbing rigged around an aluminum frame, something only slightly less uncomfortable than sitting on the deck. There'd been no cocktails. No wide-screen television, either.

I got out. There was nothing about this helicopter to suggest that it was anything other than what it seemed, a billionaire's play toy. But the Gulfstream was gone.

Perhaps whatever it was that occupied so much of Xerxes Antullis's time had required a trip away from Quartz Peak, or maybe the Gulfstream was simply in the hangar. It occurred to me that if you were going to be transporting A-bomb material, that's what you'd use: something with long range and the safety of a second engine. And customs officers don't pay much attention to private jets—terrorists fly commercial.

I went over to the second hangar. The truck I had seen there this morning was gone now, and the surrounding tarmac was empty of vehicles. I began walking around the perimeter fence, checking for any flaw or oversight in the barrier which would allow easy access. The hangar was huge, built to accommodate B-52s back at the height of the Cold War, and the entire circuit took twenty minutes.

There were no flaws. The fence was intact, razor wire topped it for its entire length, and the various gates were all securely locked. The hangar itself was a huge, windowless structure of which nothing inside was visible. I had no way of knowing whether or not the Gulfstream was in there. The only way I could find out what was inside that hangar would be by breaking in.

I returned to the first hangar, the unfenced, smaller one. There was an electrical box on the wall with buttons for operating the main doors. I pressed the top one, and the large doors gradually pulled back, allowing sunlight to flood in on the fabulous sight within: Xerxes Antullis's automobile collection.

There were perhaps thirty cars in total. The floor of the hangar had been tiled in a black-and-white checkerboard pattern, like the winner's flag at an auto race, and one of the most impressive features of the place was that there was not a single oil stain that I could see—the cars must have been very well maintained.

All were performance cars. There was a selection of American muscle cars, including a midnight blue Pontiac GTO; a long, sinuous black Dodge Charger; an elegant 1963 metallic gray Corvette with the split rear window. The most distinctive car was probably a Mercedes, a 300SL gullwing coupe—the road-going version of the car that dominated European racing in the early 1950s. The enormous gullwing doors were both open, raised high over the body. Others I didn't recognize so easily: there was a low-slung, bright yellow car which turned out to be a Maserati Ghibli; and a lovely little red convertible two-seater whose distinctive yellow prancing horse emblem proclaimed it as a Ferrari. The deck lid badge identified the model as a 250GT California.

There were some fabulous pre–World War II cars, too: a purposeful-looking Cord, a sweeping Alfa Romeo whose hood was lined with at least a hundred slotted vents, all neatly finished with chrome trim that in those days would have been applied not by machine but by hand, and a long, swooping car that looked like an Art Deco sculpture on wheels, and which turned out to be a Bugatti.

I knew enough about automobiles to know that many of these cars were highly regarded and vary rare. I suspected that the Bugatti alone would be worth more than all the money I would make in ten lifetimes—and I had been given permission to drive it. The keys to it, like all the cars, sat in the ignition.

There were no limousines. No Cadillacs, no Rolls-Royces, no luxury cars of any kind. Nor were there any examples of the many models which might be of interest for their role in the history of the automobile: no Volkswagens, no Corvairs, no Model Ts. There were only performance cars here, Thoroughbreds whose lineage could be traced directly to the racetrack. Obviously Xerxes Antullis limited his collection to those automobiles whose primary purpose was to go fast. No wonder he wanted Chassis 1075 so badly.

The one car that was missing was the little primrose E-type. It was the one that I'd been hoping to take for a drive.

I went over to the workshop that was built into one corner of the hangar. Inside was a hydraulic lift, several workbenches, a pneumatic air line, an oxyacetylene welding set, a used oil storage drum, a mountain of tools, and the thing I'd been looking for: a roller jack. I grabbed a wrench set in one hand and used the other to maneuver the roller jack past the automobile collection and out of the hangar to the GT40.

It didn't take long to remove the flat. The wheel rim was undamaged, preserving me from Binky's wrath, at least for now. The other three tires looked fine, although they'd obviously lost a lot of rubber during the previous evening. I returned to the hangar and I took my time wandering among Antullis's collection, deciding which of these many superb automobiles I would use to take the tire in to be replaced.

The Bugatti was tempting, but I was not going to drive a priceless car off the estate and in traffic, permission or no permission. Same for the other prewar vehicles. That left the postwar cars. I looked them over.

FROM the book I'd read about them, I knew that Ford had first raced GT40s at Le Mans in the year 1964. The cars were then brand-new, never properly tested, and didn't perform well. But after more failures in 1965, Henry Ford II brought in a man by the name of Carroll Shelby to take charge of their racing program. He ripped out the existing engine and replaced it with a worked version of Ford's 289. In 1966, those 289-powered Ford GT40s finished 1-2-3 at Le Mans, so far ahead of the rest of the field that they had time to maneuver for a formation finish and cross the line as a team, completing the most dominating performance by a single model in the history of the race. Then next year, in a move which must have further deflated the competition, Shelby went one better: he shoehorned a seven-liter NASCAR engine into the GT40 and called the result a Mark IV. In 1967 the new seven-liter-powered Ford GT40 Mark IVs won Le Mans, and they were unbeatable by anything but rule changes.

The GT40 Mark IV wasn't the only car Carroll Shelby stuffed with a big-block 427-cubic-inch racing engine in the late sixties. He also managed to cram the same oversized motor into a regular street car, an example of which stood before me now. I went for a closer inspection. It was a Shelby GT500 Mustang: a classic Mustang from the era, but with an extended nose, bulging bodywork, fat tires, hood fasteners, and air scoops. This one was painted iridescent gold; a vehicle with street presence, made for a town like Las Vegas. Like the other cars, the keys to the big Shelby GT500 Mustang were in the ignition. It looked like I'd found a ride into town.

I found a canvas painter's tarp in the workshop and used it to wrap the wheel before putting it in the trunk—I might have to kill Xerxes Antullis, but that was no reason to mess his cars. Then I got into the driver's seat.

The interior was standard sixties American automobile: vinyl seats without headrests, a mass of plastic interior trim, and a thin-rimmed steering wheel, but at least this one was on the correct side in this car. In addition to the usual instruments Shelby had added some of his own: a big tachometer, oil temperature and pressure, and the like. There was air-conditioning, and a combined radio–cassette player in the dash, making the Mustang a luxury car compared to the GT40. There was a tape inserted in the player. I turned the ignition switch to engage electrical power, hit the Eject button, and pulled out the tape to see what it was.

It was the Iron Butterfly. *In-A-Gadda-Da-Vida.* I felt the hairs rise on the back of my neck.

I sat a long time looking at that tape. Was it some kind of obscure message, left here on purpose for me to find? Or a warning perhaps? But who would have known I would drive the Shelby? So if it was a message, then not a message for me. But for whom?

Or maybe it was just a coincidence.

I replaced the tape and started the car. The big 427 grumbled down deep and low, rattling the whole vehicle, shaking like a Saturn V about to lift off. Normally a person would have been impressed with all that sound and fury, but after Chassis 1075 this Mustang was just a pussycat. I eased it past the other vehicles and out of the garage onto the tarmac.

I drove it slowly down to the guardhouse, getting familiar with the car. The transmission was very heavy: overengineered in typical Shelby style, built to withstand the punishing torque that he intended to pump into it from that enormous 427. But the steering was power-assisted and felt as light as a feather after the GT40.

There was a different pair on duty at the guardhouse this time. The one who approached the car checked me against a photo he had on his clipboard, presumably the license photocopy that had been taken on my arrival.

Yamina Malik ran a tight operation. I wondered where she had acquired the background for this type of work.

I looked for a black SUV like the one I'd seen in the distance by the hangar this morning—it was the sort of vehicle security people might use—but the only vehicle was the Humvee parked by the side of the guardhouse, the familiar low profile, built that way so as to show a minimum target profile for enemy ground fire, and with a mount in the rear for supporting a .50 cal. The mount was empty, but I wondered if somewhere in that guardhouse they actually had a heavy machine gun to put into the vehicle if needed.

Probably. The first rule of combat is that you can never have too much firepower, and I'd already witnessed Yamina Malik's fondness for heavy-caliber weaponry firsthand.

The guard noted the license plate, then returned to the guardhouse where he hit a button to lower the tire shredders. Unusual—tire shredders are normally installed only one way: to keep people out. Here at Quartz Peak they had a second set to keep people in, too. When the plates were down, the guard waved me through.

A mile later the big gates swung open as I approached the fence separating Quartz Peak from the rest of humanity. I drove through, and they closed behind me. I stopped to look up and down the highway, back in the real world now. It was fifty miles to Las Vegas. The road was empty, two-lane blacktop stretching endlessly in either direction. I swung the overpowered Mustang onto the asphalt and headed south.

After a while I hit the Play button on the cassette, deciding that I should listen to that tape in case there was something on it other than the music on the label. But there wasn't, just the album that I probably had last heard more than a decade ago. So I turned the volume up high to hear it over the engine noise, sat back, and drove all the way to Vegas with that strange music— half Bach fugue, half heavy metal—pounding away on a stereo which had such an excess of power that it might have been chosen by Mr. Carroll Shelby himself.

EIGHTEEN

I found the Ford dealership among a sea of auto shops and strip malls and fast-food franchises. Las Vegas is glitter on ugliness, but in this part of the city it's just plain ugliness. I stopped out front of the showroom and went inside to find where the service department was. There was a saleswoman sitting at a desk in the corner. She wore a beige silk suit and had the sleek countenance of a well-groomed predator.

On the wall to her right was a poster of a GT40, a new one. After an interval of nearly forty years Ford was again building GT40s, still challenging Ferrari, but now doing it in the salesroom instead of on the racetrack. The saleswoman must have noticed me admiring it. She came over with a smile on her face and a brochure in her hand.

"All the little boys who come in want one of these," she said, offering me the brochure. "Although they're usually a little younger than you."

The brochure was for the GT40. "Thanks," I said. "You read my mind."

"In more ways than one, I hope." She must have seen my look of puzzlement. "That's my name and number on the bottom of the brochure," she explained. "Private number," she added, in case I was a little slow.

I looked at the brochure. Sure enough, there was handwriting below the printed area.

"Jet Wilson?"

"That's me." She offered her hand, which I took.

"Lysander Dalton," I said.

Her handshake was cool and firm. "Lysander is an unusual first name," she said.

"Not as unusual as Jet."

"Just as fast as you can go."

Before I could compose a suitable reply, a couple walked in, real customers. The man was dressed in shorts with a pink polo shirt and wore the aimless smile of the perpetually stupid. The woman wore track pants, perhaps the only clothing that could accommodate her enormous avoirdupois. They looked around with that wide-eyed vacancy of people for whom competency in life will forever be a stranger.

Jet Wilson glanced at them appraisingly.

"Well now," she said with a smile, "Wildebeests at the watering hole." She returned her gaze to me. "What's a little old lion cub like me to do?"

"Before you devour them, can you tell me where the service department is?"

"Go right down past all the new cars, turn left, then left again. It's around back."

"Thanks."

"You have my number," Jet Wilson said. "You can thank me later." She gave me a wink, then turned and descended upon the new arrivals. I exited the showroom, leaving her to the kill.

When I arrived at the service department the manager and a handful of mechanics—alerted by the booming noise from the big 427—came out and began admiring the car. The manager was visibly disappointed when he learned that all I wanted was a tire changed, and thus they were not going to get a chance to work on the Shelby. In compensation I undid the fasteners, popped the latch, and raised the hood, allowing them a few minutes of blissful contemplation of what lay beneath.

Eventually they returned to work. The manager and I went around to the trunk. He did a double take when I showed him the wheel in there.

"What did that come off?" he asked suspiciously.

"A Ford," I said. "That's why I came here."

"What kind of Ford?"

"Ford GT40."

"Ford GT40s don't have tires like that," he said flatly.

"Mine does."

"Shouldn't use these," he said. "They're racing slicks. Voids the warranty."

"Actually, I think my warranty was voided long ago."

He nodded to himself, as if he had already suspected that I was the kind of troublemaker who voids warranties. "We don't carry these in stock," he said. "I'll have to order it in. Take a least a day."

"Fine. Can you deliver it when it's fixed?"

"Where?"

"Quartz Peak. Xerxes Antullis's estate. Do you know it?"

"Know *of* it," he said, "but can't say I've ever had a personal invitation. It'll cost."

"Put it on this." I handed over the American Express card, and he took it with him into the office to complete the paperwork. I stayed outside to look around.

Besides Fords, the dealership also sold Jaguars, Land Rovers, and Aston Martins—brands owned by Ford. There was an effort to separate these: the English brands had a separate salesroom and separate service facility, but they were right next door and were obviously under the same ownership. I was looking down there at the models out front when a Jaguar suddenly drove out from their service department. But it was no ordinary Jaguar—it was a primrose yellow E-type.

I only caught a glimpse of the driver before the car turned out into traffic, but there was no mistaking that great mane of wavy black hair—Yamina Malik was at the wheel. She turned south, wrong way to turn if you were heading back to Quartz Peak.

I raced into the office and hurriedly signed the credit card voucher.

LAS Vegas streets form a flat Mondrian-like grid laid on the desert, but the grid is pierced by the occasional unMondrian-like diagonal, of which the Strip is the most famous example. The road I joined was part of the grid, a long, broad, flat street stretching for miles, broken only by a series of seemingly endless traffic lights glowing bright in the early dusk of winter.

When I hit the first red, I could see the Jaguar about five lights ahead of me, similarly stopped.

My light turned green. Then, in rapid sequence, all the lights ahead also turned green. I drove at the posted speed limit but soon hit another red. Again all the lights ahead turned quickly red. They were obviously synchronized, and at this second lot of red lights the E-type was exactly where it had been before: five sets ahead of me. To catch up, I was going to have to do something to shorten the interval.

When the cross street's lights turned amber, I upped the revs and engaged first gear. The instant my light turned green, I dropped the clutch. The tires squealed for a moment and smoked slightly before finally gaining traction, sending the Shelby forward like a racehorse bolting from the gate.

This time I didn't drive at the posted speed limit. I hit the light ahead of me not long after it turned green, with the needle at seventy and still climbing. This was far faster than surrounding traffic, and I had to bob and weave a little to thread the Mustang through, but the sound of that engine must have alerted drivers ahead of me, and most of them pulled out of the left-hand lane, not wanting to get run down.

If there'd been a police cruiser on that section of road they'd have had me cold, but luck was with me. By the time I hit the next red, the Jaguar was stopped at the same light, several cars ahead.

I couldn't actually see the Jaguar, because E-types are very low, and the cars in front of me blocked the view. That was fine: it meant that Yamina Malik couldn't see me in her rearview mirror, either. I tried to figure out how best to continue. In the movies, when someone's tailing a car they stay well back, not wanting to make it obvious. When the light turned green I decided to do the same, keeping several cars between me and the Jaguar ahead.

Here's what doesn't happen in the movies: the car you are following turns right, and then the light turns amber before you get to it. The cars ahead of you stop, so that there's no way through. That's what happened to me.

Las Vegas is like Los Angeles: no one walks. That means the sidewalks are usually empty. That little stretch of sidewalk between me and the cross street was empty right now, more or less.

I turned the wheel, revved the engine, and hopped the sidewalk. A few startled citizens of Las Vegas expressed their displeasure, and when I came thundering back down onto the asphalt after having turned the corner, the drivers of the crossing traffic were positively unkind. But Yamina Malik was just ahead of me. I decided to forgo the hanging back tactic; from now on I was staying right on that E-type's tail.

It didn't matter now, because the road onto which I had turned was the Strip itself, and there was too much going on for anyone to pay attention to who was behind them. The avenue was a blaze of flashing casino facades shining brightly against the deep blue of the gathering dusk. Music filled the street, changing with each advance past one building to the next. At one casino a sea battle was underway, at another a volcano was erupting, and at the Bellagio a crowd of onlookers watched the dancing fountains perform, something which in any other city would be counted as high kitsch, but which in Las Vegas probably passed for tasteful restraint. We passed a Paris that no Frenchman would have known, a Venice that recast La Serinissima as La Ridiculossa, and even a New York City in which the subway somehow went to Ellis Island. All the time I stayed right behind Yamina Malik's Jaguar.

Eventually she pulled into the right lane and peeled off into one of the casino entrances. The casino was fronted by an enormous sphinx—this one with the nose intact, which no doubt the builders thought was an improvement upon the original. It was the Luxor, and the building itself was a massive black glass pyramid. On reflection this was the one theme which was not out of place in Las Vegas—what could be more suitable than a pyramid: an enormous building which served no productive purpose, placed haphazardly upon the desert, a monument to futility.

Yamina pulled into the entrance. There were cabs and stretch limousines and a mass of people moving with that frenzied energy which characterizes casinos early in the evening, before everyone's lost their money. A valet rushed to the Jaguar and opened the door. I stayed back now, hoping to remain unnoticed in the harsh light of the entrance, and killed the engine for good measure. Yamina got out, retrieved a sleek, brushed-aluminum attaché case from the trunk, and tipped the valet before entering the casino. The valet pulled the car over to the side rather than taking it down to the garage—cars like the E-type were parked out front for their aesthetic appeal.

When the valet came over to my car, I tipped him fifty dollars.

"Keep this one out front, too," I said.

"Yes, sir," he replied. His name tag proclaimed him as Ralph.

"You know the woman in the E-type, Ralph?"

"No, sir."

"Neither do I," I said, "but I'd like to meet her."

I took out another fifty, and held it between my fingers. "If she comes back out, think you could lose her keys for long enough to give me a call first?" Casinos are huge places, easy to lose someone in. Yamina Malik could come back out here without me noticing.

"Yes, sir," the valet replied, "that'll be no problem at all."

Ralph relieved me of that fifty with the speed of a card sharp manipulating the deck. I gave him my cell phone number, then went into the casino to find Yamina Malik.

NINETEEN

THE entrance to the casino was a wide row of plate glass doors, each separated by a long stone wall, which gave the effect of entering the pyramid though a narrow passageway, perhaps meant to suggest the way archaeologist Henry Carter, crouched and trembling with anticipation, must have first entered the tomb of Tutankhamen.

On the other side the interior opened out into a vast, cool lobby with ceilings a hundred feet high. The Egyptian theme was carried on inside, with more sphinxes, other creatures with rams' heads and lions' bodies, walls adorned in hieroglyphs and pictographs, a row of thirty-foot-high goddesses, and at the center of it all a vast temple—nominally, I learned, a copy of the temple of Ramses II at Abu Simbel—but the real object of worship lay beyond the temple: the casino itself. It occupied the bulk of the floor, a sea of green baize-topped tables stretching away in every direction. And everywhere—as ubiquitous in Las Vegas as was the scarab in ancient

Egypt—were the flashing lights and jangling sounds of slot machines.

The hotel's registration and concierge desks were to the right. There was a scattering of guests checking in or out, but none of them was Yamina Malik. No surprise there—hotel guests usually carry more luggage than a single attaché case, even in Las Vegas. I headed into the casino.

It may have been early, but there was already a good crowd at the tables—eager tourists tittering to one another as they tried to figure out how to place a chip; a high roller in brightly polished cowboy boots, laying out stacks with the bravado of a winner; and occasionally the plain bored, cigarette in one hand, fingering their chips or coins with the other, knowing that they will inevitably lose but unable to keep from playing the next card or taking the next pull of the slot machine handle. And hovering around them like carrion feeders were the dealers and pit bosses, the cocktail waitresses and floorwalkers, a casino hierarchy designed with but one purpose: to efficiently separate the gullible from their money.

There is no state income tax in Nevada, and the scene before me explained why.

I completed a circuit of the tables but found no sign of Yamina Malik. There was a bar in the center of the room, situated so that the disappointed would not have far to go to drown their sorrows. The bar was raised a foot or so above the level of the casino, making it a good place to keep watch. I took a seat at a table by the low rail which separated it from the gaming room, and ordered a drink.

For twenty minutes—the length of one martini—I saw no one resembling Yamina Malik among the many people coming and going. Then a brushed aluminum attaché case caught my eye. It was carried by a woman who had just come out of a rest room, but she was not Yamina Malik. This woman was very tall, and her hair was done in a bright platinum blond bob that went well with the attaché case. She wore a clinging hot pink dress that would have been out of place anywhere in America other than Las Vegas or Miami Beach.

Her passage across the gaming room attracted attention; she was the sort of woman for whose passage across a room the world momentarily stops spinning. Even one of the blackjack dealers paused, deck in hand and mouth agape, as she walked past his table.

I admired her, too. The dress emphasized her slender frame and long legs. The arm carrying that attaché case was also long, the skin remarkably smooth and very brown. The case must have been heavy, because supporting it cut her arm with lines of sinewy muscle under strain. I suddenly realized that I had seen an arm very much like that one earlier today, also holding something heavy at the time: my gun, in fact. I looked at the woman more closely.

It was Yamina Malik after all. The hair was a wig, but of a style and color so opposite her own that by itself it practically made her unrecognizable. With the combination of big sunglasses and glossy pink lipstick, she looked like a different person. The increased height, it turned out, was due to platform shoes with exaggeratedly high heels.

But there was even more of a transformation than the physical fact of the disguise. The woman I knew as Yamina Malik was all business, a professional, no-nonsense person. But there was nothing businesslike in the languid, leggy demeanor of this woman as she strode across the gaming floor. I had to admit that it was an excellent disguise: in Las Vegas to be outlandish is to fit right in. If it hadn't been for the attaché case I would never have recognized her myself.

So Yamina Malik had apparently spent the last

twenty minutes in the bathroom undergoing the transformation. But why? From whom did she need to
disguise herself? Or maybe there was no disguise—
perhaps she was just a woman of kinky habits. Either
way, I intended to find out.

After crossing the vast space she went to a cashier's
window. She placed the attaché case on the counter and
briefly opened it to withdraw a little silver evening bag. I
would have liked to have gotten a better look at what else
was inside that case, but I was too far away. She deposited
the case with the cashier, exchanged some money for
chips, and walked back onto the gaming floor.

At this time of the day—early evening, just before
the bulk of the gamblers hit the casinos—there are often
tables with few or even no players, but with a dealer
nevertheless standing behind it, ready to spring into action as the crowd swells. Yamina went directly to one of
these, a blackjack table that was otherwise unoccupied.
She took a seat and flashed a big, warm smile at the
dealer. He returned it with genuine good feeling: he
knew that the presence of a woman like Yamina Malik
at his table would soon attract a good crowd and the tips
that would go with it.

The dealer was right. No sooner had she taken a seat
than a balding, overweight man came lumbering along
and plopped himself right down next to her, notwithstanding the presence of four other unoccupied places at
the table. Yamina didn't seem to mind, giving the lucky
newcomer a smile even bigger than the one she'd be-
stowed upon the dealer. This new Yamina was a happy,
carefree girl.

I got up and went for a closer look. I took a wide
swing around, not wanting to get into Yamina's line of
sight. In the five minutes it took me to slowly wander
around the perimeter of the massive gaming floor, all
the places at Yamina's table had become occupied.
There was even a pair of onlookers, two guys standing

behind the last player, trying but failing to disguise sur-
reptitious glances at Yamina. The only person who was
keeping all his attention on the game was the balding,
overweight guy next to her—obviously a veteran gam-
bler, a man who had long since lost interest in anything
except the next card.

It was a fairly good-sized crowd. I decided to risk
one slow pass close behind Yamina.

I approached from behind. From my right a cocktail
waitress also approached. The costume for a cocktail
waitress at the Luxor looks like Playboy's version of an
ancient Egyptian showgirl dress. She went straight to
Yamina, who ordered a vodka-tonic. The cocktail waitress left without taking orders from the rest of the table,
which was odd. I decided to station myself at a nearby
craps table, far enough away not to be obvious, but close
enough to see precisely what happened when the waitress returned with that vodka-tonic.

Play continued. Yamina wasn't doing very well, but
she didn't seem to mind. At one point she opened her
little handbag, and from the angle I had I could see the
butt of a handgun, which I recognized as that same Para
P12 she'd been shooting with this morning. Her hand
rummaged past it and withdrew a packet of cigarettes.
She placed the packet on the table without taking one
out. She didn't take out matches or a lighter, the way a
real smoker would.

The cocktail waitress came back. I had guessed that
something was going to happen here, but even though
alerted, I almost missed it, same as everyone else did.

The waitress placed a napkin on the table, then put
the drink on top of it. Everyone's attention was on the
pair of pretty girls. My eyes were on that napkin, thinking that was the most obvious object being passed. I
barely noticed that, while reaching into her handbag for
money, Yamina's left elbow inadvertently knocked the
cigarette packet off the table.

The only other person who saw it was the fat guy next to her, at whose feet the cigarettes landed. He pushed his stool back and quickly retrieved it for her. Yamina paid for her drink and realized what had happened when the fat guy sat back up and placed the cigarette packet in the spot where it had been. She thanked him, and he said it was nothing. Play continued, and they didn't communicate for the rest of the time they were sitting together.

Neither of them realized that someone else had witnessed the exchange. The cigarette packet on the table was not the same one that Yamina had dropped. The fat guy had switched it with his own when he'd picked it up. Same brand, and obviously the exchange had been planned in advance.

At the conclusion of the next hand, the fat guy shrugged his shoulders as if to say he'd had enough, tipped the dealer, and left. He lumbered away toward the back of the casino.

Yamina's drink was still full, suggesting that she'd be here for a while—and even if she wasn't, then my fifty dollar tip would ensure that she'd remain stranded until I was called. I decided to follow the fat guy.

He went down past the shoe shine stand and out the back of the casino, where a bridge leads across to the parking lot. There were other people coming and going, but I held back fifty feet or so, not wanting to risk being noticed. He exited the bridge and walked around past the cinder block structure that enclosed the elevator and staircase, momentarily out of my sight, but from his casual walk I could tell that he didn't know he was being followed. I kept the same pace and walked past the elevators into the parking lot itself.

There was no one there. I looked around again, more carefully this time, but there was no one going to a car, no one at all. I was thinking he must have already gotten in his car, and was more carefully scanning the vehicles parked nearby, when there was suddenly an amused voice behind me.

"You're not too good at this, are you, kid?"

I turned. There, twenty feet behind me and leaning against the back wall of the elevator shaft, crumpled and smiling, was the fat, balding guy.

"I guess not," I said.

"What were you going to do when I got to the car?" he asked. "You got a car here you can follow me in?"

"I was hoping to get a license plate."

"And do what with it?"

"Use it to get your name and address."

"You got a contact down in motor vehicles?" he asked.

"No."

"Then your chances of getting my name and address from the license plate were about zip. Like I said, kid, you ain't too good at this." He stood up straight and came waddling over to me. "Let me make it easy for you." He pulled out a tattered wallet from his coat pocket, took out a business card, and handed it to me. "There's my name and address. Now come walk with me to my car. You can get the plate then, if you still want it."

He went slowly, huffing away into the parking lot. I followed, reading the business card as we went.

"Marty Blankenship," I read out loud. "Private investigator."

"Yep," he affirmed. "Was a cop for twenty. I'm retired now, but I got my license and do a little investigative work now and again, just to keep the old hand in."

"What was in the cigarette packet she gave you?"

"Cigarettes," he said easily. He stopped, pulled the packet out, and examined the label. "Lousy menthols," he said. "Only a broad would pick *menthols*." He contemptuously tossed the unopened packet into the nearby trash can, then looked around. "Now, where the hell did I leave my car?"

"What else did she pass you, Marty?" But he was too distracted to answer, trying to locate his vehicle. "Try hitting the unlock button," I said, remembering my encounter with Smiling Man. "See which one flashes and chirps."

He looked at me like I was joking. "*Flashes and chirps?* I see you ain't familiar with the typical pension of a retired cop." He continued looking around. "Over there, I think." We struck off farther into the parking lot.

"Are you going to tell me what's going on, Marty?"

"I was hoping you might tell me, kid."

"Tell you? Tell you what?"

"Who that broad is, for a start."

"You don't know?"

"Wouldn't be asking if I did."

"How can you not know? She just passed you something."

"All she passed me was a packet of cigarettes. You forget, kid, that I passed her something, too."

"Cigarettes."

"And something else."

"You mean all that fuss was for *you* to give *her* something?"

"Her idea, not mine."

"What did you pass her?"

"Can't say."

"Because you don't know?"

"Because I got standards, kid. Client confidentiality and all that stuff."

"Are you telling me that she's your client?"

He nodded in affirmation. I had assumed that he was investigating something involving Antullis, and that Yamina Malik was his inside person. It hadn't occurred to me that she might have hired him herself. "If she's your client, then how come you don't know her name?"

"She wouldn't tell me, kid. Can't say I was pleased about it, but she walked into my office in that crazy getup, offered me the case and a good retainer to go with it. Wasn't about to refuse."

"What did she want you to investigate?"

He stopped walking, turned, and looked me in the eye. "Son, that's between me and her. Tell you what though, you find my car, and I'll give you some good information." He looked around. "Olds Cutlass, 1983. Red, at least it used to be."

I spotted it three rows away. We walked over. It was a faded metallic maroon, and the left side of the front bumper hung down, secured from complete collapse by coat hanger wire. The car had bumps and dents the way trees have growth rings: one for every year of its long life.

"Nice," I said.

"Good for surveillance," he replied. "No one ever notices a piece of junk like this." He opened the driver's door, which had been left unlocked, perhaps in the hope that someone would steal it. The passenger floor was littered with empty cups and donut cartons. I could imagine him staking out some place, drinking coffee to pass time, remembering the good old days on the force.

"You got a notepad?" he asked.

"No."

"Yeah, I always forget mine, too. But I never trust to memory. Cops learn that early." He picked up a crumpled brown paper packet, scribbled something on it, and passed it to me.

"My license plate," he explained with a smile.

"Thanks."

"Now here's my information, kid."

"Okay."

He took his time, as if wanting to get something important straight before saying it. "Like I said, I was a cop for twenty. Seen a lot, you know—cops always see the worst. And Vegas is a mob city; I know how it works. The lucky ones are the ones the mob wants dead.

The unlucky ones are the ones they want to know some-thing from before they die, know what I mean?"

I nodded, remembering a village in the Philippines, strangely enough. There was no limit to human cruelty—I already knew that.

"After a while, you get a nose for bad deals. Sixth sense, if you like—you just get a feel for it." He paused, and I had to prompt him.

"Yes?"

He took a deep breath. "Truth is, I don't know what the story is here. Don't know who you are, kid, and for-give me for being honest, but I don't really care. All I can tell you is, whatever your angle is on this, do your-self a favor and just walk away. I got that sense, you know? I just know there are some bad people in this."

"I've known bad people," I said. "I'm still standing."

"Suit yourself." He closed the door, started the car, and backed out. I stood where I was, intending to nod good-bye, but Marty Blankenship engaged drive and sped away without looking at me, the way you might if you never expected to see someone again.

As I stood looking at the retreating taillights, my cell phone rang. It was Ralph the valet, calling to tell me that the woman with the Jaguar was back. "Except now she's a blond," he added, "and she's dressed like the kind of woman I wish I could afford, but can't."

TWENTY

I came back outside to the casino's entrance. It was very busy now, full of cabs and limos coming and going, disgorging their eager loads of hopeful humanity. Yamina Malik looked like a tourist attraction, standing long-legged and impatient by the E-type, still parked where she had left it, still with the top down.

As soon as he saw me, Ralph went into the office, emerging a moment later with a set of keys. He made a show of what I guessed was an apology before courteously opening the door for Yamina. This time she put the attaché case onto the passenger seat rather than locking it in the trunk. She handed him a tip, and I could tell from the look on his face that the apology had been a profitable one. When he was done he came over to where I was standing off to the side and surreptitiously handed me my own keys.

"High maintenance," he warned in a conspiratorial whisper. "Nice on the eye, but very high maintenance."

I wondered if he meant Yamina or the Jaguar. I got into the Mustang. Yamina fired up the E-type and left the casino in a roar of engine and tire noise. I followed more sedately, not wanting to damage my cover, or Xerxes Antullis's car.

We soon left the traffic of the Strip for a mixed industrial area to the west. The main thoroughfare in this area is called Industrial Avenue, an amazing failure of imagination in a city where dull concrete blocks bear names invoking ancient kingdoms or exotic Far Eastern locations. Yamina took it for a way before turning off into a broad asphalt parking lot surrounded by low commercial buildings. The parking lot was mostly empty, and all the buildings but one were dark, enterprises that had shut down for the night. The only lit building was on the far side, a nightclub.

Yamina drove the Jaguar over toward it. I stayed back, killed the lights, and waited. For ten minutes nothing happened—Yamina stayed in the car, and I could see nothing of what she was doing. Waiting perhaps, same as I was. Another car entered the lot and slowly circled before parking a few spaces from her, but the couple who emerged took no interest in the Jaguar and went straight into the nightclub. A long white stretch limo arrived, stopping directly out front. At least half a dozen people got out, women mostly, laughing loudly, dressed in high heels and short dresses. They went into the club, too.

Eventually Yamina emerged from the vehicle, long legged atop those platform shoes and still with the bright platinum blond bob. Whatever she'd been doing for the last ten minutes, it wasn't getting out of the disguise. She put the attaché case back in the trunk, locked it, then walked slightly unsteadily toward the club. Apart from the car keys there was nothing in her hands this time, not even the little silver handbag. There was no place to conceal a gun—the dress barely concealed her—which meant that she was unarmed. For Yamina Malik, unarmed was practically naked. She disappeared into the nightclub.

I got out and followed. As I approached the building I could hear the thumping bass of music coming from inside. There was a canopy above the main door, which proclaimed it to be the Pantera Club. Inside there was a small but plush lobby with another set of doors leading into the club itself. Two bouncers in black T-shirts and jeans stood guard. There was a metal detector by the interior doors, and one of the bouncers carried a pat-down wand. Now I understood why Yamina had not brought her gun. I went to the ticket window where the cover charge was collected, behind which sat a size-eight woman in a size-four dress. She smelled of cigarettes and cheap cosmetics.

"How much is the cover?" I asked.

"For how many?"

"Just me." I couldn't help looking at her enormous cleavage, which the dress did little to conceal. Neither she nor her plastic surgeon knew the virtue of restraint.

"Sorry, honey—no single men."

"How come?"

"Same in any sex club," she said matter-of-factly. "All men must be accompanied by a woman."

Ah, now I got it. The Pantera Club was not a nightclub after all, at least not a nightclub in the traditional sense.

I thanked her and left the lobby. Back outside I walked around the building while thinking it over. It seemed that my first instinct when seeing the transformed Yamina Malik had been right after all: she was simply a woman of kinky habits. The blond wig and high heels and short dress may have been a disguise, but only in the sense that they would have prevented immediate recognition, enough to allow her to quietly leave should someone she know enter the club. Or perhaps they were just part of the occasion—a girl indulging herself, dressing up for playtime.

But none of that explained the exchange with Marty Blankenship. I pulled out the cell phone and the GT40 brochure.

JET Wilson answered on the first ring.

"This is Lysander Dalton," I said. "I was in the dealership this morning."

"I remember, Mr. Dalton. I was hoping you'd call."

"How were the wildebeests?"

"Delicious, thank you."

"I take it that they didn't leave the watering hole unscathed?"

"Fully loaded Freestar," she affirmed. "It's a minivan, the only vehicle we sell with doors wide enough to accommodate a certain wildebeest's butt."

"Perhaps you'd like to join me to celebrate?"

"That would be a pleasure. Where should I meet you?"

"The Pantera Club," I said. This was met with silence. "It's over on Industrial Avenue," I added helpfully.

"I know where it is, Mr. Dalton. The question is: do you know *what* it is?"

"Certainly, Ms. Wilson. It's a sex club."

There was a long pause before she responded. "You know, most men would take me to dinner first. Or at least buy me a drink."

"Just as fast as you can go," I reminded her.

"Yes, I did say that, didn't I?" There was another long pause, then a sigh of resignation before she spoke again. "Okay, give me an hour to get ready."

I cleared my throat. "Actually, it's a little urgent."

"Urgent?"

"Yes."

"Well now, how interesting," she said. "And what exactly is 'a little urgent'?"

"Can you come right away?"

She laughed. "I'll be there in five."

IT was closer to fifteen than five. Jet Wilson finally arrived in a red Thunderbird with the top down. She emerged from the car wearing a luxuriant full-length fur coat against the cool of the Las Vegas evening. Her hair was up, and she was wearing very high heels. As she unhurriedly approached I could see a smile as she recognized me.

"Hello, Lysander Dalton."

"Hello, Jet Wilson. Thanks for coming so quickly."

She came to a stop right in front of me, very close, and in those high heels she was almost as tall as I was. Her makeup had been applied with care—urgent or not, Jet Wilson wasn't going anywhere without the cosmetic arrangements completed to her satisfaction.

"How could I have refused such a gracious invitation?"

I could faintly smell alcohol, bourbon perhaps. I wondered if she'd had a quick slug while dressing, or had already been drinking when I'd called, celebrating the wildebeests perhaps.

"That's a very attractive coat."

"Mink," she said. "Would you like to touch?" Until now her hands had been tucked under the lapels, holding the coat snug. Now she let her arms fall away to the sides, and the unbuttoned coat opened slightly, enough to reveal that Jet wasn't wearing much underneath.

"Perhaps we should go inside," I said.

Jet gathered the coat back around her as we stepped through the front doors into the lobby. Our Lady of the Implants smiled at me in recognition and carefully checked out Jet as I handed over the $200 cover charge. We passed through the metal detector and entered the inner sanctum.

Like a church, the lighting was low. We stood for a moment allowing our eyes to adjust. There were table lamps and candles and wall sconces, the sum of which suffused the place in a soft, golden light, friendly to naked flesh. The music was loud, but not loud enough to kill conversation, and was smoother and more sophisticated than the raucous adolescent hip-hop of most nightclubs.

There were many low tables, some in a sunken inner section, each surrounded on two or three sides by plush armchairs and sofas, and arranged haphazardly among potted palms and shrubs. Some were empty; most were occupied, usually by more than just a single couple. They appeared much as people might at any other upscale lounge, twenties through forties, well-groomed, expensively attired. But at one table a woman was kissing the man on her right while the man on her left ran a hand up her short skirt. At another two women were kissing with passion, obviously as a prelude to sex, while their dates smilingly looked on. Across the room I recognized the party that had unloaded from the limousine earlier: two men and five women. They were sitting around drinking and talking, but three of the girls wore nothing but underwear now.

Roving among these were cocktail waitresses dressed in fishnets and formfitting uniforms. There was a bar at one end, unoccupied apart from the bartender, and at the other a small dance floor, also unoccupied, beyond which was a raised platform with stage lights along the edge and two fireman's poles—apparently for impromptu striptease shows by the guests.

I saw no sign of Yamina Malik.

We settled into a table back by the wall, a position with a good view. A cocktail waitress came. Jet ordered a Manhattan, apparently choosing to stick with bourbon, and I ordered the same.

"So you're buying me a drink after all," Jet said,

when the waitress had left. She settled back with a smile into a corner of the sofa, still wearing the mink but allowing it to fall off her shoulders and lie completely open, now fully and invitingly revealing what lay beneath. What lay beneath was very little: a dark, paisley-patterned bustier out of whose strictures Jet's breasts threatened to overflow, a thong, stockings held up by garter belts attached to the bustier, and finally shoes whose stiletto heels probably would have been sharp enough to warrant confiscation had she tried to board an airplane.

"That's a very appealing outfit," I said.

"When the need is urgent, I try to be accommodating."

Our Manhattans arrived. I looked around as we drank. I could still see no sign of Yamina Malik's bright platinum-blond bob. But there was a second floor, accessed by a wide set of carpeted stairs on the far side of the room. I put down my glass.

"Would you excuse me for a moment?"

"You're leaving me alone?"

"Only for a minute."

"A girl could get up to a lot of mischief if left alone here," she said with a sly grin, "even for just a minute. But perhaps that's what you had in mind all along?"

"I certainly wouldn't want you to get lonely." I got to my feet.

"Oh, I don't think that'll happen," she said. "I make friends quite easily."

I made a circuitous route to the stairs, checking to ensure that I had not missed Yamina in the crowd. I found no sign of her. The emergency exit was under the staircase. I took a moment to examine it: a standard fire exit door with a low horizontal bar which allowed egress. There was a sign warning that opening the door would trigger an alarm, and I could see that it was wired. Yamina Malik could not have exited the club via this door. Therefore, unless she was in the bathroom, she was not on the first floor. I headed upstairs.

The second floor was arranged in a broad central corridor separating a series of rooms on either side. Two of these rooms were frankly intended to invite voyeurism—the walls backing onto the corridor were made of thick glass, like the walls of a racquetball or squash court. The remaining three walls were mirrored. The central feature in one room was a jacuzzi; in the other the floor was entirely covered with what looked like extra-thick exercise mats. Apparently this second room was designed to accommodate a crowd, but currently both it and the first room were empty.

I went down the corridor, cautiously opening the doors to the other rooms. Most of them were bedrooms, fitted out with the sterile luxury of a modern hotel suite. The last room on the right was very different: it turned out to be a dungeon. All of them were vacant—apparently things didn't really get going at the Pantera Club until later at night.

There were two doors remaining: one to the last room on the left, the other at the end of the corridor, and which was marked PRIVATE, NO ADMITTANCE—presumably the door to the club's offices.

I tried the door to the last room. It was locked. I put my ear up against it, listening for any sound of occupancy. I could faintly hear something within, just an occasional indistinct sound, enough to know that it was occupied, but nothing distinguishable as Yamina Malik. Yet it had to be her.

With more hope than expectation, I tried the last door, the one marked PRIVATE. To my surprise it was unlocked. I went in and quietly closed the door behind me.

I was in an extension of the corridor, but narrower than before. It was unlit, but there was faint streetlight coming in from the window at the end, maybe thirty feet away, enough for me to see. There was one door on the left, about halfway down. There were no doors on the wall to the right, but at the end of the corridor the passageway continued to the right. I began with the door on the left.

The room I entered was empty, except for equipment. The wall to the left—the one that adjoined the locked room—was glass, the other side of which was no doubt mirrored. It was set up like a police lineup room, and I was where the witness would stand, looking out on the candidates, safely concealed behind the one-way mirrors.

But what was on the other side now was nothing like a police lineup. I went over to the glass and looked more closely. There was a raised platform in the center of the other room, about the size of a doctor's examination table, upholstered in black leather, and occupied by a supine woman who, apart from a black velvet blindfold, was completely naked. Her arms were bound at the wrists and tied back behind her, over her head. Surrounding this on all four sides was a second level, about three feet wide and a foot below the other, and also upholstered in leather. There were two men on this second level, kneeling, and taking a keen personal interest in the blindfolded woman. The only other piece of furniture in the room was a lone wing chair located in a corner. This was occupied by a third man, older than the other two, fully dressed in a business suit, sitting back casually with his legs crossed, watching proceedings as calmly as if attending a chamber recital.

I couldn't see the woman's face clearly, but her flesh was pale. Whoever she was, she was not Yamina Malik.

I backed away from the wall. The room I was in was set up for more than just casual voyeurism. There was a host of video and camera gear: large cameras on heavy tripods with thick rubberized power cords lying on the floor, obviously commercial-grade equipment. I wondered if the nightclub's owners clandestinely filmed their customers, or if the setup was just for those clients who specifically wanted their exploits recorded for posterity.

The rest of the room was given over to storage: not just video gear but papers in cardboard boxes, sheets of plasterboard with a saw and a nail gun for sizing and securing them, cartons of liquor, and even spare tables and chairs—the detritus of a nightclub. I quietly left the room, leaving the quartet on the other side of those one-way mirrors to indulge themselves unobserved, and headed farther up the corridor to where it made a right turn. As I approached I could see that not all the light was coming from outside. Along with the harsh white glow of the street lighting there was the yellow incandescence of an ordinary domestic lightbulb. I came to the end of the corridor and cautiously looked around.

There were two doors, office doors with large glass panels in the upper half. The yellow light was coming from the first of these. It flickered with the shadow of someone moving about inside.

I moved forward carefully, gradually opening the field of vision to see what lay inside. There were bookshelves, occupied more by magazines and videotape boxes than actual books. Then a poster on the wall, advertising what was obviously a pornographic movie. Then the desk. There was no one behind it, but the desk light was on. Then at last, on the other side of the desk, by the gray steel filing cabinets against the wall, I saw the room's occupant. It was Yamina Malik, still in the wig, rummaging through one of the filing cabinet's drawers.

At that moment I heard the sound of a key being inserted into the door through which I'd come earlier. I heard it twist, followed by the sound of the handle being turned and the door being pushed, but whoever was on the other side had just inadvertently locked it, and so when they pushed, it didn't open.

There was a pause, then the sound of the key being retried. This time the door opened. Nothing more for a moment, not even footsteps, and I could imagine whoever it was standing there, looking at the key perhaps, going back in his mind over the sequence of events when he'd left, wondering how it was that the door had been left unlocked.

The next sound I heard was that of an automatic pistol slide being pulled to the rear. Apparently whoever it was had come to the conclusion that the door had not been left unlocked after all.

Yamina was still going through the filing cabinet, obviously unaware that someone else had entered the office space. Footsteps began coming down the passageway, and there was no time to warn her. I backed into the darkened second office and listened.

It didn't take long. I soon heard the office door being opened and some gruff command issued in a deep male voice. Then the door was slammed closed, so hard that the glass rattled. I could hear them, or at least him, the tone of heated declaratives coming through the wall, but I couldn't actually understand what was being said. I left the office and moved up the passageway, out of direct light, but close enough so that I could see what was going on inside.

The man's back was to me, leaning against the door, apparently having pushed it shut by backing up into it, probably not wanting to take his eyes off the intruder. He was a large man, over two hundred, wearing jeans and an untucked shirt from which the arms had been torn off—maybe he liked to show off his muscles, or perhaps the batwing tattoo on his shoulder. His hair was long and greasy. He was obviously holding a weapon on Yamina, but too low for me to see it.

Yamina was in the far corner, facing him, arms crossed, leaning casually on the now-closed filing cabinet, and doing a pretty good job of maintaining her cool. She would have done well in special ops: they used to teach us that there is never a reason to get flustered, because whatever happened in the last ten seconds is irrelevant—all that ever matters is what will happen in the next ten.

Batman was doing the talking. I couldn't understand what he was saying, but I understood the gesture: "Come here." Yamina stood straight and walked over, slowly, but showing no sign of fear. She came to a halt two feet away and looked at him squarely face-to-face. He raised his gun arm and put the muzzle of the weapon to her temple, then with the flat of his other hand reached into the top of her dress. Yamina's expression didn't flinch, and she remained silent. He did the talking, quieter now, and the tone sounded mocking. It was a bizarre sight, the ultimate guy who can't get a date. After a minute of fondling Yamina's breasts while simultaneously holding a gun to her head, he must have asked her a question. Whatever Yamina's response was, it wasn't what he'd wanted to hear. In a flash he brought his gun arm back, then drove it hard, still holding the weapon, straight into her face.

It was a punishing blow. He had at least a hundred pounds on her, and to the weight of his meaty fist had been added the additional heft of the weapon. Yamina went flying back onto the desk. She ended up sprawled across it, and blood came pouring out her nose. The big man laughed and began unbuttoning his jeans.

I guessed that this was my cue. There was a fire extinguisher on the wall I'd already identified as the best weapon available, a big heavy cylinder three feet long. I took it off the bracket, reversed it, and rammed it base-first through the glass, hard into the back of Batman's skull.

It wasn't the sort of thing you had to do twice. It was lights out for Batman. He went down like a sack of potatoes.

Yamina's first words as I pushed through the door against the dead weight on the floor were not encouraging.

"What are you doing here?" she asked. It sounded like an accusation.

"I came to bring you this," I said. I handed her my handkerchief, then bent down to examine the Caped Crusader.

There was a lot of blood mixing with the abundant grease and dandruff on the back of his head, but I couldn't see any shards of glass embedded in his skull. He was still breathing, which might be a good thing or a bad thing, depending on how you looked at it.

"Get his gun," Yamina commanded. She was sitting up on the desk now, handkerchief pressed to her nose, trying to stop the bleeding.

"Thanks for the tip," I said. "I wouldn't have thought of it if you hadn't told me."

The gun was several feet away, lying on the floor where Batman had dropped it. It was an old, scratched-up Smith & Wesson .40 automatic from whose frame the serial number had been filed off, and which had probably been on a dozen armed holdups in its long and anonymous life. I popped the magazine and checked the load. Unjacketed, no brass: cheap range ammo. I put the magazine back, then actioned the slide a few times, loading and ejecting, making sure the thing actually worked. Then I removed the magazine again, shook the loaded round from the breech, gathered the ejected rounds, and refilled the magazine.

"Are you finished playing with that thing yet?" Yamina asked.

"No." I checked which way the safety worked, dry-firing it to be certain, then slid the magazine back home, and stood.

"Okay, we're lovers," I said.

"What?"

"We walk downstairs arm in arm. You're all gooey, nuzzling my shoulder—that way no one sees your face." She nodded, getting it now. "We're smiling, whispering to each other now and again."

"Okay."

"We exit via the front door. Anything stops us, anything at all, we abort and use the emergency exit instead. Do you know where the emergency exit is?"

"Under the stairs." She knew her stuff. First task in any operation is to locate an alternate extraction route.

"If we abort, we split up as soon as we're through that emergency exit. You go left, I go right. Just run and don't stop, okay?"

"You'll run, too?"

"Yes," I lied. Actually I'd take out whoever came through that door after us. "If we make it through the front door, we go straight to your car. Where are the keys?"

"Over there," she said, nodding toward the filing cabinet she had been searching through.

They were on top of it, next to an open folder. While retrieving the keys I glanced at one of the documents inside the latter. It was full of numbers like a balance sheet; perhaps a financial statement. There were two small keys on the key ring, nickel-coated, but the nickel had worn away over the years: obviously the car keys. There was a third key, shiny brass, freshly cut, and bigger than the other two: a door key. Now I knew why the office door had been unlocked. I also had a pretty good idea of what Marty Blankenship had passed to Yamina in that cigarette packet earlier this evening.

Meanwhile, Yamina had found a framed mirror on

the bookcase and was using it to look at herself while dabbing away the blood. I walked over.

"God, I'm a mess," she said, more to herself than me. Actually she looked great, in a sort of bruised, puffed-up way.

"Which one's the ignition key?" She showed me. "Okay, once we're out the front door we take the car, no matter if they try to stop us. I drive, you shoot."

"Shouldn't I drive and you shoot?" she asked. "I'm familiar with the car."

"I told you I always wanted to drive an E-type; now's my chance. Ready?"

"Ready."

I snapped off the desk light, and we left the office, but on the way out, whether through accident or intent, Yamina managed to deliver a swift kick into the recumbent Batman's slack and dribbling jaw.

I checked that the corridor was clear, then we both walked out. Yamina latched onto my right arm.

"Other side," I whispered.

"Of course." She released the arm currently clutching the gun in my pocket and went to the other side. We continued toward the stairs. The jacuzzi room was occupied now. There were eight or ten of them inside, in or around the pool, laughing and drinking champagne. One of them was Jet Wilson, who seemed to have mislaid her bustier. No wonder she made friends so easily.

Going down the stairs we passed one of the bouncers I had seen out front, headed up. He glanced at us but continued past. His step was purposeful, the walk of a man with a specific destination in mind, and that destination was almost certainly the office.

"He can ID us," Yamina whispered.

"Let's hurry."

We skipped down the stairs and headed across the club, gradually forsaking the act in the interest of speed. By the time we hit the door, we were making no more pretense. I handed the gun to Yamina and made sure I had the correct key in hand.

Neither of us used the car doors: E-types are low, and it was faster just to step right in. Then we heard the shout of alarm from within, loud enough to be heard over the music. Yamina actioned the Smith & Wesson. I put in the ignition key and turned it. Nothing.

I tried again. Same result.

"Yamina, is there a trick to this?"

"Starter button." She showed it to me. "Told you I should drive."

I pressed the starter, and the car fired up as the first of the bouncers came barreling through the front door. A second followed, this one with a baseball bat in hand. The baseball bat was instructive—armed men don't carry baseball bats, because they don't need them. I engaged first and hit the gas. The E-type raced forward smoothly, light and nimble after the heavy artillery of the Fords I'd been driving lately. When they saw that we were headed for Industrial Avenue, the two raced toward a big black Lincoln in the corner of the lot. It was what I'd been waiting for: to show me which car was theirs. I hit the brakes and stopped.

"What are you doing?" Yamina cried.

I put the car in reverse, hit the gas, and went racing backward through a sea of tire smoke and axle hop toward the Lincoln.

"Turn around," I said. Yamina turned around, knees up on the seat. "Put them down." She fired a shot in their general direction, but elevated, where it wouldn't hit anyone. The two of them hit the ground—dumb thugs they may have been, but they weren't completely stupid. Since they'd felt the need for a baseball bat, I was pretty sure there was no risk of us getting shot at.

I stopped reversing twenty yards from the Lincoln. "Now take out the car."

Yamina smiled. "Okay."

She put one round into the windshield, which by itself was probably sufficient to disable the vehicle for pursuit, but then put a grouping into the front tire, near the engine so that any misses to the tire would hopefully do damage somewhere else. The big car sank on the flat.

I was thinking we were pretty safe now when at that moment Batman himself came through the front door. He was bloody and wobbly, but he was vertical: obviously I hadn't put enough force behind that fire extinguisher. Worse, there was a pump action shotgun in his hands. He did not look amused.

"Down."

Yamina was instantly down.

I put the car into first gear and hit the gas just as fast as I could. Batman pumped a round into the shotgun, aimed, and fired. It's hard to miss at close range with a shotgun. Maybe he was still groggy, or perhaps he was just a bad shot, but instead of hitting us he hit the parked car that we were racing by at the time, the windows of which shattered and collapsed in a sea of fragmented glass. A moment later we bottomed the shocks as we hit Industrial Avenue, the needle climbing through sixty. In the rearview mirror I could see Batman and one of the thugs head for another car, a low-slung, tricked-out black Corvette with fat racing tires that hadn't been in the parking lot earlier.

It seemed that Batman had brought the Batmobile.

I hit the gas and went flying down the street at twice the legal limit. Behind us I heard the Corvette before seeing it, a NASCAR-loud roar of Detroit heavy metal with the pedal to the firewall. An instant later, scanning the rearview mirror, I saw the Corvette come flying over the curb and out into the street in a shower of sparks as the suspension bottomed out, maybe a quarter mile behind us. The roar of the engine deepened as the power poured on. Whatever was under the hood of that 'Vette, it obviously wasn't stock.

It was late now, the traffic sparse, and on Industrial Avenue's wide, multilane expanse I had no trouble overtaking the two or three cars we came up to. But already that big V-8 was cutting the distance between us, and we were heading back into Las Vegas proper—it was only a matter of time before we hit a light.

Handguns are only effective at close range, and because they have short barrels they require careful aim. But with a shotgun, all you need do is point it in the general direction and pull the trigger. If they caught us, the Smith & Wesson would have no chance against that pump-action twelve-gauge.

I killed the lights, then took a sudden right on a cross street.

"Where are we going?" Yamina asked.

"The Strip. We need to put some traffic in between us and that Corvette, otherwise they'll catch us for sure."

The traffic did increase, occupying all three lanes of the street I was on. Ahead of us were the glittering lights of the Strip. Behind us, I heard the Corvette come skidding around the corner onto our street, fat tires squealing, engine at the redline. Yamina twisted in her seat as she heard it.

"They're gaining on us," she said, stating the obvious.

We crossed the last intersection before the Strip, but ahead of us the light turned amber. "Put your seat belt on," I said.

"What?"

"Your seat belt—-put it on."

"Why?"

"Why do you think?" I said. The three lanes of traffic ahead hit the brakes, slowing down for the light. "I am about to drive in an irresponsible manner."

Still she made no move to put the seat belt on. "I'm riding shotgun," she announced poutily. "I need freedom of movement."

"You'll shoot better if you're not embedded in the windshield."

The light turned red. The traffic ahead came to a halt.

Yamina crossed her arms, the way a mule would if mules had arms, and had decided not to budge. Of all the things which torment mankind, there is none so frustrating as a stubborn woman. "I'll bet in your next life you come back as one of those elderly flag ladies," she said, "the ones who work children's school crossings and—"

Whatever else she was going to say was cut off in the noise and confusion of what came next. With the traffic ahead now stopped, I turned the lights on to high beam as a warning, and pulled out into the lanes headed the other way.

The oncoming traffic slowed or skidded to a stop. I hit the horn and barged on through, going as fast as I was able, swerving through the sprawl of vehicles. There had been a green arrow on the Strip, which held back the bulk of the traffic, but as I approached, the main lights turned green as well. Eight lanes of vehicles started to pull out.

I hit the gas pedal, intending to take a best shot, but it was too late: if I continued straight now, I would clip the first row of cars. Instead, I swerved back ahead of them, in front of the cross street cars which had originally stopped ahead of me. If any of the folks on that first row had been in a hurry, they would have hit us side-on, but the Strip is a street for cruising, and people wanting to simply go from A to B take other routes. The cars braked and honked and flashed their lights, but none of them hit us.

I pulled the wheel hard left, used some extra gas to swing the rear end around, and we did a neat four-wheel drift right into the northbound lanes of the Strip. I changed down and pushed the Jaguar forward, wanting to get as much distance as possible between us and that Corvette.

Yamina wordlessly put on her seat belt.

We soon hit traffic ahead; even at this late hour the Strip was clogged, but at least now the Corvette would be somewhere well behind, bogged down in the same traffic, unable to catch up.

But not for want of trying. When the Batmobile came onto the Strip on the next light cycle, I could see them in the distance behind us, weaving from lane to lane, engine briefly racing, pushing into every opening. It made no difference; in the heavy, slow traffic of the Strip they were destined to remain well astern.

After a while Batman must have come to the same conclusion. We were stationary, stuck in a particularly heavy section of traffic, with the cross street ahead of us gridlocked. I was using the opportunity to scan the rearview mirrors when, in Yamina's side mirror, I caught a glimpse of black flashing across the gap between the traffic and the buildings behind us.

"They turned off," I said. "They're trying to use side streets to get ahead of us."

Yamina shook her head at the traffic jam around us. "They could walk and get ahead of us at this rate."

I looked around to see what avenues of escape might be available. There was a big casino across the Strip, but on this side there were lesser establishments: a water park, a motel with a sign advertising Color TV and HBO, and a place which might have been a burger joint in the days before the franchises took over, but which now had converted—in what urban planners might consider a good example of existing resource reuse—into a drive-through wedding chapel.

The traffic edged forward. I pulled over to the right lane, then up to the curb.

The place was called Chapel of Happiness and advertised itself as the "Nuptials Autorama." Painted across the overhang above the driveway was the phrase, *Say I Do—Drive on Thru.* The drive-through itself was on the opposite side of the building from the Strip and was long enough to prevent an observer from the street seeing what, if any, vehicle was inside. I pulled up to the driveway and edged inside. There was a black hose stretched across the concrete, the sort that garages used to have in the old days before people pumped their own gas, which would ring a bell inside to alert the attendant. But instead of a bell, this one played a few bars of "Here Comes the Bride."

We came to a halt. I pointed to the convex mirror fixed to the upper right-hand corner of the building. It was meant to check for vehicles around the blind side of the building before pulling out, but it also allowed us to see the traffic on the Strip. Yamina nodded in understanding; we could use it to check if the Corvette came by.

A man came out of the office. He was on the short side, about fifty, wire-rimmed glasses on an Elmer Fudd face, holding a book and hastily buttoning a long black cassock over street clothes. He smiled at us warmly.

"What a lovely couple," he exclaimed. "Welcome to the Chapel of Happiness." He came by my door and offered his hand. "I'm the Reverend Jim."

"Lysander Dalton," I replied. We shook hands. He had the firm, sincere grip of a practiced huckster. After shaking hands with me, he offered his hand to Yamina, who had to transfer the Smith & Wesson to her left hand before taking it and introducing herself. If the weapon bothered the Reverend Jim, he didn't show it—perhaps in Las Vegas it's not unusual for brides to arrive at their weddings armed. Instead, he stood back and admired the E-type.

"I do think that convertibles are so romantic, don't you?"

I guessed that the Reverend Jim was the sort of man who was never at a loss for words, and that shutting him up was going to be expensive. I pulled out my wallet and removed a hundred dollar bill, which I offered to him.

"We need to stay here for fifteen minutes or so. Will that be all right?"

"God's home accommodates all comers," he replied, while neatly relieving me of the note. He tucked it into the rear flap of his Bible, then opened it to a well-thumbed page and began reading aloud, maybe from habit, or perhaps in the hope that the cash spigot might be further opened with a little well-directed sermonizing. It took me a moment to realize that he wasn't reading in English.

"Latin?"

He paused and looked up smilingly from the book. "It does add a certain dignity, don't you think?"

A place that advertised itself as a nuptials autorama could use all the dignity it could get. "Not many people know Latin these days," I remarked. Perhaps by day he worked at Caesar's.

"I was trained in a seminary," he explained. "Latin was compulsory."

"You're a priest?"

"Ex-," he explained. "I was defrocked."

"What for?"

"A slight misunderstanding with church funds."

"Misunderstanding?"

A genuine smile broke out on his face. He leaned closer and lowered his voice. "The horse I bet on misunderstood that it was supposed to win." He winked, then stood back up straight and resumed the reading.

I turned to Yamina, who had been ignoring us while examining her injuries in the car's rearview mirror. Her nose wasn't broken, but one of her eyes was swelling.

"Cute wig," I said, hoping to make her feel better by saying something nice, but she took it as a dig.

"I can explain," she replied.

"I look forward to hearing it."

She sighed deeply, looking at the gun in her lap as if it was something curiously unfamiliar, obviously reluctant to continue. "I made a mistake once," she said eventually.

"What sort of mistake?"

"I've been to the Pantera Club before."

"Yes?"

"I was taken there by the man you leveled with the fire extinguisher. His name is Vas. I never did get a last name. I met him in a bar in one of the big casinos. He picked me up."

"Okay, so you had poor taste."

"And poor judgment," she said. "I told him what I did for a living."

"What happened?"

"Can't you guess the rest?"

"No, not really."

"He suggested we go to a nightclub. That was fine by me. It wasn't until we got inside that I discovered exactly what type of nightclub the Pantera Club was."

"And?"

"He introduced me to some of his friends," she said in the tone of someone annoyed at having to explain the obvious. "Two men and a woman. They were nice people. Young and attractive. We talked for awhile. Drank some more." She paused for a moment, and the only sound was the low Latinate murmuring of the Reverend Jim over the traffic outside.

"What happened?"

"Did you see the video room? Camera gear and one-way glass?"

"Yes."

"That's what happened. Next day, I got an e-mail. The sender's address was meaningless, just something made up for one of those free e-mail accounts. The text had a date and time and the name of a bar, obviously a meeting. It was the same bar I had been picked up in. It wasn't hard to guess who had sent the mail."

"So he wanted to see you again?"

"That wasn't all that was in it. There was an internet URL."

"And?"

"I went to the URL. There were photographs posted there. They had been taken through the one-way mirrors in that room. All of them were of me, with the three friends, from the previous evening. Very clear, very high quality. Whatever else you might say about these people, the equipment they're using is professional grade."

"Are you telling me that you're being blackmailed?"

"Yes."

"Were you identifiable in the photographs?"

"Yes, very clearly."

"No wig?"

"No, I got that for tonight. I wanted to make sure I wasn't recognized by any of the three 'friends,' or whoever had been on the other side of the one-way mirror that night."

That didn't exactly fit with what Marty Blankenship had told me: he claimed she had worn the wig before tonight, when she had first hired him. I decided not to press it for now.

"What did Vas want?"

"Money. Actually, I was relieved that it wasn't more, something to do with Mr. Antullis."

"Did you pay?"

"I'm not that stupid. Tonight was supposed to be the payoff. He told me that it would be a one-off payment, but no doubt if I actually gave it to him there would of course be demands for more. The meeting was set up for midnight, at the same bar. Since I knew Vas would be there, I decided to break into the office and resolve things my own way."

"How did you break in?"

"Lockpicks," she said. No pause, no falter. She should have been in politics.

"Did you find the photos?"

"Not exactly. I checked out the recording equipment first. It's all digital. That means no tapes, just memory. They almost certainly download the memory into a computer, but digital recording uses massive amounts of memory, so it would have to be a machine with significant storage capacity. Sure enough, I found a server in the office."

"What's a server?"

"A computer. It looks like an ordinary computer, but it's much more robust, and much more expensive. This one had a five-disc SAN array, with over a terabyte of memory. At least it used to."

"Used to?"

"I smashed the discs. Better than erasing them—erased data can be restored. No way to restore from a disc that's been physically destroyed."

"And the filing cabinet?"

"I searched there in case they back up their video to a zip drive or a minidisk. Or perhaps even had printouts of the photos that could be scanned. But I didn't find anything, not that I got much of a chance before Vas arrived. I'd assumed he would wait a while at the bar, figuring I was just late. It seems he got impatient."

"He didn't strike me as the patient type."

"Lucky you showed up."

"And to think that this morning you wanted to get rid of me."

I could see it dawning on her that there had as yet been no explanation for how I came to be in a position to drive a fire extinguisher into the back of her attacker's head. She sat up and looked at me with sudden suspicion. "Exactly how did you show up anyway?"

"I was in the neighborhood."

"What?"

"I was already in the Pantera Club."

"How come?"

"I was taken there."

"By whom?"

"A girl."

The Reverend Jim stopped murmuring and cleared his throat meaningfully, the way one guy does to warn another that the current topic of conversation is probably best not pursued.

"What girl?"

"Nice girl I met today. I had a flat on the GT40, so I came in to get it fixed. I met her at the dealership."

"And this 'nice girl' asked you to the Pantera Club?"

"Heck of place for a first date, isn't it? Anyway, I recognized you, and was going to ask you to join us for a drink. I saw you go upstairs, and so I tried doors until I found you." It wasn't a very good story, but it was the best I could come up with.

Yamina didn't immediately respond. Until now we had been leaning close, trying but failing to have the conversation in private, but now she sat back and crossed her arms, apparently displeased.

"As I've said before, Mr. Dalton, you turn up at some unexpected places. I'm not sure that—"

She stopped in midsentence. Over the traffic noise outside we could now hear a new sound: the distinctive throaty rumble of the Corvette. We both turned to the convex mirror, scanning the passing traffic. The noise was faint at first but becoming louder as the car approached. Inside the Chapel of Happiness there was no way to be sure from which direction the car was coming. If on the other side: fine—there was no easy way to do a U-turn on the Strip. But if they were on our side, then the Chapel of Happiness would present itself as an obvious place to check out.

Yamina raised the weapon and pulled the slide to the rear. The Reverend Jim, sensing the heightened tension, began reading faster. I turned on the ignition and put my finger over the starter button, ready to light up and leave in a hurry.

Then we saw it. The Corvette was on the other side, slowly rumbling down the Strip. Presumably they were searching this part of the road, trying to figure out how we could have disappeared. Even from the other side they would note the drive-through. They would come back to check it out sooner or later.

"We'll give them a moment to get past, then get out of here."

Yamina nodded in agreement. I fired up the Jaguar.

At that point the Reverend Jim breathlessly concluded his speed-reading of the Latin liturgy. He closed his Bible, smiled benignly upon us, and—reverting to the vulgar tongue—loudly proclaimed, "I now pronounce you man and wife."

TWENTY-ONE

AS we drove through the darkened desert in silence, heading back to Quartz Peak, I reviewed the lies that Yamina Malik had told me. There weren't too many. The wig had been used before tonight, unless Marty Blankenship had not meant to include it when referring to her coming to his office wearing "that crazy getup." There had been the folder of financial statements open on top of the filing cabinet, although it could have just been rapidly pulled out as she'd been searching for video or photographs. The lockpicks was an obvious lie, but perhaps Yamina had simply not wanted to mention the private detective who had apparently obtained a key for her, especially since he had no doubt done it illegally.

But there was a series of coincidences that had yet to be explained. Coincidence one: Vas's Batman tattoo. I assumed that Vas was short for Vassily, which would likely make him a Russian. Batman is not the only user of the Batman device; it is also the symbol adopted by the Russian special forces: formally called the *Spetsialnoye nazranie*, but known to the world by their abbreviated name: Spetsnaz. Their uniform patches, which as a Force Recon officer back in the Cold War I had been required to learn by sight, displayed the black spread-winged bat symbol over a blue circular target graticule. The badge is presumably designed to evoke batlike swift and silent approach by night, with the graticule implying the accurate application of deadly force—which of course is precisely what Spetsnaz are trained to do. The Spetsnaz were our counterparts, troops whose insignia and weaponry and operational tactics had been drilled into us at special ops school during endless KYE/KYF classes: know your enemy, know your friend. They had a reputation for being excessively brutal.

Coincidence two: The Gyurza handgun—Yamina's gun—is a Russian weapon, developed specifically for the Spetsnaz: high capacity, armor-piercing—unnecessarily heavy and cumbersome for normal troops, but useful in special operations.

Coincidence three: the source of the plutonium was Russian, presumably stolen from the massive Russian stockpile left over from the Cold War. Russian nuclear material is guarded by their best troops. Their best troops are Spetsnaz.

If I'd still been a soldier, I would have immediately established a satellite uplink, punched in the coordinates, and within the hour Quartz Peak, including the bunker and whatever was inside that hangar, would have been reduced to ashes and dust. But I wasn't a soldier anymore. I was Dortmund's pawn, a minor piece to be moved about on a chessboard that only he himself saw clearly.

We were approaching a lonely crossroads, where stood the only service station between Las Vegas and Quartz Peak.

"We need to get some gas," I said.

Yamina, who since Vegas had been a dark brooding

presence in the seat beside me, said nothing. I slowed and pulled in.

There was a convenience store, where the station's lone attendant at this late hour sat encased in a bullet-proof glass booth. After filling the Jaguar I went inside and moved to the far aisle by the refrigerators, where Yamina could not see me from the car. I pulled out the cell phone and dialed Dortmund.

The call was answered by the same disembodied, computer-generated voice as before. I identified myself and was immediately put through to Dortmund. At 2:00 A.M. I assumed I would be waking him up, but when Dortmund came on the line his voice betrayed no hint of sleep. Perhaps he didn't sleep, instead spending his nights endlessly prowling his study, thinking and plotting, anxiously awaiting morning for the opportunity to put his schemes into action.

"Captain Dalton," he said, dispensing with preliminaries, "my instructions to you were to provide *regular* reports of your progress."

We were obviously not amused, but I didn't have time to debate protocol.

"I think the plutonium is coming here," I said.

"Since you have failed to keep me informed, I am naturally unsure of where 'here' is."

"Quartz Peak."

He paused a few moments before responding. "You are not at Quartz Peak," he announced. "Right now you are approximately thirty miles south of it."

So the old devil had been tracking me. There was only one way he could be doing that. "You didn't tell me there was a GPS unit in the phone."

"It was unnecessary for you to know," he replied. "Perhaps even undesirable." I understood: chess masters don't explain their moves to pawns.

"And you actually keep track of me in the middle of the night?" I asked. I found the mental picture of

Dortmund sitting up in bed in his jimmy-jams watching the dot that was me moving around on the screen of a laptop vaguely disconcerting.

"I am presently in the operations center at Langley," he responded. "There has been a small incident in China which requires my attention. I should tell you that there are many things we keep track of, Captain Dalton, the least important of which might well be you." The pawn had been put in its place. "Now what is it that makes you think that the plutonium is destined for Quartz Peak?"

I explained about the radiation monitoring equipment at the bunker, the high security surrounding one of the hangars, and the fact that the Gulfstream was missing.

"That's all?" Dortmund seemed unimpressed.

"No, there's a girl."

"Naturally."

"She's the head of security for Xerxes Antullis. Her name is Yamina Malik." I spelled the name for him. "You might want to check her out."

"Would this be for the operation, or for your own personal interest?"

"Tonight she met with a Russian. Actually, she was breaking into an office he uses."

"So?"

"He had a Spetsnaz tattoo. Spetsnaz are—"

"I know who the Spetsnaz are, Captain Dalton. I was dealing with Spetsnaz while you were still wearing diapers."

"Spetsnaz troops protect sensitive installations in Russia. Like nuclear weapon installations."

"I am aware of that."

"Malik uses a weapon called a Gyurza. It's a weapon used by Spetsnaz."

"Are you telling me this Malik and this Russian are in collusion?"

"Probably."

"Then why would she have been breaking into his office?"

"A falling-out, a double cross, who knows?"

"And what exactly is their purpose?"

"Presumably the Russian represents the suppliers, probably Spetsnaz troops who decided to make themselves rich by stealing what they were assigned to protect. Malik is the link between Antullis and the Russian. Perhaps she handles the negotiations. Certainly she is handling the security for Antullis."

"And the money?"

"I don't know," I admitted. "But if we know where the plutonium is going to be, then who cares?"

"I care," Dortmund said. "I intend to stop that plutonium, Captain Dalton. If I can't do that by intercepting the plutonium, then I will do so by intercepting the money. The latter is the mission for which I chose you, and that mission has not changed. My requirement is that you intercept the money. And I think you understand that in addition I want you to ensure that the purchaser will never attempt to make a further acquisition. I had hoped that I had made myself clear before, but apparently not. So let me again state, with as much clarity as I can, that your function is to intercept the money and put an end to its source. Do I make myself clear?"

"Who was the man in Alexandria I asked you to identify?"

The sudden change in topic momentarily set him off balance. "We don't know yet," he said.

"It's been a week."

"A formal request has been made for the police records, but these things take time. You must understand that our organization has no jurisdiction on American soil. We have to work through procedures like everyone else. Citizens have rights which much be respected." Now I knew he was lying—Dortmund had precisely zero respect for citizens' rights—but if he wasn't going to tell me, there was no point pushing it. "Now, Captain Dalton, about that American Express card—"

I hit the button to end the call. Back outside, I threw the phone into the Dumpster by the side of the gas station, and returned to the Jaguar.

Yamina had turned the map light on and sat hunched over the certificate that she had been studying on and off since the Reverend Jim had thrust it upon us as we left the drive-though wedding chapel.

"I'm sure it's meaningless," she said as I got into the car. "To be valid it would have to have some sort of state seal, or something like that." She waved the certificate angrily. I wondered if it was the marriage per se that she objected to or the claim to conjugal rights that it implied. "This stupid thing is just issued by the Chapel of Happiness. And he didn't even spell my name right."

"We'll check it out tomorrow," I said. "after the honeymoon."

A reluctant and beaten-up bride she may have been, but Yamina blushed just like the real thing.

"Mr. Dalton," she said, "before you make any more remarks like that, remember that I am armed."

"Mrs. Dalton," I replied, "I do hope that you're not going to turn out to be a shrew."

TWENTY-TWO

BECKETT roused me at noon the next day. Yamina and I hadn't gotten back to Quartz Peak until 4:00 A.M., and the vigilant valet must have decided that anything earlier would have been unwelcome.

"Did sir sleep well?" he asked, putting down the breakfast tray he'd brought with him.

"Fine," I lied. One way or another Yamina Malik had been on my mind all night, either awake, or in dreams. "What's on the program today?"

Beckett brought over the paper and a glass of what might have been simple tomato juice, but hopefully wasn't. "Mr. Antullis regrets that he is unavailable today, but asks that you join him and his other guests for dinner this evening."

I drank. I was right, it wasn't plain tomato juice. He must have seen the look on my face. "I doubled both the vodka and the Tabasco," he explained. "I personally find that combination very useful in getting back on track after a late night."

"Beckett, England's loss has been the world's gain."

"Thank you, sir." He went to a drawer in the sideboard, from which he withdrew a number of small packages. "I took the liberty of selecting the appropriate accouterments for sir this evening." He held up the first box. "Cummerbund and bow tie," he said. "Black silk. I thought that sir might find those loud paisley patterns that are much favored these days a little too rambunctious for his taste."

"Definitely too rambunctious."

"And the tie is of course a real tie, not a clip-on."

"Naturally."

He held up a second, smaller box, which he opened for me to inspect. "Cuff links and studs," he explained. "Silver, inlaid with black onyx and mother of pearl in a checkerboard pattern. Distinctive without being vulgar, I think."

"Just right, Beckett. When does it start?"

"Cocktails at six, sir. Also, I have been informed that security has a delivery for you at the front gate. A wheel, as it happens."

"Good. Ask them to leave it at the garage."

"Will there be anything else?"

"No, that'll be all."

Beckett left. Breakfast turned out to be a big stack of buckwheat cakes and crisp bacon rashers, just the thing following a long night with little sleep. After finishing the pot of coffee I left the house and went down to the airstrip.

There were no vehicles outside the big hangar—presumably the contractors who worked on whatever was inside had the weekend off. The one gate I inspected was securely locked; I didn't bother doing another perimeter check. Instead I went into the workshop, found the jack where I'd left it, and took it out to the GT40. I soon had the wheel replaced and took the car for a quick burnout on the airstrip to prove the repair.

The weather was as fine as every other day in the perfect spring that was Las Vegas in late winter, but today for the first time there was a breeze coming across the desert, with the occasional gust wafting little red earth wind devils across the open runway. When I returned to the hangar I drove the GT40 right inside rather than leave it out, exposed to the elements. Binky would have been pleased.

The Shelby Mustang was back. When we'd returned last night Yamina had given the keys to the guards and told them to bring it back when they were relieved by the next watch later that morning.

The Jaguar was there, too. The body looked no worse for the beating that it had taken last night, but there was a fresh stain on the tiles beneath the engine, and I could smell the acrid odor of burnt oil.

I opened the hood. There was oil on the side of the engine, apparently having come through from that part where the head meets the block. When I checked the dipstick, the end was coated in the brown, sludgelike consistency of oil that has been mixed with water, confirming what by then I had suspected: we'd blown the head gasket last night.

Actually, I'd blown it. Yamina had been riding shotgun.

I searched the interior of the car, looking for anything that Yamina might have left behind, but there was nothing. I checked the trunk next, hoping that by some good fortune Yamina had left that brushed aluminum attaché case inside, but it was gone, too. However, the trunk was not empty. There were several packets of Jaguar spare parts, brand-new in boxes and plastic wrap, and among which was a replacement head gasket.

So that's what Yamina had been doing at the dealership yesterday. The head gasket had already been going, and Yamina had taken the car to the dealership for spare parts, perhaps using the need to do so as a good pretext for going into Las Vegas for her own purposes. But last night's car chase had been too much for the damaged engine, blowing the old gasket to the point where coolant in the water jacket had been able to seep though into the engine oil.

My father used to say that a man who never makes mistakes is probably a coward, but a man who makes them and then doesn't do his best to set things right afterward isn't much better. I fetched tools from the workshop and went to work on the Jaguar.

The hood of an E-type is the entire front of the body—headlights, fenders, everything, all hinged at the front—and so with it open, access to the engine is excellent. The E-type motor is a 4.2 liter in-line six, iron block with aluminum head. It's a big engine for such a lightweight car, and according to a footnote in my GT40 book, had proven itself in the same way as had Binky's Ford: at Le Mans. In the early sixties E-types had raced there regularly, always acquitting themselves well but never able to achieve the ultimate prize that was to go to Ford: winning the thing outright and thus dethroning Ferrari. I wasn't surprised that Xerxes Antullis had wanted one for his collection.

I drained the radiator and oil, then began disconnecting, a slow process. The engine has twin overhead camshafts, one for the inlet valves, the other for the exhaust, and so the timing belt connecting them to the crankshaft had to be loosened and removed. I closed the doors to the hangar, making sure that none of that red dirt could gust into exposed engine vitals. I loosened the head nuts and lifted up the entire cylinder head. In my hand I held a big chunk of milled aluminum with two complex camshafts driving a series of rocker arms connected to the valves, which allowed the fuel-air mixture to enter and the exhaust gases to exit. In the engine bay the cast-iron block now lay open, with six enormous pots precision-drilled into it, each occupied by a piston surrounded by compression rings, each at a different height reflecting its different point in the four-stroke cycle of an automobile's internal combustion engine. Men like all machinery, but there's something special about seeing the inside of an engine that could comfortably power a car for forty years of everyday use over public roads, or race at Le Mans. It was the ultimate expression of man's cleverness, of his ingenuity. This complex machine that lay before me now had once been mineral. Dirt, just like the dirt that was blowing across the runway right outside. Man had mined that dirt, called it bauxite or iron ore, and had refined it and shaped it and built tools to mold it to his purpose. Someone had cut sap from a tree, which eventually wound up as the rubber hose that carried water to the engine, or brake fluid to the calipers, or vacuum to the distributor. It was an amazing thing, when you thought about it. Who could help but admire a civilization which could produce something as fabulous as the engine of an E-type Jaguar? Why would anyone want to blow it up?

The gasket was black and crumbling at the point where the oil had seeped from the engine. I carefully peeled it away and wiped off the oily residue, leaving a smooth, shiny surface for its replacement. I did the same to the underside of the cylinder head, aligned it over the bolts, and gently lowered it into place.

Cylinder heads must be bolted down with precisely the same amount of pressure in each bolt. I found a torque wrench—a wrench whose handle has a little meter, telling the user exactly how many foot-pounds of force he is applying—and went to work, torquing down all fourteen bolts a little at a time, repeating the sequence over and over, making sure that the whole piece came down square onto the block. I was about to begin connecting back up when I heard a noise outside.

It was another vehicle. I went over to a window and saw an SUV go past outside, a big black one like Smiling

Man's. The engine was straining as if it was towing. There was nothing on the hitch, but the rear was down hard on the springs—whatever it was in the rear of that truck was very heavy. The windows were blacked out, and I couldn't see any faces, or even how many were inside. A sign on the side door said R & J Industries and had a telephone number in the Las Vegas area code. It stopped at the entrance to the second hangar's compound, and a man jumped down from the passenger side. I couldn't see him clearly because he was obscured by the vehicle, but now that the truck was stationary I was able to read the license plate. I went into the workshop and used a scrap of paper and a carpenter's pencil to note it down.

When I got back to the window the people in the vehicle were being joined by a woman walking quickly across the tarmac, looking around the way a person does when they would prefer not to be seen. She was long-legged and shapely, wearing high cutoff jeans and a T-shirt that had been tied at the midriff. Even without seeing her face I recognized that walk—Sorrel Tyne.

I heard her greet the man obscured by the SUV. He got back into the vehicle while she unlocked the gate. They pulled through, then waited as she relocked the gates behind them. Then she jumped into the SUV, getting into the front passenger seat easily, the way someone does who is used to the company of whoever is inside. They drove over to the hangar and opened the hangar doors, not wide, but wide enough for the truck to back up though the gap. I strained to see anything inside the hangar, but the contrast with the harsh desert light made anything in the shadows invisible. They closed the doors as soon as the truck was backed up inside.

With the gate locked and the hangar doors closed, there was nothing more for me to see—I went back to work reconnecting the engine. Whatever they were doing inside that hangar took about as long as I did to reconnect; I had the engine all hooked up, had replaced the oil and filter, and was inside the workshop looking for a timing light when I heard the truck again. I raced to the window—this time they would be facing me as they drove away from the gate, and windshields are not tinted: it was my best chance to see whoever else was inside that vehicle.

The truck pulled out from the hangar. It was high on the springs now: whatever had been weighing it down before had been unloaded. Sorrel Tyne was walking to the gate, head down, as if lost in thought, while behind her they closed up the hangar. Soon the truck caught up, slowed to say something in passing, then sped away through the gates and back to the access road out of my view.

In the brief interval as they slowed I was able to see the face of the man at the wheel. I recognized him, that same bouncer from the Pantera Club who last night had passed us going up the stairs as Yamina and I had been coming down.

Sorrel closed the gates and locked them, then walked quickly over to my hangar. I went back to the Jaguar, refilling the water, wanting to be found working if she discovered me. But she didn't come inside. Instead I faintly heard her footsteps outside, followed by a click and whir I recognized as a golf cart being set in motion as she left. Soon there was nothing but silence; she was gone.

I started the Jaguar, opened up the hangar to let the fumes escape, and went to work with the timing light and a screwdriver on the distributor's advance/retard adjustment. As I set the timing I went through what had just happened, ordering events, getting the sequence right, trying to infer exactly what it was that I had witnessed.

Sorrel had obviously arranged to meet the people in the truck. She had driven down in one of the golf carts and parked in the shade of this hangar, out of view of the house, while waiting for them to show up. With the hangar doors closed and the mechanic away on vacation, she must have assumed that it was unoccupied, and I had been making too little noise while carefully torquing down the head bolts to have alerted her.

The contractor had showed up—on a Saturday. And one of the contractor's workers just happened to work nights as a bouncer at the Pantera Club.

Sorrel had joined them but apparently preferred not to be seen doing so. They had shut themselves inside the big hangar while doing whatever it was they had been doing, which had included unloading a heavy cargo that had been in the back of the truck. They left as soon as it was done, and Sorrel closed up after them.

The timing was set, and the Jaguar was running sweetly now. A good test would have been to check the compression, but I was satisfied with the job and could see no evidence of leaking oil. I shut down the engine, closed the long hood, and began putting away the tools. When the work was cleaned up, I went for a walk over to the big hangar.

It was shut up tight, as secure as they had found it. The gates through which that SUV had driven earlier were locked. The mechanism was a pair of horizontal steel bars, one on each gate, which were locked together by a cylinder bolt lock. This was more sophisticated than the usual chain and padlock arrangement. Chains can be cut with bolt cutters, and a padlock can be relocked without a key. Not so a cylinder bolt. Now I knew why Sorrel Tyne had been down here, and why she had been the last to leave. She was the one with the key.

I went back to the workshop. There was a wall phone, an old-fashioned one with a cord, the handset blackened and greasy from use by the mechanic. I took Marty Blankenship's card from my wallet and began dialing.

He answered on the first ring, "Blankenship Investigations."

"This is Lysander Dalton," I said. "I'm the guy who was trying to follow you in the Luxor parking lot the other day."

"Yeah, kid, I recognize the voice." He paused for a moment, and on the other end I could hear a match being struck, followed by the puff of a cigarette being lit. He gave a long satisfied exhalation before continuing. "So I guess you're still standing, huh?"

"More or less."

"What can I do for you, kid?"

"You told me that if I'd gotten your license plate that night, it wouldn't have helped me anyway."

"Yep."

"Because I don't have a contact at the department of motor vehicles."

"That's right."

"Do you?"

He didn't answer immediately, and I could imagine him sitting back silently with his feet up on the desk, smoking the cigarette and calling on his cop's sixth sense while contemplating what I was asking. "You saying that you want me to make a plate for you?"

"Yes. And do some other work, too."

"Does it involve my other client?"

"Perhaps, but not directly."

"I won't investigate my own clients," he warned. "If I find that I am, I stop. And no refund."

"Understood."

"Is it a Nevada plate?"

"Yes."

"What's the other work?"

"Investigate a contracting outfit. Find out what you can about them: what their business is, who the principals are, where the money goes. I want to know if they're real or phony."

"You having renovation problems or something?"

"Or something."

"You know where this outfit is located?"

"Las Vegas. At least the telephone number I have is in the Las Vegas area code."

"You going to tell me what this is all about?"

"No."

He chuckled. "Yeah, well, guess I prefer it that way myself. I charge one hundred and fifty dollars a day, plus expenses. Three-day minimum. And I'll need a five hundred dollar retainer."

"Fine."

"How soon do you need it?"

"Right away."

He paused a moment before continuing. "Kid, nothing personal, but as a matter of policy I don't start investigating until the retainer check clears—you know what I mean?"

"Do you take American Express?"

I could hear him sigh on the other end of the line. "Well, hell," he said at last. "I must have left the AmEx machine inside my fancy car that blinks and chirps."

I took that as a no. "Do you have a favorite bar, one that you're known at?"

"Of course. I was a cop."

"Is it far away?"

"My office is above it."

"Then why not go downstairs, tell the bartender to charge six hundred dollars on the card, and then give you five hundred dollars from the till. He can keep the rest."

"You're kidding?"

"No."

"Jesus, kid. If I'd known you had that sort of money to throw around, I'd have made it a one thousand dollar retainer."

Marty called me back a few minutes later from

the bar. I provided the card number. He and the bartender completed the details of the transaction, after which Marty—flow conveniently situated—ordered Irish whiskey. I heard another cigarette being lit, now accompanied by the tinkle of ice in a glass.

"What's the license plate?" he asked. I gave him the number. There was a pause while he wrote it down. "What sort of vehicle?"

"Chevy Suburban. Black. Tinted windows." He wrote that down, too. As Marty had told me the first time we met, he trusted nothing to memory.

"Year?"

"I can never tell that anymore. It looked new."

"Yeah, they all look alike to me these days, too. When I was a kid, I could tell you the make, model, and engine size of just about any vehicle you saw. I could pick a Tempest from a GTO without even looking at the badges. Can't even tell foreign from domestic these days." I could hear the chink of ice as he took another slug. "Now, what about this contracting outfit you want me to investigate?"

"R & J Industries." I gave him the telephone number I'd seen on the side of the truck.

"What do they do? Building?"

"I don't think so. I don't know for sure, but I had the impression of some sort of light industry. Maybe sheet metal fabrication, or ventilation duct installation, something like that."

"Yeah, anything associated with air-conditioning is a growth industry in Las Vegas, that's for sure. Okay, I'll soon know exactly what it is they do, or claim to." Again he paused, probably while scribbling it all down. "How do I get in contact with you?"

"You don't. I'll get in contact with you."

Another sigh, followed by what sounded like a hefty swig of whiskey. "You going to wear a wig and make me switch cigarettes with you at a blackjack table?"

"I was thinking more along the lines of calling on the telephone."

"Glad to hear it, kid. Give me a day or two."

We ended the call. I made sure everything was squared away, then began the long walk back up to the house. It was time to shower and change for dinner.

TWENTY-THREE

A long table had been placed on the open lawn by the lake. It was formally set: white damask linens, richly patterned porcelain dinnerware, brightly polished silver cutlery, goblets and decanters made from cut crystal. Two stewards were flitting about, putting on the finishing touches. I looked more closely at the dinner plates. They were ringed in an elegant red and gold pattern, and each had a crest at the top bearing the ubiquitous intertwined X and A. In the middle of the table was a wide floral arrangement, flanked at either end by candelabra filled with long, tapering candles, unlit as the sun had not yet set. There were twelve places at the table.

Nine of the twelve guests were already gathered at the oasis, but farther down, across the water, in a little inlet of the lake that had been turned into a shady dell by a dense profusion of trees and flowering shrubs: a suitable place to have a drink while waiting for the sun to go down. I went to join them, taking a narrow stone path that wound through the undergrowth.

When I finally cleared the vegetation, the scene into

which I emerged was part charming rural idyll, part sophisticated cocktail party, part glamour photo shoot for a glossy fashion magazine, and part scene from some languorous, dreamlike Fellini film.

The clearing itself was shaded and cool, a startling contrast after the harsh desert light. The grass was different here, soft and lush, the deep green of an English garden. On one side a white-painted gazebo, which had not been visible from across the water, served as the bar and was manned by a steward who was currently topping off a highball from one of those old-fashioned soda siphons made of thick glass. Between the gazebo and the lake several plush sofas and chairs were casually arranged. These were not wooden or wrought iron like regular outdoor furniture, but sleek, low, elegant, thickly upholstered furnishings more at home in a Mullholland Drive mansion or a lower Manhattan loft— presumably they were normally stored away and only brought outside when Xerxes Antullis felt the need to take a drink by the lake.

Variously standing, sitting, or draped across these furnishings were half a dozen of the most beautiful and elegantly dressed women in the world. I walked over to join them.

Everyone was there but Antullis and Yamina Malik. Quire, apparently playing host in his master's absence, shook my hand in greeting and signaled to the steward. He was wearing a dinner suit, too, but his cummerbund had a bright paisley pattern, and the matching bow tie was obviously preassembled. Beckett would have been appalled.

There was one person at the gathering that I had not yet met. He had been sitting on the arm of a chair and chatting to its occupant, Katerina—the slender East European model—but excused himself and came to join us.

"Captain Dalton," Quire said, "allow me to introduce Captain Springfield."

Katerina laughed, her long Nefertiti-like throat arched back. "*Two* captains," she exclaimed. "I don't know whether to feel reassured or threatened." Apparently her English was just fine when she felt the urge to say something.

Springfield smiled and offered his hand. "Bobby Springfield," he said. His accent was Southern, but farther south than the northern Virginia I was used to. The Carolinas perhaps.

"Lysander Dalton," I said. "I'm very much an ex-captain, by the way."

"Army?"

"Marines. And you?" He was wearing evening uniform, what we used to call formal mess dress, but his was black with four stripes around each sleeve and had a set of gold braid wings sewn above the breast pocket.

"Air Force, retired," he said. "Now I'm Mr. Antullis's pilot. The 'captain' is what you might call honorary." He smiled the self-deprecating smile of a good old boy, but his was an intelligent face, and I knew I'd have to watch him.

"Helicopters?"

"Fixed wing multiengine, would you believe? Had to learn rotary wing from scratch when I came to work for XA." He lowered his voice. "Hate the damn things, actually. In the aircraft I was used to you could lose an engine or two, and it wasn't the end of the world. Lose an engine in a helicopter, and you better pray that the gods are on your side."

"What did you fly?"

"C130s. You know them?"

"I've jumped out of them once or twice."

"Oh heck, boy," he said with a laugh. "You're a leaper?"

"Force Recon," I admitted with a nod.

"Oh, man," he said. He shook my hand a second time. "Force Recon. I tell you, I could never look you guys in the eye. We'd be scooting in above the tree line, taking small arms fire like it's the goddamn Fourth of July, and I'm sitting there thinking that at least—God willing—I'm going to be home for dinner that night, and sleep tucked up in a real bed all safe and sound. But you people would just go and jump off of my plane right into the middle of all that stuff they were throwing up at us from below. I used to think you guys were insane." He shook his head in disbelief. "Couldn't have done that myself," he declared. "Couldn't have done that for all the money in the world."

The steward arrived. "Martini," I said. "Straight up."

He went to fetch the drink, and I turned back to Springfield to change the subject. What I wanted from him was information, not war stories. "I noticed today that the Gulfstream's gone. How did it get away without you?"

"It's down at McCarran," he said. "I took it down for maintenance yesterday, and drove back. I'll have to go down and bring it back home tomorrow."

"Got a trip coming up?"

"The boss likes to keep it handy."

"I'd like to look over it."

"Be happy to take you for a flight, if you take me for a spin in that GT40 of yours."

"It's a deal."

The martini arrived, and so we drank on it. I was planning to move the conversation around to the big hangar, and whatever was inside of it, when we were suddenly joined by Julia. She was dressed in a strapless gold evening gown whose tight bodice squeezed her breasts into two smooth semispherical rises above the top, and which were obviously under such pressure that it was only a matter of time before the laws of physics prevailed, and they burst free. She was holding a cocktail glass filled with a liquid whose color matched her dress, and which from the Angostura-soaked sugar on the rim I guessed was a sidecar.

"Gentlemen," she declared with mock seriousness. "I think that you are neglecting your duties."

"Of course, please excuse us," Quire gallantly replied. He turned to Springfield and me. "Perhaps we should join the women now, before a rebellion breaks out." He offered his arm to Julia, which she took, and the pair of them headed over to the sofa on which Sorrel sat looking out over the water.

Springfield rejoined Katerina, sitting again on the arm of her chair and resuming the conversation that had been interrupted by my arrival. Over by the side, slightly removed from the rest of us, Jeremy Caterno sat in earnest discussion with Bettina, both of them looking down on the table at what at first I thought was a magazine, but which I now saw was a musical score. Bettina's long fingers were flitting over the notes as she explained some fine point of counterpoint to Caterno.

That left Carla Fuentes and Jodie-Ann Palmer, the Argentine and the Texan. They were sitting together on the second sofa, looking at me and smiling the smiles of women with a secret. This was the pair I had first met when they had been playing backgammon by the pool, and now again there was a backgammon board open on the table in front of them, but this time they'd obviously lost interest in the game. Carla moved slightly away from her companion, and patted the space between them. I took slug of gin, and headed on over.

"Good evening," I said when I got there.

"Hello, Captain Dalton," Jodie-Ann replied.

"Please call me Lysander."

"We're glad you joined us. Carla and I had just been discussing how we had hoped to see more of you tonight."

Carla suppressed, or rather failed to suppress, a giggle. Jodie restricted herself to a sly grin and took a sip of the pink cocktail she was holding. She was dressed in a gown which seemed to have been constructed of wispy chiffon strips, and the inside of which the dressmaker had neglected to line, with the result that the outfit was basically transparent. I wondered if Jodie realized that she'd forgotten her underwear tonight.

Carla had opted for a simple short cocktail dress which showed her long, tanned legs to advantage. She leaned forward, and the front of her dress fell away so that from where I stood above her it was no longer just her legs that were revealed to advantage. The gesture may have been accidental, but I could tell from the look in Carla's eyes that it wasn't. Apparently none of the women at Quartz Peak possessed a bra.

Carla again patted the space between them in invitation. I had no choice. I sat. They squeezed up closer.

"Tell me, Lysander Dalton," Jodie began, "are you worth a solidus?"

"I'm afraid that I don't know what a solidus is."

"It's a Roman coin," she explained. "You know that Mr. Antullis collects ancient coins?"

"Yes, he mentioned it."

"Did he mention what he does with them?"

"No."

"He didn't tell you about our little Saturday evening ritual?"

"No."

Carla and Jodie looked at each other in mild surprise.

"Well, then," Jodie said, "perhaps we'd better fill you in."

Carla took up the explanation. "At least once a week we have a large formal dinner, such as we're having tonight. Sometimes it's held here at the oasis, sometimes it's on a terrace back up at the house, sometimes it's inside, in the dining room."

"Once we had dinner in the desert itself," Jodie interjected. "XA had these huge, fancy tents set up, the ground was covered with Oriental rugs, and we lay about on cushions to dine, like the retinue of some Saracen potentate."

"Sounds charming." Actually it sounded like Xerxes Antullis was some modern-day Boccaccio, acting out his own *Decameron*: a privileged retreat into a world of sybaritic make-believe. It occurred to me that there would be worse ways to spend 8.6 billion dollars.

Carla continued. "At the end of the meal, among the choices for dessert, there is always a crème brûlée or a flan or something like that. Baked into one or more of these is a coin, an ancient coin from XA's collection. No one ever knows which."

"A gift?" I suggested.

"Only us girls are served the ones that may have them."

"Then a gift for the girls alone?"

"Well yes, whoever finds one gets to keep it. But there's a little more to it than that."

"Yes?"

"The girl or girls who get them, well . . ." She leaned closer before continuing. "They stay with XA that night."

Ah, I got it now. The coins were Antullis's method of keeping things random, and thus removing the grounds for any accusations of favoritism that could lead to discord in the harem. It occurred to me that if I had my own harem, I'd probably do it that way myself.

"How very interesting," I said.

"We haven't told you everything yet," Carla warned.

"Yes?"

"Among the usual coin or coins tonight, there will apparently be a single gold solidus."

"Okay."

"A solidus is a very valuable coin."

"Then I wish you both good luck."

Carla and Jodie smiled at each other. "I'm afraid that

you still don't quite understand," Carla said. She put her hand softly on my arm. "Mr. Dalton, whoever gets the solidus won't spend the night with XA. They will spend the night with you."

I downed the remainder of the martini as the two of them closed on me in what von Clausewitz would have termed a classic pincer movement.

"We have a secret," Jodie whispered into my left ear.

"Would you like to hear what it is?" Carla whispered into my right ear.

"Okay."

"If either Carla or I get the solidus," Jodie declared, "we've decided to share."

"It doubles our chances," Carla explained. "I hope that you wouldn't mind spending the night with the two of us."

I was saved from the need to respond to this by the arrival of Xerxes Antullis and Yamina Malik.

Antullis was wearing a dinner suit, plain like mine, I thought, although later I noticed that the crest with the intertwined XA had been subtly embroidered onto the cummerbund. But in that first moment, as the two of them emerged into the clearing, it was hard to notice anything about Antullis, because the presence of Yamina Malik obliterated all else. She was wearing a long chiffon gown, azure blue but with gradations almost to green, like the gently rolling waves of some tropical turquoise sea. It was held up by a single thin diagonal strap, leaving her shoulders bare and exposing the delicious brown topography of rifts and valleys along her collarbones and across the base of her neck. She walked slightly apart from and fractionally behind Antullis, aloof and detached, the way a well-trained bodyguard does. Her eyes as they approached were not on us but on the surroundings, quickly scanning. Even going to dinner and dressed like a goddess, it seemed that Yamina Malik was on duty.

She was the only woman carrying a handbag, the same small silver evening purse she'd had at the Luxor. I wondered if it still contained the P12, or whether she'd managed to squeeze in the Gyurza this time.

Yamina held back on the perimeter of the gathering as Antullis approached, hand outstretched. "Mr. Dalton," he said, "I regret that I'm such a poor host."

I stood and we shook hands. "Not at all, Mr. Antullis. Jodie and Carla have been keeping me quite entertained."

Antullis looked at them and laughed. "I have no doubt of it," he said. "These two are double trouble."

Jodie managed to look approximately demure, but Carla merely smiled in agreement.

The steward approached, carrying a tray on which there were two drinks. Antullis took a cocktail glass filled with clear liquid like mine but garnished with lemon rind instead of an olive—apparently Antullis preferred vodka martinis to the real thing. The steward took the other—a double old-fashioned which might have contained a vodka and tonic, or perhaps just plain mineral water—to Yamina.

"I understand that you've had a opportunity to sample the automobile collection," Antullis said.

"The Shelby and the E-type," I confirmed. "I'm afraid that I blew the head gasket on the latter." I explained about the repairs I'd made that afternoon.

"I must thank you," Antullis said, "although it really wasn't necessary—my mechanic would have been happy to take care of it when he returns."

"Not at all. I enjoy working on engines, and an E-type is something special."

"Then you appreciate fine engineering, Mr. Dalton?"

"Yes, I do."

"Splendid. In that case I hope you will agree to stay on for at least a few more days. I would like to show you a very special feat of engineering—something not seen in well over half a century."

"Thank you, I'd be delighted. What is this feat of engineering, Mr. Antullis?"

He smiled and wagged a finger, "Ah, but that would spoil the surprise. I'm an entrepreneur, Mr. Dalton— you must allow me to indulge in a little showmanship." Before I could respond, he turned to the gathering. "And now, ladies and gentlemen, I believe it is time to dine."

The party left the clearing, a snaking line of dinner suits and beautiful flesh encased in beautiful clothing. Jodie and Carla walked close on either side of me, each holding an arm in proprietary ownership, as if the solidus was already theirs.

As we walked I tried hard to think of any engineering feats not seen in at least fifty years. The moonshots were a generation old, but nowhere near fifty years, and I doubted that even Antullis's ambitions stretched into outer space. There was no way to disguise civil engineering feats—bridges and dams and canals—and of course they were not candidates for half a century of inactivity anyway. The more I thought of it, the more it seemed to me that any engineering feat of more than fifty years ago would likely focus on the great event of that period: the Second World War. And that war had of course ended with the defining engineering feat of the modern era: the twin atomic explosions in Hiroshima and Nagasaki.

I stopped, suddenly recalling Antullis's specific words. He hadn't said something not *done* in well over half a century. He had said something not *seen*. And I slowly realized that of course those two explosions were something that had not been seen—outside the limited restrictions of a nuclear test site—in over half a century. And even at the test sites, ever since the ban on atmospheric testing, the explosions had been conducted underground—not physically *seen* by anyone.

I realized that Dortmund may have misunderstood the whole transaction. It wasn't plutonium that was being sold, it was a fully functional weapon. And it was a fully functional weapon that Antullis apparently intended to explode—aboveground and in plain sight—in the next few days.

So that's what he was up to: Xerxes Antullis was about to become the world's first individual citizen to go nuclear. No doubt he was purchasing more than just a single weapon, given that he was willing to explode one rather than use the fact of it as the ultimate bargaining chip. I wondered exactly what it was that he wanted to achieve. It occurred to me that there were dozens of possibilities, ranging from a relatively benign if overwrought expression of Second Amendment rights, to the formation of a breakaway nation right here at Quartz Peak. Perhaps he simply didn't want to pay taxes anymore, and thought that the purchase of atomic weapons was economically preferable to writing checks to the IRS.

Whatever the reason, there obviously wasn't much time to stop him.

TWENTY-FOUR

THE sun had set, and the candles on the table were alight now. There were place cards mounted in silver cardholders at each setting. Antullis was at the head of the table. I was on his right, two down, with Katerina between us. Bobby Springfield was opposite me, with Sorrel Tyne between him and Antullis, and Yamina Malik on his other side. Jodie was on my right.

"Do you like my jewelry?" she whispered as we took our places. I tried to find the jewelry she referred to, but apart from Yamina, she seemed to be the only woman not wearing any. "Not there," she said as I studied her earlobes for a second time. She briefly glanced down at her lap. I followed her eyes. While taking her seat Jodie had managed to pull aside the chiffon strips of her dress, revealing three shining gold rings, all in a row.

"Very attractive," I replied, "and they certainly have a charming home."

Jodie smiled and casually covered her lap with the napkin as the steward came by filling the water glasses. I looked up to see if anyone had witnessed the exchange.

Apparently not, but amid the quiet murmuring and general movement as people settled in, Yamina sat quite still, looking into her empty soup bowl, chewing her lip, and I had the impression that she was trying not to laugh.

The meal began with vichyssoise, accompanied by a honey-colored wine of impressive purity and delineation. Antullis looked at me inquiringly after I'd taken the first sip.

"Would you care to hazard a guess, Mr. Dalton?"

"Too much slate for Mosel or the Rhinegau. Rhinepfalz perhaps?"

"Close," Antullis said, "but it's a Nahe. Dönnhoff—an exceptional producer. This is the 2002 Niederhäuser Hermannshöhle. Rovani gave it a ninety-six. It's good that Parker brought Rovani on board; Parker used to underestimate the Germans, I think."

"It's an outstanding wine. You make an art of life, Mr. Antullis."

"True art is dead," he declared, waving away the comment. "All that remains is to live well."

Katerina smiled at him. "Darling, you sound like an earnest sophomore."

"And surely an odd assertion to come from an art collector?" Quire added from the far end of the table.

"Not at all. You forget that I only collect from a certain period."

"So in the century from 1870 to 1970 art was alive?"

"It was already dying, but it was not yet dead. That is what gives it its vigor. A man living comfortably, a man sure of his position in the world, is a boring man. But a man struggling for life, especially if against overwhelming odds, against forces that will inevitably crush him, that is interesting."

"Sounds like you're a fan of Greek tragedy," Julia said. "Isn't that what Aeschylus and Sophocles kept doing: prodding men into action in order to watch them fail?"

"And women, too. Don't forget Elektra."

"Or Antigone."

"Or Medea."

"That's Euripides."

"Close enough."

"I don't enjoy the fact of the failure," Antullis said. "I regret it. I just think that during the struggle, the most interesting works emerged."

" 'Do not go gentle into that good night. Rage, rage against the dying of the light'?" Julia suggested.

"Exactly," Antullis said, looking pleased with the answer. Well he might look pleased: how many potentates assemble harems whose courtesans can quote from Dylan Thomas? It would have been even more impressive if she hadn't missed a line.

"What did art die of?"

"That's easy," Quire offered. "It died when technical skill and sensitivity of feeling were replaced by fat paint brushes and bloated self-indulgence."

"I'm not sure I agree with that," Julia said.

"Nor do I," Katerina added, her voice sounding heavy and smoky, like an aristocratic émigré who had seen too much of the good life in Paris. "I rather like those things done with fat paint brushes."

"The impressionists for a start."

"Bonnard, too."

"Of course."

"Pollock."

"My favorite."

"He doesn't count for fat paint brushes. No paint brush at all."

"But surely he ranks on top in self-indulgence."

"What did he use?"

"A stick, I think."

"Or straight from the can."

"Like a good beer."

"You haven't told us why art is dead," Yamina said.

They were the first words she had spoken all night, and the table suddenly quietened.

"True," Antullis said. A new wine had been poured, a red. He held the glass up and examined the color while considering the answer. "Firstly, let me say that when I say art is dead, I mean *all* art. Not just painting or the plastic arts, a proposition which is so self-evident that it's hardly worth the discussion. But I mean everything else, too: music, literature, everything."

"But what killed it?"

"My theory is that people like me killed it."

"Like you?"

"You mean entrepreneurs?"

"No, I mean technologists. That is, the creators of new functional things, things that do stuff that wasn't done before."

"Computers?"

"Software?"

"Yes, but they just finished off something that was already dying. I think that it was the early technologies that killed art, and I think they killed it by natural competition."

Antullis stopped to try the red. I wondered if the pause was intended for dramatic effect, or if he just liked to savor good wine. He nodded, satisfied, and the steward began filling our glasses from the decanter. Antullis continued the explanation. "Consider this: until Louis Daguerre invented the daguerreotype— essentially the world's first camera—the function of a painting had been, to a greater or lesser degree, to take a picture. That is, a painting was a snapshot, something that today comes out of a camera, or is even something that your cell phone can do. But until the invention of the daguerreotype, there was no way to represent the physical likeness of things, except through painting and sculpture. Before the camera, art had *a practical function*: to preserve a visual image. After the camera, that practical function was gone, taken over forever by something that did it better at a fraction of the cost, and in a fraction of the time. From that point, painting had lost its *raison d'être*, and the present collapse into a vacuity of purpose had been determined."

"How do you know that it isn't just a coincidence?"

"Because of the timing. My theory is that there is a thirty-year period between the coming of a technology that will kill an art, and the rot setting in—thirty years because that corresponds to the time from which a man born and raised in the age of the new invention will come to his maturity and productive growth. In this case, we are talking of the first generation who, having grown up with the new technology, takes for granted that it is the function of a camera, not a canvas, to preserve images. The daguerreotype was invented in 1839. Cézanne was born in 1839. His first exhibition was in 1873, from which it is fair to say that painting no longer took representation as its primary objective. Not precisely thirty years, but you get my point. From the advent of Cézanne, Matisse and Picasso were just a matter of time. But what a long and interesting death: Cubism and the Fauves, Abstract Expressionism, and who could not help but admire that last joyous gasp: Pop Art? I can't look at a Warhol without smiling."

The main course was brought, and the discussion was by unspoken consent put on hold until its serving was complete. The dish was southwestern regional: dark chili-rubbed venison, little tamales full of spiced goat cheese, but the presence of baked polenta suggested that it was still Maria who was running things in the kitchen. The wine was Massetto, a Pomerol-like Supertuscan that went well with the food. It occurred to me that whatever other excesses Antullis might be guilty of, his diet wasn't one of them: the meal so far had not been the lavish multicourse extravaganza that I had anticipated, but two simple courses that were unassuming but well executed. It represented an avoidance of epicurean indulgence of which Epicurus himself—ever the voice of moderation—would have approved. Or perhaps Antullis's harem simply demanded it in order to retain their figures.

It was Jodie who restarted the discussion. "You said that all the arts were dead, XA. But music, too?

"Certainly."

"There is music written today. Good music."

"Yes, but it's derivative. And therefore lifeless."

"What about popular music?"

"Also derivative."

"Rap music?"

"Proof of my original thesis: art is dead." This pronouncement was met by smiles of amused agreement.

"Does your thirty-year rule apply here, too?"

"Let me ask you," Antullis replied. "When did music turn strange?"

"The Sex Pistols?" Carla offered. Perhaps she'd been a punk once herself.

"The Ramones," Julia offered, "they started it all."

"Earlier than punk rock."

"Surely you don't mean jazz?"

"No, I think jazz is an example of that great burst of energy that wouldn't have occurred had the art form itself not been dying. Perhaps jazz's peak in New York City in the 1950s is the audible equivalent of the Abstract Expressionists, who were then also at their peak, also in New York City."

"Miles Davis as Jackson Pollock?"

"And John Coltrane?"

"Definitely de Kooning. Quiet but strange."

"Okay, so if not with jazz, then when did music begin to die?"

There was silence around the table. Antullis looked down at Bettina, who until now had been silent in the discussion. "What do you think, Bettina? Was there a point where music got turned on its head, and was never the same afterward?"

"I think you mean *The Rite of Spring*," she quietly offered. Antullis nodded in agreement. Bettina took up the explanation. "Stravinsky," she said. "*The Rite of Spring* premiered in Paris, in 1913, I think. The audience rioted. People demanded their money back. Nothing like it had ever been heard before. Until *The Rite of Spring*, music was meant to be musical: to have melody. But half of *The Rite* is dissonance: noise, if you like. In academic music history, that concert is generally considered to represent the birth of modern music."

"And the thirty-year rule?"

"Edison invented the phonograph in 1877," Antullis said. "And Stravinsky was born in 1882. Until the phonograph, music was unheard unless someone played it. The purpose of music was its production. But then suddenly, with the advent of the phonograph, it could be recorded. Preserved. Endlessly reproducible, at a whim."

He sat back in satisfaction at the silence around the table. He was winning his argument. The stewards took the opportunity of the break to go around the table, asking guests what their choices were for dessert. I ordered the cheese. Most of the women ordered the crème brûlée. Carla and Jodie smiled at each other and glanced slyly at me.

A new wine was poured, and dessert brought. Katerina took up the discussion.

"You also said that literature was dead, XA. What killed that?"

"Television," several people said at once.

"A good guess, but no. I think that literature was already dying by the time television came."

"Then what?"

"Cheap paperbacks?"

"No, that's form. It's content that we're discussing here."

"Stupidity?"

"A universal constant. And therefore not a candidate."

"The movies," someone offered, and Antullis sat up straight.

"Exactly. Before the movies, the function of literature was essentially to tell a story. But then movies came along and told them better. They even show you the story, so instead of sitting back reading words, and having to picture things for yourself, the movie camera does the imagining for you. With its narrative function removed, literature collapsed into obscure introspection or imagined lyrical fancifulness. Which began with . . . ?"

"*Ulysses*," Julia said.

"Indeed. A thousand pages of stream of consciousness, but where is the story? A day spent wandering around Dublin, in which little out of the ordinary occurs. The end of narrative."

"And the thirty-year rule?"

"Louis Lumière invented the cinematograph in 1895. *Ulysses* was published in 1922."

"When was Joyce born?"

"In 1882, and died in 1941. Exactly the same years as Virginia Woolf, in case you would prefer to attribute the birth of the modern novel to her rather than him."

There was a ruminative silence around the table, followed by a few more comments on the subject, but gradually the table discussion broke up into conversations between neighbors and those sitting directly across from each other, the way dinner parties do at the end of the meal. I was eating a slice of Vacheron, and trying to think if there could be any motivational basis for acquiring nuclear weapons derived from an abstract theory of modernism, when beside me Katerina suddenly choked.

"Oh, dear," she said, removing an object from her mouth, "I almost swallowed it." She held the object over the glass, poured some water over it, and wiped it dry with her napkin before inspecting it.

It was a coin. It wasn't gold.

"Lovely," Katerina said, "but I could have died choking on it." She passed the coin to Antullis. "Darling, tell me what it was that nearly killed me."

"A silver denarius," he said. He spent a moment studying it, then smiled. *"Dictus Perpetuo Caesar,"* he read aloud, "Caesar, dictator for life."

"Which Caesar does it refer to?"

"The first, Julius," he said. "This is the coin that killed him."

"Did he choke on it, too?"

"Not exactly. You may recall from your civics classes at school that the political foundation of the Roman Republic was, like our own, based on a hatred of kings. Almost all the power of the Roman magistracy was shared: two consuls, two tribunes, and so on. It was an arrangement meant to insure that no one person ever gained too much authority, much as our own separation of powers is designed to do. The term of each office was for only a year, and of course the senate wielded ultimate authority. In the Roman Republic, it was perfectly legal to kill anyone who tried to become king."

"Until Caesar?"

"Exactly. Along he comes, fresh from the subjugation of Gaul, crosses the Rubicon, hunts down and kills Pompey, then makes himself dictator for life. There had been dictators before, of course, and Roman constitutional law allowed for their appointment in times of threat to the republic. But the tradition was for these dictators to step down, Cincinnatus-like, when the threat had passed—a tradition honored mostly in the breach, but a tradition nevertheless. Part of that tradition had been against personal representation in official business: no seals bearing one's likeness, no statues in the forum or portraits in the palaces. This prohibition extended to stamping one's likeness on coins. It was considered something that kings did. But Caesar ignored that tradition." He held up the coin. "The obverse, as you can see, is stamped with Caesar's portrait. And in case there was any doubt, he had his likeness surrounded with the phrase that must have chilled the proud senators: Caesar, dictator for life."

"Are you saying that Caesar was killed because of that coin?"

"In part. It was minted in February of 44 B.C. A month later, Caesar was assassinated, stabbed to death on the senate floor by those shortsighted men whose ire the coin had helped raise."

"You're unfair to the senators, XA. They were defending the republic against a dictator, after all."

"That's right," Julia added with a smile. "Remember, there are two sides to every coin."

"Touché," Antullis said. "Well in this case it happens that you're literally correct. Let us examine the other side." He flipped the coin around for us to see. "On the reverse is a depiction of the goddess Venus, from whom Julius Caesar claimed descent. She is shown holding Victory, plus a scepter and shield. It is meant to suggest an ancestral justification for his taking absolute power, but there was a second meaning, too. Venus is of course the goddess of love. It happened that Julius Caesar was something of a Don Juan, and was quite indifferent to whether the object of his affections was married or not. To the many senators whose wives he had seduced, this coin suggested a somewhat darker meaning. Indeed, if his intention was to goad them, it's hard to think of a better way for him to have done so. And for Brutus, the leader of the conspirators, the coin had a special significance. It was widely known that as a young man Julius Caesar had seduced Brutus's mother, and in Roman society it was generally believed that Brutus was in fact Caesar's illegitimate son." He flipped the coin into the air, caught it, and covered it with the palm of his other hand. "Whether in its obverse or reverse, this is the coin that killed Caesar."

"Heads or tails, you lose?"

"Precisely. There is a lesson here, is there not? In short: wear your power discreetly, and keep your hands off other men's wives."

By becoming a recluse and keeping a harem?

He handed the coin back to Katerina. "You fared better with this coin than did Julius Caesar: you survived; he did not."

"Beware the ides of March."

"Beware men's weak minds and frail egos," Antullis countered. "The coin was minted as part of Caesar's effort to raise funds for a Parthian war. It was a war which, had it succeeded, may have changed the course of history."

It occurred to me that I knew two power-mad lunatics—Dortmund and Antullis—and both of them were apparently fascinated by Julius Caesar. I wondered if it was a coincidence.

"Perhaps rather than falling," Antullis continued, "the Roman Republic might have instead become the foundation of a global world state. Imagine what might have been. No barbarian invasions. No Dark Ages. No Inquisition. One can't help but wish that Caesar had had the good sense to proclaim his power more subtly, and forgo the self-portraits and the Venuses."

"Perhaps," I said, "but in the end the coin was accurate."

"What do you mean?"

"Caesar got his wish: he *was* dictator for life."

Before Antullis could reply, Bettina let out a little muffled cry. "I got one," she said. Like Katerina before her, Bettina rinsed it with mineral water and dried it with her napkin. She briefly studied it before holding it aloft. "Mine's a silver denarius, too."

"Bravo," Antullis said.

Bettina and Katerina smiled at each other.

"We'll have to compare them," Katerina said. "Later, perhaps?"

"Actually, I think all three of us can compare them," Sorrel Tyne said. She tapped a spoon on the dish in front of her. The edge of a coin was poking out of her half-eaten dessert. "XA," she said with a smile, "you're a very naughty boy."

"Not at all, Sorrel. Perhaps you should examine the coin more closely."

In response she extracted it fully. Even without rinsing, we could all see that the coin was different to the other two.

"Gold," Sorrel said, stating the obvious. Jodie and Carla looked at each other in disappointment.

"A gold solidus," Antullis explained. "Fifth century, A.D. Also Roman, but by then the republic had become an empire, and the seat of government had moved to Constantinople. I hope you like it, Sorrel."

She glanced at me before replying. "I'm sure that I'm going to enjoy it very much."

THE dinner party gradually broke up. Liqueurs and brandy were brought. Antullis and Springfield smoked cigars. Some people stayed seated at the table, engaged in conversation; others stretched their legs, strolling quietly by the lake. I excused myself to go to the bathroom. I went back through the tents, found the head steward, and handed over the remainder of what I owed him.

"I wasn't sure we'd gotten the right one," he said as I counted out the notes.

"What do you mean?"

"You told me to make sure Sorrel Tyne got it. But it was the one on the other side of Captain Springfield you kept looking at, the security lady. I thought maybe you had their names confused."

"No, you got the right one."

I handed over the money, thanked him, and left to rejoin the party. When I returned, Sorrel Tyne was standing by herself, looking for me.

"I thought you must have gotten cold feet," she said.

"Of course not, Sorrel."

"Then shall we head back up to the house, or would you prefer to just ravish me right here on the grass?"

"Let's go back up to the house." She took my arm, and we left the dinner party.

I looked around for Yamina Malik, but she had disappeared.

TWENTY-FIVE

SORREL Tyne and I arrived back at the house.

"Your room or mine?" she asked when I pulled the golf cart up by the front steps.

"I've never been in a harem before, Sorrel. Give me directions, and I'll meet you in your room in a few minutes." She did so and stepped from the cart, but before leaving, she leaned back inside, very close, and whispered quietly.

"Don't take too long, Lee." Before I could reply she was gone, clattering up the steps as if late for a very important appointment. It had been a long time since someone had called me Lee. I pulled the golf cart over to the side, wondering if somewhere above, the ever-vigilant Yamina Malik was watching.

I went to my suite. When I opened the door there was an envelope on the floor, obviously having been slid underneath. It was red and smelled of an expensive perfume that I'd become familiar with earlier this evening. It contained a card, the cover of which featured a Cartier-Bresson black-and-white photograph of two

stylish Parisiennes walking down some First Ar-
rondissement avenue, circa 1950. Inside was a short
note which read, "Sorry we didn't get the coin, but why
not come by later anyway?"

There was no signature, just two lipstick prints
where Jodie and Carla had kissed the card. One of
them had three rings circled underneath, which I
guessed signified that the lip print above belonged to
Jodie. On the other side of the card one of them had
drawn a rough map with directions to whichever of
their rooms they were both occupying this evening.

The harem was certainly frisky. It occurred to me
that Caesar wasn't the only one who wasn't keeping
sufficient attention to what was going on around him. I
put the card away and went to the bedside table. There
was a silver tray on top, engraved with the intertwined
XA monogram. On it sat a bottle of San Pellegrino, a
glass, and a small saucer in which there were two
tablets—the sleeping pills that I had called up to Beckett to find for me.

I took the pills to the bar, used a spoon to crush them,
and put the resulting powder into one of a pair of champagne flutes. The champagne in the bar's refrigerator
was Krug—not the Moët I would have preferred, but it
would have to do. I opened the bottle and filled both
glasses three-quarters full. When the powder had dis-
solved, I took the glasses and left the suite to go in
search of Sorrel Tyne's room.

There were no lights on outside, and I had to rely on
the ambient moonlight to find my way along the terrace to the stairs which led up to the level above mine.
There were lanterns in the pleasure garden, not the tiki
lights favored by Hawaiian restaurants, but low Japa-
nese-style lanterns in little bamboo structures, so that
the resulting light was a soft, diffused glow. The fountains quietly splashed and gurgled. I made my way
past the trees to the inner courtyard, looking into the

shadows of the peristyle for an entrance to the seraglio itself, when behind me I heard a voice.

"I thought we'd have a swim," Sorrel said. "I love to swim at night."

She was standing by the pool, still in her evening dress.

"But I didn't bring my swimsuit," I said.

She smiled and unzipped the side of her dress. It fell from her shoulders. Apparently at least one of us was going for a swim, swimsuit or no swimsuit.

I walked over, intending to hand her the glass, but she dived into the pool before I got there. I took a seat at a nearby table, sat back comfortably, and watched the long naked form of Sorrel Tyne swim laps while I drank the champagne. There are worse ways to have a nightcap.

She stopped at the deep end after ten or so laps and pushed back her hair. "It's wonderful. Aren't you coming in?"

"No."

"Why not?"

"I'd get wet."

She laughed. "That's what I always liked about you, Lee. You always said exactly what you meant, and not a single word more."

"Your champagne's getting warm."

But instead of getting out, she pushed off the wall and began moving lazily down the pool toward where I was seated.

"Of course, it always meant that I never really knew you. You never opened up, so I always had to kind of guess what was going on inside there, you know."

"And flat."

"What?"

"Warm and flat. Your champagne's getting warm and flat."

"I never guessed that you were the kind of man who

would beat another human being to death. You have to realize what a shock it was, Lee. I was so stunned. All the time I thought you were just a good guy, you know. Loves dogs and kids. Ball games and burgers. Regular nice guy. I couldn't believe it when you turned out to be some sort of homicidal maniac."

I didn't want to get into this, but I needed to get her out of that pool and into her room. "Luke Trainor wasn't fit to live," I said. "And anyway, I didn't beat him to death."

"Because they pulled you off him," she said. She didn't say it accusingly, just in the even tone of a historian stating a fact about something too far removed in time to worry about anymore. "Whatever happened to him, by the way?"

"He's dead."

"Did you do it?"

"No, someone else did."

"Would you have if you'd seen him again?"

I paused before answering. "As it happens, I was trying to track him down at the time. The other guy got to him first. But if it had been me, then yes, I would have finished the job."

"Good," Sorrel said. "Now we both know exactly who you are."

She had reached the shallow end while we'd been raking over these old coals. Now she stood, water cascading from her body. She walked up the steps out of the pool, then came and stood in front of me, hands on hips, one knee bent, the way a bikini model might if posing in a photo shoot, except that this particular model had forgotten her bikini.

I passed her the champagne glass, which she wordlessly accepted. We held our glasses aloft in a silent toast, then drank. I looked her over, as her posture invited me to. The yellow light glistened off her wet body. Sorrel hadn't aged much in ten years, hard, flat stomach and firm breasts the same as I remembered them. Her legs were still ballerina's legs, having lost none of their fine muscle tone, despite the fact that she didn't dance anymore.

Sorrel took two or three gulps of champagne, then abruptly put down the glass. She came and sat astride me, still dripping.

"You're getting my dinner suit wet."

"Yes."

"It's not mine."

"Fuck me," she commanded.

"People could see us here."

"Yes," she said. "I like it when people watch."

I already knew that Sorrel Tyne was a woman of ravenous sexual appetites, but I couldn't recall exhibitionism as being among her quirks. The remark made me think of that room at the Pantera Club, and I wondered if she was acquainted with it.

"Let's go to your room," I suggested, but Sorrel was beyond suggestion now.

No one came by, or if so, I was unaware of them. If there were surveillance cameras on the terrace, then I just hoped they didn't have low-light or infrared capability.

Sorrel was noisy, making no attempt to restrain herself, despite the circumstances, and I could imagine coyotes miles out in the desert, wondering what was going on up on the distant mesa.

Eventually she was silent. The dinner suit was a real mess now.

After a while I reached out for the champagne glasses, being sure to give the right one to Sorrel. She drained the remainder of her champagne in a single gulp.

"Now we'll go to my room," she said as she put down the glass, "and you can finish what you started."

Sorrel resumed her shoes but not her clothes, which

she left where she'd dropped them by the poolside. We walked along the peristyle and through an archway into the interior of the harem. I had expected just rooms here, but there turned out to be a whole inner courtyard, roofed in, perhaps where the girls lounged when the heat outside became too much. There were more fountains here, and the walls were lined with low divans on which I could imagine them reading or talking or playing backgammon to pass the time. The one incongruous item was a large flat-panel television along the far wall, before which were a jumble of huge cushions on a wide Oriental rug: obviously this was where they sat and watched movies.

If my set of rooms was like something from a luxury hotel, then Sorrel's was the presidential suite. She went to take a shower while I looked around. There was a sitting room, whose doors giving onto the peristyle had intricate grills carved into the wood, as if it was a genuine harem in which the women had to remain concealed, even while looking out onto the real world. Since all the doors leading onto the peristyle were essentially the same, I realized that any of the girls could have observed us by the pool without even opening a door.

There was a bureau on one side and a desk on the other. This would be the first room I'd search when Sorrel was finally asleep. In the living room there was a sofa and chairs, a coffee table, an entertainment unit in the wall which included another wide-screen television. I put on some Miles Davis, good late-night music, and something which I hoped would cover the sounds I made as I searched later this evening. There was a bar on one side, where I mixed a pair of scotch and sodas before going in search of the bedroom. I came to a dressing room first. It was the size of a Manhattan studio apartment and contained enough clothing to have outfitted twenty women. Finally, through a pair of wide double doors, I located the bedroom, a space maybe a thousand square feet, much of it occupied by the enormous bed at its center.

On this last lay Sorrel. She was wide awake, and her eyes were glistening. I wondered if Beckett had given me amphetamines instead of barbiturates by mistake.

I went over and handed her the drink, hoping to achieve with alcohol what had so far eluded me with drugs, but then I remembered that Sorrel was a woman who could hold her liquor better than most men.

Sorrel took a sip, but then put the glass on the floor and smiled. "The oil's on the dressing table," she said.

I retrieved the oil. Sorrel removed her towel and lay on her stomach. I poured some of the oil, thick and scented, between her shoulder blades. It formed a little rivulet running down her spine. I began working it in.

"Lower," Sorrel said, but for the first time she sounded sleepy. I continued the massage, and eventually Sorrel's breathing became slow and deep—at long last she had fallen asleep.

I began in the sitting room. There was a laptop in the desk, plus writing paper and pens, but no key. The bureau held shopping catalogs and photo albums and bundles of letters tied together with ribbons. I quickly looked through the correspondence in case there was a hint as to the identity of the men who had been in the hangar that afternoon, but most of it was from old school friends whom I remembered from ten years ago. Several from her brother, a computer programmer who worked for the government in Washington. Nothing from her mother, an acquisitive and bitter divorcee who used to live in Orange County, and whose brief acquaintance had made me admire her daughter for having risen above what I guessed must have been a joyless childhood. Perhaps that upbringing had finally caught up with Sorrel.

There were some old programs from when she had been a minor in the San Diego ballet, programs I remembered the pair of us going through on Sunday afternoons, looking at the ensemble photographs and trying to pick which one was her.

I ignored the photo albums. I had long ago thrown away the photographs of Sorrel and me together, and had no interest in seeing them again.

Eventually I found the key to the hangar in a small box in back of the bureau, together with other keys, buttons, a dancing medallion, an old name tag, and the like. I recognized the lockmaker's name, and the key was distinctively large, like the key you imagine jail cells being locked with (but aren't: they are all electronic now, or at least they are in Leavenworth). It was on a ring with a second, much smaller key.

I stuffed the box into my jacket pocket. I hoped to return the key undetected, but if not, then a missing key would be a giveaway, whereas the whole box gone suggested misplacement, for who would steal buttons and name tags? When I left Sorrel's room, I had intended to go straight down to the hangar and find out what was in there that was such a big secret. I was tiptoeing across the inner courtyard when one of the other doors suddenly opened.

Jodie stood there, wearing a white baby doll negligee and high-heeled slippers with little puffs on the toes. The baby doll was filmy to the point of transparency, and was short enough to qualify as a chemise.

"We're in here," she whispered conspiratorially. Apparently she'd been keeping watch, waiting for me to leave Sorrel's room. Somewhere behind her I could hear Carla giggling.

What I wanted to do now was get to that hangar, but obviously it was not to be. I bowed to the inevitable and went to join Jodie and Carla.

TWENTY-SIX

"YOU'RE an early riser." Marty Blankenship said, after I'd identified myself over the phone.

"Actually, I'm a late sleeper," I replied. "I haven't gone to bed yet."

"That's Las Vegas for you," he said. "A petri dish for the cultivation of bad habits."

By the time I'd been released by Jodie and Carla, dawn had been breaking, negating the opportunity to surreptitiously check out the hangar while it was still dark. I'd decided to call Marty instead, and wait until tonight to discover what was inside.

"Find out anything?"

"Sure did." Marty paused, and I heard the now-familiar sound of him lighting a cigarette and enjoying the first satisfying puff. "I know all about R & J Industries," he said.

"And?"

"They're legit."

"What did you find out?"

"Registered as a corporation with the state of Nevada

for the last eight years. No tax liens. Went to the registered address, and sure enough there's a real business there, not just some lawyer's brass nameplate, which is what you often find when you actually go and visit half these so-called 'corporations.' "

"What do they do?"

"Build parts for racing cars. They're out by the Las Vegas Speedway. You know it?"

"No."

"Big complex. Several tracks. They run lots of races out there, open wheelers, dragsters, Indy cars, even NASCAR. Racing's big in this part of the world: cheap land, plenty of space for tracks, good weather all the time. Some of the racing teams are headquartered in Las Vegas, and there's a bunch of racing schools in and around the area."

"And R & J Industries?"

"They're the real McCoy. I went down to the Speedway and asked around. Most of the folks I spoke to there have heard of them. Instructor at the Richard Petty school told me they're chassis and body fabricators. Suspensions, too. Good with lightweight materials: they make bodies out of carbon fiber and chassis out of lightweight metal alloys. That's half the game, he told me: to win races you got to get the power up and the weight down. R & J Industries specializes in the second half of the equation: they're good at getting the weight down."

"They own any big black SUVs?"

"That was what I wanted to know, too. So I went down there, spent a while parked across the street. Just looking, you know. Seeing who came and who went."

I could tell that Marty Blankenship had enjoyed earning his advance. Made him feel like a cop again, most likely.

"And?"

"Three pickups, all white. And there was a long trailer with a rig for towing it, obviously for transporting

the race cars. They all had signs on the side: R & J Industries, along with the telephone number. No black
SUVs, though. No SUVs at all."

"Maybe it just wasn't there at the time?"

"Maybe. So I went in and asked."

"What did you tell them?"

"Said I saw a black SUV hit my car in a parking lot,
then drive off. Had their sign on the side. Said I wanted
to have a 'conversation' with whoever the jerk was who
was driving it."

"Did they ask how you could tell that dent from all
the others on your car?"

"Hey, that's real funny."

"Okay, so what did they tell you?"

"Said they don't have no big black SUVs. Told me
something interesting, though."

"What?"

"Those signs they have on the doors, they're not
painted. They're magnetic. Just like those things you put
on your fridge, but much bigger, of course. Guy showed
me; took me over to one of the pickups and peeled it
right off. Not easy, because they're so big they got a lot
of grip, but you can do it."

"So?"

"So, seems about a month ago two of these signs
went missing. Workman parks one of the pickups,
comes back later, and the signs are gone off of both the
doors. At the time they assumed it was just kids—you
know, some stupid prank. Who'd want a contractors'
door sign, right? But when I told him about seeing another vehicle with these signs on the doors, guy I was
talking to wanted a piece of him, too. Told me if I ever
tracked him down to give him a call, and we'd pay a
visit on the guy together."

"You buy it?"

"Yep, sure do. He was serious. Showed me the baseball bat he'd take along to help make the point."

"So what next?"

"Next thing is the license plate. Nevada DMV doesn't open 'til 8:00. I'll see my contact down there then, and get her to run the plate for me. It'll cost me, though."

"How much?"

"Won't be that kind of cost, kid. Not the sort of thing I can put on your bill." I could hear him chuckling to himself as he lit another cigarette. "By 8:05 I'll have a name and address. I'll check it out today. Give me a call tonight, okay?"

Before ending the call we agreed that I'd phone him at six that evening. We had to arrange a specific time because Marty Blankenship—ace investigator—didn't possess a cell phone. Apparently he regarded cell phones much as he did cars that flash and chirp.

IN an inversion of the usual order, I had breakfast, then went to bed. In the afternoon I went to the gym, intending to do some laps, but when I got there, the pool was already occupied. Yamina Malik was swimming smoothly and strongly up and down the lap lane. She was wearing a cap and a sleek racing one-piece, swimming freestyle, gracefully tumble turning and kicking off at the end of each lap. Now I knew where that muscle definition came from.

I sat. She may have seen me through her goggles, but if so she gave no sign of recognition and continued clicking off laps while I watched. Yamina completed another dozen or more before stopping. She pulled off her goggles, wiped the water from her face, and looked at me without expression.

"So did you make the *Guinness Book of World Records*, Mr. Dalton?"

"What do you mean?"

"Most women seduced in a twelve-hour period."

"I wasn't the one trying to destroy video of myself plus a few friends at the Pantera Club, Ms. Malik."

She looked down at the water. "Yes, of course," she said. "I'm sorry, please forgive me."

"I will if you'll give me my gun back."

"I'm afraid that's impossible."

"I'm afraid that I insist."

"Mr. Dalton, I am the head of security at Quartz Peak. I am not in the business of arming people who have access to Mr. Antullis."

"I let it go on the firing range," I said. "And I let it go again when you kept that Smith & Wesson we got from Batman. This time I'm not letting it go. I want the Anaconda returned to me."

"What do you need it for?"

"I may have to shoot someone," I explained.

She was silent for a long time before responding to this.

"If I ask you a question," she eventually said, "will you answer me?"

"Yes."

"Is the person you may have to shoot Mr. Antullis?"

"No." *At least not yet.*

Yamina seemed to think on this for a while. Eventually she hauled herself from the water. I'd seen a lot that was beautiful since I'd been a guest at Quartz Peak, but nothing that compared to the sight of Yamina Malik when she got out of that pool. Her long brown body was hugged tight by the white swimsuit, emphasizing the narrow, slender form. She reached up and pulled off the swim cap, releasing the great mass of wavy black hair beneath. Her smooth, even skin was shiny with water. She walked over to a pile of big white towels and wrapped one around herself.

"I'll have an answer for you this afternoon," Yamina

said. "I don't know what it will be yet." She grabbed her goggles and left the gym without waiting for a reply from me.

It wasn't the response I'd wanted, but it was apparently all I was getting for now. It occurred to me that in addition to being the most beautiful woman at Quartz Peak, Yamina Malik was very likely the most stubborn as well. I swam laps, trying to get that vision of her standing by the side of the pool out of my head, but it just wouldn't budge—even memories of her were stubborn.

When I returned to my suite an hour or so later, there was a cardboard box the size of a shoebox sitting on the table. Inside I found the Anaconda. It had been freshly cleaned and oiled. There was a box of ammunition inside. Black Talons, fifty rounds. Black Talons tear their targets to shreds. It seemed Yamina Malik had decided that if I was going to have to shoot someone, I might as well do it effectively.

TWENTY-SEVEN

MARTY Blankenship was on the phone when I tried calling him at 6:00 P.M. and again when I tried every few minutes after. By 8:00 P.M., after scores of attempts, all of which had resulted in a busy signal, I decided to go into Las Vegas and see him for myself.

I took the GT40. Most race cars don't have working headlights, but Le Mans is a twenty-four-hour race, and no vehicle running there could compete without them. I gassed up at the same station where I'd dumped the cell phone, and topped up with the lead additive required to keep from knocking an engine that had been built before anyone had heard of unleaded gasoline.

Marty Blankenship's address was located inside a dusty strip mall in a low-rent district on the outskirts of the city, halfway to Henderson. There was a check-cashing service, a bail bonds operation, and a greasy take-out joint doing good business in an area so forlorn that even the fast-food franchises shunned it. There was a bar, presumably the bar at which Marty had exchanged my credit card number for his retainer. There was music coming from inside, a jukebox turned up loud enough to echo across the parking lot. The only other business open at this hour was a tattoo parlor—perhaps people got tanked up at the bar in preparation for having themselves inscribed there later.

I parked the GT40 as inconspicuously as it's possible to park a $15 million race car that sounds like a loco-motive on steroids, and went in search of what Marty Blankenship's business card described as "Suite 2C." The sagging red Oldsmobile wasn't among the patrons' vehicles parked in front of the bar. I eventually found it out back by the trash. There was a bank of air-conditioning units nearby, relentlessly blowing away. Marty was right: in Las Vegas gambling is a game of chance, but the air-conditioning business is a sure thing. There was a metal staircase attached to the rear of the building, which led up to the second floor.

I climbed the stairs, which ended at a small landing where the single door bore a handwritten sign reading Marty Blankenship Investigations. There were win-dows, all heavily curtained the way windows are in Las Vegas to keep out the sun. There was no light coming from inside.

I knocked. There was no answer, and no sound from inside that I could hear. I knocked again, more loudly this time, thinking that since his car was here, Marty must be inside, and that because the lights were off, he was probably asleep.

The door came ajar under my hand. I looked down at the lock. It had been forced, and the doorframe was splintered where the bolt had been smashed away.

I ducked to the side, out of the line of fire of anyone sitting inside, and pulled out the Anaconda.

THE trouble with doing a building entry is that whoever's inside has all the advantages. They know the layout, they know the points of ingress and egress, they know which position gives the best field of fire. If they've got any brains, they'll booby-trap the obvious entrances. And when it's dark inside but lit up outside, like it was now with the strip mall's floodlighting, then whoever's inside has an extra advantage: they will see people coming in lit from behind—perfect targets—while they themselves remain hidden in shadow.

When I commanded a regular marine company, I never saw the point of risking my troops' lives if there wasn't a reason to do so. If there was a building in our way whose inhabitants were bad guys, then my philosophy was to eliminate the bad guys by destroying the building. We'd use RPGs on the flimsier structures, TOW antitank missiles if it was sturdier. For the really big stuff I'd call in an artillery barrage or close air support.

That pretty much ended when I joined Force Recon. Most special operations work is covert, conducted in territory which the opposition controls. The aim is to do what you have to do quickly and quietly, then get out before anyone realizes what's happened. My glory days of a hundred guys blowing up buildings were over, and now it was typically just a handful of us slithering in through windows or down through trapdoors, doing our work with silenced weapons and knives and explosives with timers that wouldn't go off until we were long gone.

It's good work in the open air. It's tolerable in enclosed spaces, if you have the element of surprise. But if whoever's inside knows that you're coming, and is ready and waiting, then I wouldn't recommend special operations as a particularly healthy occupation.

I crashed through the door and threw myself across the darkened room. I smashed into what was probably a table, and came to a jarring headfirst stop against the wall. I probably did more damage to myself with that maneuver than anyone waiting for me would have inflicted. I stayed absolutely still, hoping for a sound or a movement or anything at all to locate a target, but the noise of that jukebox booming up from the bar would have covered a stampede of buffalo.

The room smelled of cigarette smoke, but it was a richer, spicier smell than I associated with the Marlboros favored by Marty Blankenship, more like those clove cigarettes that became briefly popular awhile back. Gradually my eyes adjusted to the dark, and there was enough light coming through the door for me to distinguish the surroundings. I had expected the suite to be an office, but although there was a desk, the room was more like a living room, with a threadbare sofa along one wall and an old television set on the opposite side. The television had a rabbit ears antenna on top. As with many accouterments of modern life—like cell phones and chirping vehicles—cable television had apparently passed Marty Blankenship by.

The table I had hit was an old formica dining table, placed by a corner of the room equipped with a small refrigerator and stove, and which obviously served as the kitchen. I realized that this was not just Marty Blankenship's office; this was where he lived. He hadn't been exaggerating when describing the limits of an ex-cop's pension.

There was an interior door, open, which from the angle I had I could see led into a bedroom. I was pretty sure there was no one inside here now, but I wasn't going to do anything further without clearing it properly. I got up and quietly made my way into the bedroom, Anaconda held in a two-handed grip, and ready to take out anything that moved. But there wasn't anything in the bedroom besides a bed and a chest of drawers.

I cleared the one remaining room, a bathroom without a bath or a window, and about as small as you could practically make one. I went back to the living room,

closed the door and secured it with the sofa so that I'd
have warning if anyone tried to come inside, then
turned on a light.

The drawers to the desk were open. Files and papers
were scattered across the place, and the phone had
been thrown onto the floor, hence the busy signal I'd
kept getting earlier tonight. Obviously someone had
tossed the place. I looked through some of the papers,
which turned out to be from Marty's case files. They
contained surprisingly meticulous documentation for a
man who couldn't find a notebook. There were records
of interviews, diary-like chronologies of surveillances,
and careful listings of names and addresses. It seemed
that a lifetime on the force had taught Marty Blankenship the value of thorough paperwork. I could imagine
him returning to the apartment of an evening, smoking
cigarettes and drinking whiskey while carefully tran-
scribing his notes from the day's investigations.

I went into the bedroom. When I turned on the light
I discovered that the room hadn't been empty after all.
Marty Blankenship was by the wall.

In fact, he was nailed to it. He'd been crucified.

I went closer to inspect the corpse. His arms were
spread in a Christ-like gesture, as if whoever had done
this was a religious man. The wall behind was covered
in dozens of bright red rivulets which had poured down
from the many punctures in Marty's body and pooled
on the floor, turning the carpet from dirty beige into a
deep, dark, glistening maroon. Marty had been right:
whatever all this was about, there were some very bad
people involved. He should have heeded the advice he
had given to me and just walked away.

It would have taken more than one man to do this.
Someone had to have held him there. Three men, I
guessed. Two to hold Marty and one to drive in the
nails. They had stood him on an upturned trash can,
which was now on its side under the bed, where they'd

kicked it away after having secured him. Four-inch nails. There must have been fifty of them, maybe a hundred, variously driven through his arms and legs and even his torso. Torture, obviously. When they'd gotten what they wanted, they'd driven the last of the nails right through the middle of his forehead.

In the movies, when someone kills a man with a knife, it's a quick stab, then the victim falls to their knees, stomach clutched, and dies. In real life it's different. They take longer to die, for a start. And they don't fall conveniently to their knees; they usually remain standing and often try to kill you back. In the work we did, it was rarely a quick stab. Instead, after the initial entry of the blade we were taught to hold the knife in the wound, then twist and pull: twist, so as to change the blade angle, then pull, so as to pull the blade further through flesh, damaging more organs and cutting more blood vessels, thus increasing the rate of hemorrhaging and so finishing the job as quickly as possible. Even without this final maneuver, if the blade is held firmly in the wound, then the target's own natural struggling will open it up, leading to more damage and faster hemorrhaging.

There was little such damage on the corpse of Marty Blankenship. Each nail had its own small, neat puncture wound, which meant that the fifty or more that had been driven into the man must have been done in very rapid succession, before he had the opportunity to struggle. The only way to do that would be to use a pneumatic nail gun. Like the pneumatic nail gun that I'd seen in the storeroom at the Pantera Club.

I went through the apartment, wiping my fingerprints from anything that I'd touched. Then, using a handkerchief to handle the pages, I went more thoroughly through Marty Blankenship's papers. As well as those documents authored by Marty himself, there were many that he had acquired elsewhere: scans of official documents like property deeds and motor vehicle certificates of title, photocopies of driver's licenses and credit cards and such like. There were occasional photographs, smiling posed shots of teenagers whose parents would have given them to Marty when hiring him to find their no-longer-smiling and most likely runaway children. There were even some credit reports: perhaps Marty had been occasionally hired to check out the net worth of potential suitors or spouses.

Although they had been scattered about, it was easy to tell which papers belonged to which case, because Marty had entered a name and date on the top of each sheet or the back of each photo—presumably the name was that of his client and the date was when the document was produced or acquired. There was nothing dated more recently than a month ago. Nothing about the Pantera Club. Nothing that mentioned my name. Nothing that mentioned a mysterious brown-skinned client in a platinum blond wig, to whom he had surreptitiously passed a key hidden in a packet of menthol cigarettes.

It wasn't hard to figure out what Marty Blankenship's murderers had come here to find. And it also wasn't hard to figure out how they had been alerted to the fact that he was investigating them. Marty had told me himself: he was going to run the plate this morning, then spend the day checking out the owner. But now the record of who that owner was, plus everything else related to the case, was gone.

I went through the apartment one last time, checking that I hadn't missed anything obvious, and making sure that I wasn't leaving fingerprints behind. Finally I turned off the lights, pulled back the sofa, and left the apartment.

I wanted to get out of there as fast as possible, but at the bottom of the staircase the sight of Marty's aging Oldsmobile made me stop and think. There had been no notebook in the apartment—obviously whoever had killed him would have taken it with them. But there was always a chance that Marty had first written down whatever he found on a scrap of paper, perhaps even a scrap torn from the same brown paper bag he had used to note down his own license plate number for me.

I tried the driver's-side door. It was unlocked, confirming what I had suspected earlier: Marty made it a habit to leave the car unlocked in the hope that someone would steal it, so that he could then get an insurance refund for a vehicle that no one would ever pay real money for.

The interior light worked. It wasn't bright, but it was enough. I quickly found the brown paper bag I remembered from the Luxor's parking lot. I spread it out flat. The only piece missing was the part torn out for me. I checked the other side, but it was unmarked. If Marty had written down the owner of that big SUV's license plate on anything inside this car, then he hadn't used the paper bag.

The floor on the passenger side was full of trash, but apart from a donut box the seat was clear. There was an empty coffee cup in the cup holder, marked with the same franchise insignia as the donut box. When I'd last spoken to Marty, his intention was to go down to the Department of Motor Vehicles when they opened at 8:00 A.M. His contact there was apparently an old flame. I could imagine him lumbering in, two coffee cups in hand, and a box of donuts that he would have pretended was a breakfast offering, but the contents of which they probably both knew would be entirely consumed by Marty. He would have given her one of the coffee cups and asked her to run the plate. She would have keyed it into her computer terminal and given him the registered owner's name and address. If he still didn't have his notebook, she would have written it down for him. Not on official DMV letterhead, but on a piece of scrap paper. A Post-it note, perhaps.

I searched the interior for one of those little yellow adhesive notes, or any other scrap of notepaper that seemed likely, but found nothing. Perhaps she didn't make a note. Perhaps she only read it aloud from her computer screen, and it was Marty who wrote it down. But on what? On the thing that he knew he would be taking with him, of course: the donut box.

I closed the lid and checked the top. Nothing. I checked the flap, but there was nothing there, either. Nothing on the sides of the box. I checked inside, but there were only crumbs and the inverted top from the coffee, sticky with dried foam. In desperation I even checked the bottom, knowing it was futile: who would invert a donut box to write down a name and address?

I checked the coffee cup, too, since he would have had that with him. But it was unmarked, apart from logos.

I gave up. It had been a long shot, although one that was worth checking out. But in the end it was obvious that whatever Marty Blankenship had used to note down the name and address was gone.

I left the car and was halfway across the parking lot when I realized that I had not quite tried everything. I went back, hoping that checking this one last thing was not going to cost me the last few minutes before a potential witness from the bar noticed the GT40, which would lead the police investigating Marty Blankenship's murder straight to me.

I got back inside the car, opened the donut box, and turned over the plastic top from the coffee cup. There, inscribed in black marker, was what I'd been searching for:

> Vassily Goryakin
> Male 35 yr
> C/- Pantera Club
> Industrial Avenue LV

Now I knew who had murdered Marty Blankenship: that same Vas into the back of whose head I had recently had cause to ram a fire extinguisher. The same one who had seduced and blackmailed Yamina Malik. The same one whose tattoo proclaimed him to be a former member of that same Spetsnaz who were charged with guarding Russia's nuclear stockpile. And the same one who ran a nightclub whose bouncer had been secretly admitted by my ex-girlfriend into a hangar, the contents of which were a carefully guarded secret, and which was owned by a man financing the illegal acquisition of an atomic weapon.

I hadn't known Marty Blankenship well, but I'd liked him. He had been murdered because he'd been working for me. In the marines, we made it a practice to take care of our own. I was a long way from being a marine, but old habits die hard. I was eventually going to have to deal with Vassily Goryakin.

But right now, the time had come for me to find out what was inside that hangar.

TWENTY-EIGHT

IT was after midnight by the time I returned to Quartz Peak. The guards were used to the car now and waved me through. I wondered if it had been the same with R & J Industries' trucks: the guards having become so used to them coming and going that they no longer checked vehicles whose doors bore the contractor's markings.

I took the GT40 back to the airfield and left it inside the smaller hangar with Xerxes Antullis's cars. I took the flashlight and walked over to the big hangar. There were no lights on, not even the security floodlighting I would have expected around a hangar whose contents were obviously kept secret. Presumably they thought that the perimeter security was sufficient, or perhaps they had simply forgotten to turn them on.

I arrived at the gate, retrieved from my pocket the keys I had taken from Sorrel Tyne's room, and slid the big one into the lock. A moment later the gate was open, and I was moving quickly across the concrete apron to the hangar. But when I got to the side door, there was a problem. It was locked, and neither key fit. I tried several times without success before realizing the obvious: when that black SUV had been here, the only hangar doors I had actually seen open were the big ones meant for aircraft.

I went to the main hangar doors. There was no lock, or no lock that I could find. I went to the side to locate the big two-button switch like the one on the smaller hangar, but what I found here instead was a steel cabinet, locked shut, and welded to the support beam.

I tried the second key. It slid smoothly into the lock, and a moment later the cabinet was open. It was full of switchgear, circuit breakers, fire alarms, and included open and close buttons for each of the two big sliding doors. I made the breakers and hit both of the open buttons. The doors began to slowly and noisily spread apart. I stopped when they were wide enough for me to slip through and entered the hangar.

The darkness, which outside had been relieved by moonlight, was inside the hangar an all-enveloping blackness. I checked my watch, whose old-fashioned luminous dial had told me on a thousand occasions what it was telling me now: I had spent too much time on a task I had thought would be over in minutes. I would liked to have used the flashlight but wanted to get those hangar doors closed before doing so. I slowly felt my way along one of them to the point inside which was equivalent to the point outside where the switch box was located, found the controls, and hit the button. The doors ground toward each other noisily and finally closed shut with a deep clang that echoed inside the hangar like a cathedral bell. Now the darkness was total and absolute, and which for the lack of a visual point of reference was physically dizzying. If not for the floor beneath my feet, I would have been unable to tell which way was up.

I was about to turn on the flashlight when I faintly heard a sharp, metallic noise.

Lots of things make noises at night, and given that I was inside a hangar whose vast metal roof would be contracting in the cool of the evening, sharp metallic noises were to be expected. But the instant I heard the noise, I knew that it wasn't the building. Someone else was inside the hangar. I thought I even recognized the sound: the click of a safety being thumbed off.

It had come from the area where the doors had just closed. He or she had followed me into the hangar, and from the sound of the safety I assumed the intention had been to shoot me as soon as I had provided a nice clear aim point by turning on the flashlight.

I dropped quietly down and pressed an ear against the concrete floor. If I heard confident footsteps, then whoever was following me was using a night vision device, and I was in even worse trouble than I thought. But the next sound I detected was not footsteps, but a very faint rhythmic scrape: my companion was gently running a hand over the corrugated metal of the hangar doors, advancing toward me, obviously as unseeing as I was.

So we were going to play a game of blind man's bluff.

The important thing now was to make no noise. If I made a sound, any sound, he or she would have an aiming point. I backed away from the doors, over the floor, very carefully, but even so it seemed as if every movement was full of sound: the crack of a knee joint, the squelch of a rubber-soled shoe—and who would have thought that clothing itself rustles so loudly.

I stopped, made sure that my luminous watch dial was concealed under the shirt sleeve, and forced myself to remain motionless, concentrating on keeping my breathing as slow and controlled as possible. I could see nothing, of course, and had lost all sense of direction. Eventually I heard someone moving slowly past me, could almost feel the gravity of them. I held my breath.

Then I felt whoever it was, not the actual person, but the very faint movement of otherwise still air as they passed by, surely not more than a few inches away. They moved on, and after a while I was able to very gently breathe again. They were quiet, but not as quiet as me. Someone who knew they had the advantage then, someone who knew I would be unarmed.

That could be just about anyone except Yamina Malik. Yamina had returned the Anaconda to me, a weapon that I had stupidly left hidden in the car. She alone would not assume that I was unarmed.

I waited a minute, two, but heard and felt nothing more. Eventually I moved toward where I guessed the control box was. I eventually came to a wall, which I could tell when I knelt and felt with my fingers the small gap between the bottom and the floor was in fact one of the great doors. I moved right, along the door, following it with my fingers as had the person before me, until I relocated the control box. There, in the same relative position as outside, I felt the same pull-down metal lever that I'd seen outside: the fire alarm. I activated it.

It sounded more like an air raid siren than a fire alarm; perhaps they'd incorporated the old air force sirens into the alarm system when they had taken the property over. In any case, it was loud, and I could have danced an Irish jig now without being overheard. I moved quickly away from the control box—the one place my companion could have reasonably looked for me before fleeing, and stood by some drums I bumped into to await the cavalry.

They didn't take long. A few minutes later I heard the Humvee outside, soon followed by the office door being opened, and flashlight beams striking out in the darkness of the hangar. Then suddenly bank after bank of powerful floodlights came on. They gave off a brilliant white light, as bright as daylight, blinding after the total blackness in which I'd been immersed, and I had to momentarily close my eyes against it.

When I reopened them, Yamina Malik and one of the guards were standing fifty feet away, by the right-hand side. Yamina's hands were on a large switch plate embedded into the wall, and from which the floodlighting had obviously been activated.

The guard held an automatic assault rifle at the shoulder position, some sort of AR-15 variant, which from the short, heavy barrel and attached grenade launcher I assumed was a military M-4—the special operations' version of the standard M-16, and a weapon with which I was well familiar. The barrel was pointed unwaveringly at me.

"Should I stick 'em up?" I inquired.

Yamina told the guard to lower his weapon. "What are you doing here?" she asked.

"Looking around. My flashlight stopped working, and so I was trying to find the light switch. Guess I must have found the fire alarm instead."

"This is a secure area."

"Not very. The gate was unlocked, and so I walked in."

She wasn't too satisfied with this answer and thrust her hands into the pockets of her trousers. Yamina was more fully clothed than the last time she had intercepted me late at night, back when I was returning the flashlight to the GT40 after having discovered the radiation monitoring station. This time she was dressed as if for a safari: riding boots, belted khaki trousers, epauletted shirt with the sleeves rolled up. In the rush to get dressed, it seemed that she hadn't quite managed to do up all of the buttons, for which I was grateful. As far as I could tell with that unbuttoned shirt there had been no time for unnecessary underwear. No time for a side holster either: the butt of the Gyurza protruded from the waist of her trousers.

"What were you doing here to begin with?"

"I just came back from Las Vegas. After I parked the car, I took a walk around and found the gate unlocked. Sorry if I've caused a fuss."

Yamina looked inquiringly at the guard, who nodded—obviously he'd been on duty at the gate and was confirming the fact that I'd just returned to the estate.

"Are you alone?"

"Yes." There was no point telling her that I'd been followed; whoever had been in the hangar with me was long gone now. Without evidence it sounded lame, there was nothing to be done even if she had believed me, and I didn't trust her anyway.

A second guard came hurrying in through the main hangar doors.

"Perimeter's secure," he said. "No breach in the fence."

"Okay, clear the interior. You, too."

Without speaking, the two guards exchanged quick hand signals, agreeing who would take the left flank and who would take the right, then began the search. Apparently Yamina was not taking my word for it that I had been alone.

She pulled out a cell phone, dialed, and began speaking, turning slightly away from me and speaking quietly so that I couldn't overhear. For the first time since those floodlights had come on, I looked away from her to see exactly what it was that was such a big secret inside this hangar. I'd already sensed that there was something big above me, but was nevertheless amazed when I looked up and saw what it was.

It was an airship. But not just an airship, for the massive thing which filled the cavernous hangar was in another league from those benign Goodyear blimps which haunt sporting events. They are little more than mobile rubber advertising signs. This thing was far bigger, rigid, massive, and dull silver, as if it had been carved from a single huge metal billet. It had as much in common with a Goodyear blimp as a T. rex does with a gecko.

It rested on a heavily weighted, cantilevered frame that was wheeled and equipped with a big tow bar up front. By the far wall I could see parked a little yellow tractor, of the type common at all airports, that would obviously be used to bring the massive craft out of its hangar. In between the frame's forward and aft supports was a single piece of superstructure protruding below the otherwise smooth cigar-shaped body, and which was presumably the place from which the airship was controlled.

It was sleek and reminded me of a submarine, not just in shape but also in the sense of swift and silent approach, as if you could be happily walking down the street one sunny day when all of a sudden you would be in shadow, and looking up to see what had caused it, you would find this hulking dirigible right overhead. Despite being lighter than air, above all it gave the impression of imposing and foreboding mass.

Yamina Malik walked over beside me.

"Heck of a hobby," I said, with a nod at the airship. "Like model airplanes, only bigger."

"More than a hobby, I think."

"Why the big secret?"

"Showmanship, I suppose. He wants everything to be finished before he announces it to the world."

"When's he going to do that?"

"Tomorrow. It's why he asked you to stay on."

I suddenly realized what Antullis had been referring to when having promised to show me something not seen in over half a century. In 1936, the era of the airship had come to a sudden and flaming end over Lakehurst, New Jersey. Xerxes Antullis had built himself a zeppelin, something not seen since the *Hindenburg* disaster.

"What's he going to use it for?" That was the big question, of course.

"Why don't you ask him for yourself? Here comes Mr. Antullis now."

Headlights swung across the darkness outside, followed by the sound of a car coming to a stop and someone getting out. A moment later Xerxes Antullis came bounding into the hangar. I would have expected anger or disappointment, but the only thing registering on his face was a joyful pride.

"I see that you've discovered my secret, Mr. Dalton." He came and shook hands.

"And apparently spoiled your surprise, for which I apologize."

"Not at all, not at all. Twenty-four hours from now the whole world will know about her, and I sincerely hope will also be filled with curiosity to see her. And I'm glad the contractors were neglectful of the security arrangements (as I confess they have been for the last two years, notwithstanding Yamina and her predecessor's best efforts to inculcate them with the need for care) for now that gives me a chance to show you her in person, quietly, before the big hullabaloo begins."

"You've been building her for two years?"

"Yes indeed." He looked from me to the huge airship, fairly bursting with pride. "Before I sold out my interest in the XA Corporation, I often had to fly around the world for meetings and so on. I came to intensely dislike commercial flight, even in first class. Eventually, I gave up, and simply had the company use private jets, but they were often unavailable—at the wrong location, or down for maintenance, or the pilot was sick, or whatever—and so I still ended up being compelled to use commercial flights. God, how I detested them, and detest the thought of them still, although it has been many years since I took one. What really annoyed me was how poorly organized the whole thing is. Endless traffic delays in the limousine getting to the airport. Further endless delays at security. Endless delays in boarding. Endless delays in the scheduled push back. Endless delays sitting in line on the tarmac waiting for the planes ahead of you to take off, unable to stand and walk about or use the bathroom or have a drink or anything. Endless periods with the seat belt sign on, obviously illuminated not in the interests of safety but at the behest of the airline's liability lawyers. Overaged and underpaid stewardesses who would be more at home serving short-order meals at some trailer park diner. And then at the other end, that huge crap shoot called baggage retrieval. What an unholy mess. Yet there was a time, not so long ago when I was a kid, when air travel was not unpleasant. It had been enjoyable, even glamorous. It made me wonder what had gone wrong.

"Then I heard that Cunard was building a new *Queen Mary*, the *Queen Mary 2*. The conventional wisdom was that the jet age had killed all other forms of transatlantic travel, for who could compete with the speed and cost? But Cunard had obviously identified a market and were building a new transatlantic liner to take advantage of it, the world's largest passenger ship. It made me think: if there's a market for spending a lot of money to cross the Atlantic in luxury in five days, then what of a service that could do it in equal luxury, but in less than half the time?"

"You're going to use it for transatlantic travel?"

"Yes. She will leave New York of an evening, spend the next day in the crossing, and arrive the following morning in Europe. Paris, if I can get the French authorities to agree. When you think about it, although a transatlantic flight only takes six or seven hours by modern jet, in reality it takes a whole day—hours getting to and waiting at the airport, hours of delays, and so on. And those red-eyes to Europe really kill you: who doesn't need at least a further twenty-four hours to recover after one of those ghastly eastbound over-nighters? But on my airship, they will board of an evening, enjoy a civilized drink in the lounge followed by a real meal sitting at a real dining table, then retire to their cabins for sleep that is fully horizontal and unshared with one's neighbors. Each cabin has its own bathroom—no more waiting in line for the bathroom, and of course there will be showers, something that no airline offers. The next day will be spent in reading or writing letters in the library, or touring the ship, or perhaps just sitting and watching the water passing below, grateful for the temporary lull in life that my airship will afford them. There will be plenty of room, with no one forced into unpleasant and uncongenial proximity with other people. The second evening will be a formal occasion, a cocktail hour followed by a magnificent dinner—real food freshly cooked, not that warmed-over muck dished up on an airliner—then another restful night, and when they sit down for breakfast the next morning, the fields of France will be below. My passengers will arrive in Europe not just fresh, but refreshed—revived by the travel, not devastated by it."

"Sounds impressive." He'd obviously practiced that speech.

"Ah, but I've talked too much, when we have here the thing itself. Let me show her to you."

Antullis led me down the hangar along the length of the zeppelin, speaking as he walked. Yamina Malik accompanied us, whether to see the ship herself or just to keep an eye on me I couldn't be sure. "Let me give you the numbers to begin with. She is 1,353 feet in length, longer than the Empire State Building is tall, and longer than any transatlantic liner. She is twenty-three stories tall—in diameter, to be more precise. The new *Queen Mary* could fit entirely inside her. She will be by far the largest thing to have ever flown, larger even than the *Hindenburg*."

"Speaking of which, wouldn't the *Hindenburg*'s fate tend to make passengers shy away?"

"Not at all. The *Hindenburg* used hydrogen gas for lift. I use helium. Hydrogen is highly flammable, explosive even. Helium is inert. You could attack it with a blowtorch and nothing would happen. In fact, the Germans had wanted to use helium in their zeppelins, but in those days almost all the world's helium was produced in the United States, and we refused to sell it to them."

We stopped about a third down the length, and Antullis pointed up.

"Engine number two," he said. I saw a propeller at the end of an external mount extending ten feet or so from the side of the ship. It was dwarfed by the mass of the airship itself. "She has four Pratt & Whitney turboprops—that is, propellers that are powered by jet engines, same as in commuter aircraft. But mine are set on rotatable mounts, giving great maneuverability to the airship. The economics are astounding. A jetliner must use its engines for both lift and thrust. That is, their power must get the thing off the ground and sustain it aloft, while also propelling the mass forward. This was fine in the days of cheap oil, but those days are gone forever. Me, once I pay for the helium, I get all my lift for free. All I need do is propel the airship. When you work it all out, this airship will transport its one hundred and twenty passengers across the Atlantic with something less than half the fuel per passenger that a 747 uses, despite the fact that we are carrying not just those one hundred and twenty passengers but their sixty cabins, the water for their showers, the vast common areas, and so on. That makes a huge impact on the bottom line. I'm not just a dreamer, Mr. Dalton, for I mean my airship to make money."

We carried on past the control station to a point about halfway down the airship's length, where a set of steps

mounted on wheels had been pushed up against a hatchway open in the underside.

"This is where passengers will enter." We mounted
the steps into the airship. There was a small platform,
where an elegant aluminum spiral staircase led farther
up. We took it, eventually emerging into a narrow passageway.

"The cabin deck," Antullis explained. "When first
boarding, passengers will be taken directly to their cabins and allowed to settle in. Let's inspect one."

He opened the nearest door, and we went inside. The
three of us—Antullis, me, and Yamina Malik—barely
fit, for it was very compact, more like a sleeper on a
train than the cabin of an ocean liner, but it had been
very neatly fitted out and was well finished. Yamina was
pushed up against me in that confined space, and I had
to concentrate to pay attention to the tour guide.

"It's compact, of course," Antullis said, having read
my mind, "but a thousand times more luxurious than
any airline seat. The real luxury is the fact that it's private." There was a sofa which quickly converted to a
bunk, and above that a second bunk which folded down
from the wall. There was a fold-down table with a fold-
up chair. The bathroom had a sink with a mirror, a
shower, and a head.

What surprised me was the outer bulkhead. It was
transparent, a floor-to-ceiling window.

"I didn't notice any windows in the hull."

"And there aren't any, at least not in the conventional
sense. Let me explain her construction: she is basically
built as a frame covered with cloth. The frame is the primary structural element, the covering is there only to
make her aerodynamic. You would think that when I decided to build this, I would have tapped the aircraft
manufacturing industry for the expertise, but instead I
went elsewhere. Can you guess?"

I already knew, but I answered in the negative.

"I went to the auto racing industry instead. They, too, are of course concerned with maximum strength for the least weight. And I wanted the project to be fast and flexible and to be approached with fresh minds, the way that only a small team can manage, like the XA Corporation had been in the old days, not the fat, ponderous organization that it had become when I left it. So I found a small but well-respected concern right here in Las Vegas that builds racing car bodies and so on. In the end, with a lot of help, it was mainly they who physically built my airship. The frame uses precisely the same structural materials as does a racing car body: primarily light alloys and carbon fiber, but of course on a much larger scale. The exterior is Kevlar covered in a silver metallic coating, as light as could be. Since it isn't structural, I could put in as many windows as I liked, and so I decided to put in masses of them, to make the interior spaces feel open and light-filled, the very opposite of the oppressive darkness you get in an airliner with those wretched tiny windows. The windows are made of a lightweight plastic—same as aircraft windows—but much bigger and covered in a film carefully matched to the silver-coated Kevlar. I wanted the exterior to look as smooth and uncluttered as possible—you can't tell the windows are there unless you look carefully."

We left the cabin and took another spiral staircase up to the deck above, the main deck. Here, the luxury of the airship was self-evident. There were two long promenades running along either side, each of which must have been at least five hundred feet in length, and the spaces separating them were mostly not walled off, but separated by railings, so that no part was excluded from the light that would pour in from outside.

"What do you think?"

"It's magnificent," I admitted, "like an ocean liner. Is this why you became a recluse—to build this?"

He paused before responding. It was the big question,

of course: why had he suddenly decided to become a recluse, all those years ago.

"No," he said at last, "I simply became bored."

"With the life you led?"

"With the life people wanted me to lead. Believe me, Mr. Dalton, there is nothing so burdensome as other people's expectations. Come, let me show you the rest of her."

Antullis took me through the various spaces: a spacious lounge, and nearby that, a cocktail lounge with a long bar, the bulkhead behind which featured black-and-white photographs of zeppelins past. The dining room was stylish, like a fashionable New York restaurant. There was a library, a cinema, a smoking room, and a writing room. The galley was quite small but was ingeniously rigged and full of lightweight cooking appliances. The whole interior was elegant and spare, bereft of needless weight as an aircraft should be, but not at the expense of luxury—the chairs in the lounge were merely bands of leather on aluminum frames but would have passed for high chic in a Manhattan penthouse.

We went through a crew-only door to another section at the back of the ship, where they had their accommodations: cabins for the officers and bunks for the rest, and everyone shared the bathrooms back here.

Despite the vastness of the main deck, so far we had seen but a tiny portion of the interior, a fact which became apparent when Antullis took us into the heart of the airship. Here a gantry led the length of the ship, surrounded on either side by fabric cells fifty feet across, dozens of them, filled with helium, all pressing hard on each other and the frame. Occasionally between these there were smaller bags, which seemed to be weighed down with their contents. I asked Antullis what they were.

"Ballast," he explained. "Strange to say, but we deliberately carry extra weight, tons of it, in fact."

"For what purpose?"

"Two reasons. The first is trim. Although an airship is lighter than air, you only want it to be just lighter than air, otherwise it becomes difficult to control. You take on ballast—water—to trim it out at the beginning of the flight, and we move that around the ship to maintain her trim as the fuel load and fresh water load decreases during the voyage. The second purpose is if we lose lift—that is, if for some reason one or some of the helium cells leaks, and so provides less lift—we can then dump ballast, thus lightening the load to compensate. We use solid ballast for that—lead shot—since we don't have to pump that around like we do the water ballast. Indeed, we anticipate never having to use it at all."

The last stop on the tour was the control station, the only compartment in the great airship which protruded from its gigantic hull. There was a wide control panel full of engineering and system gauges plus controls for the engines. The helmsman had a seat in dead center, with the compass right in front of him and a wheel like the wheel of an airplane, which can be pushed forward or back to decrease or increase altitude. A GPS system plus an independent backup were used for navigation. I looked at some of the gauges.

"The altimeter only goes up to ten thousand feet," I noted.

"She's not pressurized," Antullis responded. "Most of the time she'll cruise at five hundred feet, which sounds a lot but which will feel like it's just above the wave tops to the passengers. The air there will be fresh and moist, not that bone-dry, recirculated stuff they make you breathe in an airliner at thirty thousand feet."

"Five hundred feet is very low. Couldn't a sudden downdraft put her in the drink?"

"She's too big. Even in high winds she remains steady. And during the ocean crossing she'll be on autopilot anyway, constantly monitoring her altitude by radio altimeter. The slightest error will cause her to correct for height above the water." He showed me the device. Unlike conventional altimeters, which rely on changes in barometric pressure to measure altitude, a radio altimeter sends radio waves directly down and measures the time taken for the reflected waves to come back up. Time taken multiplied by the speed of light and divided by two gives you altitude.

"Has she flown yet?" I asked.

"Yes, dozens of test flights," Antullis told me, "but always just in and around Quartz Peak, sufficient to prove that she actually works, and low enough to avoid the requirement for FAA approval. After we announce her to the world tomorrow, I'm going to take her out to the East Coast. We'll do our certification flights there, flying out of Lakehurst to make clear to everyone that this is no *Hindenburg.* I'm planning on taking a party of selected guests—celebrities, politicians, reporters, and so on—on a special flight to celebrate the rebirth of the zeppelin era. I hope that you will join us, Mr. Dalton."

"That's very kind of you. I'd be delighted."

"You have been good enough to share your new toy with me, so it's only fair that I should share my new toy with you." He looked at his watch. "Ah, but it's late now, and since tomorrow's announcement will be the first time I've been seen in public for a good many years, perhaps I should get some sleep."

We disembarked directly from the control room, which had its own separate door and set of wheeled stairs.

"There's one thing you haven't asked me," Antullis said as we got back down to the concrete hangar floor.

"What's that?"

"You haven't asked me what I've called her."

"Of course." It hadn't even occurred to me that she would have a name, but it was unimaginable that she wouldn't. "What is it?"

"I wanted to name her for a president, just as the *Hindenburg* herself had been named for a president, but all the good ones like *George Washington* and *Abraham Lincoln* were already taken by aircraft carriers, and when someone mentions my airship by name, I want there to be no mistaking which behemoth is being referred to. So instead, I decided to name her for some other prominent American—an artist. Can you guess which one?"

"The *Andy Warhol*?"

Antullis laughed. "No, I don't think we're quite ready for that yet." He looked fondly at the great airship. "I named her the *James Whistler.*"

TWENTY-NINE

I ate breakfast on the terrace, watching the sun slowly gather altitude, and considering what I knew. All in all, it seemed that what I knew today was less than what I'd known the day before. At the conclusion of dinner at the oasis, I had come to a fairly certain conclusion that Xerxes Antullis was intending to purchase an atomic weapon for himself, but last night much of the mystery of his cryptic comments and unexplained preoccupation was answered: he had secretly built himself a zeppelin. Apparently unable to retire quietly, the entrepreneur in him had stirred into action, and the fruits of his labors were about to be unveiled to the world. His flamboyant optimism did not seem to me to be the attitude of a man bent on acquiring weapons of mass destruction.

But there was still the fact of the radiation monitoring station. And an enthusiasm for lighter-than-air flight doesn't preclude and enthusiasm for atomic weaponry. Who knows what megalomania goes on in the head of a man who has too much money and too much power and has cut himself off from the real world for the past five years?

And then there was Marty Blankenship. Hired by Yamina Malik, then murdered—crucified—by a man who was very likely ex-Spetsnaz, and who by coincidence was the same man with whom Yamina Malik was somehow involved, sexually or otherwise.

I put aside the remains of breakfast and sat back with coffee.

The press conference at which Antullis would reveal the *James Whistler* to the world was to be held this morning at one of the big casinos in Las Vegas. Bobby Springfield and his crew were going to fly the airship down there, timing the arrival just as Antullis made the announcement. They would return to Quartz Peak, and then start out for Lakehurst first thing the next day. Antullis and his retinue, including me, were going to take the Gulfstream to the East Coast, and then a few days later the *James Whistler*'s big inaugural celebration flight would take place, an overnighter out over the Atlantic and back. The retinue would then return to Quartz Peak with the Gulfstream, leaving the *James Whistler* to complete her flight trails and airworthiness certification before entering passenger service.

The time had come to call Dortmund. I went downstairs, took a golf cart to the airstrip, and checked out the hardware in the automobile collection. That little 250GT California looked like it hadn't had a good run in a while. I took the Ferrari for a test drive up and down the airstrip a few times, enough to be able to handle it safely on a public road, then left Quartz Peak and drove across the twenty miles or so of vacant desert to the lonely gas station that I was getting to know well by now.

With a pocketful of quarters obtained from the clerk, I dialed Dortmund's number. This time I got a live human being; apparently the machine only handled calls over the secure line. She was not pleased when I explained that I was calling from a public phone. Finally Dortmund came on the line.

"Where are you?" he demanded at once.

"Don't you have a dot on the screen showing you?"

"Yes, the dot, as you call it. Well, it might interest you to know, Captain Dalton, that when that dot was inactive for twenty-four hours, I had my people investigate. They eventually found the phone. It was in a Dumpster. Do you have an explanation?"

"I don't work well with people looking over my shoulder," I explained. "Electronically or otherwise."

"Do you have any idea how much those phones cost?"

This concern for the public weal would have been more convincing if it had come from someone who hadn't dismissed a million dollars as "not real money."

"And speaking of which," he added, "we continue to encounter some untoward charges on your American Express card, which as you know was solely intended—"

"Is there any change in the status of the deal?" I interrupted.

"No," Dortmund said reluctantly, unwilling to be diverted from berating me over the American Express bills.

"The money's still not in that account?"

"As far as we know, it is not. Certainly we have not intercepted any claim that it is from the buyers, or request for proof from the sellers."

"That's all I wanted to know, thanks."

I hung up before Dortmund could respond, not wanting to endure a further scolding for my spending habits.

The money hadn't been transferred. That was what mattered. The key to all this was the money—not radiation monitoring stations, not blackmailed heads of security, not hired detectives crucified with nail guns. The money mattered. Real money: not a wire transfer, or an overdraft, or any other accounting transaction representing money, but the thing itself. Real money. Someone had to have $200 million in real money. And who but a billionaire has access to that sort of sum?

I got back into the Ferrari, swung north on the highway, and headed back to Quartz Peak.

I was halfway there when I saw the *James Whistler.* She was a mile or so away, en route to Las Vegas as flying proof of her existence. I pulled the Ferrari over to the side of the road and got out to watch her passage south.

At a distance it didn't give the impression of being especially big, but as the airship got closer, the sheer size of the thing became apparent, and when it passed by, it seemed to fill the sky. She was massive, a great, long, ribbed and tapering cylinder, her sides graduated shades of silver depending on the angle the sunlight struck it, enormous stars and stripes painted on her upper and lower vertical tailfins. She was very low, and I could clearly see the heads of the men in the control station. She was up and gone in a moment, surprisingly fast yet all but silent. I watched her disappear down toward Vegas, changing from silver to dark shadow, then at last no more than a distant smudge on the horizon.

When I returned to Quartz Peak the place was quiet. Although rarely seen in person, the fact of Xerxes Antullis's presence on the estate had been sufficient to animate the atmosphere, and the absence of the master of the house for what was perhaps the first time in five years seemed to have left the place deflated. When I asked Beckett where everyone was, he informed me that the staff were gathering around television sets to watch their boss's performance. The "lady guests," too, he informed me—and I could picture them in their interior courtyard, variously sitting or lying about on pillows in front of the big screen, voluntary prisoners watching their captor on television.

I decided to forgo watching Antullis, and went up to the library instead. The big room was deserted, alcove after alcove of books with museum-quality artworks occupying the wall space separating them. I went to the Whistler, grays and browns with a single slash of silver, muted and controlled on the surface but seething beneath, and I wondered if it was this painting that had inspired the airship's name. It inspired me—I went in search of a book that would tell me something about the man who had painted it.

I had expected to find nothing better than an encapsulated biography in an encyclopedia, but instead I came across Robert Hughes's *American Visions*, a Vasari-like account of American art through to the late twentieth century. I quickly found the section on Whistler. It was brief, but it was enough. It gave an account of his wanderings across Europe, his experiments in Orientalism, and the famous fight with Ruskin. But it also had something I hadn't known. With all his wild ways, Whistler had earned himself a nickname, an equivocal one. He had been known as the Iron Butterfly.

James Whistler was the Iron Butterfly.

I sat there for a long time after this unexpected discovery, book open, staring at but not seeing the painting in front of me, just as I had been when first meeting Xerxes Antullis. For all the effort in the intervening time, I had to admit that I really had not found out much about the man. But there was at least one thing I knew now that I hadn't known before. It was an important thing. Now I knew exactly how the money was being transferred.

THAT evening after the airship had returned, I went back down to the big hangar. It was open now, and people were coming and going, servicing the great airship and making last-minute preparations for the flight to the

East Coast the next morning. The security guard at the airship's stairs was one of Yamina Malik's men, that same ex–gunnery sergeant I'd met at the guardhouse when first arriving at Quartz Peak, and he didn't question my going on board. Once inside I went aft to the crew's quarters, then through to the interior of the vast hull. I took the same route as Antullis had taken last night when conducting the tour, along the gangway past the huge helium-filled cells. This time I paid more attention to the permanent ballast.

Like the helium, the permanent ballast was encased in fabric cells, but much thicker to cope with the weight. They were mounted on tension bars which in turn were attached to the airship's frame with a steel slip. The slip was pinned, and the pins themselves were wired with the ends of the wire joined by a lead seal, ensuring that the ballast could not be dumped by accident. Each tension bar had a large, round meter marked in thousands of pounds, showing the weight of the cell it supported, each one several tons. Below the bags were the trapdoors that would be opened if it ever became necessary to drop the ballast.

There were six permanent ballast cells, three on either side of the airship, and each weighed as much as a large SUV. I stepped off the gangway, onto a cross beam of the airframe, and inched over to the first of the cells. It had an inspection port, a heavy zippered opening that was big enough for a man to crawl through. I unzipped it and leaned inside. It was filled with lead shot, just as Antullis had told me. But when I did the same exercise with the second ballast bag, I saw at once that my guess had been right. There were more bags inside this second ballast bag, maybe a dozen in total, and something else besides: two thirty-man inflatable life rafts. I was used to these from my marine days aboard navy ships, when we would routinely have to carry out abandon ship drills. Warships do not carry lifeboats. Instead they carry these inflatables, packed tight into three-foot-long drums. If the ship sinks, these automatically inflate at a certain depth, then rise to the surface, providing you with a ready-made life raft. Since they carry thirty men, they have enough buoyancy to support several tons.

I knew what the ballast was, but opened one of the bags to make sure. There, immutable and glistening, I found bars of gold. I picked one up, incredibly heavy, and inspected it.

No hallmarks or foundry marks. Nothing which could indicate its origin.

Now I knew with certainty how they were going to transfer two hundred million dollars without leaving a trail. The ballast would be dumped as the airship flew over the Atlantic. It would sink, and then the life rafts would inflate and pull it back to the surface. By that time the airship would be past and clear. No doubt a vessel would be ready nearby to pick it up. And gold is the perfect medium: endlessly meltable and reconstitutable, erasing all serial numbers and all signs of origin but always retaining its value—the one certain way to transfer money untraceably.

THIRTY

THE Antullis party occupied the entire top two floors of the Taj Mahal, a massive and hideously ornate casino giving onto the boardwalk in Atlantic City, New Jersey. All but two of the hotel's elevators had their buttons for the floors disconnected, and those remaining two were guarded around the clock. I wondered if Xerxes Antullis was aware how closely he had emulated Howard Hughes: a fabulously wealthy recluse, who had built the world's biggest aircraft before retreating into the top floor of a casino.

Atlantic City was fifty miles away from the *James Whistler*'s location at the naval air station in Lakehurst, a good hour by car, but only a brief hop in either of the two charter helicopters that Antullis had on standby.

Antullis occupied the hotel's presidential suite on the top floor, along with Sorrel Tyne—the rest of the harem had remained at Quartz Peak, perhaps because bringing all six would have been a distraction, or perhaps in the belief that press coverage which referred in passing to "Mr. Antullis and his companion" would be more dignified than press coverage which dwelled on "Mr. Antullis and his collection of six lithesome females." The rest of the inner circle—Quire, Springfield, Caterno, Yamina Malik—all had suites on the same floor, as did I. The attendant staff—butlers, maids, valets, and even Maria the cook—occupied rooms on the floor below. The aircrew (which had flown out on the airship) and various contractors and ground crew (who had mostly flown out ahead of her on commercial) were accommodated in motels in and around Lakehurst itself.

There was a carnival atmosphere. Xerxes Antullis, after five years of self-imposed isolation, had plunged back into the world with remarkable energy. He gave endless interviews and cocktail parties, escorted politicians and business moguls on tours of the airship, and for the few days before what was to be her official maiden flight I saw little of him.

Eventually the day came. The morning was fine and cloudless, the first warm day of the coming spring, a sure sign of good luck, the locals assured us. The approach roads were crowded with vehicles that had pulled over to the side, and people lined the wire fencing that surrounded the airfield. The general public was not admitted into the air station, but there were a collection of dignitaries and of course the press, the former sitting in tiered seats as if for a parade, the latter behind temporary barriers, cameras mounted and ready, in case by some chance the helium had been mixed up with hydrogen, and they would get the shots that would make their careers.

The star of the show had yet to emerge from the massive hangar that currently housed her. Passengers embarked as they arrived rather than waiting for a formal boarding, another innovation that Antullis had decided upon after long years of frustration in airport lounges. I was still in my cabin when I felt the first sudden jerk of the tractor. We were being towed outside.

I went up to the main deck. In an airplane we would all be strapped to our seats by now, entrapped cheek by jowl for the duration of the journey, but on the *James Whistler* most passengers were standing along the promenade deck, watching the hangar slowly sliding backward as the great airship was towed outside. I recognized one or two: the senior senator from my own home state, a well-known actress enjoying an A.M. cocktail that was obviously not the day's first, the CEO of a software company that had once been a rival of XA's.

We were towed out across the tarmac, facing into the light breeze and well clear of the hangar so as to ensure no contact between it and the airship during takeoff. A band was playing, eager but faintly heard inside the cabin. The engines were started, also surprisingly quiet—in an airship a thousand feet long, they were a long way away. Soon there was the gentlest of shudders, which it took me a moment to realize was the release of the airship from the huge wheeled frame on which she had rested, and whose mass had made her heavier than air. The ground slowly sank away below, and the great airship began to gather way. The crowd cheered and people honked and the band played ever more enthusiastically. Without spilling a drop of the actress's third morning cocktail, the *James Whistler* had become airborne.

WAR is ninety-nine percent boredom and one percent sheer terror, the saying goes. This is largely true, because much of the time is spent waiting. But what the saying doesn't convey is how important that waiting is: waiting for supplies, because soldiers need food in order to fight, waiting for fuel, because tanks need gas in order to move, waiting for ammunition because facing the opposition without bullets is—like putting short in golf—pretty much guaranteed to not succeed.

In marine Force Recon, we didn't wait for food or fuel or bullets. We were trained to carry what we needed and go without all else. If there was no fuel we walked. If there was no ammunition we used knives. And if there was no food, the drill sergeant at special ops school used to tell us, then eat dirt.

Nevertheless, we would still spend hours and hours waiting. We could wait all day under the desert sun, lying down flat, buried in sand, watching opposition tanks and half-tracks and trucks streaming past us, waiting for the one we knew was the staff car. Sometimes it doesn't pay off. I waited two days in a high mountain pass once, just me and my sergeant, snowdrifts coming in but no possibility of a fire or a tent, expecting a tribal guide to come and lead us to a significant target of opportunity. He never showed up. Perhaps it was bad intelligence, or perhaps the target of opportunity took out the tribal guide—we never found out.

The point is this: waiting is part of the game. If you expect to win, then you must be prepared to wait. I knew they weren't going to dump that ballast until nightfall, for there would be too great a risk of it being seen otherwise, and even then they'd probably wait until the early hours of the morning when the passengers were asleep. Nevertheless, by lunchtime I had managed to slip unnoticed through the crew's quarters and into the main hull. I went to the same ballast cell that I'd checked back at Quartz Peak. It was as I'd last seen it. I double-checked the slip and confirmed what I already knew: there was no way to dump that ballast except by physically cutting the wire, removing the pin, then using a hammer to free the bill of the slip from the retaining ring, enabling the ballast to drop free. All I needed was a position that gave me surveillance on that slip.

I looked up. The frame loomed one hundred and fifty feet above me, with the intervening space occupied by the massive helium cells. The vertical beam nearest the gangway had a small series of rungs welded onto the side, a makeshift ladder meant for emergency use if it became necessary to do hull repairs or access the engines during flight. I began climbing.

I needed to be high, so as not to be seen, but not so high that I couldn't get an accurate shot at whoever showed up to release that ballast. At about fifty feet up I took a transverse H-beam out across the ship. The thing was only six inches wide: not good cover and not very comfortable either, but the light was fainter up here, and by leaning into the helium cell that pressed gently up against one side, I could make myself reasonably hard to see.

You can go a long time without food, but you always need water. I had two plastic water bottles with me— one empty, which I would refill with the waste from consuming the first.

Now came the waiting.

I soon learned the inspection routine: a quick walk-through every hour, and each time the crew member doing the rounds walked straight down the main gangway, looking neither left nor right, let alone up. I could have been dancing a jig and they would have missed me.

I had time on my hands and used it to think through the various scenarios that might occur when they came to dump that gold tonight. Many of the scenarios involved me shooting one or more people. It's dangerous to fire a weapon inside an aircraft. Unlike jetliners, at least the *James Whistler* wasn't pressurized: firing a .44 Magnum Anaconda on a jet at 35,000 feet would very likely prove fatal not just to the target but to everyone else on board also. If I'd had a crimping tool I would have removed some of the powder: Magnums have too much punch for the close work I was going to be doing. The rounds were hollow point, at least ensuring that they would flatten on impact, and so lessening the chance of a bullet exiting the other side of the target and damaging things that shouldn't be damaged, especially those helium cells. But if the bullets were cross-scored, they would not only flatten, they would also fragment, and thus be much less likely to exit the target, or less likely to cause collateral damage if they did. I took out the rounds from the Anaconda one at a time, and using my knife I worked two grooves an eighth of an inch deep into the nose.

It was cold where I was hiding. I'd expected that and had put on several layers of clothing in preparation. But I had no gloves, and my fingers were numb, which is probably why I dropped one of the rounds. It rolled off the beam before I could recover it, then went clattering down below, bouncing off a helium cell and landing with a loud, metallic clang onto the gangway. It rolled with the gentle motion of the airship, tinkling across the aluminum. There was no way it would be missed by the next person who came down that gangway. And if they found that bullet, then it wouldn't take them long to find me.

I checked my watch. They did hourly rounds, and the next inspection was due in five minutes. I made sure the weapon was secure, then moved across the beam to the vertical frame member and began the descent. A quick glance up and down at the bottom, checking that the gangway was clear, then I went and recovered the round. I was back at the ladder, ready to go aloft again, when I felt the barrel of a weapon pushed into the back of my head.

"Don't move," Yamina Malik said. I'd guessed it was her before she spoke, recognizing the by-now-familiar imprint of that Gyurza's muzzle in the back of my skull. "Hands on the bulkhead."

Technically it wasn't a bulkhead, but this wasn't the time to argue. She felt around and quickly removed the Anaconda. She found the knife, too. Yamina Malik was brisk and efficient: this wasn't the first time that she'd patted someone down.

She stepped back. "Turn around."

I turned around and immediately glanced at her feet. I'd wondered how I had failed to hear her approach, since I'd been able to hear those crew members on their rounds come thundering down that gangway from well away. Now I saw why: they had been wearing work boots, but Yamina Malik was wearing what looked to be ballet slippers. Above that she wore black leggings and a black turtleneck. With her dark eyes and mass of black hair, she looked like something you'd find in a comic book, mysteriously lurking around Gotham.

"Playing cat burglar?" I asked.

"I knew I shouldn't have trusted you."

"Do you know what's in that ballast cell behind me?"

"Elvis?"

"Yamina—"

"I've been doing background checks on you ever since you mysteriously arrived at Quartz Peak. You don't leave much of a trail, Mr. Dalton, except for one big exception: you were dishonorably discharged from the marines. Several of my staff are ex-marine, and they are—how can I put it kindly—not squeamish. What I'm saying here is that I don't know what it was you did, but to be dishonorably discharged from the marines it would have to have been pretty bad. The truth is, I have no idea who you are or what you're up to, but whatever it is, it's over."

"Marty Blankenship is dead."

She took an involuntary step backward. "How do you know Marty Blankenship?"

"Your friend Vas killed him."

"Killed him?"

"Nailed him to a wall."

"What?"

"He crucified him, Ms. Malik. Literally."

Yamina Malik was a controlled person, a woman always under the command of her own strong will, not given to displays of feeling or temperament. But I'd long ago formed the conclusion that beneath that crust there was a roaring mantle, a swirling lava of hot and often conflicting emotions, something which she probably didn't understand herself, and which she took pains to conceal from others. Not an introspective woman; in fact she was probably as much a stranger to herself as she was to me. But some things, physiological reactions long embedded in the genes, were simply beyond even her considerable control. Like the first crack in the earth of an impending tectonic movement, I saw her dark eyes moisten at the news that Marty Blankenship had been murdered. I was almost shocked by the sight, at the discovery that like me she must have liked the man. Whether from Olympus or the netherworld I didn't yet know, but it turned out that this little goddess was human after all.

"I think it's time we talked."

"You'll be confined to a cabin and kept under guard for the remainder of this flight," she replied. "Talk as much as you want then."

"The private detective you hired has been murdered by the compromiser of your virtue," I said.

"My virtue is fine. I've never had any personal dealings with Vassily Goryakin. Or his friends for that matter."

"The video at the Pantera Club?"

"Pure fiction."

"You invented all that?"

"It was the best I could come up with at the time."

"But why make it up at all?"

"I had to explain what I was doing there when you found me."

"And what were you doing there?"

"Vassily Goryakin was my predecessor, Mr. Dalton. That is, he was the head of security at Quartz Peak before me." She paused a moment to let me absorb this.

I recalled Antullis telling me that the agency had recommended her predecessor because he was so highly trained and experienced in security matters. Not many people are more highly trained than Spetsnaz, and the never-ending Chechen War had given them all the experience they could want, and then some. Yamina continued. "Six months ago Goryakin was fired. Now all of a sudden he resurfaces, just fifty miles away in Las Vegas, ostensibly managing a nightclub, a nightclub that I can tell you is owned by some not very charming people. Here is a man who likely holds a grudge against my employer, a very ugly man, a man who knows the security arrangements at Quartz Peak, and a man with the skills to circumvent them. It's my job to protect Xerxes Antullis. I take my job seriously, Mr. Dalton, and I was certainly not prepared to just sit back and hope that Vassily Goryakin's suddenly showing up in Las Vegas was simply a benign coincidence. I hired Marty Blankenship—anonymously—specifically to get me access to Goryakin's office. He did so. I broke in there to find out what he was up to. The rest I think you know."

Now I understood the presence of those financial statements on top of Goryakin's filing cabinet. And the wig made sense: she would not have wanted Goryakin to recognize her when reviewing the club's security tapes after his office was broken into. Yamina's Gyurza was explained, too: Goryakin would have selected it when he was head of security, since it was a weapon he was familiar with, but having been paid for by Antullis, it would have remained behind after he was dismissed.

So it seemed that whatever was going on, the woman standing before me wasn't part of it.

"Yamina, listen to me a moment. There's something you don't know about." She looked doubtful, but at least she wasn't shooting me. "What's the old ammunition dump used for?"

"Nothing."

"No, not nothing. There's some equipment down there."

"Okay, so not quite nothing," she admitted with a shrug. "There's a radiation monitoring station." It might have been a garden shed, for all the importance she attached to it.

"Doesn't the presence of a radiation monitoring station strike you as a little odd?"

"No."

"No?"

"Mr. Dalton, do you know who Xerxes Antullis's neighbor is?"

"Neighbor? He doesn't have any."

"Yes he does: the federal government. All the land to the west of Quartz Peak is owned by the federal government. Do you know what it's used for?"

"No."

"It's the Nevada Test Site, Mr. Dalton. Since the 1950s there have been more than eight hundred tests conducted there. That's eight hundred nuclear explosions, and not all of them underground. Of course there's a radiation monitoring station. Everyone who lives out there has one." She gestured with the Gyurza. "Enough talk. Get moving."

It had to be a coincidence. Or perhaps Antullis had been planning for this all along, deliberately going into seclusion by an atomic facility in the hope that any telltale rise in radiation levels from his own activities would be attributed instead to the test range. But having just played my best card and lost, none of this was going to sound convincing to Yamina right now. I turned and began walking back down the gangway.

WHEN we entered the control room, two faces turned to us, simultaneously registering astonishment when they saw that Yamina Malik was holding a weapon on me. Bobby Springfield was sitting in the captain's chair, and standing beside him was Dennis Quire. The controls themselves were unmanned, running as she was on autopilot.

"What on earth—" Springfield began to say.

"I found Mr. Dalton in the hull," Yamina said. "He was carrying this." She pulled out the Anaconda from her belt. "I suggest that he be confined to a cabin under guard for the remainder of the flight. When we land he can be escorted away."

Springfield reached for a communications handset. "Dennis, take charge of that weapon," he instructed. "I'm going to have two men come down. Mr. Dalton, you will consider yourself under arrest for the remainder of the time you are aboard my airship." But as Quire relieved Yamina of the Anaconda, Springfield slowly replaced the handset without having spoken into it. I could see the expression on his face change, and all of a sudden I knew what was coming, but before I could say anything I heard the familiar metallic click of the Anaconda's hammer being cocked to the rear.

I turned around. Quire was holding the weapon to Yamina's head.

"I'll take this one, too," he said, gently removing the Gyurza from her hand. Yamina looked one part amazed and nine parts angry. "Now, if you'd be so good as to move forward, Ms. Malik. I wouldn't want you to be tempted to try to disarm me." Apparently Quire considered her a more dangerous presence than me. He was probably right. She pushed past me to the front control panel. Springfield nodded over his shoulder. "Dennis, lock that door, will you?"

Quire locked the rear door connecting the control room with the remainder of the *James Whistler*, all the while keeping the Anaconda on Yamina and me.

"Of course, the ballast," I said. "How could ballast be dropped without the complicity of the captain?"

"Actually it could be," Springfield replied, "but it wouldn't be easy."

"What's going on here?" Yamina demanded.

"Why don't you tell her, Mr. Dalton? You seem to know what's happening."

I had nothing else to do right now, so I turned to Yamina and began the explanation. "There's gold bullion in the ballast," I said. "Several tons of it."

"What?"

"They're taking it offshore, moving it secretly so that it can't be traced."

She looked at Quire with enough contempt to have flattened most men. "You're stealing from Xerxes Antullis?"

"Merely borrowing," Quire said. "The gold will be used as collateral for another transaction."

"What transaction?"

"A profitable one, I trust. After so many years of working for one of the world's richest men, I've become rather accustomed to the trappings of wealth. I intend to retain those trappings when I retire, which I expect to do in the very near future now. Mr. Antullis's gold will be safely returned, with no one any the wiser. At least, that would have been the case before you and the somewhat curious Mr. Dalton interfered." While Quire was speaking I felt Yamina's gentle but deliberate pressure on my left arm. I briefly looked down and saw immediately what it was she was willing me to see: her fingers were on the radio altimeter dial, set at hip level between us. The other two couldn't see what she was doing. "It would have all gone so smoothly if stupid Vas hadn't gone and started stealing XA's damned coins," Quire continued. "I'll never understand what he could have been thinking of, jeopardizing a plan whose stakes were a thousand times greater than a few bits of old tin." There are certain men who just can't forgo any opportunity to enumerate the injustices they suffer—real or imagined—and Quire was one of them. While he delivered this monologue of complaints, I could tell in my peripheral vision that the airship had begun to gradually descend. Apparently Yamina had lowered the altitude setting, so that under autopilot the great airship was gently losing altitude. Since Springfield was facing back toward us, he hadn't yet realized it, and Quire was too far to the rear of the control room to notice. "Of course the idiot got himself fired. What a fool. By then we'd invested too much work and too much planning to drop the whole thing. When you got hired we briefly contemplated cutting you in, you know—it would have been so much easier if XA's head of security was with us—but in the end we figured you just wouldn't go for it."

"You were right," she said. "I wouldn't have gone for it at all."

I resisted the urge to glance out the windows, but I could sense that we were much lower now, closer to the water. I wondered exactly what it was that Yamina had in mind—if the airship ditched we'd all be in trouble.

"Well, no matter," said Quire. "I knew from the beginning you were going to be trouble, Mr. Dalton. I had hoped to shoot you as an intruder that night in the hangar, an event which would also have conveniently kept Ms. Malik occupied as she sorted it out with the authorities." He raised the Anaconda. "Never mind. You two are a problem, but a problem that can now be—"

He was interrupted by a loud alarm that suddenly started sounding in the control panel, presumably a low-altitude alarm. Springfield turned around and immediately saw that his airship was just above the water. His hands went automatically to the controls, and he pulled back on the wheel, taking over from the autopilot and pitching the airship nose up. The sudden urgent change in trim knocked Quire clean off his feet. Yamina instantly leaned across me and opened the door leading outside. A great rush of air came into the cabin, and the noise of the engines and airstream filled the control room.

"Jump," Yamina urged.

"You're kidding."

"Trust me." Without further word she pushed past me and leapt out of the airship. It didn't seem like a very good idea to me, but there are times to think and times to act. This was a time to act.

I took two quick steps and followed her out into the void.

THIRTY-ONE

I'VE jumped out of aircraft before. This was the first time I'd done it without a parachute. Although we were at low altitude, *low* is a relative term. What is low for an airship can be high for a human being. I judged that we were at least fifty feet above the waves, perhaps as much as a hundred. People commit suicide leaping off bridges at that height.

The immediate task was to set for entry. Feetfirst—hitting the water headfirst from that height would be fatal. Important not to be too stiff, in particular to keep the knees slightly bent, so as to avoid a compression fracture of the spine. I hit the water hard but clean, and went plunging down deep. I had no idea if I was injured; the adrenaline coursing through my veins now would have covered all but the most catastrophic of problems.

It took forever to get back to the surface, as is often the case with a free dive: you keep going up and up, getting closer and closer to the light, but just when you think you're there, the top always seems to recede. At last I came through and gasped for the air that had seemed would never come.

I gradually caught my breath. The adrenaline died down, and I began to feel the cold of the water. It was fine at the moment, even refreshing, but that would soon turn to a bone-numbing chill. Hypothermia would eventually set in several hours from now.

I spotted the *James Whistler*, stern to, disappearing from view, already not much more than a dot on the horizon.

A sea surface which had seemed flat from the airship was actually choppy when you were immersed in it, but at least there were no whitecaps. A long Atlantic swell rolled in from the northeast. When up on a crest of the swell I looked around, searching for any shipping that might through some amazing piece of good luck be headed this way, but the only thing I saw was Yamina Malik, bobbing in the water about a hundred yards distant. I swam over and returned to treading water about twenty feet away.

"Well, this is nice," I said.

"Better than getting shot."

"Drowning is better than getting shot? Debatable, don't you think?"

She didn't immediately reply, and I wasn't feeling that chatty myself, so we treaded water in silence. I kept looking around the horizon, hoping for a miracle.

"Is there anything you want to tell me?" she asked after a while.

"No."

Pause. "Do you like me?"

"No."

Another pause. "Not even a little?"

"No, not at all."

"Okay." She turned away.

It occurred to me that, since we were about to perish, I could have been a little more generous.

"You have courage," I said.

She turned back to face me. "Go on."

"Most women—most people for that matter—are easily frightened. Not just physically, I mean frightened in general. Scared of doing things. I don't think that's you. I don't think you're frightened by life."

"What else?"

What else. "Well, I think you're pretty stubborn."

"Is that a good thing?"

"It can be. In your case I think it is. It's the flip side of strength of character. You have determination. Strong will. You'll never be anyone's doormat."

"What else?"

More what else. "You move very gracefully."

Yamina didn't seem too impressed with this. "That's like telling a girl she has nice hair," she said.

"What do you mean?"

"It's the sort of thing people say to unattractive girls because they can't think of anything good to say."

"You're not unattractive."

"No?"

"No. Just the opposite."

"Then you think that I'm attractive?"

She looked at me eagerly for the answer, and suddenly there was the woman as she must have been as a child, face scrunched up with the serious curiosity that only little girls can muster, a question asked and ever so anxious for an unqualified answer, but already suspecting the tangential response of an adult unwilling or without the time to give a straight reply. I could picture her as she must have been at six or seven years old, skinny and gangly, all arms and legs not yet brought to grace, tall for her age, full of life and a growing intelligence that would have cleaved ever wider that separation from other little girls that her distinctive looks and strange name must have already begun.

"Yes, I think you're attractive."

"How?"

How. I tried hard to find a reply. "You have nice arms," I said eventually.

"Arms?" She held one up out of the water and examined it critically herself.

"They're long and slender, but strong, too. I noticed when we were shooting."

She twisted her arm at the wrist, first one way and then the other, then let it fall back to the water without comment.

"What else?"

Another what else. I was starting to wish she'd hurry up and drown. "Your skin," I said.

"What about it?"

"It's smooth and brown."

"You haven't said anything about my face."

"You have a beautiful face," I said. "More than just beautiful. You can see your character in your face: intelligent and alert, strong-willed, good-hearted. I like your face immensely."

"Do you love me?"

What a question. I tried to form a response. "I think that any man with a brain in his head and blood in his veins who knew you and wasn't at least a little in love with you would be either a fool or a liar. I am neither."

She considered this awhile, then nodded to herself, apparently having come to the conclusion that the reply was satisfactory. Then she ducked her head into the water, as if doing a tumble turn in the pool, and emerged from the somersault with something in her hand. It was a black plastic or metal device, about the size of a remote control. She held it up to the sky.

"What's that?" I asked.

"Communications uplink," she replied matter-of-factly.

"What are you doing?"

"Finding the satellite."

"What satellite?"

"The one that will relay our position to shore and send someone to pick us up."

"You had that all along?"

"Of course," she said with a nod. "I'd have been pretty stupid to have jumped out of the airship without this." She turned her attention from the uplink to me. "And as you've just told me, I'm not stupid. In fact I'm intelligent. And courageous. And attractive. And I have nice arms, too."

THE chopper arrived thirty minutes later. It was an old SH-3 in Coast Guard colors: white with a diagonal orange stripe across the fuselage. The winchman lowered the wire, and I showed Yamina how to get inside the strap and give the thumbs-up sign when ready for the ascent. Soon we were both inside the aircraft. We were given blankets and coffee in a thermos, but Yamina declined the latter, instead going forward to talk to the pilots. After a few minutes one of them handed her a headset, and she was soon talking on the radio, although I could hear nothing of what she was saying above the noise of the engines. Eventually she handed back the headset. After a short exchange with the captain, the helicopter banked and turned to a new heading. The winchman was called forward, too, and soon all four of them were in conference, leaving me with the coffee and a feeling that all was not well. This feeling was confirmed when the winchman came back aft and handed me a life jacket.

"You'll need this, sir."

"Why?"

"We're dropping you back into the sea."

"What?"

"We don't have enough fuel to loiter, sir. So we're going to drop you here for the rendezvous."

"What rendezvous?"

"*USS Sioux Falls*. She'll be taking you two from here."

"How come?"

"Don't know, sir. The lady arranged it."

FOR the second time in the same day I wound up bobbing in an empty ocean. At least this time I had a life jacket. There was no sign of the *USS Sioux Falls*, or any other ship. The helicopter had long since disappeared. The only thing visible besides endless water and endless sky was Yamina Malik. There hadn't been the time to question her when we'd been making hurried preparations in the helicopter. Now there was all the time in the world.

"What are we doing here?" I asked.

"You know what we're doing," Yamina replied. She looked at her watch. "Our ride will be here any minute."

"I doubt it. The horizon's empty." But before she could respond, the water around us began to well up. The current gradually increased, and it was soon bubbling furiously, as if the sea was boiling, although there had been no change in temperature. Then I felt a giant upsurge of icy cold water from below. A moment later, not more than a hundred feet away, a great black-hulled submarine broke through the surface. It seemed that the *USS Sioux Falls* was right on time after all.

THIRTY-TWO

"**OKAY,** who are you?" I asked the woman sitting across the table from me.

We were alone in the submarine's wardroom. They'd picked us up in a Zodiac, brought us on board the *Sioux Falls*, and hurried us down through the sail into the control room, where we were greeted by the captain—Commander Walt Stevenson—and several of his officers. Stevenson had explained that he needed time to dive his boat and set a course, time that we might like to use getting a hot shower and dry clothes before we all sat down to talk. Yamina and I were alone now, drinking coffee brought by a steward. Yamina was dressed in a working uniform whose name tag proclaimed it as the property of a man called Everett, a sonar technician rated petty officer second class, and from the way the clothes fit Yamina, he had probably been ordered to hand over his rig because he was the skinniest guy on board.

I'd been given khakis belonging to one of the lieutenants. Twin bars, like the marine captain's twin bars that had been removed from me after my court-martial.

Yamina and I had already discussed what had gone on aboard the *James Whistler*, coming to the obvious conclusion that Quire, Springfield, and Goryakin had conspired to steal from their employer. Now it came time to lay our own cards on the table.

"You first," Yamina replied.

There was no point in arguing precedence. I gave an abbreviated account of how I had come to be involved, ending with an emphasis as to why it was so urgent that we intercept the gold.

"You say it's going to be used to buy plutonium?"

"So I'm told."

"Who told you?"

"A man by the name of Dortmund."

"Is this Dortmund in a position to know?"

"I presume so. I've never been explicitly told exactly what his job is, but he's obviously part of the national intelligence community, and he's a big shot."

Yamina mulled on this in silence for a while.

"Your turn," I prompted.

She nodded her head, took a deep breath, and began the explanation. "Before joining Mr. Antullis, I used to work for the Secret Service," she said. "It was probably the reason he hired me. It's hard to have better security credentials than Secret Service training."

"Especially for personal security."

"Yes, but the truth is I was never part of a personal security detail. The Secret Service is really two organizations. There's the one that everybody knows about: the people who protect the president and so on. But the other side of it is actually the Service's original function: to protect U.S. financial interests. That's why the Secret Service is part of the Treasury Department. Our job is to protect government financial instruments from abuse."

"And you worked in this second part of the organization?"

"I still do."

"Still do?"

"My resignation after Antullis hired me was for show only. I was asked to apply for the job in order to get inside Quartz Peak. From time to time Xerxes Antullis takes very large positions in U.S. government-issued debt instruments. When one person owns a lot of a particular issue, we worry: they have the market cornered, and so can manipulate the price of the issue by restricting its liquidity. Take treasury futures, for example. When the futures settle, the sellers have the option of delivering from a basket of underlying physical securities. Of course they will always deliver whichever is the cheapest, and so futures pricing is based on this assumption. But what if the cheapest was owned, or mostly owned, by just one person? He could refuse to sell at fair market value. Suddenly the futures will be priced off-market, because the owner refuses to sell. It's called a liquidity crunch, and it's something we can't allow: it injures market confidence and increases the risk premium charged on U.S. debt. There has been no direct evidence of Antullis doing it, but he's one of the few individuals in the world who has regularly been in a position to do so. My job was to find out why."

"Did you?"

"No, it seems that he makes trades solely based on the expectation of getting a return on his investment, the same as everyone else does. He just does it on a much bigger scale."

"What if the trades were hidden?"

"What do you mean?"

"There were orders in that offshore account I told you about, large ones. Do you know what a CUSIP is?"

"Of course—standard issue identifiers in the securities industry. Do you remember what they were?" From her tone she obviously expected the answer to be negative.

"I do. It's easy because they all start with 912828."

"U.S. government notes," she said, obviously recognizing the numbers. "So Quire and the others were going to use the gold to buy treasuries."

"And sell."

"What?"

"Some of the orders were to sell, not buy."

"Spread trades," Yamina explained. "Looking for the price spreads between securities to narrow or widen." She was obviously familiar with the arcane world of securities trading, which is an impenetrable forest to me. "What were the other characters in the CUSIPs?"

I told her. I could tell before she responded that Yamina knew the issues.

"They were shorting fixed-rate bonds, and going long those whose returns are indexed to inflation," she said. "In other words, they were taking a big bet on inflation going up." She sat back and considered this in silence.

Apparently Quire and his associates had decided to do a little trading with Antullis's money while waiting for the plutonium sale to go through. Perhaps they were reckoning on the sale igniting a Middle Eastern war, the threat of nuclear weapons in which would surely drive the price of oil through the roof, and inflation along with it.

Commander Stevenson walked into the wardroom. He didn't look happy.

"We're at two hundred and fifty feet, just under the thermocline," he said. "We're on a course of zero-nine-zero at twelve knots. That—along with an order to 'facilitate with all haste operations as directed by Ms. Malik'—is the extent of what I know." He looked directly at Yamina. "Would you care to fill me in on exactly what those operations might be, ma'am?"

I'd known officers like this one before—good men who did their duty well but who are too easily exasperated by sudden changes to those duties, especially when the reason for the change hasn't been spelled out. We tried to avoid recruiting them in Force Recon—special operations are by their nature unpredictable, and men who can't adapt on the fly are not suited.

"Commander," I said before Yamina could respond, "if you can provide us with a chart and instruments, we'll be happy to show you exactly what it is that we need from you." Stevenson looked at me and smiled. It was exactly what he wanted: to be clearly told what was expected of him, and then allowed to get on and do it.

He reached for a mike and called the control room. A few minutes later, the three of us were huddled over a chart. As time passed we were joined by two more of the submarine's officers, and then later by some of her crew. The submarine transmitted various radio signals ashore, including one from Yamina to her bosses, telling them what was going on, and one from me to Dortmund performing a similar function. By six that evening we had finalized the planning and preparations.

It was dark outside now—actually it was permanently dark outside the *Sioux Falls*, 250 feet under the surface of the ocean—but it would also be getting dark now in the vicinity of the *James Whistler*, currently flying some 500 feet above it. It was also permanently dark 22,500 miles farther above the airship, well into space, where a RORSAT—radar ocean reconnaissance satellite—sitting in geosynchronous orbit above the North Atlantic, was currently tracking the *James Whistler* and relaying the data back to the submarine. According to the latest report, she was about 150 miles away from our position, but there was no rush. The surveillance data confirmed what the airship's flight plan had already suggested: she was heading our way.

There was nothing further for us to do now but wait. In the wardroom we ate dinner in a silence which to me was familiar, but which obviously puzzled the ship's officers. Their natural conviviality soon faded, and eventually the only activity was the coming and going of the steward, the scrape of silverware on plates, and the frequent curious but poorly concealed glance at Yamina. I wondered what they thought of her, hunched down over her food, deeply closed in now, utterly unapproachable. I didn't need to wonder what they thought of me: the seat next to mine was the last to be occupied, by a young second lieutenant coming in late off the last dog watch, nervously rushing his food and eating his bread plain rather than asking me to pass the butter. Did I really look so terrible? I supposed that I did.

To their relief we finished the meal and excused ourselves, and I could hear the quiet murmur of conversation anxiously renewed as we went down the passageway. Yamina had been given use of the captain's cabin, I had the executive officer's. We parted without ceremony: a nod of acknowledgment; should get sleep while we can.

I did sleep, but not before sitting at the executive officer's desk for half an hour, going through yet again the sequence of upcoming events as I imagined they would unfold, the contingencies for equipment failure or missed rendezvous or bad intelligence and so on. At special operations school they taught us the six Ps: *"prior preparation and planning prevents poor performance,"* and as corny as it was, the phrase was a useful one: no operation ever goes according to plan, but the better you've prepared, the better you adapt.

It wasn't late when I went to sleep, but it seemed only a moment before there was a sailor in the cabin shaking me awake. "It's zero one hundred, sir—ah, one o'clock. Captain's compliments, and the target has been located."

THIRTY-THREE

SUBMARINES don't see, they listen. In the early nineteenth century the French mathematician Fourier discovered that noise—that is, any seemingly random matrix of volume and frequency—could be decomposed into a finite set of sine waves. That's what the *Sioux Falls* was doing now: listening to the noise of the ocean on her passive sensors, and her computers were using Fourier analysis to break it down into component parts that had allowed the submarine to find, amid the mass of sounds reverberating through the sea, the telltale signs of the surface ship which we had known would have to be there to pick up the gold.

In the control room, after a quick briefing by the captain, a sonar technician showed me the results on his waterfall display: the line that was her single shaft rotating at 140 rpm, and the second line at five times that frequency, which told him that she had a five-bladed propeller. Above that a sixty hertz line: her power supply was sixty cycle, he told me, not fifty cycle like ours—obviously foreign. A chugger, he called her, steam rather than diesel, old-fashioned and slow, her bearings worn and her shaft slightly bent.

We already knew she was slow: that satellite had given us data on every ship in a hundred nautical mile radius, and it had only been this one, well out of the shipping lanes and barely making ten knots, whose course and speed took her anywhere near the *James Whistler*'s flight path. Not just anywhere near, but on a direct intercept with the airship, which made sense: double-buoyed or not, you wouldn't want to risk leaving $200 million floating in the ocean for long.

A signalman brought a message to the captain, which he quickly read before passing to me. "Looks like that's your ship."

I read the signal, barely legible in the red night lighting of the control room. The *SS Alaric* had sailed from Boston two days ago, bound for Road Town, BVI. She was a tramp steamer of 2,780 tons, an old tub of 1950s vintage that worked the less prosperous routes of the Caribbean. She was registered in Panama to an enterprise called GKD Shipping, whose ownership was unclear. The ship had a colorful history, including having been twice impounded pending the payment of fines for "undeclared cargo." In other words, her captain and crew were not averse to the occasional bit of smuggling.

I passed the signal to Yamina, who had arrived in the control room shortly after me. "That's got to be the one."

"Crew of sixteen, plus four officers," she said. "That's less than we thought."

With the two crewman from the *Sioux Falls* who would accompany Yamina and me, that would make the odds five-to-one against us. That sounds bad, but we would be well armed and have the element of surprise. Five-to-one against were better odds than I was used to.

The *Sioux Falls* had masts with radar, but Stevenson was disinclined to use them, having an old submariner's dislike of showing anything above the surface that could be detected by the target, and a particular concern that either the steamer or the airship might have embarked radar detection equipment, wanting to ensure that in the dark there was no vessel in the vicinity of the transfer to witness it, or worse, recover it for themselves. In any case, we had the satellite, and we already knew that the *James Whistler* was close by.

Then the sonar technician suddenly cried out, "Explosion bearing three-zero-five," immediately followed by "Second explosion, also three-zero-five."

The captain answered our puzzled looks. "The life rafts inflating," he explained. "Those things suddenly popping sound like an explosion underwater." The *James Whistler* had released the ballast.

"Target 2603 increasing revolutions." The control room of the *Sioux Falls*, which until now had been quiet, burst into life. The plot was surrounded by officers as bearings and cross-bearings were made to build up a picture following the *Alaric*'s sudden increase in speed, and the sonar technician was now giving a steady commentary on everything he was hearing, including what he took to be the start-up of a diesel that the officers concluded would be a generator to power the derrick that would be hauling the three tons of gold on board. The captain maneuvered the submarine to keep us bearing south of the steamer, ensuring that when she got underway again after recovering the ballast, the *Sioux Falls* would lie between her and her destination.

I turned to Yamina. "Time to get ready, I think." She nodded, and we went back to "officers' country," the area of the wardroom and officers' cabins on board a warship. A submarine is built in a series of watertight compartments, with each bulkhead pierced by a hatchway which can be sealed off with a heavy door as needed. With Yamina leading the way, I saw that she had already mastered the art of traversing these, placing her hands on the top combing and then swinging both her long legs through in a single fluid motion, without a pause in her pace, as if she had been living on submarines since she was a child.

Our gear was in the executive officer's cabin. I had expected Yamina to take hers back to her own cabin to change, but instead she simply turned her back to me and wordlessly began unbuttoning Petty Officer Everett's shirt, apparently intending to strip down right there and then. I politely turned away and got on with my own business, but after a period punctuated with ever-increasing grunts of exasperation from behind me, she spoke up.

"Can you help me?"

I turned around. When we'd picked out our wet suits from the submarine's diving locker earlier that day, Yamina had naturally chosen the smallest size. But although the smallest size suited her diameter just fine, it was obviously meant for someone much shorter. Yamina had successfully gotten the bottom part on, if having the wet suit's legs pulled halfway up your calves could be called successful, and she had her arms in the sleeves behind her, but in that awkward position she apparently lacked the strength—or the neoprene lacked the stretch—to pull the suit all the way up. She stood looking over her shoulder at me, her long back bare and glowing with a fine sheen of sweat from her efforts, her arms still in the suit behind her.

"Turn around," I said.

Yamina did nothing for a moment, and for perhaps thirty seconds we stood there mute and immobile. Then she turned around.

She was naked down to the bottom of the wet suit's zipper, which was open low below her belly button. With her arms still behind her Yamina's torso was stretched back, flattening her small taut breasts, emphasizing the fine slender line of her body, a line which between short rapid breaths fell almost dead straight until reaching the gentle inward curve at the waist. Her stomach was a flat plane. Her nipples were dark brown and hard tight. A faint undulation ran up and down her long neck as she swallowed. Her mouth was open slightly, and her eyes were unblinkingly on mine.

I stepped up and tore the wet suit from her body.

THE four of us gathered in the torpedo room, the compartment right at the front of the submarine, a big space filled with racks of the *Sioux Falls'* main weaponry. I had been in submarines before—they are a favorite method of achieving a covert insertion by sea—and knew that the torpedo room, with its expanses of unobstructed deck plating required for maneuvering the huge weapons, is the only place on a submarine with any decent space, and so it is the best venue to gather the troops for a preop briefing.

Yamina looked at the torpedoes with amazement. Torpedoes are much bigger than people imagine them to be, eighteen-foot-long monsters that weigh more than most cars, sitting in great cast metal racks with steel bands locking them in. She was looking at a Mark 48 ADCAP—advanced capability—a wire-guided weapon that could be driven onto the target by an operator on the submarine, using a joystick to send guidance signals down the miles of thin copper wire reeled out during the weapon's run. For the final phase the torpedoes are equipped with their own sonar, and the last thing the crew of the target would ever hear would be the reducing ping interval as the weapon—locked on and closing—inevitably drives in. The weapons were spotlessly clean, and not the bare metal you might expect but instead were painted a deep and lustrous green. Many of them were not torpedoes, but encapsulated Harpoon antishipping missiles or Tomahawk cruise missiles that are launched underwater through the torpedo tubes and, despite such an unnatural beginning for something meant to fly, can subsequently travel fifteen hundred miles and still go through the target's front door with absolute and unveering accuracy.

The other two people in our foursome were crew members. I had asked only that they be certified ship's divers, and volunteers. Real volunteers, I insisted, not the navy's version of volunteers, which are the sailors the senior noncoms order to put up their hands when volunteers are called for. Stevenson assured me that all twelve of the crew who were eligible had volunteered, and he had selected the two he'd most trust to back him up if things were on the line.

One was an eager Midwesterner by the name of Zborowski, and the other a gap-toothed Louisiana Creole who introduced himself as Antowaine, although whether this was his first or last name I wasn't sure. Both were E-2s and both too young for this sort of thing, which made me wonder less about them than their skipper's judgment. I wished that I had just picked from the volunteers myself. I told the black guy we'd call him Alpha and the white guy we'd call him Zulu, figuring that matching the first letter of their names was probably the easiest way for them to remember their call signs, and the coincidental alphabetical separation didn't hurt, either. I put myself and Yamina right between them: Mike One and Mike Two.

First task: equipment check. We were all suited up, suffocating in our black neoprene sheaths, but I knew they'd be grateful for that layer of warm sweat when we hit the water. Neoprene shoes which we'd stick with on board the *Alaric*, and flippers over the top, which we'd discard for the boarding. Diving watches, which we synchronized to 2:47 A.M.—time had raced by.

We each had a waterproof pack. Zulu carried one of the grappling hooks in his, I had the other. Alpha took the satellite uplink for communication with the submarine. Nightsticks and flashlights. Handcuffs for the *Alaric*'s crew. Flares, EPIRBs, and a handheld GPS if things went bad.

Weapons check. Diving knives in ankle sheaths. Beretta M9s—the military version of the Beretta 92F: standard navy-issue 9mm automatic pistols with fifteen-round magazines. The actions were stiff from lack of use. Normally officers and radio operators carry sidearms only, but in small special ops units there's no room for daintiness, and so along with the others I also carried an M-4 assault rifle, the special operations version of the M-16, with a collapsible buttstock and a big thirty-round clip, the same weapon that I had carried on dozens of ops in the past. I cradled mine like the old friend that it was, and took them through the drill: cocking handle to the rear then release, fire selector to full auto, small bursts only. No spare magazines: we were already carrying a lot of weight for a freeboard assault, and three of the four attempting it had never done one before. Besides, 120 rounds of high-velocity 5.56mm FMJ should be more than sufficient to deal with an unarmed tramp steamer crew in a surprise assault in the middle of the night.

We put on face black. Antowaine didn't really need it for color, but I made him apply it: his skin was shiny and would have reflected light. Yamina was brown enough to have gotten away without it, but she was still radiant, so I smeared some on her anyway, and hoped that the others were too young to yet know what that glow on a woman's face meant.

THE submarine had not put to sea expecting to support special operations, and so there was a lot of equipment I would have liked that she simply didn't have. There were no personal communication units. There was no body armor. No sound suppressors. For night ops our M4s were usually fitted with AN-PVS4s—short, fat, night vision devices mounted on the rail above the receiver in place of the carrying handle—but the gunner's mate had never heard of them. There were no diving boards either: on an underwater assault you carry a diving board to navigate to the target, and the embedded compass would have been helpful tonight. Another gap was grenades—I'd never done an operation without carrying at least some high explosive—but when I'd asked about them the gunner's mate had offered an alternative from his magazine inventory: underwater signal charges. These are used for basic communication between a submarine and a surface ship, he explained, loud underwater explosions that can't be missed, and which is one way a submarine warns that she's about to surface. They could be launched from underwater through a tube built for the purpose, or on the surface by hand, with a pinned lever assembly like a grenade. The casing was simple metal like a cookie tin, so there would be none of that fragmentation that makes grenades so effective, but they weighed two pounds, and two pounds of TNT makes a big bang. I took a pair, plus detonators and fuse if I needed to delay the explosion.

We went through the drill one last time. Yamina knew it by heart, but the other two needed all the repetition they could get. We would separate into two teams for the insertion phase. Alpha was the stronger and less dull of the pair, so I put him under Yamina's command. Zulu, a well-meaning but slow-witted kid, I would keep with me.

I finished the briefing and the drills. It wasn't ideal, but it was as good as we were going to get tonight. I walked over to the squawk box mounted on the bulkhead, depressed the button for the control room, and told them that we were ready when they were.

THIRTY-FOUR

A three-quarter moon sent a sliver of silver over the surface of the water, and at the edge of it the *Alaric* was visible, hull up, perhaps just a mile away now. Zulu and I could see her steaming light and port navigation light, bright white abaft and above, duller red forward and below. Whatever his shortcomings, Stevenson was a good seaman: he had calculated the *Alaric*'s course precisely, and twenty minutes earlier had dropped us into the sea with such accuracy that both her navigation lights had been visible, meaning that she was exactly head on to us. Now, two hundred feet of float line to the west, I hoped that Yamina and Alpha were seeing the same thing as us, except that in their case the color of the navigation light should be green. The only risk now was that the *Alaric* would alter course, but merchantmen rarely alter course in the open ocean.

She came on, and soon changed from a distant shape into a massive, looming presence bearing down on us. Inconsequential tramp streamer she might be, but to the four heads bobbing in the ocean that night she was suddenly a roaring immensity, bow wave flowing, engines throbbing, her monstrous passage threatening to engulf us, anonymous and unknowing, sweeping us under into her churning screw.

The float line caught. I had drilled into the other three that what followed would be unpleasant, but even I was surprised by the sudden pull, squeezing the breath from the body, sharp enough to crack a rib. Although we knew that she was only making ten knots, it was like a water skier suddenly entangled in the rope with the speedboat unnoticing, dragging us through the water, under it mostly, twisting uncontrollably, with the occasional short lurch above the surface and the accompanying opportunity to snatch a quick breath.

We hit the side, a sharp, hard thump into solid steel plate. I could make out Zulu, six feet away where he, too, was connected to the float line currently snagged on the *Alaric*'s bow. I could tell nothing of his condition, and the roaring rush of water flowing past made communication impossible, but I had the sense that he had not done well in the ordeal, and might not even be conscious. I ignored him for now and instead retrieved the grappling line, set my feet to give some angle from the ship's side, then made a toss. It caught on first try. The plan was for me to go first and secure the deck, but if Zulu was in trouble, he might need to get up sooner.

I released and moved down the float line. He was dead. I had no idea how—perhaps the harsh blow that I'd received to the shoulder when hitting the ship's side he had instead taken to the head. Or maybe he'd simply drowned. Human beings are astonishingly fragile, so very easy to kill.

I took his backpack, left the body attached so that the drag would counteract the weight of Yamina and Alpha on the other side, then made the ascent. In my marine days rarely a week would go by without doing a combat course, which usually includes rope climbs. The technique—twisting the rope around the back of one leg and over the foot, using the other foot to jam it, and thence doing the climbing with the legs rather than arms—was second nature, but even so that thirty feet or more of freeboard was a marathon for me now, and I had to make use of the knots, one at every three feet, to accomplish it. I got to the top and looked over the scuppers to check that the insertion area was clear. You would think that the aftermost deck of a merchant ship would be deserted at 4:00 A.M., but there was a man standing at the rear rail, back to me, smoking, looking out at the *Alaric*'s long, phosphorescent wake, apparently unaware that twenty feet behind him his ship was being boarded.

I used the knife, not wanting to risk alerting the crew with a gunshot, and hoisted the body over the side. If anyone else came down here for a cigarette, they could hardly fail to notice all the blood, darkness or not. We didn't have much time.

Above the wind and the sea and the engine noise I heard a metallic clang from the starboard side. I went over. Apparently Alpha was still trying with the grappling hook, and had just missed. I pointed the flashlight into the darkness below, gave the all clear signal, then went and recovered my own line, which I secured and lowered to them. After what seemed an eternity, Alpha finally came aboard.

"Zulu's dead," I said without preamble. "Do you know how to use the satellite comms?"

Alpha swallowed. It was clear that the idea people might get killed had not occurred to him, but he recovered himself well, asked no questions for which there was no time for answers, and simply nodded.

"Here's his backpack. Set up the link."

I went back to the railing without waiting for a reply, and looked over the side. Yamina came up the line as if it was she who had climbed ropes once a week, not me.

The moment she hit the deck she had the backpack open and was assembling her M4. In the torpedo room I had made them practice this with their eyes closed, and it paid dividends now: not sixty seconds after she'd hit the deck I heard the satisfying sound of the action being smoothly cocked to the rear. We joined Alpha. He had the satellite uplink—the size of a small laptop and considerably more robust—set up and working. I sent a quick signal:

> INSERTION COMPLETE. ONE ENEMY PAX DEAD. ONE CASUALTY: ZBOROWSKI, DEAD. TAKING SHIP.

Modern commercial vessels are usually constructed with their superstructure aft and the engineering spaces directly below, which leaves the bulk of the ship ahead clear for the stacking of containers, but the *Alaric* was built before the era of that now-ubiquitous module of modern shipping. In her day cargo was loaded as it came, in sacks or barrels or crates, and hoisted aboard with derricks and lowered into the cargo holds. And her propulsion was not the diesel of modern ships, which could compactly fit beneath the superstructure, but steam, which required two engineering spaces, one for the engines themselves, and the second for the boilers to produce the steam that powered them. Thus she was built with her superstructure in the center of the ship, with two large cargo holds at either end, and between them the engineering spaces.

The original plan had been for us to enter the superstructure then again split into two pairs, one taking the bridge, the other the boiler room—the only two places that would be manned and active at this time of night. After we'd taken control of those on watch, their sleeping shipmates could be rounded up at leisure. But now, with only three people instead of four, we had to change plans. I decided to take the bridge first, and left Alpha at the top of the hatchway leading down into the boiler room, ensuring that if we couldn't yet take the engineering spaces, then at least we could prevent escape from them. Yamina and I would try to take the bridge swiftly, before the personnel there could warn the engineers, but if we failed then Alpha would be well positioned to take out anyone who came racing up that ladder. Assuming that we succeeded, I would come back down and take the engineering spaces with Alpha, leaving Yamina to keep an eye on things up top.

Yamina and I began the ascent to the bridge. With the diving shoes our steps up the stairs were all but silent, but the old steamer made so much noise that we could have probably worn hobnailed boots and still climbed them undetected. We came to the highest deck in the superstructure. A passageway led forward, covered in old green linoleum tiles that were worn and lifting at the corners. There were a number of doors giving onto it—ordinary doors rather than the usual watertight steel doors of ships, for we were high enough now that if the water ever came up here then all the watertight doors in the world wouldn't have helped.

The door at the end would give onto the bridge. A last quick weapon check, and we moved forward. There were no markings on the first cabins we passed, but as we came to the end there was a lightning bolt on the left-hand door. That signified the radio operator's cabin, where he would sleep with his equipment. The cabin door opposite bore the word CAPTAIN.

We came to the door at the end of the passageway, which led to the bridge. On the other side we could hear subdued conversation from the men on watch. There would be three of them at least: quartermaster, helmsman, and the officer of the watch, plus a fourth as lookout if the steamer followed the law of the sea, which she probably did not.

"Ready?" I whispered.

Yamina nodded.

"Then here we go."

She pushed open the door, and I burst through. Four astonished faces turned to us. They were all dead quiet, two staring at the weapon in disbelief, a third staring at Yamina, and the fourth—the only one thinking—was looking at a microphone.

"Are you feeling suicidal?" I asked.

He smiled slightly, accepting the situation with grace, and said, "I am no hero, mister." He was a black man with a Caribbean accent, and from the peaked cap he wore, apparently the officer of the watch. "You are pirates, I presume?"

"U.S. government treasury agents," Yamina replied, stretching the truth.

He shrugged his shoulders, apparently being of an opinion that there was little difference between the two. "My, my," he said with a grin, "did I forget to pay the port dues again?"

"You're the captain?"

"I indeed have the honor of commanding this fine vessel. Arthur Gordon, at your service. I was wondering if perhaps we might come to some sort of arrangement—"

Before he could continue to explore the possibility of a bribe, the door to the passageway suddenly opened. The man who came in had a gun in his right hand, but it was carried casually by his side, and in his other was a cup of coffee. There was a cigarette at the corner of his mouth, whose pungent aroma I had last smelled in Marty Blankenship's apartment. He was the same man who had passed Yamina and me at the Pantera Club, going upstairs while we had been going down, after having knocked out Vas. All at once I realized what should have been obvious: how could the conspirators trust the smugglers they had hired to transport the gold? The answer was that they could not—no one would trust any ship's company with $200 million in gold, let alone this particular ship's company. So the conspirators had embarked their own people to guard it during the passage.

He looked at me for a moment in confusion, quickly followed by recognition. I don't know whether he intended to use that gun or not, but I put a three-round burst into him before he could do so. Then I turned to the captain and aimed the weapon directly at his head.

"One chance. How many?"

"Eight," he answered without hesitation. "Well, actually, seven now."

"Russians?"

"They do indeed converse in that tongue, sir."

Seven, probably all ex–Russian special forces, alerted now and with $200 million in motivation. Plus the ship's company, another sixteen, fifteen. Twenty-two against three, and with no further element of surprise. I wished now I'd brought those spare magazines, despite the extra weight.

I grabbed Yamina and raced from the bridge back down the passageway.

"What are we doing?" she asked.

"Aborting and extracting."

A head peeked out one of the cabins but quickly disappeared back inside. We flew down the stairs, and as we were coming to the bottom I saw Alpha standing, looking anxiously up at us. It was a stupid thing to do: he should have been in a crouch, back to a bulkhead and using what cover he could, staring down the approach routes along the barrel of his M-4.

A burst of automatic gunfire, deafening in the enclosed, metallic space of the ship's superstructure, and Alpha's body erupted, disintegrated. I couldn't see the shooter, but he was obviously in the passageway where Alpha had been standing. We had to regain the passageway, for it was the only way out. I leapt, fired while in midair, a long burst in hopes of compensating for inaccuracy with volume, and landed on top of Alpha's prostrate body. There had been just the one shooter, and he went down.

Down, but not out. He was wearing body armor—serious body armor: porcelain, not Kevlar. Body armor or not, the tremendous impact of the high-velocity rounds had taken him down, and probably broken a few ribs. I stood up, quickly snapped back to single shot, and put a precious round of 5.56 into his head, ensuring that he was permanently disabled.

Six left. But we were now just two.

Yamina was already crouched in the firing position, covering our rear, as if she had been trained to the task. I went back to Alpha. I was concerned not for him—he was beyond human concern from the moment those rounds had plowed into his body—but for the satellite uplink he had been carrying. It was smashed, shot right through.

I took his magazine, then knelt beside Yamina, facing forward while she faced aft. "No uplink," I said. "We can't communicate with the submarine."

A head and shoulders with a weapon glanced around the bulkhead at the end of the passageway. I recognized Vassily, and in the instant our eyes met I could tell that he recognized me. He let off a burst as he ducked back, unaimed, ricocheting wildly. I fired too, a short burst to let him know he wouldn't get us cheap, but ammunition was really too precious to waste on just making noise.

Loud shouting: Vassily yelling commands in Russian to his unseen comrades no doubt above and behind us, then quieter as he spoke to the others that were with him.

"They've sealed us up forward."

The two watchkeepers came up from the boiler room, big-eyed, scared witless, and not worth wasting precious ammunition on. They raced aft but the moment they went through the door at the end of the passageway, a burst of automatic gunfire cut them down. The Spetsnaz were obviously shooting at anything that moved now.

"They've sealed us aft, too."

"Do we go back up?"

"No. The crew's alerted now."

"Then what do we do?"

I was wondering that myself when a small can came rattling down the passageway. It came to a stop six feet away, and rolled gently from side to side with the pitching of the ship. Smoke began to come out of it. Another quick peek from the end of the passageway, too quick for even a short burst in response, but long enough for me to recognize that this time Vassily's face was covered with a mask.

"They're using gas," I said. We were covered front and rear, and above. That left only one option. "Let's go below."

I fired a short covering burst as Yamina scampered down the ladder into the boiler room, then followed.

The compartment we entered was large but gave the impression of being cramped because of the mass of machinery and valves and piping that occupied it. The whole place hummed and vibrated, a different world to the one above. The boilers themselves stood side by side athwartships, the width of the beam, massive bulk with small windows pulsing yellow from the glow of flames within. She was oil-fired, and the deck plates in front of the boilers, where the burners were turned on or off as circumstances required, were covered in the greasy black residue of furnace fuel oil. There were the condensers, the main cooling pump, rusting saltwater fire mains, bilge pumps, an evaporator dripping verdigris, rattling ventilation equipment, and miles of old leaking piping. Much of this latter was lagged, cracked, and broken, probably asbestos, and as dangerous in the long run as those Spetsnaz above us. The compartment was far louder than the rest of the ship, and hotter, too; we were soon sweating in our wet suits.

The only entrance or exit was the hatchway and ladder we had just descended. If it had been an ordinary compartment, the Spetsnaz would have used grenades, but of course that was out of the question in a boiler room. More gas canisters were of little use here: gas is used to disperse people, but we had nowhere to go, and gas wasn't going to stop us shooting at whoever tried to come down that ladder. But they couldn't just leave us here, effectively in control of the ship's propulsion. That meant they had to do it the hard way: come down and get us. I put Yamina behind a fuel pump and took cover myself behind a condenser, placed so that we had that lone ladderway in what would be a murderous crossfire. We took aim and waited as the minutes ticked by.

I could imagine what was going through Goryakin's mind above us. He, too, would be assessing the situation and coming to the ugly conclusion that he was going to lose more people before this was over. But he had no choice, and soon we could hear the noise of preparation for the assault coming from the hatchway.

Another canister, and for a moment I thought he was going to try gas after all, but when this one hit the deck plates it began to emit not gas but smoke, thick and dark and quickly reducing visibility to a few inches. It was an intelligent move; Vassily must have guessed that we wouldn't have sufficient ammunition to fire without a sure target, and with all this smoke we would never be sure. Soon I heard the rattle of a descent on the ladder. I squeezed off a short burst, not so much in the expectation of taking out the target as to just slow things down, but the result was disheartening: the bolt stayed to the rear: the magazine was empty. I quickly replaced it with the one I'd taken from Alpha, but I could hear more of them coming down that ladder, and it was clear that the end wasn't far away. The smoke was stinging my eyes and filling my lungs, so thick now that it was as effective as the CS they'd tried above.

I moved over to join Yamina. It wasn't ideal—we should have maintained angular separation for maximum effectiveness—but things were beyond that now. I withdrew the Beretta, pulled the slide to the rear, and fired a single round in the direction of the ladderway to ensure that the thing wouldn't misfire when the time came. No one fired back—they knew they were in control of the situation now, and the end was only a matter of time.

I could hear them deploying, occasional faint sounds over the constant white noise of the machinery. They were fanning out, moving wide to ensure that we couldn't use the cover of the thick smoke to sneak past them and get to that lone exit. When the deployment was complete they would advance, slowly but surely, and eventually hunt us down. We pulled back to the far side of the ship and took cover between the starboard bulkhead and a noisy cooling pump, with the bulk of a boiler hovering over us. There were no deck plates here, and greasy bilgewater sloshed around our legs. The dense smoke was stifling, and intense heat radiated from the boiler. Paint was flaking off those parts of the bulkhead not already covered in rust. The noise from the pump was deafening, its bearings obviously shot. *What a lousy place to die,* I thought, but then would a field of daisies have made dying any better?

I briefly popped the handgun's magazine and counted the remaining rounds. Yamina saw me do this, and for a moment our eyes met. We didn't say anything, but she nodded, and I could tell that she understood: I didn't intend to go down with any ammunition remaining, but the penultimate round would be for Yamina, and the last for myself.

The ship rolled, and the bilgewater washed up to our knees. There was a lot of water, and I ducked down to see where it was all coming from. It was hard to make out anything down here below the machinery and deck plates: dark at the best of times, but with the lighting dulled by the smoke I could see nothing. Yet I had a sense that the bilgewater was washing in and out with the ship's roll through more than just the boiler room. In other words, there might be another exit after all.

I took off the backpack and removed the sound charges. There was no time to prime them correctly: just an eyeball guess at three minutes' worth of fuse and an uncrimped detonator jammed into the end. If all went well, three minutes would be enough time to escape, and I just had to hope that in all this smoke the fact of the burning fuse would go unnoticed.

I leaned into Yamina's ear. "I'm going to set this charge on the boiler, and then we're going to swim out," I said, pointing at the bilgewater. "Get rid of your backpack and anything that could catch. Weapons, too."

"It leads out?" She looked doubtful.

"Yes," I said, with what I hoped was more confidence than I felt. "Just follow me."

I lit the fuse and jammed the charges into the narrow space between the boiler and the ship's side. The first shadow appeared in the smoke: they were almost on top of us now.

"Ready?" I whispered. A nod in response. I took a deep breath and slid into the dark, turgid water.

Even if it were true that the bilges ran between compartments, it was far from certain that the space would accommodate a human being. Although I could see nothing in the water I could feel the narrow confinement of the space, the beams and deck plates hitting the top of my head, and below the hull itself, scraping at my chest. It was horrendously claustrophobic, spelunking in a cave that has suddenly flooded, with just one deep breath's worth of time to find a way out. My eyes stung with the sludge of the bilgewater. The noise of the ship was amplified a hundredfold underwater, a bass rumble that had a curiously lifelike tone, as if we were deep in the cavity of some enormous and slowly aspirating sea creature. We were directly underneath the boilers now, tons of red-hot steel directly overhead, and the water was uncomfortably warm. Suddenly I could go no farther: I had hit one of the ship's ribs. I felt for the gap between it and the boiler above. I found it: a hand's-breadth, no more. Impossible for me to fit through, but skinny as she was, Yamina might make it. Yet impossible to explain, in the dark, underwater, and with lungs aching for air. I would either have to squeeze through, or we would die here.

I think it was the bilgewater which did it—the greasy slime that by now covered the wet suit had turned the neoprene into an eel-like slippery skin that enabled me to achieve what would have been impossible otherwise. I had bruised ribs, but I was through. Behind me I could feel Yamina follow.

When we emerged from the bilges it was into another large compartment, as big as before and also laden with machinery: giant turbine and massive reduction gearing—the engine room. No smoke. No people, either; if any of the ship's watchkeepers had been on duty here, they had obviously retreated until their passengers finished with the shooting. We found the ladderway and raced up.

The passageway above was deserted apart from a lone soldier, set to keep watch over the entrance to the boiler room, back to us and all his attention focused on that hatchway leading down.

I had no weapon, but no need of one. At the last moment he sensed rather that saw me, but by then it was too late: I jammed my knee into him from behind and twisted his head backward with all the force I could muster. Both his back and neck broke at the same time; either was sufficient to do the job.

I jammed down the hatch and had just clipped it shut when there was an explosion below—the charges going off—followed by the much deeper *whoomph* of the boiler suddenly releasing 400 psi of superheated steam.

Screams, then silence. The steel hatch cover had buckled upward, whether from the initial blast or from the boiler explosion I wasn't sure.

"Are they dead?"

"Braised Spetsnaz," I affirmed. Already fires were breaking out, and that second boiler would explode soon. Eventually the fire would spread to the fuel tanks, and then the ship would be blown to kingdom come. "Time to get out of here."

I took Yamina's hand. We bolted down the passageway, out to the afterdeck, and didn't break stride as we jumped onto a locker and dived over the taffrail, clear of the ship and down into her wake below.

The *Alaric* blew up a minute or two later. She was still near, having lost propulsion when that first boiler went, and it was a spectacular show, with jets of flame from that exploding fuel oil towering into the sky. She sank within a minute. There were no survivors; no one could have survived the blast. There was little in the way of wreckage, too, as if the force of the explosion had disintegrated everything, but eventually we found some ragged but serviceable life jackets.

For the third time in twenty-four hours, I was bobbing in an empty ocean with Yamina Malik. But this time we were certain of rescue, for the sound of the exploding *Alaric* was sure to have been picked up by the *Sioux Falls*.

I took advantage of the interval before the submarine's arrival to spend as much time kissing Yamina Malik as I could.

THIRTY-FIVE

A sullen fog rolled in off the Potomac with the gathering dusk, turning Washington into the Unreal City—looming and vaporous and ephemeral—a fog which transformed the city into an unknowable place, hidden and vaguely malignant, something beyond rational grasp, like quantum mechanics. Violet, too, now—but unlike dull London, Washington was shot through with an optimistic pink; fog or no fog, the trees had decided that it was spring, and the city was a sea of cherry blossoms.

I made my way slowly across Lafayette Park, lost in thought and not wanting to arrive early. Thinking of "The Waste Land" had made me think of the man I was on the way to meet (my own Mr. Eugenides). In his way Antullis was an exile, too, not that much different from Eliot—the most English Englishman that Missouri has ever produced. But Eliot's exile, despite the geography, had essentially been intellectual; a retreat into cold gray thoughts on a cold gray isle, followed by a second and blisteringly absurd retreat into an alien but accommodating religion. Antullis's exile had been of a different kind, an exile of the mind, or perhaps more accurately the spirit, as if he had decided to refuse the world what he needed most, to engage in productive activity, to achieve, the need to do.

Gradually the yellow glow of building windows came into view through the gloom. I had come to the edge of the park. Across the street lay the Hay-Adams. Antullis had a suite there, and I was shown up.

He answered the door himself, shoeless and in shirt-sleeves.

"I haven't got used to doing things for myself again yet," he said in introduction. "I seem to be perpetually late." He turned and walked back down the hall. I followed him inside. No greeting, no handshake—that much at least had not changed; as when I'd first met him, Antullis had little liking for social niceties, but by now I knew him well enough to realize that he could be gracious on demand if required, and that the absence of such courtesies with me should be taken as an obscure compliment.

We entered the suite itself. Large, but not oversized. Well furnished, but not ostentatious. No staff. Antullis was in danger of becoming a man of restraint.

"Doing things yourself?"

He picked up a cuff link from a side table and began buttoning.

"Yes. This business with Quire has given me a distaste for employing people."

"Is he still in prison?"

"No, he's out on bail. But I've hired every lawyer in the land to ensure that he goes down at the trial. Springfield, too." He grinned that old boyish grin. "I find that I have acquired an appetite for revenge."

"Good." I'm not much of a turn-the-other-cheek guy myself. "The harem?"

"Disbanded, I regret to say, but they did depart well dowered."

So in the end Sorrel Tyne had gotten what she'd wanted all along: money, although not money on the scale she had been expecting. In the abridged version of events I'd given Antullis I'd never mentioned her role.

"However, I kept Maria," Antullis added. "I may well marry her." He laughed and picked up a wine bottle, rotating it to show me the label. "In memory of her finest moment."

It was '61 Lafite; Antullis wasn't quite done with indulgence yet. He opened it and poured; no breathing, no decanting, just splashed out the way a good peasant wine should be.

We hoisted our glasses in silent cheers and drank. I felt the fluid go down, a wave of fruit crashing into a wall of slate, structured and delineated and precise. If I was ever able to craft a wine half as good as this, I would be a very happy man.

Antullis put down the glass and began putting on patent leather evening shoes.

"The GT40 isn't yours, is it?" he asked quietly, not looking up.

This was new. I should have guessed that Antullis was too smart not to have figured out that there was more to the thing than I had revealed. I took my time before replying, taking a second generous sip of the wine and replacing the glass, thinking how to best form an answer. I liked Xerxes Antullis, and I wasn't going to lie to him. But there was no way I was going to reveal the truth.

"No," I said eventually.

"How on earth did you convince Binky Benson to give it to you?"

"Not me," I admitted. "Someone else did."

He kept his eyes focused on his shoes, although by now he'd finished tying them. "Who is this someone else?" I just shook my head in response, an answer which he must have caught out of the corner of his eye.

"Then why? Were you a freelancer, looking for an exposé?"

"No, nothing like that."

"Then what?"

I had nothing to say, so I said nothing. Suddenly Antullis sat back up straight, and for the first time since asking about the car he looked directly at me. "Of course, I've got it now." He clicked his fingers and pointed. "You're some sort of government person, I'll bet. A government agent sent to infiltrate the estate." He slapped his thighs at having figured it out. "By God, you're a spy."

"No, I am someone who is used by spies."

"Is there a difference?"

"There is to me."

"And you were sent to discover what Quire was up to?" I didn't answer, happy for Antullis to believe this if he chose. "Well, if I'll be damned. I never imagined that our government was so good at these things. There the fellow was stealing massive sums of money from right under my nose, and you people figured it out."

He sat back and drank more of the wine, so I did the same. I wondered if he would still marvel at our government's efficiency if he'd known how close to killing him I had come.

"I presume the details are something you can't talk about?"

"It's best just to forget about it, I think."

"Can you tell me why the government was interested in the first place? After all, it was my money, not theirs."

"I believe that Quire intended to invest it in a way the government considered unwise," I said carefully. Technically true. Antullis just laughed, apparently happy to leave it at that.

"Well, if I'll be damned," he repeated. "You're a spy."

I didn't bother correcting him a second time, and

tried a change of subject instead. "I'm sorry the money was lost."

"Oh, forget that. I didn't even notice it missing in the first place."

"Two hundred million dollars is a lot not to notice missing."

He stood, picked up a bow tie, and moved in front of a mirror to tie it. "To tell the truth, what I feel *has* gone missing is time. It's time that's truly valuable, and what a lot of it I have wasted recently."

"No more?"

"No more. As of now, I'm rejoining the world permanently. I'll keep Quartz Peak, but no more hiding. In fact, I'm attending a dinner tonight which is likely to be well covered in the press."

"Whereabouts?"

"Over there," Antullis said matter-of-factly, nodding toward the window. Outside, the fog had lifted sufficiently for me to see across the park the White House, floodlit in the gathering dark, stark and familiar and serene.

The tie was tied. Antullis checked his watch. "I'm going to be late." He put on his dinner jacket. "Walk over with me, will you?"

"Sure." I finished the remainder of the wine in a single grateful gulp.

THE fog had completely dissipated, leaving an evening sky of the deepest indigo, with just enough light for the pale outlines of buildings to be still visible. We made our way across Lafayette Park, but just before we got to the White House gates, Antullis stopped.

"Listen, I have something to say, so I ask you to just let me say it."

"Okay."

He cleared his throat, the way a man does before he

is going to make an admission that might embarrass him. "I have more money than I could ever possibly use. You do not. If you were a reasonable man, I would offer you money, and you would accept it. However, since it is perfectly obvious that you are not a reasonable man, not only would you not accept it, you would very likely never accept an invitation from me again."

"Very likely."

"As I suspected. Therefore, I offer you nothing but friendship." He offered his hand.

"That suits me fine." We shook hands, but he held my grip.

"I haven't finished. Notwithstanding everything I just said, it occurs to me that there may come a time when you will have a need." He held up his left hand to forestall the protest that was forming. "You agreed to let me speak," he insisted, pausing until I'd settled back down.

"Very well," he continued. "The need, were it to occur, may not be yours, but for someone you hold dear. Or for an idea you hold dear. I suspect that you hold the idea of this country very dear, for example, a sentiment which I share with wholehearted enthusiasm. Whatever the case, this is what I ask: call that same number Quire gave you when he first called you. Whoever answers, tell them where and how much. No reasons, no explanations. Just where and how much. You have my word that the money will be delivered as fast as it's humanly possible to do so." He paused again, making sure that I understood how seriously he took the offer. "Good. We will never speak of it again." He finally let go of my hand. "Now, I'm told that it's considered bad form to keep the president waiting." He laughed and bounded away to the security gate without giving me an opportunity for reply.

I stood as he was cleared through security, and watched him as he continued swiftly up to the famous entrance. Before going inside, he turned and gave me a little wave, as if he owned the place himself. I had to smile. How typical of Xerxes Antullis that, having chosen to reenter the world, he would start at the top.

I turned and walked away, feeling my good humor begin to fail. I had enjoyed tonight, but tomorrow I had another appointment, an appointment which would be a different matter altogether.

THIRTY-SIX

"**THERE** was no plutonium, was there?"

Dortmund looked at me over the top of his glasses with obvious distaste but reverted without reply to the study of the typewritten card in the little silver holder that served as the lunch menu at the Mayflower Club, apparently having chosen to simply ignore the question. Or perhaps when you weigh three hundred pounds eating is the main event, something not to be diverted from by frivolous questions about fissile material. He was dressed in an impeccably tailored suit made from that same black priest-cloth fabric that he always wore; he must have a closet full of them. I wondered what he wore on weekends.

Eventually he signaled for the steward. An elderly man approached the table, bent with age, but his white linen jacket was starched stiff. He'd been hovering discreetly by the sideboard since we'd been seated, attentive but deliberately out of earshot—obviously the staff of the Mayflower Club were well acquainted with the needs of this particular member.

"The white asparagus, Gibbons?"

"Fresh today, sir."

"Wonderful, wonderful. And Dover sole to follow. Plus a bottle of the Sancerre, I think."

"Very good, sir." He left without taking my order. I wondered if it was assumed that someone who dined with Dortmund would eat whatever he ate, or if I was simply too unimportant to be fed at all.

"It's always such a fine day when the first white asparagus becomes available." Dortmund took up his sherry glass. "The coming of spring," he continued. "Rebirth, hope renewed. A fresh start." He took a healthy swig in celebration.

"There was no plutonium, was there?" I repeated.

"I heard you the first time."

"No terrorists, no sale of fissile material, no weapon getting into the wrong hands."

"No, of course not," he admitted.

"It was just about the money."

"It usually is."

"You lied to me."

"Of course I lied to you. You forget who I am, Captain Dalton. I am a professional dissembler; I lie for a living." He put down the sherry glass with the sigh of a man burdened by having to explain the obvious. "I needed to give you some sort of explanation in order to assuage what curiosity you might have, although I confess you showed precious little. And in these post–nine/eleven days, I find that invoking the threat of Islamic fundamentalists is such a splendid motivator. Besides, a little sand in the eyes never hurt anyone."

"Sixteen crew of the *Alaric* are dead because I believed you."

Dortmund looked almost bored, a ruminating pachyderm undisturbed by events lower down the food chain. "I think it was Stalin who called the death of one man a tragedy, but a million a statistic," he said. "So what is sixteen? Barely even a statistic. 'Unfortunate' perhaps, although personally I find it hard to characterize their deaths as anything beyond irrelevant. If you must indulge in sympathy for these people, then do so. But please don't expect me to join you."

The Sancerre arrived, was tasted and poured. The steward looked at me with suspicion before withdrawing—I had obviously agitated his charge, and he was not pleased. But I wasn't through agitating him yet.

"They were going to swindle Uncle Sam, weren't they?"

Dortmund didn't answer for a long time. Instead he stared at his glass, holding the base on the table with two fat fingers and swirling it slightly, the way you do with wine to release the aroma, but in this case it was just an absent gesture, something to do while calculating a response. "Might I ask how you came to this conclusion?" he said eventually.

There was no commitment in that response, but I could tell that I'd hit home. If I was to get a confirmation, I would have to lay my cards on the table. I led with my trump.

"Quire told me."

"He *told* you?"

"In a way, although he didn't really mean to. In the control room of the airship, he said that he wasn't stealing the gold, he was merely borrowing it. He said that it would be used as collateral for another transaction. A transaction he expected to be profitable."

"Yes?"

"I know what the other transaction was."

"How?"

How. Not *what,* but *how.* Now I knew that I had guessed correctly.

"When I accessed the Iron Butterfly account in the

BVI, there was a section for orders. At the time I didn't understand what those orders meant, Mr. Dortmund, but since then I've found out."

The asparagus arrived, plump pale tips that looked overcooked to me, but given the average age at the Mayflower Club, the members probably liked their food on the mushy side. The steward withdrew. Dortmund gave his full concentration to the food. He was a curiously delicate eater for such a fat man, gently prodding the asparagus for the best bits, lightly loading his fork and carefully wiping his mouth after each mouthful, an automatic gesture it seemed, perhaps intended to ensure that the dignity of his Vandyke beard was not compromised by stray food matter. Richelieu probably ate the same way.

I ate nothing. When Dortmund was finished, he took a good measure of wine, refilled his glass, and resumed the conversation as if there had been no interruption.

"And these orders were for what?"

"U.S. government bonds."

"So Quire and the other conspirators were going to convert the gold into treasuries," Dortmund said dismissively. "Hardly a swindle."

"They were selling fixed bonds, and buying inflation-indexed bonds."

"So?"

"They were taking a bet that inflation was going up. I've done some research on treasury bonds, Mr. Dortmund."

"I'm well aware of the nature of your research, Captain Dalton. Personally I preferred the lovely Ms. Houston, but I suppose that Ms. Malik does have a certain exotic, south Asian appeal."

"You're wrong by one continent and two cardinal points," I said. Dortmund looked startled; he was a man who admired precision in details and was not often accused of inaccuracy himself. Yamina's parents were originally North African, having come to America—young and penniless—to escape Nasser in the 1960s. In another man I might not have let his comment pass so easily, but Dortmund was such a hideously inhuman creature that to take issue with the remark would be like resenting a skunk for smelling bad.

So instead I just told him what I knew: that the U.S. has issued fixed-rate bonds since the second Continental Congress, but inflation-indexed bonds are new: they only began to be issued during the Clinton administration, and so their vulnerabilities are not yet explored. Instead of a fixed percentage, the return on the bond rises or falls with the rate of inflation, and so that rate of inflation number is crucial: a few basis points either way was worth millions.

"This is all very interesting, Captain Dalton. But is it relevant?"

"The rate of inflation number is a very complex and obscure measurement, not something you can do without a computer program. There are many assumptions, some questionable. For example, you would think that if an automobile which previously cost $20,000 now costs $20,100, it would be an up move in inflation, but it's possible for the index to treat this as a price *going down* because the new model has new equipment: a CD changer, say, where the old one only had a single CD slot. The final number is calculated by the Bureau of Labor Statistics. The software on which it is calculated was developed and is maintained by the XA Corporation. The scheme was dead simple: use XA's money to finance the purchase of bonds whose value would rise if inflation went up, manipulate the software to artificially inflate the inflation number, then sell the bonds and keep the profit. But you already knew all this, didn't you, Mr. Dortmund?"

He sat back and sighed. "If you must insist, then yes,

of course I knew. I told you from the beginning: the money comes first. The Russian fellow who was Antullis's head of security had access to the source code, or at least to the mechanism for keeping it safe. He had criminal connections—all ex-Russians, like himself, including the people who run the Pantera Club. We believe the ex-Spetsnaz people were recruited thus. Quire of course had the skill to make the changes to the code, and to sufficiently conceal them such that anything short of a major investigation would unlikely ever reveal the fact of the changes. We assume that he was the one who came up with the scheme in the first place. Springfield was needed for the transport of the gold. The only piece we're missing is how they were actually going to get the new code into the BLS's computer system. Presumably through a contact within the XA Corporation, which still has the maintenance contract on the software."

I knew how. Even without having discovered her letters that night, I'd have remembered that Sorrel Tyne's brother used to work as a database administrator for some government agency, and would have guessed from her involvement that it must be the Bureau of Labor Statistics. I hadn't told Dortmund's people. There was no sentimental reason for this, no residual affection—in fact since meeting her again at Quartz Peak I'd come to the conclusion that I didn't really like the woman that Sorrel Tyne had become and was fortunate that when I'd been released from Leavenworth ten years ago she had not been there waiting for me.

If they discovered her involvement themselves, then fine. But I'd known the woman—once loved her, I supposed—and so they would never discover it from me.

The sole arrived. The conversation thus far had done nothing to ruin Dortmund's appetite, and he began eating without preamble. After a while he became aware that my dish still lay untouched in front of me.

"I can assure you that they do an excellent Dover sole here. So hard to get the sauce right, I find."

"No appetite."

"I see." Dortmund paused from the dish, took a sip of wine, then sat back and fixed me with an evaluating eye. "Tell me, Captain Dalton, do you know what a trillion is?"

"It's a thousand billion."

"Oh certainly, you know the arithmetic: a thousand billion, as you say." He waved his hand dismissively. "But I don't think you really *know* what a trillion is. Let us try an exercise, shall we?"

"Okay." It was an unnecessary answer—we'd be doing the exercise whether I liked it or not. Dortmund continued between mouthfuls.

"Let's equate the number one to a second of time, shall we? That is, we'll designate a second as representing a single unit." I nodded. "Now tell me, quickly, how long is a million seconds?"

"A few days?"

"And a billion seconds?"

"Months, I guess. Maybe years."

"And a trillion seconds?"

"Decades?"

"Very good, Captain Dalton. You have demonstrated your ignorance perfectly." He triumphantly refilled his wineglass before continuing. "If a second of time were a single unit, then a million would be approximately eleven days, thirteen hours and forty-seven minutes. Less than two weeks. Not so far from your guess of 'a few days,' I think. Not a lot of time, an interval less than that between paychecks, a period which I'm told vanishes to nothing when spent on vacation."

"You don't know yourself?"

"I've never taken a vacation, Captain Dalton."

I had to admit it was hard to imagine him sunning himself at a beach resort. The local environmentalists would probably mistake him for beached whale and try to pull him back out to sea.

"And now for a billion," he continued. "If a second was one, then a billion would be thirty-two years. A long time, no? Almost half a lifetime. Very different to a million."

He was right. A billion was a very big number, bigger than you intuitively grasp.

"And now a trillion. 'Decades,' I believe you guessed. A trillion would actually be more than thirty thousand years. Thirty millennia, Captain Dalton. Thousands of generations. Not just all of civilized history, but the entire history of humanoids from the time of Cro-Magnon man—beyond the span of modern *Homo sapiens*. Yet how enticingly small a trillion sounds: just some billions, which of course are just some millions."

"Okay, but what is your point?"

"The federal debt of the United States now stands at well over seven trillion dollars, Captain Dalton. Think of it: seven *trillion*. If every dollar was just a second, that would represent the history of the human race, seven times over. It is an enormous, incomprehensible number. Fifty years ago the United States was the world's largest creditor nation. Now we are the world's largest debtor nation. The government debt is a monumental, crushing weight that has been placed upon us and upon our future by decades of weak-willed politicians plying the national Visa card in search of votes. You think I lied to you? I merely understated the problem: for that debt is a greater threat to us than a thousand terrorists seeking plutonium."

"How do you figure that?"

"Simple: our debt is financed by the rest of the world, Captain Dalton. If they choose to call in that debt we will be ruined—the economy would collapse on a scale which would make the Great Depression look like a Sunday picnic. Our debt is financed by bonds. Any threat to investor confidence in those bonds—anything which might conceivably trigger panic selling—is thus a direct attack upon the United States. And nothing would be surer to cause a collapse in investor confidence in U.S. government debt than the revelation of a scheme to manipulate their price."

"Especially if it was already being manipulated."

That silenced him. In fact it froze him. He stared at me with a mixture of horror and contempt, and remained staring at me as Gibbons came and removed the plates, swept the crumbs, returning with two cups and saucers and a silver coffeepot.

Yamina Malik had already told me all about the various schemes that she and her fellow Treasury agents uncover from time to time. Quire's was a big one, but not the biggest. Wherever there is paper representing money, then there are schemes to manipulate it, from simple counterfeiting to complex plots involving electronic transfers of nonexistent funds. Investigations are done, arrests made, prosecutions brought, just as in other areas of law enforcement. There was nothing different here. Nothing, that is, unless there was something to hide. And that something could only be this: if Quire's scheme had been to manipulate the calculation of the inflation index, then the investigation of the crime would necessarily involve the investigation of the existing process—a complex and arcane process, but anything can eventually be analyzed if it is sufficiently scrutinized. I had long ago guessed that there could be only one reason to involve Dortmund and his people: it had to be because the U.S. government's calculation of the inflation index—and the many obligations which rest upon it, from Social Security through to treasury bonds—was not something that would stand up to minute scrutiny.

This particular scheme to swindle Uncle Sam had to

be stopped, because Uncle Sam was already doing some swindling himself, and on the grandest of scales.

"It wasn't deliberate," Dortmund eventually admitted, "but when the error was detected, in the manner of public officials everywhere, they covered it up."

"What would happen if I told someone?"

"You won't," Dortmund softly replied.

"What makes you so sure?"

"Because any such accusation would inevitably lead to an investigation."

"So?"

"Investigations have a habit of leading to places best left alone."

"Such as?"

"Such as dead bodies with their skulls transfixed by furniture, not to mention an abundance of rather unpleasant but forensically useful matter left by the killer."

I'd never told Dortmund about Billy-Jo-Bob.

"How did you know?" I asked.

"Because he worked for me," Dortmund admitted matter-of-factly. "It was I who ordered your abduction in the first place."

Now it was my turn to be rendered dumbfounded.

"Please don't get high-handed on me, Captain Dalton. It was an entirely justifiable course of action. We perform complete background checks on all our employees, and we polygraph them. There wasn't time in your case, and I suspect that you would have probably refused the polygraph anyway. So I simply took the matter out of your hands. You can't seriously imagine that I would have entrusted the future of the nation's financial security to a man I knew nothing about." He paused to sip his coffee. "By the way, did you know that you have some significant unresolved issues regarding Beth Houston? Our psychological profile recommended a course of therapy to resolve these, but I suppose that now you've more or less resolved them yourself."

The port decanter arrived. Two glasses. I waited until the steward was out of earshot before continuing.

"The man I handcuffed to the SUV—the one who drugged me?"

"A CIA officer."

"Why did he follow me to Babycakes?"

"On my instructions, to verify that you did indeed go there, and that when you came out it was with the laptop. You took so much time that he assumed you'd left by a back exit. By the way, why were you in there so long?"

"Slow learner on the laptop. Why did he draw his weapon on me?"

"Because you did: when you went for your gun he instinctively went for his. We had to suppress the police report of course; he's an operations officer and thus his identity is protected. He's not pleased that you shot him, by the way."

"Who was the man I killed in the cabin?"

"Merely a petty criminal of the type we use from time to time when the work is unsuitable for genuine CIA officers. Perfectly disposable." He shrugged his shoulders in a gesture of indifference. "I believe the fellow made methamphetamines for his regular living," Dortmund added. "I rather like using meth addicts. They've always got so much *energy*."

He poured himself a generous measure of port and offered to fill my glass. But I had had enough of Dortmund. Enough of his schemes and enough of his secrets and enough of his poorly concealed joy in the successful manipulation of people.

"No, thanks. I'll just take my money and go."

"Ah, yes, the money." Dortmund slumped back in his chair. "I'm sorry to say, Captain Dalton, that there is no money."

"What?"

"Well of course there is money, but I'm afraid that it's currently lying approximately one mile below the surface of the ocean, right where you left it. Quite untouchable, although naturally you are welcome to your portion, should you find the means to recover it."

"What are you talking about? We have a deal."

"Indeed we do. And I've told you where your payment now lies."

"Have the government cut a check, Mr. Dortmund."

"The government? The government knows nothing of our arrangement."

"What?"

"My dear fellow, I've just told you how our nation's security was dependent upon the success of this operation. If the operation had been on the books, so to speak, it would have been subject to government oversight. That is, committees of *politicians* would have known about it. Of course I was not willing to take such a risk—it would have been highly irresponsible of me. Therefore I simply authorized the operation myself, quite free from the scrutiny of those weak and leaky creatures known as elected officials." He said the words *elected officials* much as other people might say *child molesters.* "So of course the financing had to be off the books, too. I had intended that the money destined for the Iron Butterfly account would be used to pay for its interception. But instead of merely capturing the *Alaric,* *you* found it necessary to indulge in some questionable heroics and sink the damn thing, along with the many tons of gold that it was carrying. Frankly, your capricious actions that night have left us in quite an untenable situation, with a mountain of bills and the means to pay them five thousand feet underwater."

Now at last I knew the reason I had been recruited: Dortmund was doing an Oliver North. Of course he couldn't have used a real CIA officer: he was running his own operation, without authorization or supervision, and had intended to steal the money with which to finance it. And apparently he considered that it was my fault that the thing had gone wrong.

"Now, it so happens that the U.S. Navy possesses a craft capable of diving to that depth," Dortmund continued. "I am intending to use it in an attempt to recover the gold." Which he would no doubt use to fund future operations that he deemed too important to be acknowledged on Capitol Hill. "As I'm sure you know, the international law of salvage is quite clear: basically, finders keepers. In short, if we recover the gold, then we will legally own it, including your portion. However, I would be willing to transfer the agreed amount to you, if you could just help us with one more little thing. There's a slight problem we're having in the south of France, and perhaps if you could just—"

I stood and walked out.

WHEN I left the Mayflower Club that day, I thought that I would never cool off. But I hadn't walked more than a hundred yards when I passed a woman who smiled at me, and I realized that she was returning my own smile. I had been grinning without being aware of it.

Many men had died recently chasing money. Money had mattered to them. Money mattered to Dortmund also. To him it was interchangeable with power, as mass is interchangeable with energy, and for Dortmund power is ambrosia. Money mattered to me, too—or at least it had. The gold that was now lying on the ocean floor—money that had been intended to relieve me of the mortgage on the vineyard—was the reason I had become involved with all this in the first place.

But the money didn't matter to me now. A woman did.

I hadn't eaten with Dortmund not because I wasn't

hungry—I'm always hungry—but because I was meeting the woman for lunch straight afterward. She would be waiting for me now, in the corner bar at the Willard, vodka-tonic in hand. A courageous woman. A stubborn woman. A woman with very beautiful arms, and much else besides.

BLACK TIGER

ROBERT BRACE

"A beautifully written debut introducing
one of the most appealing characters
I've seen in a long time."
—KYLE MILLS

It was pure luck that Lysander Dalton got up
to use the bathroom seconds before someone
shot his bed full of bullets. And it's pure
chemistry when the ex-special ops Marine
meets Valentina Mariposa. She's a sexy lawyer
who will double as Dalton's bodyguard and
hired gun in the search for the terrifying truth
behind his bullet-riddled bed.

0-425-20119-8

**Available wherever books are sold or at
penguin.com**

By 1943, the U.S. had rounded up every
Nazi spy on American soil—except one...

A GATHERING
OF SPIES

JOHN ALTMAN

0-515-13110-5

"An irresistible page-turner."
—Publishers Weekly

"Sizzling...A classic spy story."
—Stephen Coonts

"Faster-than-lightning."
—Boston Herald

*"This book has the feel of one of those great
old movies about World War II. If you were to
compare it to another novel, it would be
Ken Follett's Eye of the Needle."*
—Arizona Republic

Available wherever books are sold or at
penguin.com